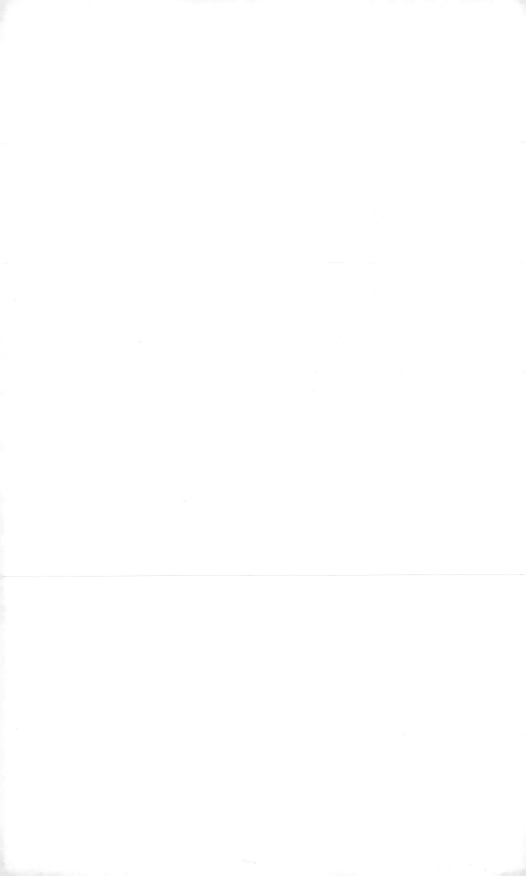

By Jason Dean and available from Headline

The Wrong Man
Backtrack

BACK TRACK

JASON DEAN

headline

First published in 2013 by
HEADLINE PUBLISHING GROUP

1

Cataloguing in Publication Data is available from the British Library

Hardback ISBN 978 0 7553 8307 8
Trade paperback ISBN 978 0 7553 8308 5

Typeset in Adobe Garamond by Palimpsest Book Production Limited,
Falkirk, Stirlingshire

Printed and bound in Great Britain by
Clays Ltd, St Ives plc

Headline's policy is to use papers that are natural, renewable and recyclable products and
made from wood grown in sustainable forests. The logging and manufacturing processes are
expected to conform to the environmental regulations of the country of origin.

HEADLINE PUBLISHING GROUP
An Hachette UK Company
338 Euston Road
London NW1 3BH

www.headline.co.uk
www.hachette.co.uk

To my wife, Nok – for all the reasons in the world.

ONE

James Bishop put on his sunglasses and got out of the silver Toyota Camry. He didn't say anything to the driver. There was no need. He shut the door, adjusted his leather jacket and checked his watch. 09.12. Then he turned and headed north along Main Street at a steady stroll. Neither fast nor slow. As though he had some specific destination in mind, but wasn't in any rush to get there.

Which was true enough to a point.

It was a warm Tuesday. Warm for early May, anyway. The sun was out, but there was also a cool breeze to take the edge off. Good spring weather. Even better when you were experiencing it outside a prison cell. Almost nine months since Bishop had gotten out and the novelty of walking around in fresh, pristine air still hadn't entirely worn off.

Parked vehicles already lined both sides of the street, but Bishop saw little actual traffic. Scratching his beard, he looked around as he walked and counted six other pedestrians. The town of Louisford, here in eastern Pennsylvania, was still in the process of waking up. Most of the stores were either still closed or just opening. That was one of the things Bishop liked about small towns. That casual indifference towards scheduled hours.

But there were also plenty of places that opened on time, day in, day out. Banks. Post offices. Franchise stores. Especially the franchise stores. They took customer care a little more seriously. Like the small Starbucks over there. Bishop could already see a small queue of people inside, waiting at the cash register for their morning caffeine fix.

But it was a franchise of a different kind that Bishop was heading towards. The one situated at the end of the street about two hundred yards away.

Bishop saw an elderly local coming his way, led by a black Labrador on a leash. The guy nodded a 'good morning' to Bishop, who smiled and nodded back. Once they'd passed each other, Bishop immediately lost the smile and carried on walking until he reached his destination seventy-two seconds later.

The cheque-cashing store was one of hundreds operating under the Standard Star umbrella. Most offered cash advances, too, but Bishop knew Pennsylvania was one of fifteen states that had either outlawed payday loans or capped the excessive interest rates to such an extent that there was no profit in it. Which probably made the banks happy, at least.

Bishop stood looking through the windows for two seconds before turning back to the street. Long enough for the interior to be imprinted on his mind in every detail.

It was still the same.

This branch had a row of four partitioned counters behind bullet-resistant glass and an ATM near the entrance. Closed circuit cameras in the ceiling covered each counter. A pair of customers – a bald, middle-aged guy and a young blonde woman – were being served at two of the counters. Following a rash of cheque-cashing store robberies over the past six months, the owners had obviously felt the need for a uniformed security guard, too. He'd been standing next to the ATM. Bishop figured late fifties. Overweight with a prominent pot belly. Probably a retired cop. Holstering an old service Walther 9mm and clearly bored beyond belief.

Bishop used a hand to brush the dark hair away from his eyes and checked the street. Empty of traffic now. He looked at his watch again. 09.14. Time to go to work.

He removed his sunglasses before pulling a pair of thin leather gloves from his pocket and slipping them on. As he reflected on how it had come down to this, he recalled a lesson that had been drilled into him more than once in the Marine Corps: that anybody's life can turn on a single event. It was true. He'd experienced one of those events already, and wondered if he was about to again. If he did, he'd have nobody to blame but himself.

Well, too late to worry about it now, he thought. *Besides, I've got no other choice.*

Then he walked over to the entrance, pulled the door open and stepped inside.

TWO

Bishop paused just inside the door. The guard watched him and gave a welcoming nod. *Public relations at work. You can wear a gun, but be nice to potential customers or you're gone.*

Bishop walked over. He put a frown on his face as though he wanted to ask a question, but wasn't sure whom to ask. The guard watched him approach. Once he'd closed the distance, Bishop turned so the cashiers couldn't see, leaned in and pulled the .357 Smith & Wesson from his waistband. Jamming the five-inch barrel into the guard's ample midsection, he said, 'You know what this is, so don't do anything dumb. They don't pay you enough.' At the same time, he used his right hand to unlatch the guard's holster and pull out the Walther.

'Hey,' the guard said, wheezing. 'Are you crazy? You can't do this.'

'I am doing it,' Bishop said, sliding the magazine out one-handed and stuffing it in his pants pocket. He also ejected the chambered round and saw it land on the floor. 'Relax and keep your voice down. A couple of minutes from now, this'll all be over.' After checking to make sure the guard carried no extra ammo, he placed the Walther back in the guy's holster and said, 'What's your name?'

'My name?'

'Yeah, your first name. What is it?'

The guard looked at him like he'd lost his mind, but Bishop noticed he'd stopped wheezing. 'Randolph,' he said.

'Is that Randolph or Randy?'

'It's Randy to my friends. To jerks like you, it's Randolph.'

Bishop smiled. 'Okay, Randolph. Now I figure you're the one holds the keys to the front door, right?' Bishop already knew this was so,

4

but wanted Randolph to get in the habit of answering his questions. Simple psychology, but it made things easier in the long run.

'Yeah,' Randolph said.

'Good. What say we go over and lock it so nobody else walks in. Right now.'

Still keeping his back to the cashiers, Bishop walked slowly with Randolph to the entrance and watched him pull a key chain from his utility belt. The guard picked a key, inserted it into the lock and turned it a hundred and eighty degrees clockwise. 'It's locked,' he said.

'Not that I don't believe you,' Bishop said, 'but try pushing the door for me.'

Randolph pressed a hand against the frame. The door didn't move.

'Good,' Bishop said. He took the keys from the guard's hand while he studied the street outside. Still empty except for the occasional vehicle passing by. 'Okay, Randolph. Let's go over to the counters now.'

Randolph turned and Bishop stayed at his back as they walked towards the rear of the store. Bishop quickly stooped down to pick up the extra round he'd dropped as he passed. He didn't want Randolph getting any ideas. When they were a couple of feet away from the counters, Bishop said, 'Walk over to the first counter and just stand there.'

He waited as Randolph did as he was told, watching the two cashiers' faces. The woman serving the bald guy was the first to notice something was wrong. The eyes behind her glasses grew wide when she saw Bishop. She said something to her male colleague, who was in conversation with the woman customer. The man immediately stopped talking and stared at Bishop with his mouth open.

'Okay, everybody,' Bishop said. 'Hands where I can see them. I'm here for the company's money, not yours. So no heroics.'

The two customers jumped at his voice and turned round. The blonde woman saw the cannon in his hand and took a sharp intake of breath. The bald guy said, 'What? Hey, wait a minute. I ain't even—'

'Everybody relax,' Bishop said, cutting him off. 'This'll soon be over and then you can all go back to your normal lives. But right now, I want you and you,' and he pointed the gun briefly at the two customers, 'to stand over there with Randolph and just be quiet. I'm calm right now, but if you play up I'll get angry and you really don't want that. And keep your cell phones in your pockets. They make me angry, too.'

Bishop watched the woman nudge the man. Then they both shuffled to the left and stood next to Randolph a few feet away.

'Don't worry,' Randolph said. 'Everything'll be fine. Just do what he says.'

The bald guy snorted and just looked at him. 'You kidding me, Randy?'

'No, he's not,' Bishop said. 'Now shut up.'

He stepped forward and faced the male cashier at the third window. Placing the revolver in plain sight on the counter, he glanced at his name badge and said, 'You stay right there, John. Don't move.' He turned to the bespectacled woman, noted her name badge and said, 'Leanne, I want every note in the place except singles. You'll put them in a bag fast as you can and when you're done you'll pass it through to me. Got that?'

Neither cashier moved. Neither of them said anything. Bishop knew they probably felt safe as houses behind the thick wall of glass. And that the only reason they weren't running out the back was because of the two customers on this side. He also knew one of them had already triggered a silent alarm somewhere, but he'd planned for that.

Bishop tapped the gun barrel against the glass and said, 'Leanne, the only thing separating us right now is a three-quarter-inch thick layer of polycarbonate. You know why they call this glass bullet-resistant and not bullet-proof?'

Leanne's eyes were orbs. She swallowed and gave a small shake of her head.

'It's because they don't want to get sued for false advertising.' He tapped the glass with the barrel again. 'Now this is a .357 Magnum loaded with light-grain, 125-gram hollow-points. And the main advantage of using a light-grain round is it travels a lot faster than a normal bullet. Fast enough to zip right through this glass like it was rice paper.

I've seen it happen. Which means there really isn't anything separating us at all. Randolph, I'm guessing you were a cop once. Convince Leanne I'm not making this up. I don't want to have to give John here an extra eye to prove my point.'

Randolph said, 'He's not making it up. Get the money.'

Neither cashier moved. They were probably still in shock. Bishop needed to get things moving. He tapped the barrel against the glass again. 'Three,' he said.

He paused. Tapped again. 'Two.'

Pause. Tap. 'One.'

John suddenly came out of his trance and said, 'No, *don't*. Please.' He turned to Leanne. 'Quick. Get him the money.'

Bishop watched Leanne jump off her stool and look round the room. She knelt down, picked something off the floor and came back with a small canvas sack. Then she started rummaging around under the counter and sorting through notes.

'When you finish here, Leanne, don't forget to get the rest from the manager's office out back. I'm sure he'll help once you fill him in.'

Leanne nodded as she worked and Bishop turned to look at the three in the corner. He ignored their stares and checked his watch. 09.17. It changed to 09.18. Then he heard the sound of sirens. Two vehicles, it sounded like. And not far away. Maybe three or four blocks at most.

'Faster, Leanne,' he said, and then heard the sound of a horn out front. He turned and saw the silver Toyota right outside. The driver, Sayles, was behind the wheel looking back at him, moving his head back and forth like a rooster. Then he looked behind as the sirens got louder. Sayles beeped the horn once more. He stared at Bishop for a long moment. Then he shook his head, revved the engine and just took off.

Without expression, Bishop watched him disappear. Sayles was there, then he wasn't. Just gone. Bishop allowed a long breath to escape from his lips.

The sirens were getting much louder now. Probably already at the next block. Looked like from here on in he was on his own. Bishop stared at a spot on the floor for a moment and then at the three people in the corner.

Well, not alone, exactly.

He focused on the woman. Early twenties. Very pretty, if pale. Five-six, slim, with straight blond hair down to her shoulders and large blue eyes. Wearing a long-sleeved baseball shirt and jeans. Gold band on the third finger of her left hand.

She must have felt his gaze on her. She turned her face from the direction of the sirens and stared at him. Bishop thought she looked plenty scared.

'What's your name?' he asked.

She paused. Swallowed. 'Sonja Addison.'

Bishop heard the screeching of tyres in the street outside and then the sirens cut out entirely. He turned and saw flashing red lights reflected in the store windows opposite, but that was all. Turning back to the girl, Bishop reached into his back pocket. He pulled out a set of nylon flex cuffs and said, 'Okay, Sonja. Step over here.'

THREE

'Leave her the hell out of this,' Randolph said, taking a step forward. 'You want a hostage, take me instead.'

Bishop raised the gun. 'Real decent of you, Randolph, but you'd only slow me down. And you can stop too, Leanne. That money won't help. Sonja, come over here now.'

The girl looked up at Randolph, said, 'Thank you, anyway,' and then slowly walked towards Bishop. He thought she already looked resigned, as though she'd expected nothing less at this point.

'You're making a big mistake, pal,' Randolph said. 'That lady's—'

'Oh, my God,' someone said at Bishop's right.

Bishop turned and saw a red-haired man entering the cashier's room behind John and Leanne. He wore a short-sleeved shirt and tie and had a cell phone in his hand. Bishop knew this was the store manager. Probably come to see what all the noise outside was about. He was gaping at everybody in turn, but his gaze finished up at the gun in Bishop's hand.

'You missed all the fun,' Bishop said. 'But for now, lose that phone and keep your mouth shut like the rest of these good people. I don't want to hear another word from anybody unless I ask a direct question.' He waited as the guy placed the cell on the floor, then said, 'Okay, Sonja, put one of these loops around your left wrist and pull the slack so it's tight.' He waited as she did as instructed, then said, 'All right, now put your other hand in the second loop.'

Sonja slipped her right wrist through and Bishop put the gun in his waistband and used both hands to tighten it. But not too much. He let go and Sonja dropped both hands to her waist. Holding the gun again, Bishop turned to the counter she'd been standing against and saw a Mexican-style shoulder bag by the window.

'You keep your car keys in there?' he asked.

Sonja nodded.

Keeping his eyes on her, Bishop reached in and rummaged around. Then he pulled out a key ring with four keys attached to it. The worn leather fob had a Ford logo in the centre. 'What model, how old and where's it parked?' he asked, tucking them in his pocket.

'It's a fifteen-year old Mustang,' she said. Her soft voice only wavered a little. 'Just out front and to the right. About four or five cars down.'

Bishop nodded. He knew where it was. 'All gassed up? Don't lie.'

'Tank's three-quarters full, I think. Please don't hurt me.'

'I won't if you do what I say,' Bishop said. 'Take these.' He handed her Randolph's keys. Then he turned her so she was facing the entrance. He put his right hand on her right shoulder and felt her flinch at the touch. His left hand pressed the barrel of the gun against her neck. Up close, he could smell the apple conditioner she'd used this morning.

'Let's go,' he said. 'Slow and easy, understand?'

'Yes,' she said, and began walking slowly towards the front of the store.

Crouching a little, Bishop matched her, step for step, until they reached the door. He looked through the glass and saw two white Crown Vics parked at angles in the middle of the street. One on either side of the store. Behind the one on the left he saw the heads and shoulders of two male deputies. One held a handgun aimed at the storefront, the other a twelve-gauge Mossberg pump.

Bishop turned to his right. Two more behind the second car. Male and female. Similarly armed. The guy looked to be Bishop's height. Six, six-one, maybe. Beefy, wearing a moustache. His partner was crouched behind the front fender. Dark-haired, from what he could see. Bishop guessed there'd be others covering the rear. And this was just the beginning. More would come. Further back, a number of people were lining the streets to watch the spectacle. Bishop waited as the cop with the moustache reached into the car, pulled out a bullhorn and brought it to his mouth.

'*You in there. This is the police. We have you surrounded, front and back. Throw out your weapon and exit the store with your hands up.*'

Bishop felt the girl stiffen at the amplified words. 'Not very original, is he?' he said into her ear. 'Use the large black key to unlock the door and then push it open. Slowly.'

Sonja looked down and then chose the same key Randolph had used. She inserted it in the lock. Turned it counter-clockwise until it stopped. Then Bishop moved with her as she leaned forward, pushing the door open as far as it would go. Fresh air wafted in. It seemed a hell of a lot warmer outside than he remembered. Or maybe it was just him. But he was impressed with the girl's composure so far. She was a lot calmer than she had any right to be.

He put his mouth to her ear and said, 'Tell them your name, that I've got a gun pointed at your head and that we're coming out now.'

Sonja took a deep breath and yelled, 'Please don't shoot. My name is Sonja Addison. This man has a gun at my head. He says we're coming out now.'

Bishop looked further down to the right and saw the dark blue Mustang parked next to the kerb about a dozen yards past the Crown Victoria, pointing north.

The cop placed the bullhorn on the roof and aimed his gun at Bishop. 'Let the woman go and drop the weapon, mister. Now.'

Ignoring him, Bishop said, 'We'll walk to your vehicle now, Sonja, but we're gonna do it sideways with you in front of me. Like a couple of crabs. Don't worry, they're not about to shoot you to get to me.'

'Look, maybe if you just—'

'Don't talk,' Bishop said. 'Start walking now.'

He nudged her forward until they were both outside, then Sonja began edging herself towards the Mustang. Bishop mirrored her movements exactly, like they were dance partners. He kept the gun at Sonja's neck all the way, his head behind hers. He didn't need to see the cops to know they were there. All he cared about was getting them to the Mustang. Twenty feet away now. Fifteen.

'I won't warn you again, mister,' the cop shouted. 'You're just making things worse. Drop the piece. *Now.*'

Bishop said nothing. Just kept edging his way to the vehicle in tandem with Sonja. He knew the cop was bluffing. There were witnesses all around. Five feet to go. Then three. Then two. When Sonja came to the passenger door, she stopped. So did Bishop. He reached into his pants pocket, found the car keys and handed them to her.

'Unlock the door and open it.'

'I don't know if I can,' she said. Bishop could feel her body trembling. Her hands shook too, jangling the keys. Delayed shock. He'd seen it plenty of times before.

'Take a deep breath, then put the key in the lock. Don't think about anything else.'

Bishop waited patiently as she took several deep breaths. Then, after some fumbling, she inserted the key on the second attempt. She unlocked it and pulled the key out. Then she grabbed the handle and pulled the door open.

'Good,' he said, manoeuvring them so their backs were to the cops. 'Now we're gonna get in together. I'll be keeping the gun on you as I slide into the driver's seat, so make sure you stick close. Ready? Go.'

Clutching Sonja's shoulder tightly, Bishop ducked down and pulled them both inside in less than a second. He slid himself over to the driver's side, holding on to her all the way. 'Reach over and pull the door shut,' he said.

Keeping the gun at her side, he watched Sonja lie across the passenger seat, stretching her arms until her fingers touched the inner door handle. She got a good grip and pulled it until it clicked shut. Then she sat back up again, her body close to his.

'Now start the engine for me.'

Sonja stared into his light blue eyes, her expression blank, then took another deep breath before inserting the key in the ignition. She turned it and the engine caught immediately. Bishop pressed the button to lock the doors and stepped on the gas, watching as the tachometer needle swept over to the right. The engine still sounded smooth, despite the high mileage. It was a standard 3.8 litre V6 with a manual stick shift. Not as powerful as later models, but a definite improvement over the '80s version. That had been a bad decade all round, but especially for Mustangs.

He checked the side mirror and saw the deputies had moved to the other side of their vehicle for cover, the other two joining them. In case Bishop decided to pop off a few shots to slow them down. But he had no intention of doing that. He wasn't an idiot.

Pulling his safety belt across, Bishop said, 'Move over and buckle up.'

He watched as she edged over and used both hands to pull the belt over herself. Once he heard the click, Bishop stuck the gun into his waistband and pushed the gear stick into second. Then he swung the wheel to the left and stepped hard on the gas.

FOUR

The Mustang screeched away from the kerb and took off like a dog let loose from a trap. As he gained speed, Bishop checked the rearview and saw the beefy cop back there yank open the door of his vehicle and get in. He was already backing up as his female partner jumped in the passenger side. Bishop heard sirens and then saw flashing lights.

Soon, they became dots in the distance. But they wouldn't be for long.

Bishop changed gear and checked his speed. Fifty. Sixty. Seventy. The roar of the engine soon overrode everything else. The Mustang wasn't pretty, but it could sure move. He still had to put some space between them, though. Time was against him now. *Every*thing was against him now.

He glanced at his passenger. She was staring straight ahead with wide eyes, her lips set in a straight line. Her face was white and she looked as though she'd rather be anywhere else but here. *Join the club*, he thought. At least she was quiet. Bishop faced front and saw the road was clear ahead. Houses and trees sped past in a blur. A few vehicles passed by, heading back towards town. Soon it was just trees and forest on either side. Farm country.

And about a quarter mile behind him were the tootsie-roll lights. Right now, they'd be calling for back-up. Aerial as well as ground units. That would take time. But how much? No way of telling. Bishop was already up to ninety when the road began a long, slow curve to the left. He kept his speed steady and lost sight of the police lights behind him. Once the road straightened out again he saw the State Route 4022 intersection coming up ahead. As he approached, Bishop tapped the brakes, brought them down to forty-five and swerved left into the two-lane road without stopping. Luckily, there was no traffic. Just empty road. Fields and farms on either side. He began picking up the pace again and soon saw the cruiser make the same turn. Still a quarter mile behind him. That was good. As long as they got no closer.

Bishop covered another mile without them gaining. Two miles. Then, in the distance, just before Jacob's Cemetery, he saw what he wanted. The turnoff for the second leg of State Route 125, the heavily forested road bikers came from all over the state to ride. Mainly for its steep mountain climbs and its legendary, blind hairpin turns. He slowed as he approached, then took the right turn and increased his speed again on the straight. Sixty. Seventy.

Dense forest began surrounding them on both sides. A pick-up passed by, going south, closely followed by a convoy of four motor-bikes. The cops were still back there behind him. The road began to ascend gently as he entered the Appalachians. A low guard rail lined the right side of the road now, protecting drivers from the steep drop-offs on that side. If you could call something that only reached your knees protection. After a couple more miles he saw the road take a sharp left turn up ahead. Slowing to twenty just before the turn, he negotiated the car round it before speeding up again. Then two more bikes whizzed by. Followed by a FedEx truck. Then more empty road. Bishop took them back up to seventy.

By the time he slowed down for a sharp right up ahead the cruiser still hadn't appeared in the rear-view. He slowed to twenty-five, took the bend and was halfway round when he felt the rear end slide to the left. Sonja cried out and reached out to grab the dashboard for balance. Bishop ground his teeth as he steered into the slide, then shifted down into second and felt the tyres gain purchase again. *Careful, boy, careful.* Once he came out of the curve safely, Bishop kept pushing, pushing, pushing. Sixty. Seventy. Eighty.

This section was on a gentle descent and acceleration was easy. Almost too easy. Cliff face at his left. Guard rail at his right, followed by a sheer drop into the forest ravine below. He glanced at the rear-view and saw empty road. No cops yet. He knew he was making good time on the corners. Then he downshifted as he saw the yellow sign ahead. Another arrow at a right angle. This one pointing left. A blind hairpin turn. One of the worst.

Then he saw the turn, with the guard rail following it round. Beyond it were trees and a drop to nothingness. This time he reduced his speed down to twenty again. He kept his eyes focused on the few feet of black asphalt directly in front of him, gripping the wheel until his knuckles were white. But there was no time to waste. Halfway round, he pressed down hard on the accelerator again and by the time they shot out of the hairpin they were moving at over forty miles per hour.

Sonja suddenly raised her cuffed hands and screamed.

Directly ahead, a massive eighteen-wheeler was heading right for them down the centre line. Wide enough to take up both sides of the road. And only fifteen feet away from them.

Less.

FIVE

Deputy Louise Fletcher held on to the dashboard as her partner, Deputy Garry Cavanaugh, carefully steered them through the bad hairpin turn. Every cop in the area hated this road. And this was the reason why. As soon as they were facing the straight, she saw what lay ahead and shouted, '*Stop!*'

Cavanaugh jammed both feet on the brakes and the Crown Vic immediately jerked to a halt. They both stared at the scene in front of them.

'Holy shit,' Cavanaugh said.

An eighteen-wheeler had stopped almost twenty feet away, the cab turned at an angle to the long box trailer it was carrying. The long stretch of road behind it was empty. For now. Fletcher watched wide-eyed as the truck driver ran over to the missing sections of guard rail and peered down into the ravine below.

At the Mustang.

Without a word, Cavanaugh pushed his door open, jumped out and ran over to join the young driver, a heavily built black man in a baseball cap. Thinking quickly, Fletcher slid over into the driver's seat and carefully backed up until she was on the other side of the hairpin. So Richardson and Baynard, following half a mile behind, wouldn't smash right into the back of them. She switched off the siren, too. The flashers she left alone.

Then she got out and ran back towards the broken guard rail, where the truck driver and Cavanaugh were standing at the edge, looking down into the gorge. She was only a few yards away when she heard the sound of the gas tank exploding below. Cavanaugh and the trucker jerked their heads back at the concussion and then Fletcher was alongside both men, looking down through the trees. A hundred and fifty feet below, Fletcher saw the smashed-up remains of the blue Mustang they'd been pursuing lying amongst the foliage. A moment later the wreckage was completely obscured by flames and smoke.

Fletcher searched for a way down, but there were no handholds and the drop was too steep. Impossible without proper equipment. And that wasn't likely to arrive any time soon. Fletcher pulled the two-way from her belt as a second explosion shook the air. The truck driver lost his balance and fell back to the ground.

As she put a call in to Jean at Dispatch, she saw Cavanaugh look back at her briefly and shake his head. They both knew it was hopeless. But she still requested an ambulance ASAP, and told Jean to notify the fire department three towns away. Then she turned back to see the young driver looking up at both of them as though only just noticing he wasn't alone.

He raised the visor of his baseball cap and said, 'He was just *there*, officers. I mean, deputies. He just came out of nowhere, going *way* too fast. Then he must have seen me and just lost . . .' The guy shook his head and looked at the ground. 'Oh, Jesus. He was going too fast. There was nothing I could do. He just . . . Oh, man.'

'You see anybody get out?' Cavanaugh asked, looking down at him.

The driver kept shaking his head as he slowly got to his feet. 'I didn't see nobody, man. He just swerved and went right over. Jesus, he was just going too fast and I pressed down on the brakes. What else could I do?'

Fletcher shook her head as she watched the smoke rising into the air. 'Nothing, sir. Nothing at all.'

SIX

'How long before we can leave?' Sonja whispered from the passenger seat.

Bishop removed the wig that had been annoying him for hours and dropped it on the dash. Brushing a palm back and forth over his buzz cut, he sat back and let out a deep breath as the adrenalin left his system. 'Not too long. Once they take our driver's witness statement, they'll let him go. An accident scene like this, they'll want to get this rig moving before it starts blocking traffic.'

'God, I hope so,' she said, still shaking. 'Just knowing the police are a few feet away scares me half to death.'

'Try and relax. They're seeing exactly what we want them to see.'

'So am I finally safe from *him*?'

'Well, you're officially dead. Or you will be in a few days. I figure you can't get much safer than that.'

Sonja looked at him without smiling. 'I thought we really *were* dead a couple of times back there. My car never handled that good before.'

'That's because your car's currently at the bottom of that ravine where we planted it earlier. We've been preparing this one for weeks to make it as identical as possible to yours, then swapped them last night while you were asleep.'

She leaned over and checked the speedometer. 'The mileage is all wrong and I never even noticed,' she said. 'Not even when I was driving into town this morning.'

'You had other things on your mind, I guess,' Bishop said, turning to watch the large shape of Luke Shelton at the rear of the trailer.

He was carefully arranging the crates of soft toys back there until

19

they reached all the way to the roof. After all this hard work and effort, Bishop thought it would be pretty sloppy to get caught out by a routine inspection. God, after all, was in the details. Luke worked fast, just like he had when he'd guided the Mustang inside. The truck hadn't actually been moving towards them, of course, although it had seemed that way at first glance. Hence, Sonja's scream. It had merely been idling. Waiting for Bishop. As soon as he'd come out of the hairpin turn, he'd steered the car precisely through the thin gap between truck and guard rail. Once through, he'd performed a 180-degree handbrake turn and seen Luke at the rear of the truck, waving him in. Bishop had then quickly guided the vehicle up the ramps and inside, after which Luke retrieved the ramps and shut the rear doors after them. The whole thing had gone like clockwork. But then, after all their practice runs, it wasn't surprising they'd got it down to a precise science.

Bishop removed the .357 from his waistband and placed it in the glove compartment. It joined the Swiss army knife he'd used to cut Sonja free from the cuffs. Then he adjusted the rear-view mirror. His pale blue eyes focused on the lower part of his face as he slowly peeled off the fake beard and moustache.

Sonja turned to him. 'What if they check the dental records of . . . of the girl in the car? You know, with our regular dentist?'

'Then they'll find definite proof that the burnt female body down there is one Sonja Addison. We took the trouble to switch your dental X-rays with hers a while back, so don't worry.'

She gave a nervous laugh. 'Sorry, I'm just . . . I still can't believe this is actually working out.'

Bishop turned to her and smiled. 'Now might be a good time to start believing it.'

She nodded reluctantly and faced front again. Bishop studied her profile for a moment, thinking back to the chance encounter three weeks ago that had started all this. He'd been waiting at a stop sign just outside Louisford when her Mustang had bumped into the back of his BMW. It was a ten-year-old model he'd bought last year, using some of the money the city of New York had paid out for his wrongful imprisonment. He'd been racking up the already high mileage by driving aimlessly across America, trying to figure out what he wanted to do next, when Sonja had entered the picture.

There was barely any damage to either car, but Sonja just went to pieces like the world had come to an end. It was puzzling. She didn't seem crazy or anything. Just very highly strung. And scared. After managing to calm her down a little, Bishop drove her to a snack bar and made her drink something hot. He wasn't in any rush to get anywhere, and her behaviour interested him. After an hour of talking about everything except her problem, she finally came out with it. Slowly at first, then it all came in a rush.

She talked about her lawyer husband, Carl, and the daily beatings he inflicted upon her, both physically and mentally. She described the gruesome methods he used to keep her in line, and why she only wore long-sleeved shirts these days. But mostly she talked about how impossible it was to escape. Carl would either kill her, or go to the ends of the earth to find her. And he had plenty of influential friends to help him. For years, every local cop had known that if they had a legal problem they could retain Carl Addison's services for next to nothing. He believed in supporting his local police force. Which meant he was owed a *lot* of favours.

She also told Bishop how she'd recently overheard telephone conversations that convinced her Carl was also in the pocket of some big drug dealer over in Reading. That had earned her a major beating that resulted in a broken collarbone. She still had the bruises. After that, Bishop hadn't needed any more convincing. At the tender age of twenty-three, she was far too young to have to face that kind of fear every day. That she also reminded Bishop of someone he knew who'd been in a very similar situation just made his decision that much easier. And that situation had ended very badly because of him. He felt that by helping Sonja he might atone for a past mistake that haunted him to this day.

Bishop wasn't the impetuous type, though. Never had been. He did plenty of research of his own before committing himself. He'd learned the value of on-the-spot reconnaissance from his time back in the Corps, where accurate intel could mean the difference between life and death. Even more so when he entered the close protection business a couple of years after his discharge. In this case, before he did anything, he needed to be absolutely sure Sonja was on the level. He researched her whole life. Bishop's occasional girlfriend, Jenna Falstaff, had even chipped in to help by utilizing her unique information-gathering skills. In the end, everything Sonja had told him checked out.

That he still had that open offer of contract work for Equal Aid, the non-profit organization dedicated to helping victims of violence, had given him momentary pause for thought. They would have snapped up a case like this in no time. *And* financed it. But Bishop's bitter feelings towards the man behind the organization were still too strong for him to make that call. Besides, he wasn't exactly short of money right now. He could afford the expense.

He turned and saw that Luke had finished with the crates. It looked good from this side. He'd made them three deep, so they wouldn't topple over during the journey back to New York. Luke was sitting on one of the spare crates, looking as though he'd rather be anywhere else. To be honest, Bishop didn't really want him here, either, but he'd needed a team he could trust for this and he didn't have that many to choose from. Fortunately, Jenna's brother, Ali, had been only too glad to help after the business last year. He still felt he owed Bishop for his sister's safe return after an old nemesis of Bishop took her hostage. With himself taking the truck driver role, Ali'd then persuaded Luke and another pal, Leon Sayles, to fill the other parts. One thing was for sure, though, Bishop wouldn't ask them again. As far as he was concerned, any debts Ali and Luke felt they'd accrued had been paid in full.

Sonja broke into his thoughts and said, 'Can I ask where you got the . . . you know?'

Bishop smiled. 'The bodies? They were already dead, if that's what you're worried about.'

She gave a half-chuckle. It was a nice sound. Soft, but genuine. Bishop wondered how long it had been since anyone had heard it.

'I guessed that much,' she said. 'I was just wondering, that's all.'

'City and hospital morgues are full of Jane and John Does. You wouldn't believe how many. Usually overdose victims, like our friends back there. And if you do your research, you'll usually find an attendant who'll take a bit of extra cash to turn the other way for five minutes. And maybe fudge the records a little, too. That answer your question?'

She wrapped her arms around herself and nodded once.

'While I think about it,' Bishop said, 'you better hand over that ring. A break like this has to be clean. Just the clothes on your back and nothing else. That includes jewellery.'

'It'll be a pleasure,' she said and twisted the gold band a few times until she was able to ease it over the joint.

As she handed it to him, Bishop noticed part of a silver chain at the neck of the baseball shirt. 'The necklace, too.'

Sonja placed a hand over her chest. 'Don't make me give this up. Please.'

'Why?'

She pulled it out and held the talisman in her palm. It was a small silver pentagram set within a circle. Five lines of equal length joined together to create the simplest regular star polygon. Bishop had always felt a certain satisfaction in its symmetrical perfection.

She said, 'My mom gave me this when I was six, after my dad died. She told me it's supposed to protect the owner from evil.'

'Didn't really do its job, then, did it?'

'Well, you're here. So who's to say?'

Bishop could have argued the point, but didn't. Most people needed to believe in something outside themselves. Even if it was only a good luck charm. He reached over and turned the piece over, studying it closely. When he was sure there were no special inscriptions or markings of any kind, he dropped it back in her palm. He figured there must be millions of these things in circulation, so where was the harm?

'Okay,' he said. 'This you can keep.'

'Thank you.' She placed it back under her shirt. 'So from now on, I'm Selina Clements, right?'

'Right. Start thinking of yourself under that name and keep practising your signature until it feels totally natural. Then once we get to the city, Ali, our driver, will finish up your new IDs and get you in the databases. Tomorrow, we'll start the drive to your new apartment in Arizona. Only you and I will know about it. The first six months' rent has been paid to get your started, but after that it's down to you.'

'We're not flying?'

Bishop shook his head. 'Too many screening checkpoints and security cameras in airports these days. I don't want to risk your face ending up on a TSA database so soon after your death. Besides, the journey will give you some time to start planning the new life you got ahead of you.'

She leaned her head back against the seat rest and shivered again. 'A new start,' she said quietly. 'Now *there's* a scary thought.'

SEVEN

Five weeks later, on a bright June day, Bishop was at the house on Staten Island, raking the last of the new gravel across the backyard and making sure it was all evenly laid out. The two-storey home had been passed down to him and his sister, Amy, after their parents' deaths over twenty-five years ago. But it hadn't been used much since and had fallen into partial disrepair. Amy had no use for it and had made it clear the place was all his if he wanted it. So a fortnight ago, he'd finally taken on sole ownership. After placing the BMW in hibernation in the garage, he set to work making the place habitable again. Whether he planned to stay there was another matter, but it was always good to have roots somewhere. And the property taxes were minimal. For the moment, he was just enjoying the physical labour and the good weather. And trying to convince himself he wasn't just marking time.

As he worked his thoughts returned to Jenna. With all the recent driving he'd barely seen anything of her the last few months, and not for lack of trying on her part. It hadn't escaped his attention that she'd begun to cool off a little in recent weeks either. Not that he could really blame her. He didn't know what was wrong with him. There sure wasn't anything wrong with her. Just the opposite, in fact. She was smart, beautiful and funny. And totally trustworthy. She'd proved that from the moment they'd met last year. With the whole world against him, she was the only one who'd believed in him. The *only* one. He knew he'd have to sort his head out and make a decision soon, though. Jenna wouldn't put up with the situation for too much longer. In fact, for all he knew, it could already be too late.

The vibration of the cell phone against his leg broke him out of his reverie. He leaned the rake against the wooden fence, reached into his pants pocket and pulled it out. It wasn't a number he'd seen before, and he had a good memory for those kinds of things. Photographic, or to give it the proper term, eidetic.

He took the call and said, 'Yes?'

A woman's voice said, 'Who am I speaking to, please?'

'This is Bishop,' he said. Her voice had sounded fairly young. He guessed early forties, but it was hard to tell with women. 'Your turn.'

'Well, we haven't met, but my name's Michelle Gardiner. Does that mean anything to you?'

Bishop didn't have to think about it for long. He knew Sonja/Selina's mother was called Michelle. And Gardiner had been Selina's maiden name before she got married to Addison. 'Yeah, it does. What can I do for you, Ms Gardiner?'

'Please call me Michelle.'

He walked over and sat on the concrete stoop in front of the kitchen door. 'So how can I help you, Michelle? And how did you get this number?'

'My daughter gave it to me. She's the reason I'm calling.'

'Uh huh. Tell me, how many letters are there in your daughter's first name?'

There was a pause. Then she said, 'Six.'

Which instantly told him Selina had been in contact with her mother since her relocation. Even though Bishop had advised her not to for at least a year. That could be bad. Just how bad, though, he still needed to find out.

'And how have you been keeping in touch with her, Michelle?'

'By public phone. We arranged the system before the . . . well, you know.'

'Tell me,' he said.

'Well, I gave her the number of a payphone near me. We arranged a day and a time for her to call me there, very soon after she moved away. The day after, in fact.'

'Go on.'

'We talked about things. You know, about what you did to help

26

get her away from *him*. About . . . well, everything, really. Except her new address. We both knew that would be a bad idea. Then at the end, I gave her the numbers of four more payphones in my area. She said she'd call the fourth number at the same time the next week from a different payphone.'

Watching a couple of kingbirds land on the apple tree in the Robinsons' backyard across the way, Bishop nodded to himself. Not a bad system. Fairly random. Not perfect, of course. Nothing was these days. But not bad. Not bad at all. Both mother and daughter had obviously given this plenty of thought.

'So that's what she did,' he said.

'Yes. Then at the end, we made a date for her next call. May 16. She said she'd call the third number next time, but from a different payphone.'

'And did she?'

'No,' she said. 'That second conversation was the last one we had. That was almost four weeks ago and I've been a nervous wreck ever since. That's why I'm calling you. I'm convinced my daughter's gone missing and I don't know who else to turn to.'

EIGHT

Bishop pulled the door open and entered the crowded diner. He looked round and immediately picked out Michelle Gardiner. It wasn't difficult. For a start, she was the only woman there on her own. But mostly, it was because she was so clearly an older version of her daughter.

She'd asked Bishop to meet her in this place off Easton Avenue in Somerset, New Jersey. Not far from where she lived. She was sitting at a booth in the corner, next to the window. She'd obviously seen him emerge from the cab outside and now gave him a sad-looking smile as he walked towards her booth.

'Michelle,' he said and sat down opposite. Straight away, he could see she was just as attractive as her daughter, but in a more subtle way. Blond hair cut to the same length, but in a different style. Bishop added a few years to his initial guess. Late forties, probably. Similar facial features too, but with added lines and bags under her eyes. She clearly hadn't been sleeping much lately. She wore a long-sleeved V-neck shirt and jeans. But no jewellery. Not even earrings.

'And you must be Bishop,' she said. 'Even if you hadn't told me what you'd be wearing, I'd have recognized you from my daughter's description. She was very complimentary.'

Bishop gazed out the window. 'She should look beneath the surface more often. That's what got her into trouble in the first place.'

'Well, she's still young,' she said. 'What can you do?'

Bishop turned back and saw she was looking down at his right hand. Or more specifically, the missing part of his pinkie finger. Since he really didn't want to get into the specifics behind it, he said, 'You've known all along, haven't you? About Selina's vanishing act, I mean.'

She nodded and took a sip from her coffee cup. The hand holding it wasn't too steady. 'Son— Sorry, *Selina* and I have always had a very close relationship. We became even closer once she married that Addison creep and I became her only outlet. So yes, she kept me up to date with how you were helping her, although she didn't really go into details.'

'And nobody else knows?'

'There isn't anybody else, Bishop. Just her. And me.'

'No boyfriend or partner in the background?'

She gave him that sad smile again. 'I've lived alone a long time. I find . . .'

Just then, a waitress appeared at their table and handed Bishop a menu. He handed it back to her without looking at it and asked for a black coffee without sugar. Once she was gone, Michelle continued, 'I had a hard time finding someone who could live up to Selina's father after he died. And over the years I've gotten used to my independence. I've come to like it a lot. Although I have to admit, I could have really used somebody to talk to recently.'

'Because you think Selina's missing.'

'I'm *sure* she is. She wouldn't go almost a month without contacting me, Bishop. She just wouldn't.' She sighed and used two fingers to rub at her temple. 'Another damn headache. It seems I get one every day now. These past few weeks, I swear I've been steadily going out of my mind. I can't talk to anybody about it. I can't call the police, for obvious reasons. And I can't raise the kind of money detective agencies charge. And what would I say, anyway? I don't know what to do.'

The waitress came back, placed a mug on the table and filled it with coffee. Then she refilled Michelle's and went away again.

Bishop took a sip, made a face, and put it down again. 'So the obvious question is, why didn't you call me sooner?'

'Because I lost the number. Or I thought I had. I wrote it down on a scrap of paper, see, and then forgot all about it until I actually wanted to call you. That was about two weeks ago. I searched everywhere and thought I'd thrown it out with the garbage by mistake. I almost went crazy trying to find it.'

'Selina didn't give you my name?'

Michelle shook her head. 'No, she was adamant about that. Said you were deadly serious about security and she respected that. I practically had to force your phone number out of her. And then this morning, I finally found the note lodged at the back of one of the drawers in my work desk. You can't imagine how relieved I was.'

Bishop could imagine, all right. He felt the same way. He'd called Selina a few times during the first week to make sure she was settling in okay and then decided to let her be, knowing she'd phone him if she had any problems. He'd planned to check in with her again later this week, but that wasn't good enough. They'd been out of contact for almost a month now. If not for Michelle, he'd still be in the dark about this. Angry at his own lapse, he moved his cup in a circle and said, 'Look, I know she's your daughter, but has it occurred to you that Selina's a highly attractive single woman in a town where nobody knows her? I mean, she wouldn't have to work too hard to open up her social life if that's what she wanted. And it could be she's found herself a job already.'

'She has,' Michelle said. 'Our last conversation was only a brief one, just an update really, but she said she'd been doing some waitressing at a local diner. You know, until she figured out what she really wanted to do. She said it was tiring, but she sounded happy she was doing something.'

'There you go. So she's working a shift. Meeting people. Maybe she's met up with someone who's taking up what time she's got left over. It happens.'

She gave him that sad smile again. 'I know what you're saying, and yes, that's possible. But she'd stay in contact somehow. I just know she would. The bond between us is too strong. I was the only one she could turn to when she was with *him*, and that only made us closer. I can't make you believe me, but I just know something's wrong.'

Bishop said nothing. Just looked down at his coffee and took another sip, despite how it tasted. He *did* believe Michelle, that was the problem. If Selina had kept her mother in the loop till now, she wouldn't then cut her out all of a sudden. Not without a damn good reason. It would go against everything Bishop knew of her character. Which meant something or someone had prevented her from doing so. And was still preventing her. But without further information, the possibilities were endless. He needed to narrow those possibilities down to probabilities, then go on from there. And not just for Michelle's peace of mind, either.

He sat back and, without warning, found his thoughts returning to Laurette Chounan. The girl he'd failed to protect thirteen years before. And the main reason he'd decided to help Selina with her problem.

During Bishop's final year of military service, his FAST unit had been stationed in Port-au-Prince, Haiti, for something called Operation Fairwinds. They were there to provide security for the Navy Mobile Construction Battalion and the Air Force engineers tasked with repairing roads, hospitals and schools in the area. It was tiring work and the days were long, hot and unforgiving. One evening, Bishop, knowing his men needed a night away from the base, had taken them to one of the few decent bars in the area and it was there he first saw Laurette. She was drinking with a bunch of her girlfriends. He watched her for half an hour before she finally spotted him and smiled back. Then he introduced himself and they began to talk. She was very pretty, with skin of the darkest brown and light green eyes. The kind of eyes that promised the earth. Later that very night, she delivered on that promise.

After that they began to see each other whenever they could. Bishop was soon smitten with her, and she with him. They were a good match in almost every department, not just the physical. He'd even started to think about his imminent discharge and how that might affect their relationship. Maybe he'd get serious with her. It wasn't beyond the realms of possibility. They were both still young. And when you were young, the possibilities were endless.

Then, after a month, Laurette just disappeared. Vanished. Bishop couldn't find her anywhere. If anybody in her apartment block knew where she was, they weren't talking. It didn't stop him. He searched every place he could think of. He tried all their haunts, questioned all her friends, and got absolutely nowhere. He was getting more desperate with each passing day, when a week later she turned up again. At first she wouldn't let Bishop into the apartment, and then when she finally relented he saw why. Her face and body were covered in ugly cuts and bruises, and her entire left arm was in plaster.

It took a while, but Laurette finally gave him the name of the man responsible. Jean-Robert Develaux. An old boyfriend and ex-gang member who still thought he had unrestricted access to her whenever he felt in the mood. She pleaded with Bishop to let it go, told him she was just grateful Develaux hadn't used a knife on her. His specialty, apparently. Her pleas were wasted on Bishop. Every part of him wanted to pay this Develaux a personal visit, and soon. But Laurette had no idea where he lived any more.

It took Bishop a few days of asking questions around town, that's all. Money usually gets you the answers you want in most parts of the world. Port-au-Prince was no different. He finally tracked Develaux down to a tin-roofed shanty a few miles outside Cité Soleil, one of the worst slums in the western hemisphere. Once night came, Bishop, disguised in a ski mask, broke into the two-room house. Then he just waited.

Develaux showed up at three in the morning, wasted to the gills, with a girl on his arm. Bishop immediately knocked him out, then pushed some money into the stunned girl's hands and told her to leave. She didn't need much persuading. Thirty minutes later, when Develaux regained consciousness, Bishop calmly and systematically beat him to a pulp. He used only his hands and made sure no part of Jean-Robert's body was left untouched. Then he broke both of the man's wrists for good measure. He told Develaux, in rough French, that if he ever went near Laurette again, he'd cut off his dick, or worse. Then he left.

That was his biggest mistake. Leaving Develaux alive.

Three weeks later, Laurette paid the price for that mistake.

They'd reverted to seeing each other fairly regularly once more, but after several days without any contact, Bishop got a bad feeling and found his way into her apartment. The first thing he saw was all the dried blood everywhere. Then he saw what was left of her body and face. It was barely recognizable as human. He knew straight away that Develaux had made her last moments on earth as painful as humanly possible, no doubt relishing every second of her agony.

Bishop closed off his emotions and felt himself turn cold. From then on, he devoted every off-duty moment to locating Develaux again. The old shanty was a washout, as he knew it would be. But there were other leads, and he followed all of them. Two months later, he finally found him alone in a run-down, fly-ridden third-storey apartment close to the harbour. He broke in silently, then used Develaux's own knife to do what he should have done three months before, making sure the murderer experienced exactly what he'd put Laurette through. And then, once he felt he'd got the point across, he slit the ruined thing's throat from ear to ear and calmly watched its remaining life seep into the floorboards. Bishop didn't particularly feel proud of what he'd done, but he was satisfied with the end result. One less piece of shit in the world was no bad thing.

But it didn't bring Laurette back. Or rid Bishop of the guilt he felt over her murder. He wasn't sure anything ever would, until Selina came along and unwittingly offered him a chance of absolution. In his own mind, at least.

As he slowly came back to the present, he noticed Michelle frowning at him from across the table. She said, 'Please tell me what you're thinking, Bishop.'

He said, 'I'm thinking I need to go pay your daughter a visit.'

NINE

At 01.15 the next morning, Bishop stood at the rear entrance to the Heritage Apartments in Saracen, Arizona. The complex was located on a quiet, residential street about two miles from the centre of town. He saw only two other vehicles in the rear parking area. Probably due to the poor lighting on this side. But that was why he'd chosen it over the bay at the front. He didn't want to advertise his presence if he could help it.

He'd flown this time. No need for the cloak and dagger routine any more. He'd taken the 20.30 Delta flight from JFK and landed at Sky Harbour Airport in Phoenix at 23.25, Arizona time. After hiring a Ford Taurus he made the drive in less than ninety minutes.

Heritage was made up of a number of loosely arranged two-storey buildings, all interconnected by concrete footbridges and stairways. Each block overlooked a communal garden area. A few trees here and there gave a sense of enclosure to the place. Even in the darkness it looked tranquil. Just one of the reasons he'd picked it out for Selina.

Bishop took the spare keys from his pocket, glad he'd decided to have copies made in case of emergencies. He figured this qualified. Of course, he could always pick the lock, but it was usually best to go the legit route whenever possible. He unlocked the gate, walked over to the second building on the left and climbed the steps at the side. Upon reaching the second floor, he kept walking until he reached No. 40 at the end.

He used the other two keys to silently unlock the door. If he found Selina inside, he'd apologise for the intrusion. But he didn't think he would. He slowly pushed the door open a few inches until he felt a slight obstruction on the other side. He listened for a few beats, but heard nothing. Inside, there was only darkness. He stepped through the gap and closed the door behind him. Then he felt along the wall and turned on the lights.

He was in the short entrance hall that emptied out into the living room at the end. The bathroom and kitchen areas both opened off from the right. Directly to his left was the bedroom. His first impression was that the place was empty and had been for a while. The air smelt musty. The windows clearly hadn't been opened in some time.

Bishop began to get a bad feeling in his gut.

And then there was the obstruction he'd felt behind the door. The accumulated mail still lay in a messy pile and Bishop crouched down and carefully went through it. Most of it was junk mail and flyers, but there were a couple of bills halfway down. One from the gas company, and an energy bill from APS. The post date on the gas bill was fifteen days old. Twenty-one days for the electric. Then more junk mail, more flyers. And that was it. So Selina hadn't been here in at least three weeks. Probably longer.

The feeling in his gut intensified.

Bishop stood and checked the bedroom first. It was empty and the bed had been made. He gave the other rooms a cursory inspection and soon discovered they were also empty. All the drapes were drawn. There were no pictures on the walls. No books in the bookcase. The apartment had come furnished, but it still felt unused. Selina hadn't yet imprinted her personality on the place. It was still waiting to be lived in.

There could be a plausible explanation. She might have fallen hard for a guy and moved in with him straight away. Just let everything else go to hell and decided to live for the moment for once. Highly unlikely, of course. Especially with what Bishop knew of Selina. But he couldn't entirely rule it out. Not yet.

He sat down on the living-room couch. Resting on one of the arms was a fat Stephen King paperback open to its spine. Selina looked to be about halfway in. He flicked through the pages and found no hidden notes. On the coffee table were some fashion magazines, a three week-old copy of the *Saracen Post*, a bookmark advertising a local bookstore and some recent water ring stains. The room was free of other personal effects.

Bishop got up and entered the bathroom again. The only noteworthy item in the medicine cabinet was a box containing 60 Xanax pills. Two of the six blister packs were empty already. Which meant Selina was still suffering from regular anxiety attacks. Not exactly surprising after what she'd been through.

In the kitchen, the refrigerator held some TV dinners, some canned soft drinks, a half-full bottle of white wine and various vegetables, now rotten and discoloured. There was a second-hand portable TV on the counter. He found some new cutlery, crockery and glasses in the cupboards, some cleaning products under the sink, and that was pretty much it.

In the bedroom closet Bishop found some Levis, a few skirts and a wide variety of shirts on hangers. All long-sleeved. Nothing in any of the pockets. He then checked the wooden dresser under the window. The first drawer contained underwear Selina bought in New York. The second contained pyjamas, some towels and a short chemise nightie.

Bishop remembered Selina's innocent delight upon seeing the nightie in the clothes store. Addison hadn't approved of nightwear of any kind. Not even her necklace, which she said she always took off before going to bed. So that eliminated the boyfriend theory. If she was shacked up with somebody, she would have taken the nightie, too.

Turning to the bed, he saw the night stand was a woodgrain thing with two deep drawers. A lamp, a digital clock and a pair of reading glasses fought for space on the top. He sat down on the bed, opened the first drawer and found a couple more paperbacks that looked new. The second drawer contained a small flashlight, some pens and a small, unused notepad.

Bishop closed the drawer and stared at the wall, absently scratching at the day-old whiskers under his chin. He'd expected to find a few examples of Selina's ID lying around, but there was nothing. No purse, either. Not a single thing that might have identified Selina Clements as the occupant. Even the rental contract was missing.

Bishop frowned. The details here just didn't add up. Firstly, nobody carried around *all* their documents with them. It just wasn't done. And second, the open book on the couch indicated Selina had been doing some reading before going to bed. Yet the open bottle in the refrigerator and the water rings on the table suggested she'd also been sipping from a glass of wine while she read. Which meant she'd had enough time to tidy up after herself, but not to insert the bookmark and keep her place.

Then there were the drapes and the made bed. At this time of year, the sun came up at around 05.00. And he knew there weren't any all-night diners round here, which meant her shift must have started at a fairly reasonable hour. Some time later than 05.00, he figured. So if she'd made the bed prior to leaving the apartment the next morning, why keep the drapes drawn when it was light outside? And she'd left her supply of Xanax behind, too.

Details. That's all he had. He needed more.

Bishop closed his eyes for a few moments, and when he opened them again he got off the bed and pulled the night stand away from the wall. And there it was, on the carpet. What he'd been searching for all this time without knowing it.

Selina's silver pentagram necklace.

The one she wore everywhere, except to bed. She must have left it on the night stand and it had fallen off somehow. As soon as she woke up, she would have found it and put it on. Ready for the day ahead. But she hadn't.

Now everything fitted together in Bishop's mind. All the pieces made sense. Whoever snatched Selina had done it in the early hours. Probably more than one person. They'd also taken along her important personal effects and made an attempt to tidy the place up, to make it look as though she'd left of her own accord. They'd washed the wine glass and replaced the bottle, but they'd forgotten about the open book on the sofa. And the Xanax. Nor had they thought to open the drapes. The necklace was the wild card. Selina might well have knocked the night stand in her sleep so that it simply slid off, remaining hidden and undisturbed until this moment. Waiting for Bishop to find it.

Bishop crouched down and picked the necklace up. Looked at it for a moment before putting it in his pocket. Everything else in here was replaceable, but Selina would want the necklace back for sure. If she was still alive. And if she wasn't, the people who took her would soon join her. That much he could guarantee. First, though, he needed to find them.

And he had a good idea of where to start.

TEN

At the offices of Addison & Fraser, Attorneys-at-Law, Carl Addison made sure all the lights were turned off before picking up his briefcase and making for the front desk. It was past nine and he was the only one left. The others had gone home hours ago. Addison locked up, then walked to the third floor elevator and pressed the button. The doors opened immediately. He got in and sighed as he pressed for the basement car park. It had been a long day, most of it spent trying to get to the bottom of a particularly complicated tax case on behalf of Len Chappell, millionaire owner of Chappell Construction. He felt tired and irritable.

When the doors opened again he walked towards his Lexus, the only vehicle left in the car park, and thought about what to do for dinner now he was a single man again. No more meals waiting for him when he got home. But then Sonja had never been much of a cook anyway. That was something he'd only found out *after* they'd gotten married, of course. Dumb bitch. Although he had to admit that was partly his fault. He'd always been more interested in the chase than the catch. Still, at least she was finally out of his hair. Maybe he'd simply skip dinner tonight. He wasn't really hungry anyway.

Addison unlocked the Lexus, got in and started her up. He drove over to the entry gate, swiped his card at the machine to raise the barrier, then pulled out onto Vercer and drove west.

Pity about the Mustang, though. It hadn't been the prettiest thing on four wheels, but it could sure move. On the other hand, as soon as that hefty life insurance payout of Sonja's came through, he could easily buy another Mustang to replace it. But a Mach 1, this time. The genuine article. Up till now, he'd had to be careful how he spent the money he got from his extracurricular work, but now he'd have a legit source to explain it away things would be different. He still found it hard to believe how well life was working out for him these days, but then it wasn't like he hadn't worked hard for it.

All good things come to those who wait, he thought.

And that was another thing. Now the Sonja situation was finally resolved, he was back in Gaspard's good books again. Not the same as before, of course. Not yet. But he would be. The drug boss didn't have many bagmen he could trust and he knew it. Not with Addison's respectable credentials. With a little patience, he'd be Gaspard's number one choice again soon enough.

Yes sir, after a brief bad spell there, everything now seems to be working out just fine.

He turned on the radio and for a change tuned into a country and western station as he drove, hoping they'd play a ditty about a dead wife. Something to give him a chuckle.

Ten minutes later, he entered his street. It was a short cul-de-sac containing only six houses, three on each side. Addison's was one of those at the end, set well away from his nearest neighbour. He'd always appreciated the privacy it gave him. Especially those times when he'd needed to discipline Sonja.

After pulling into his driveway, he got out and approached the front door. Another bonus was that the single-level house didn't feel so crowded now Sonja was gone. He could just put his feet up and relax. Right now, a couple of cold ones from the refrigerator sounded just fine and then he'd hit the sack. Gaspard had said he'd probably need him tomorrow. In which case, it would be a good idea to get a decent night's sleep while he could.

He opened his front door and entered the hallway. He was turning to push the door closed when he saw movement out the corner of his eye. Then something slammed against the back of his neck and he felt himself falling, falling.

By the time his head hit the floor, Carl Addison was already unconscious.

ELEVEN

First, there was movement behind the eyelids. Then Addison began moving his head slowly from side to side. Like he wanted the dream to last a little longer. Bishop sat in a chair several feet away and waited patiently for Addison to regain full consciousness.

They were in Addison's basement. Bishop had brought him down here and positioned him directly underneath the only light bulb. Bishop wasn't planning on wasting the lawyer. Not unless he absolutely had to. That's why he wore the black ski mask and leather gloves. And for the psychological effect, as well, he had to admit. Nobody likes seeing a man in a ski mask, especially when they're tied to a chair in a dark cellar. Then there was the small work table Bishop had placed next his own chair. And the items he'd placed upon it. They'd have their own effect too.

Addison slowly opened his eyes. He furrowed his brow, trying to figure out the new reality in which he found himself. Then he raised his head and looked straight at Bishop. His eyes grew round. He looked down at his bonds and said, 'Huh?' He tried to move his arms and legs without success. 'Hey, what is this?' he said, rocking his body from side to side.

Bishop let him. He'd already tested the chair and found it pretty sturdy. There wasn't much danger of it toppling over unless Addison lost it entirely. Bishop just sat there and watched as the man fought uselessly against his bonds. Waiting for him to adjust.

Finally, Addison became still and said, 'What the hell is this? You must have made a mistake. I'm just a lawyer, for God's sake. What do you want with me?'

Bishop switched his gaze to the desk at his side and knew Addison would be looking, too. He'd see two clear glass laboratory jars, each containing a clear solution and each bearing a white label. The first read *Sulphuric acid – H_2SO_4.* The second read *Hydrochloric acid – HCl.* Addison would know what they were, even if he couldn't make out the words from where he sat. They belonged to him, after all. Bishop had found them upstairs. In front was a large, empty beaker. Next to it was the gun that Addison kept in his bedroom drawer. A black 9mm Sig Sauer P226. Fully loaded. At the back were eight wads of bank notes stacked in two piles. Bishop had searched the basement and found them in a lockbox buried under an old filing cabinet in the corner. Four hundred thousand dollars in total. Drug money. Had to be.

Bishop picked up a $50,000 wad and tossed it on the floor between them. He then picked up the bottle of sulphuric acid, pulled out the stopper and carefully filled the beaker.

'What?' Addison said. 'Hey, you don't have to do that. Just tell me what you want, okay? I'll tell you what you want to know. We'll work this out. Just *talk* to me.'

Bishop said nothing. He just picked up the beaker, leaned forward, and slowly began pouring the acid onto the wad of notes.

The effects were immediate and impressive.

Holding his breath to avoid the fumes, Bishop watched, fascinated, as the notes began to turn brown and flaky before dissolving completely. The stuff ate through it at a rapid speed, as though he were observing it via time-lapse photography. He kept pouring until he'd made a deep hole in the bundle. When the beaker was empty, Bishop watched the acid consume the bundle from the inside out, as if it were a living organism. It was amazing to look at. Really incredible. Even Addison was silent, the awe clear on his face. After another minute, all that remained of the bundle of notes was a few untidy piles of discoloured powder on the concrete floor. And fumes.

Bishop sat back in his chair and said nothing.

Addison finally looked up. He was blinking rapidly. Bishop saw real fear in his eyes now. Fear of the unknown, probably. He was trying to figure out the reason behind Bishop's actions and coming up blank. To him, destroying money made no sense at all.

'I don't understand what you want,' he said. 'Just tell me what you want.'

Bishop said, 'Powerful stuff, huh? Sulphuric acid.'

Addison nodded. 'Yeah. Yeah, sure.'

'Know how human skin reacts if it comes into contact with this shit?' Bishop motioned his head towards the other jar. 'Or, even better, hydrochloric acid?'

Addison shook his head.

'Sure you do, Addison. Why else would you keep these in the house? Tell me what happens if you were to squeeze a few drops of hydrochloric acid onto . . . an arm, say. Let's make it a woman's arm. Like your wife's.'

'My wife? But she's . . .'

'Dead. I know. In that bungled loan store robbery. I read all about it. Taken hostage by some guy and they both die in a gas tank explosion when the getaway car speeds off a cliff. That must have taken some arranging, huh?'

'What are you talking about?'

Bishop nodded at the remaining bundles of cash. 'That wasn't enough for you, was it, Addison? You wanted the three hundred grand from her life insurance, too.' Bishop let his voice become more animated. He needed Addison to believe he was a real loose cannon. That he was capable of anything. Which was partly true. 'So you dreamt up this robbery scenario and arranged it so she dies at the end. Real convenient. And the robber. Who was he? Some poor loser you represented once? You promise him a big fat paycheck if he did this one favour for you, or did you always plan to kill him, too?'

'What? I didn't know him and that's the truth. I deal with things like tax law, employment law and personal injury cases. My partner, Ben Fraser, he's the one deals with criminal cases. And why would I want Sonja dead? She was my wife. I loved her.'

'Yeah, she showed me exactly how much you loved her. All those acid burns over her arms, for example. Told me how she'd get a new one any time she did something to displease you. And how you threatened to use hydrochloric acid on her face if she ever talked.'

Addison looked at the floor. Then at Bishop again. 'You knew her?'

'I loved her,' Bishop said, hoping the pain in his voice sounded genuine. It was essential for the role he was playing. 'And she loved me. She told me everything. We were planning on disappearing together when you stuck a spanner in the works.'

'Look, whoever you are, I had nothing to with her death. You've *got* to believe me. There was no way I could have organized something like that. It was all too random. The police were in pursuit of the car all the way and saw everything. It was just a bad hairpin turn and an eighteen-wheeler they didn't see coming. That's all. Her death was an accident. I'm telling you the God's honest truth. Ask anybody.'

Bishop studied Addison closely as he spoke. There are many ways to tell if a person's lying. Not so many if the suspect's restrained, but enough. Bishop had gotten to know almost all of them over the years. Too much or too little eye contact, for example. Or glancing up and to the right. Or unnatural pauses as they think about what to say next. Added to which was his gut instinct, which rarely let him down. And much as Bishop hated to admit it, the guy was speaking the truth. Or the truth as he knew it. He really did believe she'd died in that crash. Which meant he couldn't very well be behind her disappearance, too.

Bishop just sat and stared at him, thinking. He'd been so sure Addison was the one. Or that he had some connection to those who'd taken Selina. Had he been totally off the mark? Frowning, he let his eyes wander over the items on the table. He stared at the wad of notes, then picked up the top bundle. Flicked through it once. Fifty thousand dollars. The kind of money people got killed over every day. *If in doubt, follow the money.*

'Your friend in Reading,' Bishop said. 'Tell me about him.'

Addison didn't meet Bishop's eyes. 'What are you talking about? What friend?'

'Your wife told me you did regular errands for some drug bigshot in Reading. So what are you, his bagman? Or do you help launder his cash? What?'

Addison didn't say anything, but he didn't really have to.

'So was this guy aware your wife knew about his operation, and your connection to it?'

Bishop watched Addison's facial muscles relax as he gave a one-shoulder shrug. It was another tell and Bishop could almost guess the next words out of his mouth.

'He didn't know Sonja at all,' he said.

'So that's how you want to play it, huh?' Bishop moved his hand towards the gun.

'Look, you better kill me now if that's what you plan to do anyway. *He* will if he even *suspects* I've talked. You might as well get it over with.'

Bishop's hand passed over the gun and grabbed the bottle of hydro-chloric acid instead. He pulled the stopper out and filled the beaker again. It gave off an evil-looking vapour that dissipated on contact with the air. He touched his palm against it. It was very warm, even through the leather of his glove.

'Kill you?' Bishop smiled at Addison. 'Who said anything about killing?'

TWELVE

'Apparently,' Bishop said, 'when this stuff makes contact, all you feel at first is this unbelievable stinging sensation. That's what I hear, anyway. After that you can actually start to feel your face coming away in pieces. Really horrible. But you'd know all about that, right? Probably described it all to your wife in Panavision detail.' Bishop made a show of looking at his watch. 'Look, it's getting late. Tell you what, I'll just repeat the question one more time and we'll go on from there, okay? Did this guy in Reading find out about her knowledge of his organization and your connection to it, or didn't he?'

Addison took his eyes from the beaker and looked at Bishop. 'He found out.'

'That's better. How?'

Addison looked at his feet. 'I might have mentioned it to one of his people in passing. How my wife kept nosing into things she shouldn't.'

'And he passed it on.'

'He must have. Next thing I know, I'm being called into his private office and—'

'His name.'

Addison sighed, defeated. 'Gaspard,' he said. 'Joshua Gaspard.'

'And how do you fit into his operation?'

'I'm just a middleman, that's all. I collect cash from his senior lieutenants on a semi-regular basis and deliver it personally to him. He prefers using professional people like me who aren't about to be stopped and questioned by the police. But all his people know that I'm not to be touched.'

'A man of respect, huh? Okay, go on. He called you into his office, then what?'

46

'Well, he said he'd spent a lot of money to make sure he stayed in the shadows. Only a handful of people know he even exists and that's the way he likes it. He told me he didn't care that Sonja was my wife, he just wanted her gone now she knew his name. He said I had to take care of it personally, or he'd take care of me.'

'So you *were* planning on killing her.'

'I didn't know *what* I was going to do, and that's the truth. I swear to you. But it didn't make any difference, because a couple of weeks later she was dead anyway.'

Bishop said nothing, but he was thinking how fortunate his timing had been. If he'd left it another week or two to extract Selina, he might well have been too late. Addison would have put it off and put it off, but Bishop had no doubt he would have ended up justifying her murder to himself. The guy was pond scum from his soles on up. But at least now Bishop had another lead. And he also had a plausible reason to ask for more information on this Gaspard without raising Addison's suspicions.

He said, 'So it didn't occur to you that this Gaspard could have arranged the loan store robbery as a way of taking your wife out? If they hadn't swerved to avoid that truck, the robber could have had orders to kill her and then disappear.'

'Sure, it crossed my mind, but I couldn't exactly ask him, could I? What would be the point anyway? What was done was done.'

'I'll have to ask him myself, then.'

Addison made a face. 'Believe me, you've got no idea what you'd be up against.'

'Why don't you fill me in? You can start with his address.'

Addison sighed. 'It's a place called Equinox Tower. A fifteen-storey apartment block on 5th and Franklin, in the central business district. He owns the whole building. He keeps the seventh floor for himself and his men and rents the others out to tenants to keep it respectable. He operates all his business from there and rarely goes out himself.'

'Why not the penthouse?'

'The word is, he doesn't like heights much. Nobody knows for sure. Maybe the seventh floor is as high as he can go without bringing up his lunch.'

'You've been in there and know the layout,' Bishop said.

'I've been in there, but only as far as the first apartment. The one you see on the left as soon as you come out of his private elevator. That's where he has his office. Sometimes I hand the money to him, sometimes it's one of his men. I know he's knocked some of the walls through so most of the other apartments are kind of connected. I couldn't tell you which one's his, but it's probably one of those they left alone.'

Great, thought Bishop. *So much for accurate intel.* 'What about building security?'

'Well, you need a special key card to get into the place, and there are cameras all over the lobby. I always use his private elevator at the rear and it's guarded round the clock. Other than that, your guess is as good as mine. There's probably not much more, though. His men say he keeps everything pretty low-key to avoid drawing attention to himself.'

Bishop thought that sounded about right. If the place also doubled as a normal residential apartment block, Gaspard couldn't exactly treat it like a fortress. Tenants wouldn't stand for it. Besides, that's what his bodyguards were for. 'So what's he look like?'

'He's about five-eight or -nine, I guess. Stocky. Early thirties, but his hair's already turning grey. He keeps it long and ties it back. Small, deep-set eyes, and he's got a small star tattoo on his throat. Whenever I've seen him, he's always been wearing a tracksuit.'

'And his bodyguards. Tell me about them.'

'Black suits and black ties. Shaved heads. Fairly big. The usual.'

'Uh huh. And when you make deliveries, what kind of bags do you use?'

'No bags. Black Samsonite attaché cases every time. Gaspard says he likes how they smell when they're packed with money. He claims it's the best smell in the world.'

Bishop nodded. He remembered seeing three empty ones in Addison's bedroom cupboard.

He then reached down behind the table and pulled out a black nylon holdall he'd brought along. Inside was a police-issue M26 Taser gun and five spare cartridges he'd found in Addison's study. When you've got friends on the force, you get all the best stuff. And there was also the $50,000 brick he'd placed in there while Addison was unconscious. Well, $45,000 to be precise. The one he'd destroyed had simply been four hundred and fifty sheets of newspaper carefully cut to the same size and surrounded at each end by twenty-five hundred-dollar bills. He wasn't about to destroy a small fortune just to make a point. He wasn't stupid. This money belonged to Selina. If anyone had earned it, she had.

He transferred the rest of the cash into the bag. The 9mm, too. It might come in handy in the future. He zipped the bag closed and stood up. 'Well, that's it, then.'

Addison stared at Bishop. 'You . . . you're going to let me go?'

'That's the question, isn't it?' Bishop said. 'Thing is, I been trying to get your wife's acid scars out of my mind and I just can't do it. She suffered a lot of pain at your hands, both physical and mental. I'm thinking that you'll just find somebody else and do the same thing all over again.' Bishop turned and picked up the full beaker. It still felt warm to the touch. 'Unless I teach you a lesson.'

Addison started fighting against the ropes again. 'Whatever you're thinking,' he said, his voice rising, 'don't do it. I'm begging you.'

'Are they the same words your wife used on you? When she begged you to stop burning her arms, was she crying? I imagine she was. That's how people like you get your rocks off, isn't it?'

Addison was struggling frantically now. 'You've got it all wrong. I've got a bad temper, that's all. Sometimes it gets out of hand, but I'd never have used acid on her face. That was all show. Look, please. Doing this to me won't bring her back.'

'You're absolutely right,' Bishop said. 'It won't.'

Then he threw the contents of the beaker in the man's face.

Addison's screams were deafening in the enclosed space. He jerked his body back with enough force to topple the chair. Bishop watched him land on his back and thought he sounded like an animal with its fur on fire. He kept thrashing around like a man possessed, screaming incomprehensible words at Bishop.

Bishop just smiled. He picked up the bag and walked over to the stairs and began climbing. The bonds would probably take at least a day to get through. If not, one of his co-workers was sure to find him.

At some point, Addison would also grasp that although his face stung a little, it wasn't actually falling off. Maybe he'd realize he'd been suckered with hot tap water. Or maybe he wouldn't. Bishop didn't really care. Right now, he had more important things to think about.

THIRTEEN

Vaughn Mayfield followed his two prospects into the elevator and then hit the button for nine. He smiled at them both as the doors silently eased shut, but kept his attention mostly on the woman. 'Hot' didn't describe her adequately. Rhian Lerner was incredible-looking. He'd been captivated from the moment he met them outside the building.

The black skin only helped. It really brought out her large eyes. Made them seem like they were boring right into his brain whenever she looked at him. Like right now, for instance. And that coy, enigmatic smile she was directing his way held more than just professional interest. He was sure of it. He'd met enough horny women in the real estate business to know the signs. She clearly wanted Vaughn as much as he wanted her.

Her white boyfriend, Dennis Ackroyd, was oblivious. He just stood there in his suit, watching the numbers change. Which made a certain kind of sense. Vaughn knew he was some kind of accountant. A good one, evidently, if he could afford the rent on one of these apartments. They weren't cheap. He was fairly tall, but stoop-shouldered, with thick glasses. Vaughn thought he looked completely out of her league. He was guessing she probably stayed with Dennis for his money and got her kicks elsewhere. Which was fine by Vaughn.

'How come there's no seven on the panel, Vaughn?' Rhian asked. 'Is it unlucky or something?'

'Not at all. That whole floor belongs to the owner of this building and he's very serious when it comes to his privacy.'

'Oh. So he's got his own private elevator, then?'

'Exactly right. Here we are.' The elevator came to a stop and the doors slid open. 'After you, Rhian,' Vaughn said. 'Dennis.'

He followed them out and then led them down the left-hand corridor.

'This is it,' he said, stopping outside 906. Shifting his thick binder to his other hand, he pulled a chain of keys from his pocket, found the right one and opened the door. 'There are two empty apartments on this floor, but this one's south-facing. I think you'll like it.'

'Let's see, shall we?' Rhian said and went in first. Mayfield watched that tight little butt wiggle underneath the jeans and then Dennis blocked the view as he followed her inside. Vaughn closed the door and joined them in the living room straight ahead.

The next ten minutes he spent showing them round the large apartment, pointing out all the extra features, like the balconies outside the main rooms and the gym on the top floor. He emphasized the building's security and told them he'd even throw in an extra parking slot in the underground car park for free. He *really* wanted Rhian to take the apartment.

They were in the master bedroom when she said, 'What do you think, Denny? From where I'm standing it all looks perfect.'

'Yeah, it seems okay,' Dennis said, looking out the window. He didn't sound too excited or impressed. Vaughn guessed he was long accustomed to giving Rhian whatever she wanted, whenever she wanted it. But then, most men would.

Rhian turned to him. 'It wouldn't kill you to show some enthusiasm, you know. You were exactly the same when we . . . Hey, what's wrong, baby? You feeling okay?'

'Not really,' Dennis said and turned with his hand pressed against his stomach. In the sunlight, Vaughn could see he looked a little pale. 'Probably that seafood we had last night. I told you what happens when my system comes into contact with fish.'

'Your *system*.' Rhian rolled her eyes at Vaughn. 'That's all I ever hear about these days. Well, you better take yourself to the bathroom then.'

Vaughn said, 'You know where it is, don't you, Dennis?'

'Yeah, sure,' Dennis said and shuffled by Vaughn as he made his way out of the room.

Rhian sat on the bed and patted the mattress. 'This is a big old thing, isn't it, Vaughn? Two people could get up to all kinds of mischief on here, I bet. Why don't you take a load off? Dennis may be a while; he's got a very weak stomach. Among other things.'

Damn, she doesn't waste any time, does she? Vaughn smiled, placed his keys and binder on the bed and sat down beside her. 'So you like the apartment, Rhian?'

'I sure do. How many others are available in this building?'

He reached for his folder and opened it to the second page. 'Well, we've got 904 also on this floor. Then there's 1507 on the top floor and . . . let's see, another one on the fourth floor's just come on the market. That's just a one-bedroom, though.'

'But the other two are like this one?'

'More or less. They're both two bedrooms. One's north-facing. The other's on this side.'

Rhian nodded. 'I don't suppose you've got a floor plan, do you? So I can get a sense of where everything is in relation to each other. Like for the fire exits and elevators.'

'Sure, I should have a few copies in here.' He turned to the clear wallets at the back, flipped through to the ninth floor, then pulled out a folded sheet and handed it to her.

'You got one for the fifteenth floor, too? That's where the gym is, right?'

'Oh, sure.' He found the layout for the top floor and passed it over. At the same time, he angled himself so their thighs were touching. Rhian smiled, but didn't move away. He watched her profile as she looked over the plans and said, 'There are some great restaurants around here, Rhian. We could arrange a time and I could show you a few if you'd like. If Dennis didn't mind.'

She smiled at him. 'Dennis wouldn't have a say in the matter. I go where I please and do what I want.'

'I can see that.'

She looked at him and said, 'We could do dinner next week, maybe. Why don't you tell me about some of the hot spots around here. Maybe we can try some of them out, too.'

Music to my ears. Vaughn smiled as he began listing the wildest nightspots in the area, all the while watching Rhian's eyes sparkle in hedonistic anticipation. He was sure she'd be an absolute animal in bed and he couldn't wait to give her a test drive. After a while, though, it dawned on him that he hadn't heard from her boyfriend in some time.

'Is Dennis okay, you think?' he said. 'He's been gone awhile now.'

Rhian frowned as she looked at her watch. 'Hmm, well, I wouldn't worry too much. Maybe you could just knock on the door and see if he's okay.'

'Right.' Vaughn stood up and walked out. In the entrance hall, he knocked a couple of times on the bathroom door and said, 'Everything okay in there, Dennis?'

There was no response.

'Dennis?' Still no sound. He turned the handle. The door was unlocked. Vaughn poked his face round the door and saw an empty bathroom. No Dennis. *What the hell?*

He turned to his right and saw the entrance door was unlatched. Which wasn't good. Unauthorized people wandering around the building could reflect very badly on him. Vaughn jogged over and pulled it open. Then he heard a weird wheezing sound and stepped into the hallway. And there was Dennis, thank God, leaning against the wall. He was out of breath and sucking on an inhaler of some kind. He looked in a bad state.

'Asthma attack,' he said. 'I get them . . . every now and then. I didn't want you . . . to hear me choking. It's kind of embarrassing. But I'll be . . . okay now.'

Man, what a pathetic wreck, Vaughn thought. *No wonder Rhian likes to play the field.* But he smiled and said, 'Hey, no problem. You've seen everything, anyway. If you want to wait here, I'll just go grab my keys and folder and see if Rhian's ready to leave.'

Dennis just nodded and Vaughn turned to go back inside. He was already thinking about which restaurant he'd take the guy's girlfriend to next week. And for what he had in mind afterwards, it needed to be one fairly close to a hotel.

FOURTEEN

On the busy sidewalk out front, Mayfield shook hands with them both and said, 'Don't forget, guys, you call me any time you got any questions, okay?' He glanced quickly at the woman he knew as Rhian. 'Any time at all.'

'Thanks,' Bishop said, still playing dumb.

'We'll definitely be in touch, Vaughn,' Jenna Falstaff said, giving him a sultry smile.

Vaughn grinned back, then turned and marched off down the street to wherever he'd parked his car.

Bishop took off the glasses and rolled his shoulders, ironing out the kinks that came with stooping for so long. 'So when's the wedding?'

'Not exactly subtle, is he?' Jenna said with a sigh. 'I think I need a long shower after all that. Boy, the things I do for you.'

'Don't give me that. You were enjoying yourself. I saw you.'

'Well, maybe a little,' she said. They began walking towards the narrow side street that bordered Equinox Tower's west side. 'So did you have enough time?'

'Just about. He caught me out of breath but the inhaler explained it away.' They stopped at the corner of the side street. It was more an alley really, but it allowed them to get clear of the lunchtime sidewalk traffic. 'What about you? You get the floor plans?'

'Naturally.' She reached into her shoulder bag and handed them over. And a key. 'For 1507,' she said. 'He's sure to notice it's missing before too long, though.'

'Well, I should be safe enough for a few hours, at least. After that, it won't matter.'

'What if this Addison's already gotten free? He'll try to warn Gaspard, won't he?'

'Not if he wants to keep breathing. Admitting he gave Gaspard's name to a complete stranger would be like signing his own death warrant, and I don't think even he's *that* dumb.'

'Well, if you say so. But I think you're taking a big risk.'

Bishop shrugged and looked at Jenna for a moment. Then he leaned forward and kissed her. 'Thanks for helping. I really appreciate it.'

Which was something of an understatement. Last night, his internet research at Addison's revealed the sole agent for Equinox was an outfit called Slocombe Realty. He'd then called Jenna and asked if she'd be willing to come down to Pennsylvania to help him out with something. She hadn't been too happy about it, but she eventually agreed to pick up the few items he asked for and then drive straight down. He couldn't think of anybody else who'd do the same.

Jenna touched her lips with two fingers. 'Wow, was that an actual kiss? From *you*? And just what else was I was gonna do, James? In case it's escaped your attention, this is about the closest thing we've had to a date in months. It seems you're always busy, or is it that you've got yourself a new squeeze and I'm just being slow?'

'You know better than that.'

'Do I? So what is it, then? Has the thrill gone already?'

'Look, let's not do this now, huh? Not here on the sidewalk. Not when I got a dozen other things on my mind.'

'Seems to me you've always got something on your mind,' Jenna said with a snort. 'And as far as I'm concerned, now's as good a time as any. Besides, what's the big obsession about finding this Selina girl, anyway? I'm getting the impression she means a lot more to you than you've been making out.'

'She's just someone who needs help, that's all,' he said. He really didn't want to get into all the whys and wherefores right now. Or his history with Laurette Chounan. It would take far too long.

Jenna shook her head in obvious aggravation. 'See what I mean? As talkative as ever. Well, let me tell you, I've had a lot of time to think about us over the last few months, and I've come to realize I might have made a big mistake. I know our relationship was all based around some pretty strange circumstances, but enough time's passed that that's no longer an excuse. Everything's been kind of been one-way for a while now, and that's not good enough. I don't expect the earth, but a little honest commitment from you would sure go a long way.'

'You're right, Jenna,' he said. 'But I told you right from the start I'm not used to long-term relationships. Maybe I'm just not cut for them. I don't know.'

'Yeah, I remember. I didn't really want to believe you then, but I'm starting to now. Look, James, I don't wanna fall out with you, but this is really frustrating. We rarely talk these days, and even when we do nothing gets said. I'm thinking maybe we should just draw a line under this while we're still on friendly terms.' She gave a long sigh and said, 'I don't expect a decision from you right this second, but you need to decide what it is you really want and give me an answer. And soon. Because I won't wait around forever.'

'I understand,' he said. 'We'll talk, I promise.'

After a short silence, Jenna nodded and kissed him on the lips. To Bishop, it felt chaste. Like she'd already made her decision. He wasn't sure if that was a good thing or not. He pulled away and said, 'I better go.'

'Bet you say that to all the women,' Jenna said with a half-smile.

Then she turned and joined the rest of the pedestrians on Franklin without looking back. In less than a second, she was part of the crowd. Then she was gone.

FIFTEEN

For a brief moment, Bishop toyed with the idea of going after her. But the impulse passed quickly. He had work to do. Instead, he turned and continued deeper into the alley.

The narrow cul-de-sac went on for about three hundred yards or so. He passed several vans parked on either side. On his left, a fat delivery guy was carrying large boxes from the rear of his van and handing them to another guy in a doorway. Neither man gave Bishop a glance. On the right was an unmarked trade entrance to Equinox Tower, but he wasn't planning to gain entrance that way.

Bishop kept walking and stopped at the fire exit door further down. It was solid steel and set flush against the wall. Almost. He also knew it was equipped with an AC powered alarm, set to go off any time the locking bar was pushed open from the other side.

Jenna's comment about 'strange circumstances' had been a reference to his prison escape last year and the ensuing fallout. But the time he'd spent inside for another man's crime hadn't been entirely wasted. His cellmate, for instance, had always been eager to show him different ways to get into buildings. And Bishop had always been a good listener.

Earlier, while Jenna kept Vaughn distracted, Bishop had run down eight flights until he reached this door. He'd taken his tools from his jacket pocket and gone to work on the control panel located close by. After disconnecting it from the mains, he'd had to work fast before security noticed something was up. He quickly located the contact switch in the doorframe. Then he removed the two wires in the device, twisted them together and left them disconnected. After reassembling the device, he'd reconnected the control panel to the mains and pushed open the fire door. There had been no alarm. He knew the control system still received the same voltage whether the contact switch was open or closed. As far as it was concerned, everything was functioning correctly.

He'd then inserted a small rubber wedge to keep the door from fully closing and sprinted back up the stairs. Out of breath, he'd reached the apartment about five seconds before Mayfield's head appeared outside the door.

Bishop stepped over to the grey dumpster a few feet beyond the fire exit and looked back. The delivery guy was locking the van's doors and making ready to go. Bishop waited another minute as he got in, started her up and slowly pulled out into Franklin.

After a final check, Bishop opened the dumpster lid. He reached in and moved a couple of black garbage bags out of the way at the back until he found the undisturbed attaché case he'd hidden this morning. He pulled it out and walked back to the door. Thanks to the wedge, about a centimetre of the door's edge was jutting out of its steel frame. He moved to one side, used the fingers of both hands to get a purchase on it and carefully pulled the door open.

He picked up the attaché case and slipped inside, closing the door fully behind him. He then took the floor plans from his pocket and looked from one to the other, memorizing every detail.

Each floor shared the same basic layout, with nine apartments of varying sizes around the perimeter. The largest apartment was the one on the north-west corner. No. 901, according to the plans. On the fifteenth floor it was taken up by the gym. It took up most of the northern side, with a short hallway separating it from its much smaller neighbour on the north-east corner. Another hallway separated it from its immediate neighbour on the western perimeter. Which meant it was the only completely segregated apartment.

No. 701 would be Gaspard's room. Bishop was sure of it.

That it wasn't on the top floor already showed good sense on Gaspard's part. Back in his close protection days, Bishop had always hated it when clients demanded the penthouse. They were showy and difficult to defend against. Somewhere in the middle was always better. 701 had easy access to the fire stairs without being too close. It was also right next to Gaspard's private elevator. Had to be, since the only place for it was in that hallway between 701 and 702.

Satisfied, Bishop pocketed the plans and continued walking down the empty hallway until he reached the stairwell. He listened for a moment, heard nothing, then began climbing.

He saw nobody all the way to the seventh floor. Same as when he'd used the stairs earlier. In Bishop's experience, fire stairs in the more expensive apartment blocks were rarely used by tenants. Those afraid of elevators could usually afford to find somewhere closer to the ground to live. Bishop just hoped that theory would hold true in this case.

The stairway door was made of steel with a gap of about three or four millimetres at the bottom. More than enough. Bishop knelt down and opened the attaché case. He pulled out the gun, checked it and placed it in the back of his waistband. Some extra ammo went into his pocket. He then took out the Medit industrial fibre-optic scope he'd asked Jenna to get from her brother's apartment. Boasting a tiny 1.0mm diameter insertion tube, it was the smallest scope on the market, and ridiculously expensive. The nature of Aleron's business meant that clients seeking his particular talents occasionally offered to pay in black market merchandise rather than cash. Ali had mentioned once that he currently had a box of these things in his basement and was holding on till he found a buyer willing to pay the right price. Fortunately for Bishop, it seemed he was still waiting.

Bishop listened for any sounds above or below, but again heard nothing. He then lay on his stomach to the side of the door and slowly inserted the tube partway into the gap. He looked through the eyepiece and saw part of a door opposite. Manoeuvring the Teflon-coated tube to the left he saw a dimly lit hallway that ended in a right turn about two hundred feet away. Same tasteful, dark brown colour scheme as the ninth floor. Nobody in sight.

He moved the tube to the right and saw the bottom half of a man in a dark suit. Panning upwards, Bishop saw he was leaning against the wall about ten feet away, close to the corner so he had a clear view of both corridors. He had close-cropped hair and was doing something on his cell phone that required both hands. Probably playing a game. He was also wearing lightly tinted aviator sunglasses, which made Bishop happy. There was no reason at all to wear sunglasses in here, so the guy clearly just wanted to look cool. Excellent. Still, Bishop wasn't about to underestimate him. That's how mistakes got made.

Bishop got up, put the scope back in the case and took out a roll of duct tape and the cheap, disposable Samsung cell phone he'd picked up earlier. He placed the phone on the floor a few feet from the door, picked up the case and climbed the stairs to the next turn. He peered back and estimated the distance to the door was about twenty-five feet. Should be okay.

He pulled his own cell from his jacket pocket and pressed a single key. Almost immediately the Pink Panther theme tune echoed through the stairwell from the Samsung down below. Bishop crouched down on a step out of sight and took the gun from his waistband. Checked it once more.

And waited.

SIXTEEN

After one hundred and seventeen seconds, Bishop heard the sound of the door opening.

Bishop just stayed where he was and kept counting as the ringtone started up again. He gave the guy two seconds to cover the immediate area as he looked for the phone's owner. He gave him another to realize one of the tenants must have dropped it on their way up or down. Bishop waited a further two seconds, then emerged from his place on the next landing, gun pointed downwards.

The guard was in the act of picking up the cell phone with his left hand. He had an automatic in his right. The moment he stood up, Bishop aimed the M26 and fired.

The compressed nitrogen in the Taser cartridge immediately propelled two darts at a speed of one hundred and eighty feet per second dead centre into the man's chest, along with thirty-five feet of insulated wire and fifty thousand volts of electricity.

The guard's hands snapped open into claws and both gun and phone fell to the floor. Bishop sprinted down the stairs as the man landed on his back like a sack of wet towels, convulsing violently as the voltage surged through his nervous system. Bishop quickly wrapped the roll of duct tape around the man's wrists four times and tore it off. Then the same with the ankles. All the while, the man's eyes remained locked on his every move.

Bishop calculated five or six seconds had passed since he'd fired. That was the average time for a person to stay incapacitated after being hit with one of these things. Sure enough, the man's convulsions suddenly stopped on the six second mark.

'Son of a *bitch*,' he said, and kicked out at Bishop with his feet.

Bishop sidestepped neatly and stamped his own heel into the man's stomach. The guard let out a whoosh of air and curled up onto his side. Bishop knelt down, tore off another length of tape and pasted it over his mouth. He still needed to ask this guy some questions, but he'd have to make do with yes or no answers. He couldn't risk him calling out for reinforcements.

'Don't move,' Bishop said.

The guy finally stopped struggling, but kept glaring at Bishop.

Bishop pulled out his cell phone and ended the call. The stairwell went quiet again. He was already sick of that song. He pocketed the other cell and checked the guard's gun. It looked like a Colt M1911 except the magazine extended out from the handle by about two inches. It was an OTs-33 Pernach, a lightweight Russian 9mm machine pistol he'd heard about back in his close protection days. Illegal as hell. He checked the 27-round magazine and saw it was full, with one in the chamber.

In his wallet, he found a driver's licence made out to an Anthony Holland. He also found a compact Motorola two-way radio clipped to his belt, which he attached to his own.

He removed the guard's sunglasses, put them on and went back for his attaché case. After reloading the M26 with another cartridge, he studied the bound man. Bishop was six-one and this guy looked about an inch shorter. But they were about the same weight. Bishop was one hundred and seventy-five pounds and this guy couldn't be much over one-eighty. Hair was slightly shorter than Bishop's buzz cut, but Bishop couldn't do anything about that.

He crouched down and pulled out the ninth floor plan. 'Okay, Holland,' he said. 'Now pretend this is the seventh floor and point out Gaspard's room for me.'

The guard paused, then used both index fingers to stab at 905 in the south-east corner.

Bishop sighed and stood up. *Why do they always have to do it the hard way?* He aimed the M26 at the man's crotch area. The man's eyes grew wide. Bishop shrugged and pulled the trigger.

The darts entered Holland's testicles and he doubled up like a bear trap as electricity coursed through them. He rolled onto his side, jerking uncontrollably, his face a picture of agony.

This time it took about seven seconds for the spasms to stop. Bishop waited for the man's breathing to return to normal and said, 'Everyone's allowed one mistake. That was yours.'

He reloaded the Taser, stuck it back in his waistband and brought out the Pernach. He pressed the barrel of the machine pistol against the man's left kneecap and said, 'Don't lie to me again, understand?'

Holland stared wide-eyed at the gun, then at Bishop. He nodded twice. Bishop picked up the floor plan and showed it to him again. 'Gaspard. Where?'

The bodyguard pointed at the apartment on the north-west corner. 701.

'Good,' Bishop said. 'How many other guards in the corridors?'

Holland raised a single index finger.

'Where?'

The man pointed at the small hallway between 701 and 702. Which more or less confirmed Bishop's guess about the elevator's location.

'How many people in the other rooms?'

Holland frowned, then raised nine fingers.

'How many of them women?'

Holland thought again. Four fingers this time.

'Is Gaspard alone?'

A head shake.

'He's got some of the girls in there with him?'

Holland nodded and showed two fingers.

'Okay,' Bishop said, 'thanks.' He slammed the side of the gun into the man's temple and watched the eyes roll upwards. He figured he'd be out for half an hour, at least. He unfastened Holland's shoulder holster, inserted the weapon and put it on under his own jacket. Then he picked up the attaché case, pulled open the door and entered the seventh floor corridor.

He stood still for a moment, listening. He could hear the sound of muffled laughter from one of the apartments in the hallway to his right. It sounded feminine. Then a male voice said something. More laughter.

Bishop turned left and stopped when he heard one of the doors ahead opening. He put down the case and took his cell phone from his pocket. Leaned against the wall and started pressing random buttons. In his peripheral vision, he saw a man step into the hallway carrying a sports bag. Bishop hoped the glasses and subdued lighting would work in his favour. The man glanced in Bishop's direction as he closed the door.

'That Tetris'll make you go blind, Tony,' he said in a rough voice.

'Mm hmm,' Bishop mumbled without looking up. Just kept pressing buttons. He saw the man shake his head and walk away from him. Then he turned at the junction and was gone.

Bishop listened. After a few moments, he heard voices and then the faint sound of an electric motor in operation. Had to be the private elevator. The guy was going out.

He breathed out again, picked up the case and followed the same route, passing doors along the way. At the end, he stopped and peered right. The hallway was empty with a single door halfway down on the left. Gaspard's apartment. Bishop could also make out soft slapping sounds coming from the elevator alcove at the end. He smiled to himself. It was the sound of cards on a table. The other guard was playing solitaire. *Real pros, these guys.*

Bishop entered the hallway and kept walking. As he approached the door he unclipped the walkie-talkie from his belt and brought it to his right ear, partly obscuring his face if the guard decided to get nosy and check.

He knocked on the door. After a few moments, a muffled voice said, 'What?'

Bishop lowered his voice a couple of octaves to match Holland's and said, 'Tony.' He placed the case on the floor and gripped the Taser gun in his rear waistband. This was the worst part. He'd have a split second to decide whether to shoot Gaspard or not. And if he did and the guard heard it and poked his head round, Bishop would be momentarily defenceless. And a moment like that could last a lifetime.

He waited.

Bishop then saw a movement at his far right and knew it was the guard. He kept the walkie-talkie at his ear and willed the door to open. *Come on, Gaspard. Open up. I don't have all day.* The guard was still there. Still looking at him. Pretty soon he'd wonder why Holland had a walkie-talkie stuck to his face and come see for himself.

Then Bishop heard the sound of tumblers dropping and the door opened a few inches. Bishop looked in and saw a man with a greying ponytail walking away from the door dressed in a tan bathrobe. He was talking on a cell phone. *Perfect timing.* He'd caught the guy while he was in the middle of a call and distracted. Bishop picked up the case, calmly stepped inside and closed the door after him. He turned the key in the lock and pulled out the Taser.

He was in a vast living room that offered a panoramic view of the city. Gaspard was walking over the thick white carpet towards the windows, still talking while gesticulating with his free hand. He didn't sound happy. To Bishop's left were two doors, one closed, one partly open. Through the open door, he could see part of a large bed and a woman's foot. Further away to his right were two more doors. Both of these were closed.

Bishop aimed the M26 at the middle of Gaspard's back and just waited.

When Gaspard finally flipped his phone closed and turned round, he opened his mouth to speak and that's when Bishop fired.

SEVENTEEN

Bishop slapped the back of his hand hard against Gaspard's face and he jolted awake immediately, his eyes darting in every direction as he tried to figure out why the world had gone topsy-turvy on him. The effects of the chloroform had undoubtedly slowed down his mental processes a little, so Bishop gave him a moment.

Gaspard looked down, or 'up' in his case, and finally got it. His eyes bugged out and he let loose a long, satisfying scream, muffled only by the duct tape over his mouth.

They were on the balcony of apartment 1507 on the south-west corner. Or rather, Bishop was. Gaspard was just outside it, hanging upside down with his hands secured behind his back. Bishop watched him through the glass panel of the railing. Right now the only thing preventing Gaspard from dropping one hundred and sixty feet to the side street below was the Sterling 8mm mountaineering rope he'd tied around the man's ankles and waist. This rope was looped through the ribbed grille of a stainless steel, ceiling-mounted LED light before finishing up at the sliding balcony door, where it was tied to the handle.

Bishop figured if you wanted to make somebody talk, a good start was to have them wake up to their worst nightmare. And it looked like Addison had been right about Gaspard's acrophobia. Hauling him up five flights of stairs had been tiring, but the result was worth it.

Bishop approached the railing, looked down and said, 'Some drop, huh?'

Gaspard had finally stopped screaming. But he still looked far from calm. The star tattoo on his throat seemed to be moving of its own accord and there was a damp patch at the front of his tracksuit pants that was steadily growing in size. Bishop looked across the way. Of the buildings opposite, the tallest was seven storeys high, so they were safe from any observers from that direction. And a protruding wall gave them privacy from their immediate neighbour to the right. He couldn't have picked a better spot if he'd tried.

Bishop looked down at his captive and said, 'Now, in a few moments I'm going to take that tape off your mouth and we're going to talk. I'm going to ask you some questions and you're going to answer them.' He reached down and picked up a kitchen knife he'd found in the apartment behind them. 'And one thing I can absolutely guarantee is that if you scream, shout, or say anything above a whisper, I'll cut this rope. Do you understand?'

Gaspard nodded his head frantically, his forehead twice striking the glass panel in an effort to get his point across.

'And since I've already been given answers to some of these questions, if I catch you lying at any point, same result. Are we clear?'

Gaspard was nodding so much his body started to sway from side to side. Which made him start panicking again. Bishop sighed and came forward to stop the rope from swinging. He didn't have time for this. It was already half an hour since he'd set off that ringtone in the stairwell. There was no telling when one of the other guards would notice Gaspard and Holland were missing and organize a floor-by-floor search. He needed to be gone from here.

Once Gaspard was still, Bishop reached down and ripped the tape from his mouth. Gaspard let out a loud sigh and then clamped his mouth shut, breathing heavily through his nose. His body swayed a little from the breeze.

Bishop crouched down so their eyes were level through the glass partition. As with Addison, he'd have to go the indirect route to get the information he wanted. He couldn't very well accuse Gaspard of snatching Selina when she was supposed to be dead. But if Bishop continued to play the role of an aggrieved lover convinced she'd been killed by Gaspard, he'd be all too eager to prove that she was still breathing if he could.

'Now listen up,' Bishop said. 'An easy one to start you off. Sonja Addison. You recognize the name, right? Think carefully and answer.'

Gaspard swallowed and said, 'Yeah, I know the name.'

'That's a good start. Next question: when did you first find out she was aware of the connection between you and her worthless husband?'

'I don't . . .' Bishop began to rise and Gaspard said, '*Wait*. Wait. One of my men, Wynant. He told me.'

'After Addison let it slip?'

'Yeah. Who are you?'

'Just somebody who cared for her a great deal, that's all you need to know. Now the robber of that cheque-cashing store who took her hostage, how did you recruit him?'

There was a long pause. Gaspard said, 'What are you talking about?'

'Well, I can't see you using one of your own men for the job, so he must have been an outsider. Where'd you find him?'

'Wait a minute. You think *I* was behind that robbery a month back?'

'Yeah. You ordered Addison to take care of his wife, but after a couple of weeks I think you got impatient and decided to take matters into your own hands. So you arranged a robbery where she got randomly picked as a hostage. Probably instructed your guy to kill her once he lost the cops on his tail. Tell me, when he swerved to avoid that truck and they both ended up in that ravine, did you feel like the luckiest man on earth, or what? A real, honest-to-God accident falling right in your lap like that.'

Gaspard slowly shook his head. 'Hey . . . Hey, now, you got it all wrong. If Addison told you this, he's given you bad intel. You gotta believe me.'

'So you didn't tell Addison you wanted her dead? That what you're telling me?'

'I . . . Okay, I admit I lost my temper when I found out she was butting into my business. But I don't go round wasting civilians if I can help it. That's bad business. And I like a low profile. So I told him to deal with it himself if he wanted to stay on my good side.'

Bishop just looked at him. Gaspard had to know he was balancing on a knife edge here, so he couldn't afford to give a single wrong answer. No outright lies so far, but he still wasn't as desperate as Bishop wanted him. That had to change.

He got up, then reached down and placed the tape over Gaspard's mouth again. 'Sorry, Gaspard. And you were doing so well up to that point. I'm sure you had her killed, so you know what happens now.'

Gaspard struggled frantically, causing his body to swing from side to side again. He made noises under the tape that made it clear he had things to say if only Bishop were to let him. Bishop just turned and picked up the knife, then stepped over to the section of rope that went from the ceiling to the door handle. He pressed a finger against the cable, testing the tautness. Let go and watched it vibrate.

The drug boss was almost crazy with fear now, shouting under the tape, his head knocking against the glass so much Bishop thought it might crack. But Bishop just gripped the rope with one hand, and with the other started to make slow cutting motions with the knife. Then after a few moments he frowned and turned to Gaspard. As though he were deciding whether to give him another chance or not.

He released the rope and walked over to the railing. 'Scream and you drop,' he said. Gaspard stopped struggling and nodded twice. 'Last chance. If you got something to say, speak. And it better be good.' Bishop reached down and ripped off the tape again.

'Please,' Gaspard said breathlessly. 'Don't do this, man. You're making a big mistake. I'm telling you the truth, I swear to God. When I heard about the crash I was on cloud nine, I admit. At first I thought it was Addison's doing, but he ain't smart enough. Like you said, I put it all down as a gift from the skies. Look, man, I understand about revenge, but it was an accident. That's all. Just an accident. I had no hand in this, I swear. Come on, pull me up. Please, I'm begging you.'

Bishop looked at him and already knew he was telling the truth. If Gaspard had been behind Selina's kidnapping, he would have offered to swap her for his life by now. No question. And Bishop couldn't see him kidnapping her and then offing her. Not when it was simpler just to smother her in her bed. No, Gaspard wasn't the man he was after.

Which meant Bishop was right back at square one again.

EIGHTEEN

The town of Saracen, Arizona was located off Route 60, about a hundred miles northwest of Phoenix. With the I-10 running almost parallel about fifteen miles to the south, there was never much traffic on the 60 and today was no different. Bishop was driving a rented Chevy Impala this time. That's all the National guys had left at the airport, but he didn't really care as long as it got him where he wanted to go. He'd actually planned to get here yesterday, but every flight except the one this morning had been full. Even in first class.

At 13.03, he passed the town limit sign – *Welcome to Saracen, Arizona. Pop. 10748. Home of the original desert-dwellers!* – and a short while later made a left onto Saracen Road. He carried on for a couple of miles, drove through the centre of town and out again, and took a few more turns until he reached the Heritage Apartments.

The complex looked much better in the sunlight. Like a little green oasis in the desert. Bishop parked up in the same spot as before, grabbed his overnight bag from the passenger seat and got out. After the air conditioning of the car, the heat was like a short slap in the face. Not that he was complaining. Heat was always preferable to the cold in Bishop's opinion, and at least there was no humidity. Anyway, he wasn't here for the climate.

Yesterday, after leaving Gaspard hanging for his men to find, Bishop had considered his next move. And it hadn't taken long to figure out the only avenue left was to return to Arizona, follow in Selina's foot-steps and see what he could dig up. Because Bishop was now sure her disappearance had nothing to do with her previous life. Which meant the people who'd taken her only knew her as Selina Clements, newly arrived resident of Saracen. They'd seen her around town, found out where she lived and grabbed her for reasons as yet unknown. So Bishop would stay here until he discovered those reasons. And from there, the road was sure to lead to Selina. One way or another, he'd find out what happened.

Bishop passed through the open gate at the rear and followed the same route as before. Since the rent was already paid up for another five months, Bishop saw no reason to let Selina's apartment go to waste.

Along the way he passed an elderly couple on the ground floor, sitting in chairs outside their front door. The woman smiled and said, 'Afternoon,' as he approached. Bishop returned the greeting. The man said nothing, just watched him as he passed.

Bishop climbed the stairs and let himself into No. 40. He picked up two envelopes from the doormat, both addressed to the previous tenant. One was an invitation to apply for a Visa card, the other plugging an obscure overseas lottery.

Bishop showered, then pulled a grey T-shirt, a white button-down shirt and some fresh black chinos from his bag and put them on. Then he went next door to No. 39 and rang the bell. Thirty seconds later the door opened and a wide-hipped, dark-haired woman in her mid to late thirties glared back at him, holding a mug of something hot. She had prominent bags under her eyes and didn't look too happy. But maybe she always looked that way.

'Help you?' she asked.

'Yeah, sorry to disturb you, but I'm from No. 40 next door. My name's Bishop.'

'Congratulations.' She leaned against the wall of her hallway and gave him a half-smile. 'Mine's Andrea. So you're my new neighbour, huh?'

'Well, that's what I wanted to talk to you about. Do you know the woman who was here before?'

Andrea frowned. 'Quiet, blonde girl? Selina, wasn't it?'

'That's her. Selina Clements.'

'We spoke a couple of times. Why?'

'She's my girlfriend. I was supposed to join her here, but I haven't talked to her in a month and there's no sign of her in the apartment apart from a few clothes. I'm real worried.'

'You haven't talked to her in a month?' Andrea raised one eyebrow as she took a sip of her drink. 'That sure don't sound like no boyfriend I ever heard of.'

Bishop gave a strained smile. 'I did try, but her cell phone's out of service and she hasn't had a landline put in. I've been overseas finishing up a contract job, and this is absolutely the earliest I could get away.'

'What about her folks? You could have called them and they could have maybe filed a missing persons report or something.'

'Selina hasn't got any family. There's just me.'

'Oh, okay. Well, like I said, I only talked to her a couple of times. She was pretty shy and kept herself to herself. And I work nights, so our paths didn't cross that often. I do know she worked in one of the diners in town, though.'

'You know which one?'

Andrea shook her head. 'I don't eat in town much. Just pass through it on the way to work and back again.'

'Can you remember the last time you saw her?'

She looked at a point above Bishop's head as she took another sip. 'It was about a month ago, I think. I know it was the day they arrested that drugged-up rapper in LA for crushing his girlfriend's skull with a pipe. I was coming home from my shift after hearing it on the car radio and Selina was just going out to work. She said guys like that should go straight to the electric chair without passing *Go*. I remember being surprised, 'cause that was totally unlike her. She didn't usually have much to say, although she was always polite to me. And don't ask me for the exact date, 'cause I couldn't tell you.'

Bishop didn't need to. He remembered reading the story in the *Times*. It had been May 15. And Selina was scheduled to call her mom the next day. Which meant she must have been grabbed that same night. And it was now June 12, making it four weeks to the day since she'd been taken.

'And she didn't seem worried about anything else when you spoke to her?'

'It was just a quick conversation, that's all, and I was pretty tired. But she didn't seem any more nervous than usual, if that's what you mean.'

'Was she dressed in her work clothes when you saw her?'

'Uh huh.'

'You remember the colour of her uniform?'

She furrowed her brow as she took another swallow. 'Uh, it was light blue, I think. Yeah, that was it. Light blue, with white collars.'

'Okay. Can you let me know if you remember anything else? If I'm not in, you can leave a note under the door.'

She shrugged. 'Sure, but I really don't know anything more. Look, don't forget to go to the police and file a missing persons report, okay? Maybe they can help.'

'I won't forget,' he said and turned to go. 'Thanks.'

NINETEEN

As Bishop drove back into town, he thought back to Andrea's parting suggestion. She meant well, but filing an official missing person's report was about the last thing on his mind.

Selina's new name would hold up under a certain amount of scrutiny, but there was no telling how much damage a full-scale investigation might do. And any detective who dug deep enough would eventually find himself with a lot of unanswered questions. Like how come the missing person has a credit history that only goes back a year? And how come she has no relatives and no friends? And even if by some miracle the cops *did* locate her, where would that get him? They never reveal the missing person's whereabouts or give out any kind of contact information. They're not even allowed to pass on a message.

No, this wasn't something he could trust to the police, even if he wanted to. Bishop needed to do this himself. He wouldn't be able to rest otherwise. He possessed enough self-awareness to know the obsessive gene in his DNA was calling the shots now. He'd screwed up by not staying in regular contact with Selina. Now he needed to make things right again, if he could.

He reached the outskirts of the main part of town, found a space on the street and parked. He got out and started walking, breathing evenly. Working off the anger he felt at his own stupidity and thoughtlessness. It was still lunchtime, but the streets weren't exactly crowded. With an area covering fourteen square miles, Saracen was one of those mid-size Arizona towns with too much space and not enough people. But he guessed that was all part of the state's attraction. That and the slower pace. And the weather, of course.

Feeling somewhat calmer, Bishop stopped outside a dingy antique store. A fat guy in his fifties was sitting on a chair beside the entrance, reading an old crime paperback with a man's bandaged face on the cover.

'Good book?' Bishop asked.

'Better than most,' the man said and looked up. 'What can I do you for?'

'I'm looking for a diner around here where the waitresses wear light blue uniforms with white collars. You know the one I mean?'

The man brought his eyebrows together. 'Seem to me that'd be Tod's Café. So you're into uniforms, huh?'

'Not so much these days. Where can I find this Tod's?'

'Just keep going down here two more blocks, then take a right into Willingham. You'll spot Tod's down on the left. They do a mean chilliburger if you're interested.'

'I am now. Thanks.'

Bishop followed the directions and found Tod's Café less than five minutes later. Situated on a large lot, it was a typical single-storey building with lots of glass at the front and a tall, bold-lettered sign outside. He walked in and saw the place was already half full. He checked his watch. 14.06. The lunchtime crowd was still going strong.

He took a booth next to the window at the end and sat with his back to the wall. Old habits, dying hard. One of the waitresses, a heavy-set brunette in her late twenties, came over and handed him a menu. Her nameplate read *Sandy*. He said, 'The guy outside the antiques store said you do a great chilliburger here, Sandy. That right?'

'Flynn? Yeah, he's dead on. He recommend a side order, too? Because our onion rings are something else, believe me.'

Bishop handed the menu back and said, 'Looks like my choice is made, then. And can I get an iced tea with that?' She nodded as she wrote down the order and Bishop said, 'Tell me, Sandy, did you know Selina when she worked here?'

She paused and looked at him. 'She was a pretty, blonde girl, wasn't she?' Bishop nodded and she said, 'We said hello to each other a few times, but you really need to talk to Gloria. They used to time their breaks so they could go out back together.'

Bishop looked around and saw three other waitresses. 'Which one's Gloria?'

'See the woman over there serving the old couple, about my age with longer hair? That's her.'

Bishop saw her. 'Do me a favour, Sandy. Ask her to come over when she gets a spare moment?'

'Sure thing. I'll be back with your drink.'

Bishop watched Sandy walk up to Gloria and say something while pointing in Bishop's direction. Gloria looked over and gave a brief reply before moving off to another customer. Sandy hadn't said so, but Bishop assumed she smoked during her breaks, which caused him to wonder if Selina had started smoking too. Bishop wouldn't have been surprised. He knew waitressing was pretty high on the list when it came to stressful jobs.

A minute later, Sandy returned with his drink and said, 'Gloria said she'll stop by when she can.'

'Thanks.'

Bishop sipped at his drink and studied the room. Like him, there were plenty of guys on their own. Manual workers as well as guys in shirts and ties. A few joked with the waitresses as they passed by. Regulars, probably. There were also one or two women dining alone. One in the booth across the aisle kept sneaking glances his way. Without looking directly at her, he could see she was both attractive and of Latino extraction. Probably waiting for her boyfriend. He gave a mental shrug and turned his thoughts back to Selina, wondering how many customers had joked with her when she worked here. The way she looked, guys probably came here when they weren't even hungry, just so they could talk to her. Maybe more than just talk. A few of them must have worked up the courage to ask her out. Had she turned them all down, or had she decided to risk a date with one? It didn't seem likely, but he couldn't discount the possibility.

'Sandy said you wanted to speak to me?'

Bishop looked up to his right. The thin form of Gloria was standing at his side with one hand on her hip, head tilted slightly. Her blue-grey eyes were focused on his. There was a hint of defiance in them that he liked.

'I'd just like to ask you a few questions about Selina, if you don't mind,' he said. 'I hear you two were friends.'

'Are you a policeman or something? 'Cause you sure don't look like one.'

'I'll take that as a compliment. No, I'm just another friend who's concerned for her welfare. She's been missing for a month now and I want to find her.'

'Oh. Well, I can't talk now, this is our busiest period. You'll have to wait until my next break.'

'Okay. When's that?'

She paused, chewing on her inner cheek as she studied him. 'Well, if you're out back in about an hour, we can talk for as long as it takes for me to finish my cigarette.'

'I'll be there,' he said.

TWENTY

Gloria took a Marlboro Light, placed it between her lips and lit the end with a match. 'I didn't get your name,' she said, blowing out a plume of smoke as she shook the match out.

'Bishop,' he said. They were in the rear car park, out by the dumpsters. Gloria had come out a few seconds ago, nodded once to Bishop and slid a brick over to keep the rear door from closing. As far as Bishop could see, they were alone out there.

She leaned back against the wall, one arm tucked around her waist. 'So what makes you think Selina's missing? She could have just taken off, you know. No law against it.'

'Did she seem the spur-of-the-moment type to you?'

'Not really, but then I only knew her for a short time.' She offered him her pack of cigarettes. He shook his head and she said, 'Don't blame you, it's a bad habit. I gave the same warning to Selina, but I didn't need to. One drag was enough for her. Poor girl almost coughed up a lung.'

'But you still shared breaks.'

'When we could. She kind of latched on to me for some reason, but I didn't mind. I liked her. She was shy as hell, but she had this mystery about her, too, like she'd experienced plenty already. Not that she ever talked about it.'

'She wouldn't.'

Gloria arched an eyebrow. 'Bad?'

'She only just got out in time. This was a fresh start for her.'

'And that was thanks to you?'

'I helped.'

She looked at him for a moment as she took a long drag of the cigarette. 'Must be nice to have a friend like you. All right, so what do you want to know?'

'How long had she been working here at Tod's?'

'Just over a week, I guess. Eight or nine days.'

'And then on May 16, she just didn't turn up for work?'

'Was that the date? Then yeah. I tried calling her cell to see what was up, but all I got was an "out of service" message. I do remember thinking it was weird she never came to pick up her last few days' pay, though.'

'When you talked, did she seem worried about anything? Or did she mention any problems?'

Gloria pursed her lips and slowly shook her head. 'To be honest, she let me do most of the talking, which was fine by me. She was pretty quiet on the whole, although she did tell me she was only doing this until she figured out what she really wanted to do, and that she might apply for an evening class at some point and learn a skill. But I think she just liked listening to me, you know?'

Bishop turned as an SUV containing a family of four pulled in, looking for a space. 'Was she seeing anybody that you know of?' he asked.

'Guys, you mean? She didn't mention anybody, but that might not mean anything. We never really reached the diary-sharing stage.'

'But women talk about the men in their lives, don't they?'

'Not all of them, Bishop. Give us some credit.'

He smiled. 'Sorry. What about customers? Any of them give her special attention?'

Gloria snorted and smoke exited her nostrils. 'She wasn't exactly short of admirers, if that's what you mean. You should have seen some of the tips she was getting from our male regulars. Unbelievable. Although I don't think she ever really understood why. She didn't mind putting it all into the kitty either, which made her better than okay in my book.'

'And nobody sticks out in your mind? Somebody who showed more than casual interest in her?'

Gloria chewed her inner cheek again, then took another drag. She watched the father lock the doors of the SUV and follow his wife and two kids as they walked round to the front entrance. Then her eyes narrowed.

'Something?' Bishop asked.

'There *was* a guy, but I couldn't tell you his name or anything. He came with some workmates one lunchtime shortly after Selina started. Then all of a sudden he's in here every lunchtime on his own. Always sat in Selina's section too. Good-looking guy.'

'What was he, an office worker?'

'Not unless they suddenly dropped the dress code around here. Auto mechanic would be my guess. He wore dark overalls with the sleeves rolled up, probably so he could show off his muscles. His pals were wearing them too. They were all pretty loud, I remember.'

'And did he come in on the day Selina didn't show?'

Gloria furrowed her brow again. 'Hey, now you mention it, no, he didn't. And I can't remember seeing him since then, either.'

'Can you remember what he looks like?'

'Um. Well, he's shorter than you. Maybe five-nine. Stocky with round shoulders. Fairly muscly. Light brown hair, shaved at the sides. He looked pretty intense, I can tell you that.'

'Do you recall seeing any kind of logo on the overalls? Like the name of a tyre, or a garage? Something?'

Gloria sighed and said, 'Hey look, I'm not out there taking notes, you know. I'm too busy trying to solve earth-shattering problems like why there's an onion ring in someone's fries, and what am I gonna do about it. Or why somebody got rye instead of white bread, when I know for a fact he specifically ordered rye in the first place. I don't have time to notice everything.'

'I understand. Well, thanks, anyway.' Bishop turned to go.

'Hey, Bishop,' she said, and he stopped and looked at her. 'I didn't mean to snap. It's just been a busy day, okay? Busier than usual, I mean. Hold on for a minute while I think.'

'Sure.'

Bishop leaned against the dumpster and watched the cigarette. There was about an inch to go before she reached the filter, but people rarely let it get that far. She took another lungful and looked skyward as she breathed out. It would sure save time if she could give him something more to go on. But if she couldn't, it was no big deal. It just meant he'd have to keep working the streets like any good investigator until he found the guy. And he *would* find him. He was just deciding in which direction to start when he felt Gloria staring at him. He looked up at her.

'Jennings,' she said. She was smiling.

'Jennings?'

'Or Pennings. Something like that. On his chest pocket. In green. Not obvious from a distance. I remember passing by his table and wondering whether it was his name or not. But it looked more professional, like for a company.'

Jennings or Pennings. Bishop smiled and took a twenty from his pocket. He folded it lengthways and offered it to her. 'Thanks, Gloria. I really appreciate your time.'

'Hey, I didn't talk to you for profit.' She dropped the remains of her smoke and stamped on it. Pulling the door open, she nudged the brick aside with her foot and smiled at him. 'Promise you'll let me know when you find her and we'll call it quits, okay?'

'I promise,' he said, and watched the door close behind her.

TWENTY-ONE

Bishop crossed Saracen Road, then walked two blocks before going east down West Central Avenue. He'd driven down here before, back when he was scoping the place out for Selina, and remembered this was where the majority of the local government buildings were located.

It took him less than ten minutes to find the public library. It was a modern, hundred-foot square, single-storey adobe building with four matching pillars out front, two on either side of the tinted glass entrance.

Bishop liked how almost everything around here was single-storey, with the occasional two-storey building here and there to break things up. But then, Arizona had the luxury of plenty of space to play with. It made a refreshing change from New York, though, where construction only ever went in one direction: upwards.

He passed between the pillars and entered the building. Once inside, his first thought was that they'd accidentally set the air-conditioning to freezing, but after a few seconds his body decided it wasn't that bad. He slowly scanned the room until his eyes landed on the reference section in the north-west corner. He walked over, passing some female students and an old guy carrying a stack of military tomes, found himself a local Yellow Pages and took it to an empty table.

He opened it up and went straight to the *Automobile* section near the front. There were lots of sub-sections and he started with the first: *Body Repairs & Painting*. It was always best to be thorough, and he knew many of these places employed their own team of mechanics. There were seven businesses listed in the Saracen area, but none of the names came close to sounding like Jennings. He kept turning the pages. *Automobile – Dealers. Automobile – Parts & Accessories. Automobile – Rentals.* Nothing.

But *Automobile – Repairs & Servicing* presented him with a real possibility. Twenty-four businesses were listed, but it was the second one that caught his eye. *Bannings Automotive.*

Bishop thought it wasn't too big a leap to get to Jennings. Or Pennings. Gloria had said she only got a quick look, after all. He carefully scanned the whole page. There was no display ad for Bannings, only a listing with the address – *17 E. Richards Ave., Saracen* – and a phone number. He memorized them both and kept turning the pages, reading through the *Automobile – Tires* and *Automobile – Wash & Detailing* sections to make sure. Nothing else even came close.

He rose and put the directory back where he'd found it. Then he went to the maps section on the next shelf along. He pulled out one of the street maps of the town and unfolded it. East Richards Avenue was out on its own near the southern tip of the town. Three miles from here, according to the scale. He memorized the directions and replaced the map.

Then he left the library and went back for his vehicle.

TWENTY-TWO

Bannings Automotive was a flat-roofed, prefabricated steel building and the last structure before East Richards Avenue came to a natural end. There was a narrow dirt track that continued left, but past that it was just sagebrush, cacti and fenced-off desert until you got to the mountains far off in the distance. On the other side of the road was a fenced playground with a hoop at each end. A couple of kids were dribbling a ball around without much enthusiasm as they watched Bishop's car make a U-turn and come back.

Bishop parked the Chevy on the side of the road and got out. He walked towards Bannings and saw a single door entrance for customers on the far left, next to a small window. Further down were three large, shuttered entrances from which the sounds of engines, drills and hydraulic machinery could be heard.

Since the closest neighbour was a flat, windowless building Bishop had passed fifty yards back, he figured they probably didn't get too many complaints about the noise.

He peered into the first shuttered entrance. There was a pick-up on a lift. A guy in dark blue overalls stood underneath, using a drill on something on the underside. He wore a moustache and looked Hispanic. Bishop felt sure Gloria would have mentioned that so he tried the next one. This had another car on a lift – an old BMW this time – but at ground level. One mechanic was in the driving seat, fiddling with something under the steering wheel. Bishop could see he was too skinny to be the one. Another guy was leaning over the engine, shining a pencil light at something. Bishop stepped inside for a better look.

The man saw Bishop's shadow and raised himself up. He was in his early twenties and had the right height and build, but Bishop immediately discounted him. Gloria had said the man he was after was good-looking, and this guy most definitely did not qualify. He had a large, bulbous nose and there was a lopsided quality to his features that was hard to ignore.

'Help you with something?' he asked.

'No thanks,' Bishop said and moved on. The third area had a lift, but was otherwise empty. Bishop could see through to the rest of the garage inside. It was a vast open space, half of which was taken up by stacks of old tyres. Hundreds of them all over the place. Numerous vehicles lay in various states of repair and Bishop could hear a loud radio playing some kind of death metal over the machinery noises. He began to walk in that direction.

'Where you going, mister?'

Bishop stopped and turned. The same man was glaring at him from the entrance, fists against his hips.

'Inside,' Bishop said. 'I'm looking for somebody who works here.'

'*I* work here.'

'You're not the one I want to talk to.'

'Oh, yeah? What's the matter, don't you like my face or something?'

Bishop raised an eyebrow. 'No comment.'

The man's eyes grew smaller and he pointed at a sign attached to the wall that read *Employees only past this point*. 'See that? It means you better come back here. Right now.'

'What, before you turn ugly?'

The man took a step forward and said, 'Shit, you looking to get your ass kicked, is that it? 'Cause I'm the man for that.'

Bishop sighed and turned away, carrying on past the lift and into the garage's main work area.

The lighting in here wasn't great, but Bishop could see well enough. He was watching the ground. Specifically the shadows. When he saw a long shape extend from the shadow following him, Bishop swivelled and grabbed the hand just about to land on his shoulder. With his .other hand, Bishop gripped the man's index finger and pushed it back as far as it would go, stopping just before the bone was due to snap. The man grunted and quickly fell to one knee to stop it going any further.

'We don't have to do this,' Bishop said, keeping the pressure on while the man clamped his lips shut. 'A broken finger's no good to a man who works with his hands, and I doubt you get medical coverage in this place. So why don't you just go back to what you were doing and forget we ever met? How's that sound?'

'Good,' the man said with gritted teeth.

'Excellent,' said Bishop and let go. He watched as the man gripped his finger and got to his feet. Then he turned and walked back to the BMW. His skinny partner who'd been watching the proceedings quickly darted back inside the car before he was noticed.

Bishop turned back. Everybody else was still working. Nobody had been watching. The loud radio probably helped, although part of him wondered how anybody could work with that racket going on. *Doesn't anybody write actual songs any more?* Bishop saw a pair of legs sticking out from underneath a Chrysler. He nudged the guy's foot with his toe and waited as the mechanic rolled himself out and squinted at Bishop. He was about Bishop's height and had long curly hair down past his shoulders.

'Forget it,' Bishop said. 'My mistake.'

The guy frowned, then shrugged and rolled back under the vehicle.

Bishop walked between more vehicles until he reached a Chevy pick-up with its hood removed. A man in overalls was leaning in with his arms wide apart and his back to Bishop. His head moved in time to the noise blasting from the radio on a table a few feet away. He was about five-nine. Stocky and well built. His hair was clearly shaved at the back and sides.

Bishop walked over and faced him from across the engine. The man looked up and frowned. Bishop studied him quickly. Mid-twenties. Straight nose, piercing eyes, symmetrical features. Everything in its place. He guessed it was a good-looking face. Anyway, this had to be the guy. He was the only one left.

Bishop walked over and pulled the plug on the radio. The garage went blissfully quiet for a moment. Then the sounds of tools and revving engines filled the air again.

'What the hell you think you're doing?' the man said.

'Couldn't hear myself think,' Bishop said. 'You and I need to have a talk.'

The man snorted and said, 'Yeah, right.' He began moving towards the radio. 'Whoever you are, you better get on out of here before I throw you out.'

'I have already had this conversation with Waxworks back there,' Bishop said. 'And I really wouldn't touch that plug.'

The man halted. Looked over at his less attractive buddy, who was back working on the BMW. Then at Bishop. 'What *is* this? Who are you, anyway?'

'Just somebody who wants some answers.'

The mechanic scratched his forearm. 'Look, what's this about? You a cop?'

'Why? Were you expecting one to show up?'

The man's eyes seemed to look in every direction but Bishop's. 'I don't know what you're talking about.'

'And I think you do.' Bishop had already noticed another shuttered door at the side of the building, raised halfway. He pointed to it and said, 'Through there. You first. Let's go.'

TWENTY-THREE

Once outside, Bishop saw they were in a large, enclosed yard with wire fencing all around, concealed from the road thanks to two rows of old oxyacetylene cylinders lined up against one side. Bishop also saw two manual gas pumps next to the building that looked like they'd been around since the fifties, but the strong smell of fuel out here indicated they were still in working order. Also scattered around were wheel dollies, towing equipment, car ramps, manual forklifts and various other pieces of garage equipment.

As the guy fiddled with a pack of Juicy Fruit, Bishop looked up and noticed a small security camera attached to the roof antennae, aimed towards the front of the building. He turned back to the mechanic and said, 'You can start with your name.'

The guy stuck a stick of gum in his mouth and said, 'Gary Hewitt. You gonna tell me yours?'

'Mine doesn't matter.'

'Well, if you're a cop, you gotta show me some ID.'

'I'm just a private citizen, which means I don't have to show you anything.'

Hewitt's brows came together. 'So what's this all about?'

'It's about a waitress at Tod's who's gone missing. You know who I'm talking about.'

Hewitt looked at the ground and began carefully folding the gum wrapper into a small square. After a while he said, quietly, 'Selina.'

'Correct answer. Now tell me what you did with her.'

Hewitt looked up. '*Did* with her? I don't get you.'

'No?' Bishop moved a step closer. 'Well, maybe you can get this. I talked to people who can place you at Tod's diner for every day she worked there, always sitting in her section and talking to her every chance you got.' Bishop was only guessing at that part, but it was educated guesswork. 'And then a month ago, on May 16, she doesn't show up at the diner and neither do you. And nobody's seen her since. Now from where I'm standing, that kind of puts you in a bad spot.'

Hewitt looked at the ground again and began unwrapping another stick of gum. Bishop noticed his hands weren't entirely steady.

The death metal started up again inside. Bishop said, 'I also notice you don't act too surprised when I say she's been missing all this time. Which means you know why.'

'Look, I didn't do *any*thing to her, man. That's the truth.'

'Convince me. Take me through it. You showed up at the diner with some of these guys one lunchtime, right? And once you laid eyes on her, what was it, lust at first sight?'

'At first, sure. But once I got talking to her I realized she was real nice with it, and I ain't met too many women like that recently. Not with looks *and* personality.'

'Sure. So what then? You kept asking her for a date and she kept turning you down, right?'

Hewitt stopped chewing. 'Huh? What makes you say that?'

'You kept going back. If she'd said yes at any point, you wouldn't have bothered. So what'd you do next? Start following her home when she quit work?'

'Why would I do that?'

'Because you sound like the type who can't take no for an answer. You probably don't get turned down by women too much, so you'd want to know why this one was different. I recognize the obsessive type.'

Hewitt snorted. 'Hey, I'm no stalker. That ain't my scene at all.'

'No? So what did you do?'

'Nothing. Just parked outside her place a few nights to see what the wind blew in.'

Bishop watched him shrug, as though that kind of passive surveillance might not really count as stalking. But Bishop didn't care about that. He'd had a feeling all along Hewitt knew more than he was telling and this sounded like the inroad he'd been waiting for.

'And you saw something,' he said.

'Hey, Selina wasn't seeing anybody, okay? I was just—'

'I know she wasn't,' Bishop said. 'That's not what I meant. You were there on the night of the 15th, or the morning of the 16th. I want to know what you saw.'

Hewitt rubbed at the stubble on his cheeks and glanced inside quickly before turning back. 'Okay,' he said, 'but the whole thing was kinda weird.'

TWENTY-FOUR

Bishop leaned against one of the fuel pumps and folded his arms. 'I'm listening,' he said.

Hewitt sighed. 'Well, I was at the rear parking bay where I could just about make out the door to No. 40 on the second floor. I'd parked there the two previous nights, and usually gave up around eleven and went home. But this time I must have been real tired, 'cause the next thing I know I'm hearing footsteps outside and my head's resting up against the window. I look at the dashboard clock and see it's two fifty in the morning.

'I was still half asleep, but I raised my head and noticed this ambulance parked on the other side of the lot. But the lights weren't on or anything. The back door was open and two paramedics were carrying this stretcher inside. And it sure looked to me like there was somebody on it.'

'You couldn't make out any details?'

'I got tinted windows and it was pretty cloudy that night. And I was still groggy. I didn't really think anything of it, you know? There's plenty of old timers at that Heritage place, so I just figured one of them croaked that night. That would explain why there weren't no flashing lights. No big deal. So I just sat there and waited for them to go.'

Bishop watched Hewitt unwrap a third stick of gum and place it in his mouth. 'Then what?'

'Well, one guy stayed in back. The other one got in the driver's seat and shut the door real quiet. Then it was just more waiting while I tried to stay awake. Mostly I just wanted to get home, but I didn't want anyone seeing me there. I thought they'd drive off or something, but the ambulance just stayed put. After about a minute, it occurred to me to check Selina's door and that's when I saw a third guy come out and lock the door behind him.'

'Another paramedic?'

'I guess. He was carrying a small bag and wearing the same clothes as the other two.'

'Which were what?'

'Black pants and light, short-sleeved shirt with those badges on the shoulders. Like you see on TV. Anyway, he came back down, got in the passenger side and then they just pulled out and slowly drove off. That's all I saw.'

'Not quite,' Bishop said. 'Tell me about the ambulance.'

Hewitt thought for a moment. 'Well, it looked like a white Ford E350. Maybe a F350. You know, the kind that looks like a box with a cab stuck on front? Type I or Type III, they call them. The same models most hospitals use.'

'Any markings?'

'Uh, yeah. Two horizontal stripes across the body and cab that ended in a jagged M shape, like the heartbeat on an ECG. Don't ask what colour, everything's grey at that time of night. And if there was the name of a hospital on the side, I sure didn't see it.'

'Licence plates?'

'From that distance, in the dark? Forget it.'

'You didn't notice anything else?'

Hewitt scrunched his brow as he chewed. 'Well, when it pulled away, I looked at the rear doors and saw the stripes and that heartbeat squiggle again, but it was different. It didn't look like an M any more, you know? Like maybe they'd pasted it on upside down by mistake.'

'Okay,' Bishop said. 'So what then? You just went home and forgot all about it?'

'Hey, what you take me for, man? I checked the next day, okay? I called the nearest hospitals and asked if they brought in a Selina Clements the night before, except nobody knew what the hell I was talking about. I tried, man. What else was I supposed to do?'

Bishop shook his head. 'You saw an otherwise totally healthy young woman being placed in an ambulance in the middle of the night, which then drove off with no sense of urgency whatsoever, and didn't feel that warranted a call to the cops?'

Hewitt made a harsh sound through his nose. 'That'd go down real well, wouldn't it? And when they ask me what I'm doing in the parking area at three in the morning, what do I tell them? That I'm just checking that the girl I seen in the diner is sleeping okay? I don't need that kind of rep, man.'

'You could have made an anonymous call.'

'Nothing's anonymous in this town. It would have come back to me.'

Bishop doubted it, but saw little use arguing the point. Besides, what was done was done. All that mattered now was to move on with this new information.

But at least it meant Selina was still out there somewhere. Waiting to be found. She had to be. This had been a professional job by people who'd done it before. And it wouldn't be to snuff her out. They'd taken her for a specific reason. The ambulance and paramedic cover was a neat touch, too. Just in case they ever got stopped. It could even be real, although he thought it unlikely. Paramedics worked in twos, not threes. That was something he'd have to check next. But he still had a couple more questions.

'Tell me what you remember about the men, what they looked like, anything that sticks in your mind.'

'Well, it was dark like I told you. The first two I couldn't even tell you if they were fat or thin. I was still trying to keep my eyes open.'

'But you got a good look at the last guy, right?'

'Well, he was big. About your height, maybe taller. And thickset. Wore a small beard like this.' Hewitt used a finger and thumb to make a circle around his mouth and chin.

'A goatee,' Bishop said. 'Was his hair long or short?'

'Short. It didn't look like he had much left on top, but I can't be sure.' Hewitt showed Bishop his palms. 'That's everything, man, I swear. Now I gotta get back to work before the boss notices I'm missing.'

'One more thing,' Bishop said.

Hewitt turned back. 'What?'

'Which hospitals did you call?'

TWENTY-FIVE

Bishop drove back into town and slowed when he saw a Mail Boxes Etc. The dashboard clock said it was 17.07, and he figured most places would be closing up fairly soon. He found a spot and parked, then went back and entered the store. As he'd expected, it was one of the smaller branches. But big enough for what he was after. In addition to the mail boxes, packaging supplies, mailing accessories, printers and copying machines, he also saw a passport photo booth over in the far corner.

Ten minutes later, he emerged with his purchases. Then he got into his car, started the engine and pulled out into the light traffic.

Hewitt had given him the names of the three closest hospitals. One of them, Saracen Medical Center, was on the west side of town. Bishop didn't need the map. He'd already seen it once before when he'd made his initial recon of the area. Instead, as he drove though the residential streets, he thought about what he'd learned so far and wondered if it was enough. He knew he was doing all he could. Following every lead and moving from one step to the next. Keeping the momentum going. But it still rankled that he'd discovered Selina's disappearance so late. He knew every day not spent searching for her was a day wasted. And it was coming up to a full month now. That wasn't just a cold trail. It was freezing.

But he wouldn't quit. He couldn't.

He drove on. The houses became more scarce the further out he got, and in their place he saw various business premises, a couple of used car lots, a number of storage companies and a large industrial park full of warehouses. He took a left when he saw the turnoff he'd been looking for and drove on for another mile. Saracen Medical Center was at the end.

Three low buildings of varying sizes made up the centre, each with its own large parking area. He drove past the main building and followed the signs for *Emergencies*. They finally guided him to the third building. There was a large sign out front with *EMERGENCY* in dark red letters. He drove on round the back and saw a covered rear entrance for the emergency vehicles. There were two ambulances already parked in nearby spaces.

Bishop parked, got out and walked over. Even from a distance he could see the vehicles didn't fit Hewitt's description. They were the right colour, but that was all. These ambulances looked like cargo vans with slightly raised roofs. No stripes on the sides, either. Just blue and yellow checkers running along the bottom and the name of the hospital in big letters on the rear doors.

He turned and walked back to his car. He hadn't really expected to hit paydirt so close to the scene of the crime, but he had to check anyway. On to the next.

The driver of the Ford Fusion stayed in the main car park with the engine running. She knew the Impala would return. There was only the one road in and out. It was just a matter of waiting, that's all. And she was good at that. In her line of work, you had to be.

And here it came now. She caught a glimpse of this Bishop behind the wheel, looking straight ahead with that same focused expression she'd seen before. It was a look that told her he wasn't the type to give up once he started out on something. That was something to think about. She might have to take some action soon.

She let the Impala pass by and just sat there for a few more moments. There was no rush. She'd already planted the low-frequency tracker under his vehicle back at the auto repair place, so she had some breathing space. You couldn't get away with shadowing somebody in this state without them noticing sooner rather than later. Not unless you had an edge.

The Impala had already disappeared from view. She counted to twenty to make sure, then pulled out of the parking area and drove off in the same direction.

TWENTY-SIX

Bishop got back onto Saracen Road and when it joined Highway 60 turned right, back the way he'd come.

It was almost dusk by this time and in his rear-view Bishop could see the sky start to turn orange. Out of habit, he once again took note of the buildings as they whipped by. There weren't many. Another business park with a smattering of large warehouses. Some ranches here and there, both private and for tourists. A dilapidated old aircraft hangar in the distance. The abandoned remains of a roadside motel with a decrepit arrow-shaped sign out front. The ever-present RV resorts and trailer parks with those great names, like Sunrise Paradise and Eden Park. Then it was just desert. And the road.

After twenty-eight miles, he passed through Aguila and then took the turn onto State Route 71. After another fourteen miles of that he joined the US 93 and headed north-west. Soon after, he left the highway and followed the signs that pointed him to the town of Garrick.

He stopped at the first gas station he saw and went inside. There was a selection of road maps near the till and he took one for Garrick, handed the proprietor a ten and said, 'Do you know where the medical centre is?'

'Sure do,' she said as she gave him his change. 'Want me to mark it for you?'

'That'd be great.'

She smiled, unfolded the map and used a pen to draw a cross on the east side. 'Right there on East Clifford Avenue. It takes up the whole road, so you can't miss it.'

'I won't,' he said. 'Thanks.'

It took him less than five minutes to find it. The town of Garrick was about half the size of Saracen, but the hospital more than made up for it. It took up several acres and was made up of five connected buildings, each with its own parking area. The main building was four storeys high. The rest were the usual two. Bishop checked all the front entrances and didn't see a single ambulance. Finally, he followed the sign that pointed him to *Emergencies*.

It was almost dark now and Bishop switched his headlights on. He followed the service road round and parked in the most remote lot. After deactivating the ceiling light, he opened the door and got out. He walked the rest of the way down the road, then through an open entranceway towards the rear of the main building.

He was in a service area illuminated by spotlights, semi-sheltered by an eight-foot high brick wall running round it. Bishop saw a covered entrance to his left with sliding access doors similar to the ones at Saracen. No doubt electronically operated via infrared sensors at the top of the doors. They usually were. There was a call button in the wall to the side.

Adjacent to the doors, jutting out like an afterthought, was a solitary, one-storey utility structure with no windows and a single metal door. There was a dark passageway separating it from the hospital. Beyond that, facing him, was a continuation of the main building with a raised area for deliveries. He saw several shuttered doors, an ice machine, a row of seats and a small table outside. There was also a large, unoccupied mobile unit parked in the corner with *Give blood – the gift of life* written on the side.

But no ambulances.

Bishop went back to his car, got in and saw it was 18.58. One would turn up soon, he was sure. The odds were with him. There was always an emergency somewhere. He moved the car so it was facing the way he'd come, sat back in his seat and got as comfortable as he could. Then he just stared out the windshield, watching everything that moved.

A minute later, he saw a car pull into the next parking lot ahead. Some Ford or other. It looked vaguely familiar, but then there were plenty of Fords around. He soon lost sight of it behind some other parked vehicles.

He slowed his breathing and waited.

TWENTY-SEVEN

At 20.52, Bishop saw flashing red and white lights in the distance, coming his way. There was no siren. The ambulance followed his route down the service road, took the curve and passed in front of him. Bishop had enough time to take note of the box shape and horizontal lines on the side as it sped by, then it disappeared through the entranceway.

Bishop got out and ran over, staying out of sight behind the wall. The ambulance was backing up to the emergency doors, where a male nurse in scrubs waited, clipboard in hand. The lights above the entrance gave Bishop a clearer view of the vehicle. It was definitely a type I or III. That box shape was unmistakable. It was white and had two horizontal stripes that ended in a jagged heartbeat graphic. It almost looked like an M.

The vehicle stopped and the nurse pulled the rear doors open and helped the paramedic in the back lower the patient and gurney to the ground. The paramedic went back for an oxygen canister and held a mask to the patient's face. Bishop noticed he was wearing the same kind of clothes Hewitt had described: dark pants and white short-sleeved shirt with badges on the shoulders. Then they both rolled him or her through the doors and into the building. Bishop instinctively started counting. Ten seconds later the automatic doors began to close.

Same kind of clothes. Same kind of ambulance. That wasn't coincidence. But he still needed to investigate further.

Next step was to get inside. Problem was, you couldn't just walk into a hospital and nose around like in the old days. Everybody wore identification now. Even visitors. Besides, visiting hours at most hospitals ended at 20.00, and entering that way wouldn't allow him the freedom of movement he needed. Which left just one option.

Bishop turned his attention to the driver. He was still sitting in the ambulance, writing something down and checking his watch. Then he yawned, opened the door and stretched as he got out. He ambled over to the raised area, jumped up and took one of the seats. He pulled something from his shirt pocket, stuck it in his mouth and lit it. Then he took his cell phone from another pocket and started pressing buttons with one hand as he smoked.

Bishop stayed by the wall and calculated the distance to the ambulance. About forty feet, more or less. The driver was still playing with his phone. Bishop moved to the left until the ambulance shielded him from view. Then he took a deep breath and sprinted towards it.

Three seconds later he came to a stop next to the rear cabin, breathing deeply through his nose. He checked the back. The stripes continued along the rear doors and there was the same heartbeat graphic, only smaller. It still looked like an M. Which meant this couldn't have been the ambulance Hewitt had seen. But right now it could still prove useful.

Bishop sidled over to the passenger side door and glanced through the window. The driver hadn't moved. But Bishop was more interested in the vehicle's interior. There was a dark windbreaker in an untidy heap on the passenger seat. Bishop had never looked a gift horse in the mouth, and he wasn't about to start now. He wanted that jacket.

He crouched down and grabbed the door handle. He took one last look at the driver, then opened the door a couple of inches. Not wide enough to activate the interior light. He reached in, pulled the jacket through the gap and gently closed the door again.

Bishop quickly went through the pockets. There was a wallet in one and he opened it up. Credit cards. Some cash. Driver's licence. The usual. But not what he wanted. He put it back and tried another pocket. He felt something plastic and brought it out.

It was the guy's hospital ID.

The laminated kind, with a mylar strip and alligator clip attached to it. At the top of the card was the name of the hospital. On the left, an illustration of the caduceus – the winged staff entwined by two serpents from Greek mythology. On the right, a head shot. In the centre it listed the owner's name as Albert Williamson, gave the date of issue and his ID number. Then a thin barcode at the bottom. On the back was a list of the hospital's alert codes, specified by different colours.

Perfect.

After another glance at the driver, Bishop opened the door and dropped the jacket on the seat. Chances were he wouldn't notice the ID was missing for some time yet. And even then he'd figure he'd simply dropped it somewhere and go get a replacement. No big deal.

Remembering that shadowy passageway he'd seen earlier, Bishop went to the rear of the ambulance and took another look. It was about twenty feet from the emergency doors. Good enough. Since the utility building concealed him from the driver, he walked over and entered the passage a little way until the deep shadows enveloped him entirely.

He leaned against the wall and watched the sliding doors. For the next few minutes, other than breathing, Bishop barely moved at all. Then he saw movement to his left. In the reflection from the driver's side window, he saw Williamson walking back to the vehicle. The driver then leaned with his back against the door and continued doing things on his cell. He yawned again. Bishop guessed he was at the tail end of a long shift.

Bishop watched him for a while, then moved his eyes at the sound of the emergency doors opening. He saw the second paramedic exit with the gurney and knew he now had ten seconds before the doors closed. And he could cover the distance in less than three.

He saw Williamson look at his partner and put his cell in his pocket. Without saying anything, he turned, opened his door and got behind the wheel.

Two seconds had passed. At three, the second man hefted the now empty stretcher into the rear cabin and slid it forward.

At the five-second mark, the paramedic stepped up into the ambulance and turned to reach for both doors.

At six, he pulled them both closed.

Bishop sprinted for the open doorway, hoping Al the driver wasn't looking in his wing mirror.

He reached the entrance in less than three seconds and darted through the opening and slammed against the wall opposite. Then he heard a faint hum and the glass doors began to close.

He'd made it. Question was, had he been spotted?

TWENTY-EIGHT

He turned and saw the ambulance doors were still shut. Nobody was investigating. They hadn't seen him. He watched the rear tail lights come on and then the ambulance slowly pulled away to the right.

One obstacle over with, he thought. *Now, on to the next.*

Bishop saw he was at the end of a long, well-lit corridor. Halfway down was a set of double doors, currently closed. He couldn't see anybody through the glass panels, but that wouldn't last. He needed to move. And what he really needed right now was a locker room.

He walked down the hallway, checking each door as he passed. One bore the legend *Records – 2b*. Then came *Records – 2a*. Most doors had no identification at all. These were all locked. But on the left side he came across one that said *Supplies*. It was also locked.

Good thing he never left home without his tools.

He looked at the lock for a few seconds, then brought out his key ring. On it were three different-sized 'bump' keys he'd made the year before to practise with. His old cellmate had shown him how. The one he picked was just a normal house key, but with the five evenly spaced, triangular grooves filed right down to the minimum setting. He looked both ways, then inserted it fully into the lock. He pulled it out one notch, using his index finger to apply a little torque pressure from one side. Then he took his Swiss Army knife from his pocket, tapped it against the key and felt it catch against the tumblers. He turned the key all the way and unlocked the door.

And people say you never learn anything useful in prison.

Once inside, Bishop closed the door and felt around in the darkness until he found the light switch. He was in a narrow, windowless room with ceiling-high shelves on either side and a metal cabinet at the far end. Amongst all the spare bed sheets, pillows and towels, he also spotted a whole section devoted to green scrubs. But best of all was a shelf loaded with piles of doctors' white lab coats. Looked like he wouldn't need a locker room, after all.

He flipped through until he found a size 42 and pulled it out. He put it on, but it felt a little tight around the shoulders. He tried the next size up and that fitted perfectly. Then he went over and opened the door to the metal cabinet. Inside were stationery supplies, surplus chart holders, name panel pads, and some aluminium portfolio clipboards. He took two pens and one of the clipboards and closed the cabinet.

Next, he took the items he'd purchased earlier from his pocket and laid them out on an empty shelf.

A strip of passport photos. A Tombow glue stick. A small tube of Super Glue. A thin X-Acto knife with a No. 11 blade. He also added his pocket knife to the collection.

He extracted the miniature scissors from the multi-tool knife and used them to cut one of his photos so it was slightly larger than the one on the ID. Then he used the extra-fine X-Acto blade to make a long slit in the right side of the laminated plastic where the card began. Picking up the Swiss Army knife again, Bishop chose the flat-edged screwdriver tool and inserted it between the plastic and the card, moving it around a little to work the space. He took the photo, used the glue stick on the back and pushed it under the plastic with the tip of the screwdriver. After a little manoeuvring, he got it so it covered the old photo entirely and pressed his thumb against it until he was sure it would stay. Finally, he used a drop of Super Glue to seal up the slit in the plastic and waited for it to dry.

After fifteen seconds, he picked the ID up and studied it closely. The photo didn't protrude from the surface too much, and the cut he'd made in the plastic was only noticeable if you were looking for it. Bishop felt it would get him through a casual inspection. As long as the person in question didn't know the real Albert Williamson, that is.

Pocketing everything else, Bishop clipped the new ID to his shirt pocket. The pens he stuck in the coat's upper pocket. Jenna had once said that if you look and sound the part, people will generally believe you're who you claim to be. And she would know. All he needed now to complete the picture was a stethoscope, but you couldn't have everything. The clipboard would have to do.

Bishop listened at the door and heard nothing. He stepped out, switched off the lights and relocked the door behind him. Then he continued down the corridor and pushed through the double doors.

And almost walked right into a nurse coming out of a room to his right.

'Whoa there, doctor,' she said, backing into the food trolley just behind her.

'Sorry about that,' he said. 'Don't know my own speed sometimes.'

Through the open doorway behind her Bishop saw a patient on the bed, eating from a tray. Looked like he'd caught them during suppertime. Good timing.

'No harm done,' she said and frowned at the double doors behind him. 'Were you looking for something, Dr . . . ?'

'Williamson,' he said, and quickly flashed the ID. 'No, my patient puked up on me and I was just getting a spare lab coat from the supply room, that's all.'

'Ha. Welcome to my world. Was it bad?'

'You ever seen *The Exorcist*?'

The nurse laughed and said, 'I'll tell the kitchen to lay off the pea soup for a while.' Then she took another tray from the trolley and opened the next door along. 'Evening, Elaine. How we doing? Just *look* at the feast we prepared for you this evening . . .'

Bishop shook his head and carried on walking. That was too close. He was aware he could slip up and say the wrong thing at any time. And the more encounters he had with hospital staff, the more likely it was it would happen.

About fifty yards up ahead the corridor opened out into a large open area with lots of glass. Just the kind of exposure he hoped to avoid. Bishop continued walking until he noticed a large chart on the right-hand wall. He moved closer and saw it was a floor plan for the whole building.

Bishop checked his current position on the first floor and saw that the area up ahead led to the main reception. But before that, about twenty yards away on the left, were the stairs. He scanned the rest of the floor, as well as the three above. Not memorizing everything. That would take too long. Just enough to get a general sense of the place.

This corridor contained the only patient rooms on the first floor. The rest was taken up by the intensive care units and various admin departments. The second floor contained cardio, radiology and a number of other departments. Patient accommodation took up most of the third and fourth levels. He took special note of the locations of the nurse stations.

Out the corner of his eye, Bishop saw somebody walking this way from reception. It looked like another nurse. Not wanting another encounter so soon, he strode over to where the stair entrance should be. He found the door without a problem, pulled it open and entered the stairwell.

He climbed to the third floor, opened the door and looked down to his left. The same long corridor as downstairs. All he could see in this one was a trolley about thirty yards down. A nurse was taking something from the middle. Looked like another food tray. She and the tray disappeared into one of the rooms. He turned to the right and saw the nurses' station about fifty yards away with another corridor just beyond it on the left. Another nurse, her blond hair tied back into a ponytail, was leaning on the counter with a phone at her ear. She paged through a medical file while she listened. Then she replaced the phone, picked up the file and walked off down the left passageway.

Bishop stepped out onto the floor and walked in that direction. When he reached the counter he looked over. The station was currently unattended, like he'd hoped. But it wouldn't stay that way for long. He needed to work fast.

He stepped through the opening and saw three computers on the desk under the counter. All the screensavers were activated. He jiggled all three mice and the screensavers disappeared. Two of the screens asked for passwords to log on to the hospital database, but he got lucky with the third one. The user hadn't logged off.

Placing the clipboard on the desk, Bishop sat down and paused when he noticed a pad of blank CMS 1500 health insurance claim forms under the counter. Figuring something was better than nothing, he tore off three sheets and stuck them under the clipboard's metal spring-loaded clamp.

He turned back to the computer and scanned through the desktop folders. There was one titled *Admissions*. He double-clicked on it and another folder opened up with a number of sub-sections, all arranged by date. He couldn't make sense of the names and figured it was some kind of hospital code. He knew the medical community had a language all their own.

Bishop clicked on the first entry and a spreadsheet instantly filled the screen. It contained a long list of names with more dates and times alongside. These had to be patients and their admission dates. The first one was an Eamonn Baxter from the morning of June 1. He scrolled down. The last was a Rosalie Warner, who was admitted on the 12th at 20.56. He looked at his watch. That was just sixteen minutes ago. Which meant it had to be the patient Williamson and his partner just brought in. He was impressed. They sure didn't mess around in here. Or maybe they did. That was what he was here to find out.

He tried the next folder down. More names and dates, but for May this time. Bishop scrolled down till he reached the 16th. A lot of admissions that day, but he was only interested in the overnight ones. He calculated that if Selina had been taken at 03.00, that meant the ambulance would have gotten here by 04.00 or thereabouts. He looked at the entries for that time period:

5/16 – ADM. 03.02. MARIN, Colleen. 4–19. D.G. 328.
5/16 – ADM. 03.43. ECCLES, Angelina. 3–05. D/C 05/23 – 17.42.
5/16 – ADM. 03.59. WHITLOCK, Caden. 3–12. D/C 05/20 – 11.18. K.G. 199.
5/16 – ADM. 04.14. EASTMAN, Mary. 4–29. A.T. 423.

The next patient after Eastman hadn't been admitted until almost six o'clock, so that just left these four. Bishop immediately discounted Colleen Marin because of the time factor, and Whitlock for a more obvious reason. Which left two possibilities: Angelina Eccles and Mary Eastman. One of these women could well have been Selina under an assumed name. *Another* assumed name, that is.

Just then a female voice behind him said, 'What do you think you're doing?'

TWENTY-NINE

Bishop turned round to see the same blonde nurse glaring back at him. Her eyebrows were set in a straight line as she walked round the counter towards him. She looked ready for war.

Bishop quit out of the program and put on his best disarming smile. 'Hope you don't mind. I just needed to check on something and there wasn't anybody . . .'

'Yeah, yeah,' she said, facing him across the counter. 'But this section right here? Where you're sitting? We call it a *nurses'* station, which means it's for *nurses*. If it was for doctors, it would be called a *doctors'* station. Which means if you need some help with something you come and ask a *nurse*. You see where I'm going with this?'

'I'm beginning to get the picture,' he said as she came through the opening. The name on her badge read *Helena Thornhill*. Picking up his clipboard, he got up and turned to her. 'Would it help if I said I was sorry, Helena?'

'It might.' She turned from the screen to look at him for a moment. He could see the anger slowly fading from her features. The use of her name probably helped. But the frown still remained. She glanced at the part of his ID that was visible and said, 'You know, I don't recall seeing you before.'

'Well, I'm only here for today. I was sent over from St Joseph's in Phoenix to do a special consult on an ICU patient, and just needed to double check the exact time he was admitted. I couldn't make it out from the notes they give me.' He shrugged. 'You know what doctors' handwriting's like.'

'Do I ever.'

'There you go. I didn't think there'd be a problem, Helena; the nurses at St Joseph's are all pretty easy-going about this kind of thing. But I'll get out your way now, okay?'

The nurse showed him her palms and smiled. 'Hey, forget it. I guess I get a little over-possessive about my workspace sometimes.'

'That's understandable,' he said, turning to go. 'Well, I better get back.'

She nodded and sat in the seat he'd vacated, while he walked down the corridor in the opposite direction to the stairs. Taking that route again might raise the nurse's suspicions even more. At the end he turned left and saw the elevator bank up ahead. He stood before the right-hand doors and pressed the 'up' button. He needed to check one more thing before he left. Assuming *D/C* stood for discharged, that meant Mary Eastman was still in the building. In room 4–29 on the fourth floor. His next stop.

As he waited, a female doctor and a male nurse exited a room at his left and came over to stand in front of the elevator next to him. The nurse pressed the 'down' button. Bishop took a pen from his pocket and pretended to go over the blank forms on his clipboard.

After ten long seconds, Bishop heard a *ping* and the doors in front of him opened. The elevator was empty. He stepped in quickly with his head still down and pressed 4. The doors closed and he breathed out again. At the fourth floor, he stepped out and turned right, studying the room numbers as he passed. There was a 4–15 on the left. Then a 4–16 on the right. Looked like he was going in the right direction. He carried on, but slowed when he saw another nurses' station up ahead on the left, just before another intersection.

He opened up his clipboard again and moved his finger along as he walked. He was aware of the two nurses in the station, but didn't look up. Just kept walking straight ahead, checking his imaginary medical charts. Once he felt he was out of range, he looked up and saw a large window and a long bench marking the end of this passageway about twenty feet away. He checked the door on his left. 4–25. And two more doors to go.

Bishop stopped outside the last door and looked back. Just a single figure in the distance. Looked like a patient walking around. He turned back to the door to 4–29, gripped the handle and turned. Except he couldn't. The door was locked.

That was unexpected. Bishop had never heard of hospitals locking patients in their rooms before. Not even felons. They might assign a cop to stand watch outside, but that was about as far as they went. He took out his keys again and used the same technique as before. Five seconds later he opened the door and stepped inside.

It was a normal private room with a window, a bed with rails on each side and a small en-suite bathroom on the right. There was a patient lying in the bed. It was clearly female. The bed sheets covered her body all the way to the chin. She had blond hair, but that was as much as he could tell for certain. The rest of her head was wrapped in bandages.

Bishop looked at the foot of the bed, but didn't see a chart. Or a chart holder. Even though he'd seen plenty of spare ones in the supply room. So this patient apparently didn't warrant a medical history. Which was unusual. The only item on the small bedside table was a call button. He looked around and couldn't see any personal effects either.

'Mary Eastman?' he said, approaching the bed. 'Can you hear me?'

No response. No movement except the steady rise and fall of her chest.

Bishop moved closer and touched her shoulder. 'Mary Eastman?' He leaned in closer and said into her ear, 'Selina, is that you under there?'

Again, no response. Probably doped to the gills on God knows what. But there was an easy way to tell if she really was Selina. Bishop reached down, about to pull back the sheets to expose her arms, when somebody said, 'Hey, what you doing in here?'

Bishop turned and saw a male orderly walking slowly towards him from the doorway. He was wearing a scowl along with two days' worth of stubble. About Bishop's height, but much wider in the shoulders.

'We're in a hospital,' Bishop said. 'I'm a doctor. This is a patient. Which part of that don't you get?' He studied the man's white scrubs and saw no identification. 'Who are you anyway?'

'That's none of your business. Only authorized personnel are allowed in here and you're not authorized. And this door was locked when I left. How'd you get in here?'

'What are you talking about? It wasn't locked. I was told to check up on this patient and that's exactly what I was doing when you barged in.'

The orderly stopped a couple of feet from Bishop. 'I don't think so, pal. I haven't seen you around here before. I'm thinking maybe we should go talk to somebody about this.'

Bishop opened his mouth to reply when he noticed a shadow in the corridor outside. Then another orderly appeared at the door. Shorter than the first one, but just as wide, with a noticeable paunch. This was starting to get out of hand. Bishop knew he had to make a decision right now, while he was still an unknown quantity.

'Sure, let's go,' he said, and nodded towards the doorway. 'Your girlfriend coming with us?'

When Stubble turned his head to look, Bishop dropped the clipboard, bent his left arm and slammed the point of his elbow into his face. Right between the eyes. Stubble grunted and fell to the floor with his hands at his forehead. Bishop spun round just as the second man charged towards him.

It took fractions of a second for Bishop's mind to sift through the seven possible hand strikes. He chose the 'spear hand'. The only move that would give him the extra three inches of range he needed. Even as he thought it, he set his legs wide apart, knees bent for perfect equilibrium. At the same time he pressed together the fingers of his right hand, straightening them so the whole hand resembled a spearhead. The orderly was less than two feet away. Bishop could almost smell the guy's breath. Bishop pulled his right elbow back, then in one rapid movement just shot his arm out to its full length, his fingers sinking into the orderly's stomach like it was a pillow. Bishop immediately pulled his arm back then dived out of the way as the man's momentum swept him past the foot of the bed.

The man made a sickly, gurgling sound and fell to the floor with his hands wrapped around his waist. Bishop heard him make heaving sounds and turned back to the bed. Stubble was already getting to his feet, ready for the next round. Bishop dropped his shoulder and delivered a short side kick into his solar plexus and the man fell back into the bathroom.

Retrieving his clipboard from the floor, Bishop pulled out his keys and ran for the door. Slamming it shut behind him, he inserted the same bump key as before and did everything in reverse. When he heard the lock bolt slide home, he then inserted the key all the way and bent it back until the metal snapped. Bishop heard a weight crash against the door. He slowed his breathing and walked back down the corridor. He passed the nurses' station and smiled at the single nurse sitting there. She gave him an uncertain smile back.

He passed the elevator bank and the second nurse station without seeing anybody and pushed open the door to the stairs. Once he reached the ground floor, he stuck his head out and listened. No alarms. No running people. He stepped into the corridor and turned right. Fifty yards to the rear emergency doors. He didn't run, just walked at a steady pace like he belonged. Just a doctor going about his business.

Bishop finally reached the doors and stood under the sensor. They slid open and he stepped outside. Then he turned at a movement at his left and something struck the base of his skull. His legs went and as he fell to the ground his final thought was, *Didn't this happen already?*

Then everything went black.

THIRTY

Bishop's own coughing woke him up. He must have been hacking away for some time. His lungs already ached from the effort. Then he heard the crackling roar of flames all around him. It was also unbelievably hot. He raised his head from the concrete floor and tried to focus, but all he saw was black smoke in every direction. Swirling around like a furious living organism. It thinned at his left for a moment, revealing writhing orange ribbons in the background. Then the gap closed and he was staring at the smoke creature again.

Last thing Bishop remembered was coming out of the hospital and feeling a sharp sensation at the back of his skull. And now he was here. In a burning building somewhere. Ignoring the throbbing pain in his head Bishop got up and turned a complete circle, trying to make out details, but it was impossible. There was just too much smoke. He could see a few feet in front of his face and that was all. His eyes were already stinging.

And there was that nauseating stench of burning rubber everywhere. The air was thick with it. He remembered those stacks of tyres he'd seen at the Bannings place and wondered if that's where they'd brought him. Figuring that if the fire didn't get him, the toxic fumes would. Some choice. Which meant he needed to find another alternative. And fast.

Bishop removed the lab coat and ripped off the arms. He stuck one in his back pocket and tied the other around his lower face like a bandana. It wasn't much help, but his coughing subsided a little. Keeping low to the ground, he picked a direction and began walking. It only took three steps before he saw a burning vehicle in front of him. He moved round it and collided with another one, also on fire.

He saw similar shapes all around him, all aflame. He avoided some burning tyres and then his foot came into contact with a large soft object.

Bishop knelt down and waved his hand back and forth, trying to disperse the smoke enough to see. It was a man. He was lying on his back with his head in an unnatural position. His neck had been broken. The light from nearby flames allowed Bishop to recognize the face immediately. It was the mechanic he'd questioned this afternoon. Hewitt.

Poor guy had been a creep, but that hardly warranted a death sentence. But his presence here indicated this *was* the Bannings place.

That was both good and bad. Good because Bishop could remember the basic layout, even in the dark. Bad because it was also a prefab steel building. These things were built to be fire resistant, but that was no consolation to anybody trapped inside. The exterior would hold together while he got turned into a TV dinner.

Still coughing, Bishop got to his feet and continued in the same direction, calling to mind everything he'd seen of the place this afternoon. The placement of the three shutters at the front, along with the customer entrance at the other end. And that small window next to the front door. Maybe he could get out that way. But he needed to get his bearings first.

His outstretched fingers suddenly touched a steel wall and he yanked his hand back. His fingertips felt like they'd touched a furnace. He turned right and kept walking with the wall at his left until his knee knocked against a sturdy metal object. He moved his hand along it until he recognized it as one of the car lifts. And just past the lift would be the last shutter.

Now he knew where he was. And the customer entrance was at the other end of the building. Great. He'd wasted valuable time going the wrong way. He didn't bother checking the shutters. He had no doubt they'd be securely padlocked for the night. Instead he retraced his steps and aimed for the other end, avoiding more burning tyres and vehicles along the way. The smoke was definitely getting thicker now. And his coughing was getting worse.

Two minutes later, Bishop's fingers touched the opposite wall. And behind it would be the customer entrance. He turned left and soon came upon a door in the wall. He tried the handle. Locked, naturally. He took a step back and delivered a side kick just below the handle. And again. On the third kick, the door crashed inwards and Bishop ducked inside.

He could see straight away the fire had already found its way into this section. Probably from all the oil saturating the floor area. But the smoke wasn't quite as thick as before. Not yet anyway. He saw a connecting door on his right. He turned to his left and took a few steps until he found the customer entrance. It was a steel door. He moved his hand down and found the locking bolt and a large padlock. No real surprise there.

He moved along until he came to the window he remembered seeing. And then just stared at it for a moment in disbelief. There was an inner steel grate covering the whole frame with thick circular bars set vertically and horizontally. He couldn't see a single screw, which meant the whole thing had to have been welded to the steel wall.

You've got to be kidding.

Bishop grabbed it with both hands and pulled with all his weight. It didn't budge a millimetre. He got more leverage with his feet and tried again, every muscle straining with the effort. Nothing happened.

Bishop let go and tried to control his coughing. He refused to be discouraged. There was always a way out of any situation. Always. He'd put that belief to the test on numerous occasions and found it to be true every single time. Fire or not, today would be no different.

He searched the room for anything that he could use on the grille or the padlock. But there was nothing even remotely strong enough. But he did find a working flashlight in one of the file cabinets. He switched it on and ran the beam over the room. On the wall was a row of framed Employee of the Month awards, each with a different headshot. He saw Hewitt up there, along with all the other mechanics. Then a large bookcase full of box files and folders. Some of them already on fire. Useless. He returned to the connecting door he'd seen earlier, pulled it open and was faced with more smoke. He was in a windowless office with shelves of auto supplies along the walls, but no tyre irons. Nothing of any use. He ducked as an aerosol exploded from the heat and paint splattered the wall. Then another one blew.

Bishop tried the next door along and entered a short corridor with a restroom on his left and another door at the end. That one opened onto another windowless office. Probably Bannings'. The fire hadn't reached this far yet, although there was still plenty of smoke. Bishop ran to the desk and went through the drawers. He slammed the last one shut and then saw two bright red, twenty-litre jerry cans under the desk. The first was empty, but the second one was full. He unscrewed the cap and smelled gas. Good.

With a new exit route forming in his mind, Bishop picked up the full canister and shone the flashlight around the room one last time. He stopped when the beam hit two small black boxes on Bannings' work desk. One had a cable going into the back of the computer drive and another going into the electrical outlet in the floor. That had to be the modem or router. The other box had a single cable sticking out of it that ran up into the ceiling.

Where the security camera was.

Putting down the jerry can, Bishop shone the light over the box. It was about the same size as a pack of cigarettes, but half the thickness. On the back he saw a *WD* logo and underneath that, *ITB*. With a thin smile, he unplugged the hard drive and left it there for the moment.

Next, he checked the restroom. It was small and narrow, but it contained a shower. Bishop turned on the faucets and stood under for almost a minute until he was completely soaked. Then he grabbed the hard drive and the jerry can and went back into the supplies room. He quickly searched the shelves until he found a twelve-foot long fuel siphon hose and a rubber-coated tape measure. He wrapped the hard drive in the hose's plastic packaging, stuffed that and the tape measure in his pocket and looped the siphon tubing around his shoulders. Then he picked up the full jerry can and went to the front office.

The reception was full of black smoke now. Bishop entered the garage area and was almost blown over by the heat. He heard a muffled explosion over the noise of the flames and guessed a gas tank had just exploded. It wouldn't be the last. Bishop aimed for the opposite wall and began walking, using his flashlight to help avoid the obstructions. There were burning tyres everywhere he turned. He was about halfway across when there was a flash of light to his left, followed by the sound of another explosion.

Bishop kept on and when he finally reached the far wall, turned left. Towards the shutter door he and Hewitt had used earlier. He noticed his clothes were almost totally dry again, every drop of moisture completely evaporated from the heat.

Another vehicle exploded behind him. Bishop was also finding it much more difficult to breathe. The fire was sucking up all the oxygen like a vacuum. He didn't have much time left. Finally he reached the shutter and put down the can. He knelt down and saw there was about an inch of space to play with at the bottom. That would be enough.

Bishop took the tape measure from his pocket and placed it under the shutter as a wedge. Then he unscrewed the cap on the jerry can and inserted one end of the hose into the opening. He placed the other end between his lips and began sucking. When the gasoline started flowing down the tube, he took it from his mouth and fed it through the gap.

Towards those two gas pumps outside.

He started counting, figuring it would take about ninety seconds to empty the can completely. He then took the bandana from his face, twisted it a few times and inserted half of it into the opening at the top. Then he took the other sleeve from his back pocket and looked behind him. He saw large flames through the black smoke and made his way towards them. When he reached them he saw it was another stack of burning tyres. A very large stack.

Bishop got as close as he dared and threw one end of the sleeve into the flame, waiting until he was sure it was alight before pulling it out. He was still counting. Sixty-three seconds had passed. The jerry can wouldn't be empty yet. He ran back to the shutter door with the burning rag, knelt down a few feet away and threw it towards the canister. He saw it come into contact with the other jacket arm. When that caught fire too, Bishop dived face down on the floor with his hands over his head.

He knew he was done for if this didn't work. Burned alive in the ass-end of nowhere. He could think of better ways to die. And far less painful ways. Some part of him wondered how quick it would be when the time came.

Five seconds later, the world exploded.

THIRTY-ONE

The force of the blast rocked Bishop's body and the noise almost deafened him. Then it was just the sound of the fire again. He took his hands from his head and turned to look. There was a huge, ugly fissure in the side of the building, about twenty feet from the shutter door. Black smoke was pouring out through the gap, anxious to reach the outside world.

Somebody *had* to have heard that.

Bishop got up and ran over to the opening. Another explosion rocked the building and he fell to the ground. Either the second fuel pump or one of those oxyacetylene tanks. Seems they weren't empty, after all. But he needed to get out of here before anything else went up.

He got to his feet again and saw the wide fissure started about a foot from the floor, with jagged metal lining the edges like Stone Age knives. Bishop ran straight at it and dived through, rolling when he hit the ground on the other side. He slammed against one of the wheel dollies and got up and ran for the fence. He climbed up and over, then kept running, making for that dirt track he'd seen before. A few seconds later he got to the sagebrush and dropped to the ground, still coughing.

He looked back and saw flames poking through the gap along with the smoke. Even in the darkness, he could see an immense dark cloud hovering over the building. Then there was another explosion, like before. Then another. The oxyacetylene tanks. Had to be.

Finally, the coughing subsided and Bishop got his breath back. There hadn't been any more explosions. All he could hear was the faint crackle of flames from inside the building.

Then he heard sirens. In the distance. But obviously coming this way. Somebody must have seen the smoke and called 911. Which meant this whole area would be crawling with emergency services pretty soon. Including the police. And they couldn't find him here. A suspicious-looking stranger near a burning building in the middle of the night was every cop's dream. But which way? The sirens were coming from the north, and if he went south or west the desert would just swallow him up. Which just left this dirt track he was on.

Then he remembered the hard drive in his pocket and pulled it out. If the cops did pick him up they'd confiscate it as evidence for sure. And while he was fairly sure whatever was on there would clear him of any wrongdoing, it was a sure bet they'd never allow him to see the actual footage for himself. Plus it would also open up a whole bunch of questions Bishop had no intention of answering just yet.

Which left just one option.

Bishop stood and turned slowly in a circle as he looked at the ground. There. About ten feet away. There was a large cholla cactus on its own amongst the sage, with a few rocks close by on the right. He walked over and studied them. The largest was about a foot long at its widest diameter. He knelt down and hefted it. Weighed about twenty-five pounds. Putting it down, he noticed one of the smaller rocks had a pointed edge on one side and he used it to start digging into the hard desert soil.

When he was done, Bishop took out the hard drive and placed it carefully in the two-inch deep hole. Then he filled it in and placed the large rock on top. Good enough. The sirens were only a few blocks away now. He could already see the flashing lights in the distance. He needed to move. The more distance he could put between himself and this place, the better.

He started walking east along the dirt track and saw it made a gradual turn northwards. He stayed with it, took the turn and stopped when he heard the unmistakable sound of a car engine somewhere in front of him. He stood motionless and listened. Higher than usual RPM. As though the car was in too low a gear for its speed. Then a vehicle suddenly appeared from the left about a hundred yards up ahead. Must be another road down there. There were no headlights. He couldn't be sure, but it looked like it was travelling in reverse. He watched it move across the landscape, then it turned onto the dirt track, still with its back to him. And it kept coming his way. All he could see was a dark shape and the two reversing lights on either side as they got closer and closer.

Even after what he'd just been through, this was definitely one of the weirdest things Bishop had seen in a while. Whoever was driving sure knew how to handle a car. He just stood there and waited, curious to see what happened next.

When it was twenty feet away, the brake lights came on and the car skidded to a complete stop. Then the rear lights disappeared, leaving the vehicle in darkness. Over the din of the approaching sirens, he could hear the engine idling. Then the passenger door opened. The interior lights didn't come on, but he could still make out a shape in the driver's seat.

Bishop walked towards the car and when he reached the door bent his head and looked inside.

The driver was female. She was calmly staring back at him with large, dark eyes and an unreadable expression on her face. From the lights in the dash, Bishop could see it was the same Latino woman who'd been checking him out in the diner earlier. Wearing a denim-type shirt and jeans, she looked to be in her late twenties or early thirties, with long black hair tied back in a ponytail.

She revved the engine once and said, 'I don't have all night, Bishop. You getting in or not?'

Bishop raised his eyebrows at the sound of his name. Then he got in.

THIRTY-TWO

Bishop buckled his seat belt while the woman took off down the track at a steady 30 mph. She still hadn't turned her headlights on. There were no lights around here and the existing cloud cover meant navigating by moonlight was almost impossible. *Almost* being the operative word. Bishop figured her night vision must be phenomenal. He'd once read that people who suffered from colour blindness often see better in the dark, and wondered if that explained it.

She gave him a quick glance and said, 'Nothing to say at all?'

He let out a long breath and looked at the dash clock. 01.29. 'Mostly, I'm trying to figure out how you know my name.'

'I have my ways.'

'Uh huh. So you going to tell me yours, or shall I just call you Mystery Girl?'

'Clarissa Vallejo, at your service,' she said, and downshifted. She took a left turn and few seconds later they were on smooth asphalt with the occasional house passing by on either side. Bishop could also see some streetlights way off in the distance. She took another look at him and said, 'What's that smile for?'

'Nothing. I just never figured my guardian angel would be turn out to be Mexican.'

'Mexican *American*, if you don't mind. We live in politically correct times.'

'Right. So where are you taking me?'

'Where do you *want* me to take you?'

So he was being given a choice. That was promising. Bishop thought for a few seconds and decided it might be best to avoid Selina's

123

apartment this evening. Or morning. No point in tempting fate. 'You know any decent motels around here?' he asked.

'Well, the one I'm staying at isn't too bad, and there seem to be plenty of vacancies. It's just a couple of miles outside of town on Route 60.'

Bishop frowned at her. 'You're at a motel? I had you down as a local.'

'How'd you figure that?'

'You seem to know your way around this place pretty well. And in the dark, too.' When she didn't respond, he said, 'But a motel outside of town sounds perfect right now.'

She snorted. 'Yeah, I expect it does. You could definitely do with a shower. Have you seen yourself?'

Bishop swivelled the rear-view round and a stranger stared back at him. One with a black and white face. The soot stains started halfway up his nose and continued up into his hairline, while the part of his face that had been covered by the bandana was practically unmarked. He looked down at himself and saw that his previously white shirt was also dark with soot and torn in several places. And he reeked of smoke. Yeah, a shower might be a good idea at that.

'So was it you who called in the cavalry?' he asked.

'Yeah. Took me a while to find you, but once I spotted the smoke I just followed that and figured you'd be at the end of it. I spent a long time trying to find a way in, but after realizing it was completely impossible I dialled 911. Man, that place was locked up *tight*. I was round the other side when I heard the explosions and figured that was you making your escape. How'd you get out in the end?'

Bishop told her about the old fuel pumps at the side of the building, then said, 'Why were you looking for me?'

'I'm your guardian angel, aren't I?'

'I don't believe in guardian angels, Vallejo.' He watched her for a moment. 'I like the way you get round my questions without actually answering them. Is that a special skill you learned somewhere or is it an inherent thing?'

'A little of both, probably.'

'So how long you been keeping tabs on me? Since the diner?'

'Uh huh.' Vallejo came to an intersection, stopped and looked both ways. Bishop remembered the map from the library. The next intersection up ahead would put them on Saracen Road. But instead, Vallejo finally switched on her lights and turned right on Christchurch. Bishop had yet to see another moving vehicle on the streets.

'What'd you do? Place a tracer under my car?'

She nodded as she drove. 'At Bannings' place. I waited in my car and watched you talk with that waitress, then followed you from there to the library, and then to the garage. I saw how you got into that medical centre in Garrick, by the way. Have you ever tried doing anything the easy way? You know, with*out* breaking the law?'

Bishop shrugged. 'Laws are useful, but sometimes they can slow things down. Speaking of which, most concerned citizens would have suggested dropping me at the police station by now. That'd be the next logical step for somebody in my position.'

'You want me to take you there now?'

Bishop looked out the window. 'Not really. I don't have much faith in the police solving my problems.'

Vallejo took a left, then drove up to the Saracen Road intersection and waited. They'd passed by the main section of town now and were still the only car on the streets. She pulled out and kept on in a northerly direction. 'Why's that?' she asked in a light tone.

'I had some bad experiences with them a while back. And the few I've met since haven't altered my opinion of them. I find the less we have to do with each other, the happier I am.'

'In that case,' Vallejo said, 'we might have problems.'

THIRTY-THREE

Bishop slowly turned to look at her. All of a sudden he was glad he'd taken the trouble to hide the hard drive. 'Am I under arrest?' he asked.

She gave a smile. 'Why, you kill anybody recently?'

'Not recently, no.'

Vallejo glanced at him briefly before turning her attention back to the road. 'I wish I could tell whether you're joking or not. Still, I'm pretty sure it wasn't you who started that fire back there and that's all I care about at the moment.'

'That's a load off my mind. So who the hell are you?'

'Well, if you want my full title, it's Officer Clarissa Vallejo, but I couldn't arrest you even if I wanted to. You're completely out of my jurisdiction for a start.'

'Which is where?'

'A place called Corvallis, in Oregon.'

'I've heard of it. So what's the other reason? You get pulled off active duty or something?'

Vallejo was silent as they came up to the turnoff for Route 60. She turned left and said, 'Suspended.'

'Suspended, huh? Why, you kill somebody?'

'Touché. Why don't we wait until we get to the motel, and then we'll talk some more. Unless you want to crash first, that is.'

'I think I can stay awake a while longer,' he said and turned his attention to the road ahead. Beyond the headlights all he could see was darkness. He found the melody from that old song 'What a Difference a Day Makes' running through his head. A guy he'd interviewed this afternoon gets murdered a few hours later. And Bishop would have been all set to join him, but for those fuel pumps outside. But the fact that somebody wanted him dead meant he was getting somewhere, and in less time than he could have imagined. It was a shame poor Hewitt had to pay the price, but Bishop could hardly be blamed for that.

And now this cop. He wondered just what Vallejo's interest in him was. And if she already knew his name, how much more did she know? He generally liked to keep as low a profile as possible, but a little research would have unearthed his recent past easily enough. Nobody was safe from the internet these days. Bishop certainly wasn't.

'That's it up ahead,' Vallejo said.

Bishop had already spotted the tall sign in the distance, all lit up. As they got closer he could make out the name, *Amber Motel*, laid out in a hand-drawn typeface.

Vallejo pulled in to the court and stopped the car just past the office. She turned to him and shook her head. 'Bishop, you do look a sight. Maybe I should sign you in, huh?'

'Good idea. How much are the rooms?'

'Forty-five dollars a night.'

He pulled two crumpled twenties and a five from his pocket and handed them over. She got out and he turned in his seat to see her press the buzzer. After about thirty seconds, the office lights came on and a young Asian guy came and unlocked the door. Bishop turned back and studied the layout of the place. It looked like a throwback to the 1950s. Besides the front office, he counted about twenty rooms laid out to form three sides of a square. Parking spaces in front of the rooms. In the middle of it all was an enclosed pool with two large palm trees at each end. The only other vehicle was an old Lincoln parked next to the office.

Soon, the driver's door opened and Vallejo got back in. She handed him a key with a large *8* on the fob and said, 'If anybody asks, you're Raymond Vallejo, my stepbrother.'

'Whatever you say, sis.'

'And don't call me "sis".'

She drove to the far corner of the square and parked in front of his room. They both got out and he saw her approach the door to No. 7.

'Come by when you're ready,' she said. 'I'll leave the door unlocked.'

As Bishop dried himself off he stared at his reflection in the mirror. He looked presentable again, even if he felt dead on his feet. He gazed at the ancient pink scar on his shoulder. Jenna had once said it looked like the outline of a gecko lizard sitting there, waiting to pounce, although Bishop had never been able to see it. But now he could finally make out the basic shape, distorted though it was. Like one of the Magic Eye pictures where the image is right there in front of you all the time. You just need to look.

Ditching the ruined shirt, Bishop donned the rest of his clothes and knocked twice on Vallejo's door. When he heard a voice say 'Come in' he entered a room that was the same as his, but in reverse. Tiled floors, double bed, TV, fridge. A table and two chairs by the window. Bathroom at the rear. Like seventy-five per cent of motel rooms everywhere. Vallejo was sitting on the bed with her back propped up by two pillows, watching him as she sipped from a glass tumbler. The TV was tuned into some wildlife programme, but with the sound muted.

'Well, you look human again,' Vallejo said. 'You want something to drink? I got white wine, Diet Cokes or water in the fridge. Take your pick.'

'Thanks.' Bishop got up, opened the refrigerator door and pulled out a half-full bottle of Santa Margherita. He took a tumbler from the top of the TV, poured some of the wine into it and took it back to one of the chairs. He sat down, took a swallow and said, 'You know, I could throw more questions at you, but I think it would save us both a lot of time and effort if you just told me what you're doing here.'

Vallejo leaned back until her head touched the wall. 'I'm here for the same reason as you, Bishop. Searching for a missing woman.'

'But not the same woman.'

'No, not the same. But similar.' She smiled. 'You'd be surprised.'

'What's her name?'

'Samantha Mathison.'

'Mathison,' he said. 'So she's not a relative?'

'No.'

'And how long has she been gone?'

Vallejo sighed. 'Almost three months now.'

'That's a long time.'

'You think I don't know that?' She finished off her wine and made a face. 'I can count, too. You think I don't wake up every morning wondering what the hell I'm doing here when Sam could already be . . . ?'

Vallejo closed her eyes and banged her head lightly against the wall. Getting control of herself again. She got off the bed, walked over to the fridge and took out the wine bottle.

Bishop watched her, thinking. Quietly, he said, 'This Samantha sounds like more than just a friend.'

'That obvious, huh?' Vallejo took her refilled glass back to the bed. 'And thanks for using the present tense. Yeah, Sam's a *lot* more than a friend to me. That surprise you?'

'Nothing surprises me.' Bishop shrugged. 'We are who we are.'

Vallejo raised her glass to him. 'That's a great philosophy to have. I just wish more people shared your view.'

'I thought Corvallis was a college town. Aren't kids pretty open-minded about that kind of thing these days?'

'Not if you're a cop with an image to protect. People expect you to act in a certain way. Anything less is considered a weakness, and you know how kids love to jump on weaknesses. My fellow officers aren't much different. They all tend to see things in black and white, especially when it comes to women. All of which means I've learned it's safer to be circumspect about my private life. You'd probably be the same in my position.'

Since Bishop had never much cared what people thought of him, he doubted it. But he let it slide and said, 'So tell me why you're out here on your own, when you could be running things through official channels with the full weight of the law behind you.'

Vallejo looked at him. 'Because everyone else believes Samantha died three months ago, in the same fire that killed the rest of her family.'

THIRTY-FOUR

Bishop sat back in the chair and said, 'I think you'd better start at the beginning. How long have you known Samantha?'

Vallejo drank some more wine and said, 'I first met her two years ago. My partner and I were assigned to check out complaints of a suspicious character lurking around one of the wealthier neighbourhoods. My partner checked the area while I went in to get a description from the resident who called it in. That was Samantha.' She shrugged. 'What can I say? I liked her and I could tell she liked me, even though she was married with a kid.'

'And things progressed between you two from that point on.'

'Right. But on the quiet. She was only twenty-four and wasn't ready to leave her husband just yet and I loved being a cop. And of course, she absolutely *adored* her boy, Mark. Neither of us wanted to screw things up, so we just enjoyed our time together for what it was. And we always made sure to stay clear of Corvallis for our liaisons.'

'Okay. So fast forward to three months ago.'

Vallejo gazed at the moving pictures on the TV and rubbed her eyes. 'It was March 17. About three in the morning. We were on the other side of town when we heard it on the scanner. A 911 call reporting a house fire on Samantha's street. I remember telling my partner we should get over there to help with crowd control, but by the time we arrived it was all over. There was almost nothing left. Just a black, smoking husk of a building where Sam's house used to be. Tell the truth, I can't remember much else of that night. I must have been on autopilot or something.' She closed her eyes. 'God.'

Bishop gave her a few seconds, then said, 'How many died in the fire?'

'Three. They found the burnt remains of a man, woman and child upstairs, all in the same room. And before you ask, the medical examiner identified all three as the Mathisons.'

'But you don't believe that.'

'Well, I can't comment on the husband as I never met him, and little Mark was usually out at kindergarten. But I know for a fact the third victim wasn't Samantha.'

'Tell me how,' he said.

'Well, you know how we usually identify fire victims when they're too badly burnt for normal identification.'

'Usually from dental records.'

'Right. So I saw the photos the medical examiner made of her teeth, okay? And they weren't Sam's. I knew them like my own, believe me, and if she had a gap between her front upper incisors before that night I would have noticed. Yet there it was, in black and white. A little gap about a millimetre wide. Not only that, but it seemed she'd grown three new wisdom teeth overnight.'

'You're saying Samantha had three of her wisdom teeth extracted?'

'Either that or they never erupted. The two upper ones were missing and so was the lower one on the left side. Yet the female corpse had all four of hers still in place.'

Bishop rubbed a palm over his scalp. 'And you're absolutely sure Sam was missing those three?'

'Well, we both enjoyed kissing, you know what I mean?'

'Fair enough. So I take it they checked against the family's dental records and found a perfect match against all three?'

'Yeah.' Vallejo brought her eyebrows together. 'You don't sound surprised.'

'Let's just say I've had some first-hand experience at this kind of thing. So did you tell your captain about it?'

'How could I? Nobody even knew Samantha and I were friends, let alone lovers. I brought up that gap in the front teeth, saying it wasn't there when I went to her house two years before, but he just said she must have been wearing caps that melted in the fire.'

'What about the fire? Did the investigators determine the cause?'

'Accidental, if you can believe that. They traced it all back to some faulty wiring on the refrigerator. Said it could easily have sparked off late at night and just spread through the house in no time. Apparently it's one of the most common causes for house fires every year.'

'So at that point you decided to follow things up on your own.'

'Well, I had to. Nobody else was gonna do anything about it. Besides, I knew how weird it sounded. Once you accepted the basic premise that it wasn't Sam, you had to accept the fact that somebody had gone into her bedroom in the middle of the night, killed the husband and son, replaced Sam with a freshly prepared corpse and then set the place alight before taking off. And it had to be more than one person. Maybe two or three. That kind of thing just doesn't happen in places like Corvallis. Or most other places, to be honest.'

Bishop looked down at his glass, rotating it slowly between finger and thumb. He was thinking of the similarities between his missing person and Vallejo's. Especially the time of the disappearance. 03.00 or thereabouts. Similar MO, except in this case the kidnappers were willing to sacrifice a father and his son to get what they wanted. Either chloroformed or smothered them while they were asleep. And both women were about the same age, early to mid-twenties. Both beautiful, too. Some coincidence. If you believed in that kind of thing.

He said, 'Somebody saw an ambulance outside the house that night, didn't they?'

Vallejo stared at him, a small upturn at the corner of her mouth. 'How'd you guess?'

'You're here, aren't you? And I imagine the witness was somebody not too reliable, or your fellow officers would have followed up on it. Probably a homeless guy or a neighbour coming back from a late night poker game, smashed out his skull.'

'You'd have made a pretty good detective, Bishop. It was option one: the homeless guy. I was becoming a real pain in the ass around that neighbourhood, let me tell you. I was convinced somebody saw something, but nobody did. Got to a point my captain was getting so many complaints about me, he threatened me with suspension if I didn't lay off. Like *that* was gonna stop me. So I started hanging around the area in the early hours of the morning to see what turned up, and one time I saw this homeless man going through the trashcans.

'He wasn't too friendly at first, but once I bought him a bottle of Mad Dog, I couldn't shut him up. He finally admitted he'd been in the neighbourhood that night when he saw this ambulance pull up outside Sam's house. This was about an hour before the fire, he said. He didn't think anything of it and moved along. But when he passed by about half an hour later the ambulance was still there, backed up against the garage with the rear doors open.'

'He notice any details?' Bishop asked.

'Well, he said the licence plate had a cactus on it. Which narrowed it down to a single state, at least. Couldn't make out the registration, but he said it was one of those boxy ambulances with an electronic heartbeat on the side.'

'Sounds familiar.'

She smiled. 'Doesn't it. And that was all I could get out of him. But I thought I had enough to take back to my captain and get the case reopened. Which was probably a mistake, in hindsight.'

'He didn't take it too well, huh?'

Vallejo sighed. 'Accused me of wasting everybody's time and obsessing over something that was dead and buried. We had a heated argument about it and I ended up slugging him.'

Bishop raised an eyebrow. 'You punched out your *captain*?'

'Right on the jaw. He got a beautiful purple bruise out of it. I got a one-hundred-and-twenty-day suspension, effective immediately.' She shrugged. 'What can I say? Sometimes, my impulses get the better of me. But the upside was that I had time to do some travelling. I drove out to Arizona the next day and started checking out the hospitals for similar ambulances.'

'Arizona's a pretty big state.'

'Don't I know it. I started at the north-east corner and kind of worked my way across, then down. After three weeks without any luck I ended up here in Saracen. I'd just crossed the town's medical centre off my list when I decided to stop for lunch at Tod's Café. So

I sit in a booth and this waitress with *Selina* on her nameplate walks up and hands me a menu. And right then, it was like all the air in my lungs had just *gone*.'

'Yeah, you mentioned there were similarities between the two women.'

Vallejo shook her head. 'You don't get it, Bishop. I swear to God, I thought I was actually looking at *Sam*.'

THIRTY-FIVE

Bishop stared at her. 'What are you talking about?'

'I'm telling you, Bishop, I thought I'd found Samantha Mathison in this little diner in the middle of nowhere. It was like a scene out of *The Twilight Zone*.'

'But it wasn't her,' he said. 'It couldn't have been.'

'Of course it wasn't. But the eyes and some of her facial character-istics threw me for a moment there. It was only when she asked if I was all right that it kind of broke the spell. Selina's voice was much softer than Sam's. And then I started noticing all the other differences between them. For a start, Selina's nose was much shorter and she had a wider forehead, plus her shoulders were smaller than Sam's. Also, Sam wasn't as fair-haired as Selina. I could go on, but still . . .'

'You mention any of this to Selina?'

Vallejo ran her fingers through her hair. 'Well, I told her I knew somebody who looked a lot like her and she just smiled. That was another thing that was different. Selina's smile didn't feel natural. Almost like she'd forgotten how to do it, you know what I mean?'

'Yes. So what happened then?'

'Well, she was pretty busy so I just ordered something and let her go. I gave her a good tip when I left and then drove off. But when I got back on route 60, I spotted this motel and took a room for the night. Seeing Selina there gave me a faint connection to Samantha and I wanted to prolong it for a little while longer. It felt like an omen or something.'

'That's understandable.'

Vallejo smiled. 'I guess I just wanted to speak to her again, even if it was just to hear her voice. So I napped for a few hours, watched some TV, then went back in the evening. But her shift had ended so I knew I wouldn't see her until the next morning.'

'You remember what day this was?'

'Sure. May 15.'

Bishop nodded. 'Selina was snatched that night.'

'Yeah, I guess she must have been. She wasn't there the next day. I just figured she was off sick, and that it was another sign that I should move on, so that's what I did.'

'But Garrick's less than fifty miles away. You telling me it took you four weeks to get from here to there?'

'Hey, give me a break, huh?' Vallejo got up off the bed, stretched, then came over and sat in the chair opposite. 'Life doesn't always go the way you planned, okay? One reason I remember the date so well is because on the 17th I was called back to Corvallis. The department's public affairs division decided my case was to be reviewed. They actually wanted to extend my suspension to six months, which meant I had to go and fight my corner and be on call any time the bastards wanted to interview me. That was a whole three weeks before I could get back on Sam's trail.'

'Okay. So when did you make the discovery at Garrick Medical Center?'

'Two days ago. After I spotted one of their ambulances, I came back here, got a room and tried to think about what to do next. It's not as easy for me as it is for you, Bishop. I'm kind of between a rock and a hard place. I'm still a cop, so I can't just do what I please. But I'm also suspended, which means I only have limited resources available to me.'

'I assume you used one of those resources to find out who I was.'

She smiled. 'A cop buddy of mine simply traced the registration to a local rental company and got your name from them. Piece of cake. So, yeah, the last two days I'd go over to Tod's for lunch, partly to think through my strategy and partly in the hope Selina might reappear. But she never did and I wasn't about to ask after her. And then you show up in the booth opposite and do the asking for me. I found that pretty interesting, the fact that she'd gone missing just after I saw her.'

'I can imagine. So then you decided to follow me.'

'Wouldn't you, in my position? After all, you practically fell in my lap. But I knew I'd made the right decision when you made for the Garrick hospital. I parked up in the next lot and waited to see what you'd do.'

Bishop remembered seeing a Ford pull in and realized that had probably been Vallejo. 'How much did you see?' he asked.

'Well, about an hour after you went in the back, I saw a man come out and get into your Impala. Then he got out again. He was holding something that looked like a cell phone and walking around the car, watching the screen. Then he disappeared from view for a few seconds before getting back in the car.'

Bishop said, 'He found your GPS tracker.'

'That's right. I just wish I knew how he did it. Those things are hard to detect. Anyway, not long after, I saw this large van pull out from a nearby space. Then the Impala pulled out and followed close behind. That's when I knew something was rotten in Denmark. It was a good bet you were in the back of that van, and I knew they'd be even more alert now that they'd found the tracker. And I was right.'

'Where did they lose you?'

Vallejo drank from her glass. 'Somewhere on the 60 between Aguila and Wenden. Again, I don't know how. I had to keep my distance, and they must have waited until the right moment then just poured on the speed and left me for dust.'

Bishop turned to the window, made a gap in the drapes and looked out into the empty forecourt. 'Unlikely. I've seen you drive. They probably just pulled in somewhere and waited for a few cars to pass by before moving out again. That's what I'd do.'

'Yeah, you could be right. But all I could do was keep going and hope they'd taken you back to Saracen. I drove around the streets for hours and finally lucked out when I spotted that black smoke in the distance. You know the rest.' She finished her wine and said, 'Okay, Bishop. Now why don't you tell me how *you* got into this mess?'

Bishop turned from the window, finished his own drink and realized how shattered he felt. But Vallejo had been a good sport so far, answering all his questions without complaint. She deserved the same respect. So he summarized the events in Louisville over five weeks before, covering the faked death. Selina's relocation here and her subsequent disappearance.

'Jeez, Bishop,' she said. 'You do this kind of thing often?'

He shrugged. 'Selina was a special case, that's all.' Then he went over the events of today, going over everything Andrea, Gloria and Hewitt had told him earlier.

'Hewitt?' she said. 'That was the mechanic at the garage?'

'Yeah. Unfortunately, he's still there.'

Vallejo gave him a look. 'Explain that, please.'

'After I came to, I stumbled over Hewitt's body. His neck was broken.'

'Shit. And you didn't feel that was worth mentioning before now?'

'I hadn't got to that part yet. Besides, we can't do anything for him now. But it explains what my pals were doing for those missing hours while you were searching for us. No doubt staking out Hewitt's place until they could grab him without witnesses, and then setting the fire with both of us inside.'

Vallejo slowly nodded and said, 'But how did they find out Hewitt was talking to you in the first place? I only knew about it from following you.'

Bishop yawned. He couldn't help it. Then he said, 'They probably paid someone to keep an eye on him for a while since he was one of the few people with a connection to Selina. Along with instructions to call a number if anybody came around asking questions. That's probably how they anticipated my visit to the hospital.'

'Maybe,' she said. 'But there's something else. Your pals parked your car right in front of the garage's customer entrance, which means the police are going to want to talk to you fairly soon.'

'They'll have to find me first,' he said. 'You want to hear the rest?'

Vallejo sighed. 'In for a dime, in for a dollar. Go ahead, I'm listening.'

So Bishop continued with his summary. He told her about the names he'd found on the nurses' computer, followed by his encounter with the bandaged patient in room 4–29 and her two beefy guardians.

Vallejo said, 'You think this Eastman woman could have been Selina?'

'It's possible. Another few seconds and I would have known for sure.' He told her about the acid welts on Selina's upper arms and said, 'All I know is two women are snatched. Both physically similar. And that hospital's involved somehow. I just don't know how deep it goes. And I don't know why.'

She frowned. 'Some kind of plastic surgery scam, maybe. There has to be a reason why Eastman's face was covered in bandages. But it still doesn't make any sense. Selina and Samantha are both beautiful woman, so why change something that doesn't need changing?'

'It could be they wanted to make them *more* alike.'

Vallejo looked at him. 'That's a very good point. But why?'

Bishop stood up and rubbed the back of his neck. 'I don't know. I'm just thinking out loud. Let's sleep on it. We've got an early start ahead of us.'

'We going back to the hospital?'

'First thing,' he said. 'We're going to find out who Mary Eastman really is.'

THIRTY-SIX

Vallejo drove them past the Garrick town limits sign at 09.17 the next morning. It was another clear, sunny day and already hot enough to justify the air conditioning. Before leaving Saracen, they'd also made a brief detour to Heritage. Once Bishop felt confident nobody was watching the place, he'd entered No. 40 and changed into some fresh clothes.

He had been tempted to go and retrieve the hard drive, too, but he figured there'd still be police in the area. Besides, it was safe enough where it was for the time being.

As they drove down Garrick's main street, Vallejo glanced at Bishop and asked, 'You given any thought to how we're going to get in this time?'

Bishop emerged from his thoughts and said, 'Yeah. Through the front door. Visiting hours started at nine.'

Vallejo made a face. 'You think that's wise?'

'Maybe not, but I don't think I can use the same trick twice. Anyway, I know where I'm going this time. And they're less likely to try anything during daylight hours.'

'That's assuming the whole hospital isn't somehow in on this.'

Bishop looked sideways at her. 'That's conspiracy talk, Vallejo. And I don't see how it could work anyway. With that many people working there, word would get out. It always does. No, I think for the most part the hospital's staffed by professionals who are just doing their job. Although somebody at the top *has* to be aware of what's going on in room 4–29. And maybe a few other rooms, too.'

They both lapsed back into silence. Less than five minutes later, they entered the medical centre's main car park. Vallejo found a space not far from the main entrance and parked.

She turned to Bishop. 'You might still get recognized, you know.'

He reached down and opened the glove compartment. Inside was a pair of lightly tinted sunglasses and a generic baseball cap he'd bought earlier. He put them on and said, 'That should do it. Besides, only a few people actually saw me last night.' He turned to her and said, 'There is one other thing.'

She reached for her seat belt. 'What's that?'

'You're not coming.'

She paused and looked at him, her face a mask. 'Is that right? I assume you got a real good reason, because I'm really looking forward to hearing it.'

'I've got two. Look, I said they probably won't try anything, but I can't be sure. And if something goes wrong, I'd rest a lot easier knowing you're out here as back-up.'

Vallejo leaned her head back against the rest and stared at something in the distance. 'That's strike one,' she said. 'I hope the second reason's more convincing.'

Bishop smiled despite himself. She reminded him of a couple of female Marines he'd served with in another life. They couldn't be intimidated, either. But then he'd never had any use for toadies and sycophants. Not for as long as he could remember. Strength of character was all that mattered to Bishop. Besides, a little friction in these kinds of situations often worked wonders.

'Okay,' he said. 'If Mary Eastman *is* Selina under a different name, I'm goint to try and bring her out with me.'

'What, just walk right out with her over your shoulder?'

'I'm hoping I can be a little more subtle than that, but I may have to improvise. And to do that I need to know I can call you on my cell and you'll be waiting outside with the engine running. We might need to move fast and I know you can drive.'

Vallejo just stared at him. After a few moments, she said, 'You never actually told me why you're doing all this, Bishop. Are you in love with Selina or what?'

He snorted. 'Why? Are you in love with Samantha?'

She paused, frowning. 'I don't know. But she *is* important to me.'

'Exactly. You don't have to love somebody to care about them. Look, I simply removed Selina from a very bad situation and set her up here so she could start again. But somebody came along and decided to reverse all that before she got the chance. Some people might be able to say "screw it" and walk away, but I can't. You might as well ask me to juggle elephants.'

'You still feel responsible for her.'

Bishop shrugged. Talking about this kind of thing always made him uncomfortable. And if he'd avoided going into any detail with Jenna about his feelings for Laurette and Selina, he sure wasn't going to start now. Instead, he said, 'I'm just a guy who always finishes what he starts, that's all. So are you with me on this, or not?'

She puffed out her cheeks. 'You are *so* going to get me into trouble, Bishop. Honest to God, you are.'

'You're already in trouble, so what's a little more?' He opened the door and got out. He was about to close it when he turned back. 'Were you ever in the service, Vallejo?'

She frowned again, smiling a little. 'No, but my dad was in the Marines. Why?'

'Just curious.' He nodded to her and said, 'Stick around. I'll be in touch.'

THIRTY-SEVEN

Bishop pushed through the glass double doors and saw that the only way in was through a metal detector just in front of the reception area. He walked over and the sullen, overweight security guard on the other side of the counter handed him a plastic tray. Bishop placed his keys on it and stepped through. No alarms went off. The guard handed him back his keys and waved him on like she had better things to do.

He walked over to the long, curved, chest-high reception desk straight ahead. Seated behind it were three women of varying ages. The one on the right was in conversation with a male nurse. The receptionist in the middle was talking on the phone as she worked on her computer. The one on the left was writing something with her head down.

Bishop walked up to this one and said, 'Hi.'

The woman looked up and gave him a toothy smile. 'Good morning, can I help you?'

'I'm here to visit my aunt, Colleen Marin.'

'Just one moment, please.' She turned to her computer and started tapping her fingers on the keyboard. Bishop just hoped this Colleen was old enough to have a nephew in his mid to late thirties or he'd have some awkward explaining to do.

After a few seconds she said, 'That's room 4–19.' She stood up and pushed a ledger across the counter. 'If you could just sign in here. And I need your first name for your ID.'

Bishop gave it to her and took a pen and scribbled something illegible in the space provided. As the receptionist printed out a card, he watched her neighbour finish her call, then pick up the phone

143

again. She pressed a number and started speaking, and Bishop could hear her words amplified over the hospital PA system: '*Paging Dr Blue. Will Dr Blue please go to ICU room 1–32 immediately? That's ICU, room 1–32, for Dr Blue. Thank you.*'

Bishop remembered the hospital codes he'd seen on the back of Al Williamson's ID. 'Dr Blue' meant a patient was suffering a cardiac arrest. The codes were obviously used so as to not alarm the visitors or other patients.

'Here you go.'

Bishop looked down and the receptionist handed him a plastic pouch with a clip. There was a card in front with *James* in large type, then *4–19* and a bar code at the bottom.

'If you can wear this while you're here,' she said, 'and hand it back when you leave. You'll find the elevators just through these doors to your right.'

Bishop thanked her and clipped the ID to his shirt pocket. He pushed through the doors and soon found the elevators. When the next one arrived he got in and pressed for the fourth floor. When it came to a stop he stepped out and looked to his right.

Same as before. The corridor went on for another hundred feet or so with 4–29 right at the end. And just before that, on the left, was the nurses' station. And whoever was on duty wouldn't be able to miss Bishop as he walked past. But seeing the receptionist downstairs had given him an idea.

He approached the station and saw only one nurse on duty, sorting through some files. That was good. More than one and it wouldn't work. The nurse saw Bishop and came over, still holding the files. Her nameplate said she was *Jackie Hernandez*.

Bishop said, 'Hi. Could you tell me which direction for the men's rooms?'

'Sure. Just go back past the elevator and take a right. Restrooms are about thirty feet on the left of the corridor.'

'Thanks,' he said and moved back in that direction. When he came to room 4–19 a few doors down, he turned the handle and quietly pushed the door open.

The room was mostly in darkness. The drapes had been pulled across, but enough light came in for him to see the figure in the bed. Colleen Marin was an elderly lady and looked to be asleep. At least, he hoped so. Otherwise the hospital might find themselves with another cardiac arrest on their hands.

Bishop stepped inside and closed the door. The room had the same layout as 4–29. There was a call button on the bedside table and a phone. He picked up the phone and carried it into the bathroom and closed the door. He pressed *0* and after two rings a female voice said, 'Reception.'

'Yeah, this is Roger over at Radiology,' Bishop said. 'I've been told to ask if you can page Nurse Hernandez on the fourth floor. We need her to come over here and pick up some patient files? It's fairly important and her phone's busy.'

'Right now?'

'That would be great. Thanks a lot.' Bishop ended the call, then placed the phone on the bedside table as before. He went over to the door and pulled it open a crack. He waited, and forty-three seconds later heard the call for Nurse Hernandez come over the loudspeaker.

Shortly afterwards, he saw her walk past the door towards the elevator bank. He gave it another twenty seconds before he peered out the door. She was gone. Bishop took a last look at Colleen and exited the room, quietly closing the door behind him. Just before he got to the nurses' station, he looked round and was pleased to see the area currently unoccupied.

He walked on and stopped outside 4–29. He was about to bring out his keys again, but decided to try the door handle first.

It was unlocked. That wasn't good.

He pushed the door open and saw the room was empty. No Mary Eastman. The bed was still there, but there were no sheets. Just a bare mattress. Nothing to show anybody had been here, except a faint medicinal odour in the air.

Bishop scowled. They sure hadn't taken any chances. Mary Eastman had either been switched to another room or moved to another location entirely. But if here, which room? Perhaps they'd updated the database with her new room number. It was a slim hope, but one worth checking while he still had the chance.

He was about to turn for the nurses' station when he heard the unmistakable sound of a revolver being cocked behind him. Then a voice said, 'Don't move. You're under arrest.'

THIRTY-EIGHT

Bishop walked through the hospital lobby with his hands cuffed behind his back and the uniformed cop at his side. Upstairs, Bishop had seen *Officer P. Blake* on his nameplate. He was a solidly built guy a couple of inches shorter and a decade younger than Bishop. As they were passing the front desk, all three receptionists stopped what they were doing and stared.

Bishop stared back and came to a sudden halt before the one who'd helped him. He pointed with his chin to the ID badge clipped to his shirt.

Blake said, 'Move your ass,' and tried to push him along, but Bishop kept his ground.

The receptionist slowly got up from her chair, reached over and unclipped the ID from his shirt before sitting down again. 'Thank you,' she said.

Bishop smiled, and when Blake nudged him in the back again allowed himself to be led through the metal detector and out through the front doors.

There was a cruiser waiting directly outside with *Saracen Police Department* in large letters on the side. He guessed they must have a fairly good relationship with the Garrick police if they were allowed to make arrests within the town's borders. Bishop didn't know where the car had been parked, but it was a safe bet they'd been waiting on the off-chance that he'd show up here again. But it wasn't like he'd had a whole lot of options. And he'd still been too late. They probably moved Eastman last night.

As Blake unlocked the rear door, Bishop saw Vallejo's Fusion, still parked in the same space. He could make out her face as she watched him from the front seat. That was one thing he'd done right, at least.

Blake placed a hand on Bishop's head and pushed him down into the back seat and shut the door. The car smelled faintly of aftershave and fast food. The driver turned his head and watched Bishop with small eyes. Through the steel mesh partition, Bishop could see old shaving cuts all over his neck.

'Didn't think we'd find you so fast, did you?' he said with a smirk.

Bishop blinked and said nothing. Just looked out the side window. The Miranda warning was full of good stuff for somebody in Bishop's situation, but the right to remain silent was his absolute favourite. You couldn't incriminate yourself if you stayed quiet.

Blake got in the passenger seat and said, 'Okay, Vern. Let's go.'

Vern grunted, then faced front and put the vehicle into gear and started off.

At no point during the journey did Bishop turn to look out the rear window. He could already feel Vallejo back there in the distance. He didn't need to see her. Most of his time was spent coming up with possible reasons for his arrest. As far as he knew, there were no legal ramifications for impersonating a doctor unless you were dumb enough to give out medical advice as well. Although manslaughter was a distinct possibility. That fat orderly last night hadn't looked too good when Bishop last saw him. A 'spear hand' strike could cause all kinds of problems, not the least of which was internal bleeding.

More likely, it was to do with the fire. Vallejo said his hire car had been there for all to see. But Bishop wasn't about to ask. He didn't want to give these two the satisfaction of telling him to go screw himself.

Forty minutes later, Vern entered West Garfield Avenue and turned in to the police station. The large, one-storey building was hard to miss, mainly because of the cantilevered flat roof that extended out on all four sides by about twenty feet. As an example of unconventional modern architecture, Bishop thought the structure held up pretty well.

There was a large visitors' car park out front, separated from the station house by a small access road. Vern parked in a bay outside the front entrance. Blake opened the rear door and used a hand to help Bishop get out. Then they marched him into the station.

Inside, everything was polished wood, chrome and glass. All very modern. The air conditioning had been set to the default 'freezing' mode, like the library yesterday. Maybe it was an official mandate around here. Bishop saw two short rows of visitors' seats at his left. Ahead, a desk sergeant sat behind a long counter, watching them. There were two corridors, one at each side of the desk, that presumably provided access to the rest of the station.

The two uniforms led Bishop towards the counter. The desk sergeant, a dark-skinned man with long sideburns, turned to his computer and said, 'Okay, let's have your name, date of birth, address and telephone number.'

Bishop said nothing. Just looked back at the sergeant without expression.

'We couldn't shut him up on the drive over here, sarge,' Blake said and handed over Bishop's wallet. 'Here you go. His name's James Bishop. Everything else is in there.'

The sergeant slid the wallet over, opened it and pulled out Bishop's driver's licence and social security card. He tapped his fingers against the keyboard for a minute, then placed the cards back in the wallet and slid the wallet back to Blake. He turned away, took a clear plastic zip lock bag from one of the cubby holes, stapled a form to it and slid that over, too. 'Okay, take him over to Hannah.'

Blake led them down the left-hand corridor and stopped outside the third door down on the right. Vern opened it and went in first, followed by Bishop, then Blake.

It was a grey room with grey walls and a grey ceiling. A single, circular ceiling light provided the only illumination. To his left, Bishop saw an expensive-looking digital camera on a tripod, pointed towards the left-hand wall. Directly ahead was something that resembled a small ATM, but with a glass panel instead of a keypad. On the right was a desk bearing a computer, a scanner, a printer and lots of other things. Behind it sat another uniformed cop. This one was a large, bespectacled Latino woman with long curly hair. She looked up from some paperwork and then stood up and came round the desk.

'Hey, come on, guys,' she said, tilting her head. 'I'm gonna need access to his hands.'

Vern took his revolver from his holster. Blake said, 'Okay, Bishop, I'm going to uncuff you then bring your hands to the front and cuff you again. You twitch without warning and my partner over there *will* shoot you. Understand?'

Bishop nodded and didn't move a muscle throughout the whole process.

Once that was done, Hannah led him to the wall, handed him a number holder and told him to face forward. Bishop held it at chest level and looked directly at the camera. Then he gave his left profile. Then the right. It wasn't the first time he'd gone through this procedure. He knew the routine.

Next, he allowed Hannah to lead him over to the fingerprint scanner. No need for messy ink in the twenty-first century. Hannah took his left hand and pressed his thumb against the glass plate for ten seconds. A red light swept back and forth under the plate as the laser scanned his print. Once the rest of the left hand was done, she took his right and frowned when she noticed the missing third joint of his pinkie finger.

Bishop just smiled at her.

Hannah shrugged, began printing his thumb, then turned at the sound of the door opening behind him. 'Hey, chief,' she said.

Bishop turned too, and saw an overweight, grey-haired man of medium height standing in the doorway, looking back at him. He was wearing a dark blue, short-sleeved uniform with four gold stars on each lapel. Bishop saw *L. Emery* printed on his gold name badge. He had a heavily lined, jowly face and appeared to be in his late fifties or early sixties. His pale grey eyes looked at Bishop with deep suspicion.

Emery turned to Blake and said, 'This is the one?'

'That's right, sir,' Blake said. 'Bishop. We just brought him in this minute.'

Emery nodded and looked back at Bishop for a few more moments. Like he was cataloguing him. Then he closed the door and was gone.

What was that all about? Bishop thought.

Hannah shrugged again and then carried on printing Bishop's remaining fingers. Once she was done, she said, 'Okay, boys, he's all yours again.'

He was led out the room and the trio moved on down the corridor. Near the end of the hallway, Vern opened a door on the left and they all stepped through.

Straight away, Bishop knew he was in an interview room. It had all the hallmarks. It was small, windowless, and contained a desk and three chairs, one of which was clearly more uncomfortable than the others. That would be his. A one-way mirror took up most of one side and there was a small closed circuit camera in a corner near the ceiling.

Vern stood near the door with his hand on his holster again. Blake didn't warn him this time. He just said, 'Turn around and place your hands on the desk.'

Bishop complied. Blake searched him thoroughly, but found nothing except his keys and cell phone. He threw them onto the desk along with his wallet.

Blake pointed to the steel folding chair in front of the desk and said, 'Sit down.'

Bishop ignored that chair and sat in the one behind the desk instead.

'Not there, shit-for-brains,' Vern said.

'Forget it, Vern,' Blake said.

Blake filled the zip lock bag with Bishop's possessions, handed him a ballpoint and told him to sign his name on the form stapled to the bag. Bishop signed. Blake took the bag and pen, tore off the bottom part of the form and handed it to Bishop. Then he and his partner left the room.

Bishop pocketed the receipt. Then he sat back in the chair, put his feet up on the desk and closed his eyes.

THIRTY-NINE

Bishop knew they were watching him, trying to get a read on his body language. Either via the camera or through the one-way mirror. It was straight out of Police Interrogation 101. Leave the suspect alone for a while and see how he reacts. Bishop almost smiled at that. If they'd wanted to see him sweat they should have turned off the air conditioning first.

After about twenty minutes of pretending to sleep, he heard the sound of the door being unlocked. It swung open and two men in shirtsleeves and ties entered the room. One was a slightly overweight man in his late forties holding a plastic cup of clear liquid. He had grey, thinning hair and heavy-lidded eyes. The other was probably early thirties with strawberry-blond hair, a long face and a nose that was too straight to be totally natural.

Bishop slowly lowered his feet from the desk before one of them did it for him. Neither man made any move to remove Bishop's cuffs. Or offer him the water. And Bishop wasn't about to ask.

The older one glanced at the two remaining chairs and remained standing with his back against the wall. He hitched his pants up and took a sip from his cup. 'I'm Detective Levine,' he said. 'This here's my partner, Detective Shaw. Looks like we got a situation here, doesn't it, Bishop?'

Shaw perched on the edge of the desk and looked down at Bishop with a faint smile. 'You know, you look pretty relaxed for a guy who's just been arrested. But then, you ain't exactly a first timer at this, are you? We been checking up on you. That trouble you had back east last year, for instance. And then that business that started it all, three years before that. Tell me, Bishop, is it just me or do people have a habit of dying around you?'

Bishop remained silent. So they knew his history. So what? He was just waiting for them to get down to the business at hand.

Still watching him, Shaw said, 'You want to tell us where you were between the hours of ten p.m. and two a.m. last night?'

Bishop kept his breathing steady and said nothing. So this was about Hewitt. He couldn't say it was entirely unexpected, but he wasn't exactly happy about it, either.

Shaw tilted his head. 'Didn't think so. Here's an easier one then: why'd you murder Gary Hewitt?'

Bishop stayed silent. ·

'Because we found his body at the Bannings place last night with his neck broken. What was left of his body, I mean. You know about the fire they had over there, right? What am I saying? Course you do; you started it. We found your hire car right outside with your rental agreement in the glove compartment. Didn't take us long to get a photo from that and we been showing it to people all night. Seems you been a busy boy recently.'

Levine said, 'See, we know you went to visit Hewitt yesterday at the garage, Bishop. We've got witnesses who saw you. They said you were very threatening. We've got one man who says you assaulted him when he tried to stop you from entering the premises. Claims you almost broke his hand. And we've got another who says you pressured Hewitt into going outside with you so you could talk in private.'

'Except it wasn't so private,' Shaw said, still smiling. 'The same witness stood nearby and heard part of the conversation. He says you accused Hewitt of killing some girl. Who was she, Bishop? An ex of yours?'

Bishop breathed a little easier. So whoever had overheard the conversation hadn't gotten Selina's name. That was something, at least. Maybe the radio had drowned out that part. He made a mental note never to diss death metal again.

Levine continued, 'After that it gets pretty confusing. There's some missing hours before you turn up at the hospital in Garrick, somehow wearing a doctor's uniform and ID. Two orderlies discover you in a patient's room and chase you out. Then three hours later, we get an arson attack at Bannings Automotive with your car outside and a man inside with his neck broken. A man who you had a major argument with earlier that day.'

'Let him hear your take on it, Val,' Shaw said. He crossed his arms and leaned in closer to Bishop. 'This is always my favourite part. Feel free to butt in if you got something to add. My partner won't mind.'

Levine gave Shaw a look and said, 'You're searching for some woman. We don't know who yet. Whatever leads you're following bring you to Hewitt, who you believe either killed her or had some involvement in her disappearance. He denies killing her and possibly suggests you check out the local hospitals. You end up at the one in Garrick and, instead of waiting for visiting hours, decide to gain access by impersonating a doctor. You start checking rooms, and soon after, two orderlies confront you and force you to run. You drive back to Saracen with murder on your mind. You feel Hewitt's led you on a chase and you're seeing red.'

Bishop could sense Shaw watching him through all of this, but kept his face a mask. To be honest, he was impressed they'd found out so much in such a short amount of time.

'So you kidnap him and take him back to the garage,' Levine said. 'It's nice and remote there with nobody to interfere. God only knows what you did then. Possibly tortured the poor man until he gave you what you wanted. Then you broke his neck, probably without thinking, and set the whole place alight to cover up the crime.

'Except it didn't all go to plan.' Levine frowned. 'Maybe the fire spread too fast and you had trouble getting out. Whatever happened, you had to leave your car behind and hot-tail it out of there on foot.'

Shaw leaned in again and said, 'We already know you got a history of violence, Bishop. With your background, you could probably break the guy's neck in your sleep. So that's *means* taken care of. You believe Hewitt was behind this girl's death or disappearance and you wanted to make him pay. So that's *motive*. And let's face it, with that car of yours on the scene and no alibi, you sure got the *opportunity*. So that's three for three in anyone's book. Care to comment?'

Bishop looked at the one-way mirror. Then at the camera. Then at the two detectives. Nothing had changed. He still had nothing to say. Not yet, anyway.

Levine pushed off from the wall. 'This is your chance to set the record straight, Bishop. We know you did it, we just don't know all the reasons behind it. If you told us what those reasons are, it might make a difference when it comes to trial. So we'll leave you alone so you can think on it for a while.' He caught Shaw's eye and motioned for the door.

Shaw got off the desk. 'That's right. Give it some serious thought. We'll be back real soon, okay?'

Levine opened the door and both men left the room.

Bishop sat back and stared at a spot on the wall, grateful for the silence again. Those two had given him an earache. But at least now he knew how much *they* knew.

He turned his thoughts back to the hard drive he'd hidden, and how he didn't want to use it unless it was absolutely necessary. At the moment, it was his only connection to the people who'd taken Selina. If he turned it over to the police, he'd have nothing. But it was also the only way he could put himself in the clear. Assuming it held footage of the people who'd grabbed him, that is.

But one thing was for sure, he couldn't stay locked up in here. Selina's trail was cold enough as it was. The only evidence they had on him at the moment was circumstantial, but it would be enough to hold him for forty-eight hours, at least. And that was forty-seven hours too long. He needed to get out on the streets again. He considered getting himself a lawyer, then have him get word to Vallejo to pick up the hard drive, copy everything onto a duplicate and hand the original to the cops. Not an ideal solution, as it would refocus the police's attention onto the real killers and he didn't want that. No telling how they might react if they thought they'd been exposed. But right now, it was the best he could come up with.

He also thought about how fast they'd placed him at the break-in at the Garrick hospital. And the way they were waiting for him this morning. Who'd made that connection? It wasn't exactly obvious. Unless somebody in the police department was involved. That was always a possibility. One of those orderlies from last night could have called their police contact and filled him in when it became obvious Bishop hadn't been killed in the fire. But in that case, why involve the uniforms, when it would be a lot easier to finish the job and kill Bishop outright?

He kept himself occupied by running through a variety of different scenarios, none of them particularly satisfying, until Shaw opened the door seventy-seven minutes later. He was alone this time and the smirk was absent from his face.

'On your feet, Bishop,' he said. 'Your alibi showed up.'

FORTY

Shaw nudged Bishop back down the hallway towards the front desk without another word. Probably didn't trust himself. He waited until Bishop had reached the lobby before unlocking the cuffs, his upper lip curled into a sneer.

'I'll be seeing you again, Bishop,' he said, then moved off down the hallway without looking back.

Maybe you will, Bishop thought. He turned and saw Vallejo sitting in one of the visitors' chairs. She stood up and gave him a big smile when she saw him. He noticed the desk sergeant watching them both and immediately got it. She was here as the concerned 'girlfriend', looking out for her man. Bishop wondered how much that must have stung. He smiled back and she came over and wrapped him in a lover's embrace. Feigned though it was, Bishop found himself enjoying it. Being held by attractive women never got old.

'You can hug back,' she whispered, 'but if you go anywhere *near* my ass, you die.'

'That's a shame,' he whispered back, holding her round the waist. 'And you got such a nice one, too.'

For appearances' sake, they squeezed each other for a few more seconds until Bishop pushed himself away from her. 'Let's get out of here,' he said.

'You read my mind. I'll meet you outside.'

Bishop went to the desk and handed the sergeant the receipt for his few possessions. After pocketing his cell phone, keys and wallet, he joined Vallejo on the steps outside. Then they walked into the visitors' car park, passing a number of vehicles until they reached the familiar Ford Fusion. Vallejo unlocked it and they both got in.

She turned to him and sighed. 'I just falsified a police statement for you, Bishop. That's the first time I've ever committed a felony. Didn't I say you were going to get me into trouble?'

'Better watch out,' he said, removing the back of his cell phone. 'I'll have you robbing banks next.'

She grimaced. 'Don't joke. You know, I was getting concerned. They kept me waiting for over an hour before bringing you out.'

He paused and looked at her. 'That's interesting. I wonder what they were doing.' After a moment, he went back to dismantling his phone. 'So what did you tell them?'

'Well, I said I followed you back from the hospital and wanted to know why you'd been arrested. When the desk sergeant said it was about that fire last night, I told him you couldn't have had anything to do with it since you were in bed with me all night.'

'Oh, yeah, I forgot all about that,' Bishop said as he closely inspected the phone's inner workings. 'How was I, by the way?'

'Unbelievable, as usual. Just a pity you're not my type. What the hell are you doing?'

'Seeing if they put a GPS tracker in here.'

'That's illegal without a warrant, and they wouldn't have had time.'

'You're forgetting not everyone's as upstanding as you,' he said. But there was nothing in there. He was sure of it. Bishop began reassembling the phone again. 'So how did you explain my Chevy being at the scene?'

'I said you'd taken it in when the front brakes started giving you problems. I brought you back to the motel in mine and then we retired for the night. I kept it simple.'

'That's usually the best way,' he said. Except it now meant he couldn't give the hard drive to the police even if he wanted to. Once they saw Vallejo had given a false statement, she'd be in even worse trouble. And Bishop wasn't about to allow that to happen. Not after what she'd done for him.

'Thanks for the alibi, Vallejo. I mean that.'

She shrugged and said, 'You'd do the same for me, wouldn't you?'

'Well, I would now.'

Her eyes turned to slits. '*Hijo de puta.*'

'That's not nice, Vallejo.'

'It wasn't meant to be. So where to next?'

Bishop put on his seat belt. 'Back to the same spot where you picked me up last night. I left something there I need to pick up.'

FORTY-ONE

Just over an hour later, after having retrieved the hard drive from its hiding place and gotten some late breakfast at a Denny's, they both returned to Vallejo's motel room. Bishop made a brief trip to the bathroom to splash some water on his face and came out to see Vallejo placing her laptop upon the table.

Bishop moved the other chair next to hers and sat down as Vallejo opened up the computer. The wallpaper that greeted them showed a version of the famous *Jaws* movie poster, but with Alfred E. Neuman in place of the female swimmer.

Bishop turned to look at Vallejo. 'I didn't expect that.'

She shrugged. 'My dad kept a big collection of old *Mad* magazines in the attic when I was a kid, okay? Let's not make a big deal out of it. So why didn't you tell me about this hard drive before?'

Bishop placed the device on the table. 'I didn't know if I could trust you, did I?'

'And now you do?'

He smiled at her. 'For a cop, you're okay, Vallejo.'

'Is that supposed to be a compliment?'

'If you knew me better, you wouldn't need to ask.' Bishop took the USB lead she'd brought over and connected one end to the laptop and the other to the black box. A second later, a hard drive icon showed up and he used the touchpad to open it up. The folder listed hundreds of .mpeg files going back a week. The newest was from this morning. From the looks of things, Bishop guessed the camera software automatically saved the footage in one hour increments. That made things a little easier. He counted down the files with yesterday's date and double-clicked on the seventeenth one.

The QuickTime player opened up and then the screen was filled with a wide-angle aerial view of the garage forecourt at 16.00 yesterday. There was no sound and the colours looked muted. Bishop could see the line of parked vehicles out front, as well as a segment of East Richards Avenue. In the lower right corner was yesterday's date and a running time counter, which was about the only way to tell this was actual footage rather than a still shot.

'Exciting stuff,' Vallejo said.

'Isn't it.' Bishop moved the cursor to the timeline at the bottom, clicked on the playhead and began slowly dragging it to the right. Still nothing happened, just at a faster speed. Then at 16.08.42, Bishop came into view from the right. He went back a few seconds and then let it play in real time.

'The image quality could be better,' Vallejo said. 'If I didn't already know that was you, I might not have guessed.'

'Probably Bannings counting his pennies,' he said. 'High-definition video on these things isn't cheap.' Soon Bishop's digital alter ego disappeared offscreen. He thought for a moment, then leaned forward and dragged the playhead to 16.18.00.

Vallejo looked at him. 'What are you doing?'

'It was around this point that somebody turned the radio back on inside.'

'You're speaking in riddles again, Bishop. What are you talking about?'

'Let's just watch and see.'

They viewed the footage in silence. A minute passed. Then two. At 16.20.53, a figure emerged from the lower-left of the screen. From the direction of the car lifts. Bishop recognized him as the skinny mechanic who'd been working on the same car as Waxworks. He held a cell phone to his ear and was walking around in circles, listening and talking. Then at 16.21.42, he put the phone in his pocket and went back inside.

'I don't get it,' Vallejo said. 'What just happened? And what's it got to do with the radio?'

Bishop ran his palm across his scalp and told her about turning off the radio when he'd first talked to Hewitt. 'But somebody switched it back on shortly after we went outside. Really loud heavy metal, or whatever they call it nowadays. Thing is, one of my interrogators at the station said a witness heard part of my conversation with Hewitt. That could only have been the lookout you and I hypothesized about last night. Nobody else would have cared. He probably crept up to the side shutter and listened in as best he could. But when the radio came back on the racket must have drowned out the rest of our conversation. At which point, I figure he would have given up and called his contact. Telling him about my showing up on the scene, asking Hewitt questions about some woman.'

'Sounds reasonable.' Vallejo rewound the footage and watched the mechanic talk on the cell phone again. 'You know his name?'

'Maybe. Let me think.' Bishop closed his eyes and thought back to those Employee of the Month pictures he'd seen for a few seconds in the front office. There'd been five of them in a row. All with head shots above the names. The glum face of the skinny mechanic had been on the fourth one along. It was clear in his mind. But what was the name underneath? Joe something. Or maybe John.

Concentrate, dammit. The name's right there. All you need to do is focus.

Twenty seconds later, he opened his eyes and smiled at Vallejo. 'Rutherford. John or Joe Rutherford.'

'Hey, not bad. So, what, you think he was involved in the fire?'

Bishop shook his head. 'I think he's just a guy who was offered some easy money to perform a simple task. Nothing more than that. But he's another connection to the people we're after. And there'll be a number on his cell phone I'd really like to see. But that's for later.'

He closed the .mpeg file and opened up the first of today's. 'Right now, I'm more interested in seeing who tried to kill me.'

FORTY-TWO

It opened with the same view as before, except it was obviously night-time and there were no vehicles parked outside. Illumination was provided by a spotlight at roof level. Something about the starkness of the scene reminded Bishop of those old Bogart movies from the forties he used to love watching. And still did, come to think of it.

He reached for the controls and speeded things up a little. He was almost halfway across the timeline when Vallejo said, 'Right *there*.'

Bishop had spotted the movement too, and was already dragging the playhead back. When he got to 00.24.37, he let it play in real time.

They saw the beams from the headlights first. At 00.24.44. Then a light-coloured panel van pulled into the forecourt and parked at an angle. Looked like a Merc, judging by the grille. But Bishop couldn't make out the plates. Not in this light and not at that distance.

'Sure looks like the same one I saw at the hospital,' Vallejo said.

Bishop watched as a thickset man in a dark suit got out the passenger side and stood there with his hands at his sides, looking around as though he owned the place. Bishop could make out a goatee on his face and not much hair on top. Most of his features were bleached out from the harsh light, but this had to be the same man Hewitt had seen. From the erectness of his stance, Bishop thought he might possibly be ex-military. In any case, Bishop was looking forward to meeting him in the near future.

Then Bishop's rented Chevy Impala appeared. It came to a halt on the road and Goatee pointed down to the shutters at the end. The Chevy drove off in that direction. At the same time, the van's driver got out. He was wearing casual clothes and looked like one of the orderlies Bishop had encountered at the hospital. Goatee said something, then walked offscreen towards the customer entrance while the driver went to the van's rear and pulled the doors open.

Less than a minute later, Goatee reappeared and joined the driver. Bishop then watched the two men carry a third from the van's interior towards the customer entrance, his head swinging down like a rag doll's. Hewitt. And he was clearly already dead.

'Jesus,' Vallejo whispered.

Both men came back and pulled out Bishop, then carried him inside, too. It felt weird watching it. Since he'd been unconscious at the time, it was hard to believe that was actually him being carried to his funeral pyre. But there it was, in living black and white.

'How come they didn't waste you along with Hewitt?' Vallejo asked.

'Two random homicides in a quiet desert community would have opened up too many questions. This way was smarter. As a stranger in town, I'd get the blame posthumously and everybody would be happy. Case closed. It was just their bad luck I regained consciousness in time and managed to get out.'

They kept watching, but after a minute of nothing happening Bishop began fast-forwarding. The killers were still inside, no doubt making their preparations. He was nearing the end of the hour when he noticed more movement. He wound it back a little and resumed watching at 00.55.54.

All three men came into view again. They stood this side of the van and Goatee looked back at the building while the other two lit cigarettes. Goatee seemed to be saying something and then the other two laughed. Probably asked why they hadn't lit them inside, or something similarly feeble. Then they all got in the van. Goatee rolled down his window and leaned out as the driver turned the van round and drove them back the way they came.

Until we meet again, Bishop thought. *And we will. You can be sure of it.*

He quit out of the file and sat back in the chair. Alfred E. Neuman grinned back at him with that idiotic smile. *What, me . . . Worry?*

Vallejo said, 'So did you recognize any of them?'

'Well, the one in the suit matches the description Hewitt gave me of the leader of the team who took Selina. And the other two could have been the orderlies I fought with at the hospital. Couldn't swear to it, though.' After a moment's silence, he turned and saw Vallejo chewing on her lower lip. 'What is it?'

'We *have* to deliver this to the police, Bishop. And don't look at me like that. These people killed one man and tried to kill another. And God knows how many others. We might not recognize them, but somebody around here might if we allow them to see the footage.'

Bishop scratched the back of his neck. 'That would be a major mistake, Vallejo.'

'Tell me why.'

'Two reasons. First of all, you've just told the police I took that Chevy to the garage myself, after which you brought me back here and boffed my brains out.' He waved his hand at the laptop. 'Clearly not so. Which means you'd have to admit you falsified your statement and say goodbye to whatever's left of your career.'

'Oh, shit, I forgot about that.' She rubbed her forehead. 'And the other reason?'

Bishop said, 'I think the police might be involved, too.'

FORTY-THREE

Vallejo looked at him for a long moment. 'That sounds like conspiracy talk to me, Bishop. Didn't you warn me against that this morning?'

'I didn't say the whole department. For all I know, it's just one rotten apple.' But even as Bishop said it, Shaw's face loomed large in his mind. He was a definite contender.

'You got anything to back that up?' Vallejo said, stepping over to the refrigerator. 'Or is this just another one of your hang-ups against anyone with a badge?'

'All I've got right now are questions,' he said. 'For instance, I was arrested for the Hewitt killing, so why were those two Saracen cops waiting for me at the hospital in Garrick? How did they know I was the same guy who showed up last night pretending to be a doctor?'

Vallejo filled two glasses with Evian and handed one to Bishop. 'You tell me.'

Bishop drank some of the water and tapped a knuckle against the screen. 'I think one of these three, probably the big one, gave my description to his contact at the Saracen PD and let them handle it. Probably mentioned my visit to the hospital last night and that it might be an idea to post a couple of uniforms in case I decided to return. And like an idiot, that's exactly what I did.'

'But why involve the police at all? They could have just waited for you to show up, then buried you out in the desert.'

Bishop shrugged. 'Maybe the man at the top decided it was better to stick with the original plan. I mean, he'd already invested all this time and effort on setting me up as a fall guy for Hewitt's murder. Easier all round if he let the police catch me so they can wrap up the case quickly, then everybody's able to carry on with their business as normal.'

'But the evidence against you was all circumstantial. Any half-decent lawyer would have cast enough reasonable doubt in the minds of the jury to get you off.'

'I've a strong feeling I would have been found dead in my cell long before that. A suicide would prove my guilt better than any trial. A lot neater, too.'

Vallejo thought about that. Then she said, 'So that alibi I gave you must have really thrown them for a loop.'

'And then some. They probably didn't even know you existed before this morning. You can bet they do now, though.'

Vallejo finished her drink and said, 'Okay, Bishop, you've convinced me. We hold on to the hard drive. So what next?'

Bishop looked around the room until he spotted the small air ventilation grille near the ceiling. 'I'll hide the hard drive,' he said. 'You see if you can find out where this Rutherford lives.'

FORTY-FOUR

According to the online White Pages, a Jon Rutherford lived at the Rio Alamos Apartments on West McKinley Avenue, out on the western outskirts of town. Apartment number 132. Vallejo got them there in less than twenty minutes.

To Bishop the whole place looked cheap and depressing. The complex took up most of a block, with a large part of the acreage set aside for parking. The two-storey apartment buildings dotted around were simple rectangular blocks devoid of any character, with no trees or greenery in sight. There was barely any shade anywhere.

Vallejo drove through the entrance and turned left at the fork in the access road. She followed the road all the way round until they found the building that housed apartments 121–160. The car park for this section was mostly empty. And on a Saturday, too. Bishop guessed this was the kind of place that always had vacancies. Vallejo parked a few spaces along from a ten-year-old blue Toyota Camry. Bishop could remember seeing something similar outside Bannings' yesterday and wondered if it was Rutherford's.

They got out and walked over to the stairs at the side of the building. There was nobody else around that he could see. Apart from the occasional vehicle passing by on McKinley, the place was quiet.

As they climbed the steps, she said, 'Has it occurred to you that this guy might not be too anxious to talk to you?'

Bishop said, 'Believe me, he'll be desperate to tell me everything in no time at all.'

'That's the problem. I *do* believe you.'

At the top, they walked along the walkway until they reached No. 132. Bishop stood to one side of the door. Vallejo took the other.

Again, old habits died hard. For both of them. Bishop rapped on the door a couple of times and waited.

There were no sounds from within. None at all. He knocked again, looking at Vallejo. Bishop began to suspect that maybe that wasn't Rutherford's car downstairs. Or maybe he'd gone out to get drunk now that he'd found himself unemployed.

'Hey, you smell something?' Vallejo asked, sniffing the air.

Now that she mentioned it, he did. 'That's gas,' he said.

He bent down to the keyhole and breathed in. The smell was definitely coming from within. They needed to get inside, fast. He took his keys from his pocket and found one that looked right. He inserted it and did his bump trick again. He turned the handle and pushed, but a steel security chain prevented it from opening more than a couple of inches. And the smell was a lot stronger now.

'Take a deep breath, Vallejo,' he said. 'And try not to leave any prints.'

Bishop took three steps back and then launched himself at the door. His right shoulder smashed into the chained section and it crashed open. Covering his nose and mouth with the crook of his elbow, Bishop plunged ahead down the hallway until he found the kitchen on the left.

It was a mess. The kind of mess you'd expect of a young guy living on his own. Dirty plates and cutlery everywhere, except in the sink. There was also a refrigerator, a washing machine, a breakfast table, two chairs – and a gas stove.

The oven door was open. A male figure lay on his stomach with his head all the way inside. The dial for the gas was the maximum setting. Bishop turned it to the off position. He checked and it was Rutherford all right. The skin was already cold. He'd been dead for at least a couple of hours. Possibly longer. Turning round, Bishop saw Vallejo at the doorway, her hand over her nose and mouth. He pointed to the window. She nodded, then grabbed a cloth from the sink and unlatched it, opening it as wide as it could go.

Bishop quickly patted the body down. In one of the pants pockets there was something that felt like a wallet. In another, a set of keys. He pulled these out and saw one with a Toyota symbol on it.

He stood up, grabbed a dirty rag from the kitchen counter and said, 'You'd better open all the other windows before somebody passes by with a cigarette. And see if you can spot Rutherford's cell phone around here somewhere. I'll go and check his car.'

'Right.'

Vallejo left the kitchen and Bishop retraced his steps to the front door. He peered out and saw nobody in the immediate vicinity. Once down the steps he walked over to the Toyota and unlocked it. Using the rag to pull the door open, Bishop got in and gave the interior a once-over. There was plenty of junk on the carpet and in the glove compartment, but no cell phone anywhere. He got out, locked the car again and went back upstairs.

Vallejo met him in the living room and said, 'Nothing. You?'

Bishop shook his head and said, 'I didn't think they'd be that dumb, but it was worth checking.'

He turned, walked back to the kitchen and looked down at the sad figure of Rutherford. The bodies were really starting to pile up now. And he didn't think it would stop any time soon, either. The only way it might would be if Bishop gave up and went home. And that wasn't about to happen in this lifetime. More likely, they'd just try to kill him again. He hoped so. Bishop was tired of groping around in the dark. He needed some facts to go on. And the best way to get them would be from the horse's mouth. He felt confident that if he got his hands on one of them, he'd soon be able to make him talk.

Standing beside him, Vallejo said, 'Sure looks like suicide, doesn't it?'

'But we know better, don't we?'

'So Rutherford's just another loose end they needed to tie up?'

'That's right. Hewitt had a link to Selina and he's gone. Rutherford had a link to the bad guys and now he's gone. They tried to kill me. These are serious people, Vallejo. Whatever we've stumbled onto is big enough that they can afford to waste anyone with even the slightest connection to them or their victims.'

'But it kind of means we've also come to a dead end, doesn't it? Unless you've got some other lead you've been keeping secret?'

Bishop had been thinking about that on the drive over here. About what to do if Rutherford wasn't around. And he'd found his thoughts returning to those admissions entries on the hospital database. At the end of most entries had been a pair of initials and a three-digit number. He hadn't thought much about them at the time, but now he had a pretty good idea what they signified.

'I might have one,' he said. 'Come on. Every second we stay in this place is a second too long. We can make an anonymous call to the cops once we're away from here.'

Bishop relocked the front door and they made their way down to the car without meeting anybody. Once Vallejo got them back on the road, Bishop told her what he'd seen on the computer back at the hospital. 'I think those initials represent the physician assigned to each patient. The number could be the physician's pager number or pass number. The one on Mary Eastman's entry was A.T. 423. And that's somebody I'd really like to talk to.'

'So how do you figure on finding out his, or her, name? I'd say that hospital's pretty much out of bounds for you now, so you can forget about accessing that database again.'

Bishop shrugged. 'There must be a registry somewhere that lists physicians that practise in the state. And since Mary Eastman's face was covered in bandages, we could narrow it down further by focusing only on plastic surgeons. There can't be that many with the initials A.T.'

'Don't be too sure, Bishop. They *are* two of the more common letters in the alphabet.'

'You got any better suggestions?'

She turned to him. 'You know, I just might.'

FORTY-FIVE

The *Saracen Post* newspaper offices were located in another large, one-storey building on West Central Avenue, overlooking the park. Two blocks down from the library. A pretty sensible location, Bishop felt. Or it would have been before the internet came along and levelled the playing field for researchers everywhere.

Vallejo parked in one of the angled spaces directly outside and turned off the engine.

Bishop looked out the window and said, 'So what are we doing here?'

'My first evening here,' she said, 'I went to a bar in town and got talking with a woman and a couple of her friends. Once her friends left, we stayed on. She said her name was Kaitlyn McGowan and that she worked at the local paper. We kept drinking and I ended up telling her more than I should have. I probably sounded deranged, talking about this phantom ambulance going round stealing women in the middle of the night, but she was real sympathetic. She also said I could call her again any time I felt like just talking to someone.'

'People say a lot of things when they've had a few beers, Vallejo. They don't necessarily mean them.'

'I *know* that, but she still might be able to help. Besides, what have we got to lose?'

'Nothing,' he said and opened the door.

Once they entered the building they found themselves in an empty reception area. Newspaper and magazine racks shared wall space with a number of framed paintings. Probably from local artists. There was a large desk ahead with a computer and phone, but no receptionist. And no sign of one, either. But Bishop noticed a hallway to the right and heard voices coming from that direction.

They walked down the short passageway and entered what looked to be the newsroom. It was a large open-space area with about fifteen desks scattered around. Half of them were occupied by men and women either talking on the phone or working on computers. Or both. On either side were a number of private office areas, few of which looked occupied.

A pale young man working at one of the desks close to the hallway turned from his screen and smiled at Bishop and Vallejo. 'Help you, folks?'

'There was nobody in reception,' Bishop said.

'Yeah, I know. Sheila had to rush home for another family emergency.' He turned to a large, bespectacled woman two desks down. 'Third one this week, wasn't it?'

'Fourth,' she said without turning from her screen.

The man turned back. 'My mistake. Fourth. So you got a hot story for us, or what?'

Vallejo looked round and said, 'I don't see Kaitlyn. Is she in today?'

The man searched the room. 'Well, she was here a few minutes . . . Hey, there she goes now.'

Bishop followed his gaze and saw a slim, attractive woman leave one of the offices on the left and walk towards a desk in the corner, next to a window. The privileges of rank, no doubt. She had a batch of folders under one arm and was carrying a cup of something while she talked on her cell phone.

'Okay if we go over and talk to her?' Vallejo asked. 'I know her.'

'Go right ahead,' the man said and returned to his screen.

They made their way through the room until they reached Kaitlyn's corner desk. She was still talking quietly on the cell phone and lifted a finger – *one minute* – to indicate they find themselves a seat. Bishop rolled two free chairs over from a nearby desk and they both sat down to wait.

Bishop studied Kaitlyn McGowan. Dressed in a long-sleeved shirt and jeans, she was about Vallejo's age, maybe a little older, with straight light-brown hair down to her shoulders. He detected little make-up on her face. Maybe a hint of eye shadow around the hazel, almond eyes, but that was all. Her face already contained everything it needed to make it attractive.

She finished the call and placed the cell phone on the only clear spot on her desk. She smiled at Vallejo and said, 'Hello again, Clarissa.'

Vallejo smiled back. 'Good memory. How are you, Kate?'

'Busy, as always.' She lifted her mug and took a sip. Bishop could smell the faint aroma of coffee. 'Good to see you again.'

'And you.' Vallejo looked around at the people working. 'You didn't tell me the *Post* was a daily paper.'

'Weekdays only. Saturdays, some of us usually come in and finish up our lifestyle stories and features, ready for the following week.' She tilted her head at Bishop. 'So who's your good-looking friend?'

Bishop introduced himself and said, 'You the boss around here?'

She shook her head. 'That honour goes to our wealthy founding father and owner, Stan Neeson. I'm just the editor, as well as senior reporter, although that's not saying much.' Kate sat back in her chair and looked at him. 'So you're James Bishop, huh?'

'Why? Am I famous?'

'I think *in*famous probably fits you better. I heard your name mentioned in conjunction with the Bannings fire on the police scanner this morning.'

'Oh, that. It was a just case of mistaken identity, that's all.'

She turned to Vallejo. 'Is that right?'

'Absolutely,' Vallejo said with a straight face.

Kate turned back to Bishop, a faint upturn at the corners of her mouth. 'Hmm. So tell me, what brings you to my humble corner?'

'I was hoping you could help us out with something,' Bishop said.

Kate frowned and looked at Vallejo. '*Us*? Is this about your missing friend? Samantha, isn't it?'

Vallejo opened her mouth to speak and Bishop said quickly, 'That's right. I'm an old friend of Clarissa's and we're working together on locating Sam.' He didn't want to bring Selina's name into this if he could help it. And the fact that Kate was already aware of Samantha's existence would simplify things a lot.

'Go ahead,' Kate said, 'I'm listening.'

'Well, I've been checking around nearby hospitals, unofficially, and I may have found a lead a few days ago. See, I got a glimpse of some old paperwork with the name S. Mathison on it. It looked like a patient's assessment sheet and most of it was illegible, although I could clearly make out the word *blepharoplasty* in there. Which is eyelid surgery, isn't it? And at the bottom the physician had signed his initials along with a number: AT 423. So maybe that's an ID number or something.'

'So?'

'So, I think this guy is probably a plastic surgeon, so maybe he belongs to one of the medical associations, if there's one that specializes in that. This is the first sign we've had that Samantha's still walking around so we really need to talk to him. I wouldn't know where to start, but you must have plenty of contacts who can point us in the right direction.'

Kate was watching him closely. 'Is that it?'

'That's all we've got. Can you help?'

Kate looked at each of them and then took another sip of coffee. 'There *is* an association for that kind of thing. An offshoot of the AMA, called the AFFCRS. The American Federation of Facial Cosmetic and Reconstructive Surgery. But I don't think that would help much.'

'Why not?'

'Because cosmetic surgeons aren't legally required to register. It's like a lot of these organizations. Most only join so they can have a few extra letters after their name. Looks good on the business card.' She took another sip of her drink. 'It doesn't really matter, anyway.'

'No? How come?'

'Because I already got a pretty good idea who this A.T. is.'

Vallejo shifted in her seat. Bishop said. 'Care to share?'

Kate shook her head and smiled. 'Not on your life.'

FORTY-SIX

Bishop arched his eyebrows. 'Something I said?'

'You tell me. Was that story you gave me really the best you could come up with?'

'But I wasn't lying about Sam,' Vallejo said. 'She's the whole reason I'm here.'

'Oh, I believe *you*, Clarissa, but I don't believe she's the reason *Bishop's* here. Unless I'm a worse judge of character than I give myself credit for. Which I'm not.'

Bishop sat back in his seat. 'So why *am* I here?'

'Well, I don't know, do I? But I'm pretty sure you're not an old friend showing up to help out your old buddy. I mean, what took you so long? And for that matter, why didn't Clarissa find this reference to Samantha before now? It's been a month, after all. I may not know her that well, but I can tell she's no dummy. If you found this elusive paperwork, then so could Clarissa. Especially as she's got a lot more motive to go digging than you.'

Kate carefully placed her mug on the desk and sat forward. 'Now I'm not against helping you guys out, but I really hate being lied to. I'm kind of eccentric like that. That's why I do what I do. So I suggest you put your heads together and rethink your strategy in dealing with me, then maybe we can start over. What do you think?'

Bishop sighed and turned to Vallejo. 'I can see it's my lot in life to be surrounded by strong, forceful women.'

Vallejo shrugged. 'I can think of worse fates.'

'Actually, so can I,' Bishop said.

He turned back to Kate. She reminded him a lot of Jenna. Not physically, but in other areas. Mainly the low tolerance for bullshit.

And the fact she didn't pull her punches when voicing her displeasure. Bishop had always liked people who spoke their minds. And he found himself liking this Kate. So the truth, then. But not the *whole* truth. Not with Selina's future safety at stake. Kate was still a reporter, after all.

'Okay,' he said, 'the name of the woman I'm searching for is Selina Clements.' He went on to tell her about how he'd helped Selina, but only in broad strokes. He told her about his relocating her out here, followed by her sudden disappearance a month ago. Vallejo also mentioned the jarring similarities between her and Samantha. Kate listened to it all without interruption.

Once they were done, she said, 'That's better.'

'You believe that over the far simpler story that I'm just helping Vallejo out with her problem? I thought it sounded pretty good, myself.'

Kate smiled. 'It's a matter of context. I might have believed it if it had come from Clarissa's lips, since she's a friend. Coming from a total stranger like yourself, however, I tend to be a little more dubious.'

'Maybe I'm a friend, too,' Bishop said,

'We'll have to see, won't we?' Kate said with a smile. 'So this Selina. What was her name before you changed it?'

Bishop just slowly shook his head.

'I thought you said we were friends.'

'A friend wouldn't ask that.'

Kate looked at him for a moment. Bishop thought she was deciding whether to get angry or not. Then she smiled and said, 'You're right. Sorry.'

'Accepted. So what does A.T. stand for?'

Kate let out a long breath. 'Well, I'm ninety-five per cent sure it stands for Adrian Tatem. And before you ask, he's a plastic surgeon. Or a *cosmetic* surgeon, as they like to be called nowadays.'

Bishop said, 'He's local?'

'Kind of. He's got a place here in Saracen, but he doesn't really mix with other residents. Standoffish kind of guy. Nobody really knows him that well.'

'But you seem to.'

She shrugged. 'I know *of* him. That's not really the same thing, is it?'

'Okay, so tell me what you do know.'

'Only that he moved here from L.A. with his wife about three years ago. Got themselves a fancy walled compound on the east side of town. Like I say, I don't know much about the guy, but I did a little digging and found out he used to be under exclusive contract to one of the big Hollywood studios. Prime Pictures.'

'I've heard of them,' Vallejo said.

'Most people have.' Kate found a rubber band on her desk and started stretching it between her fingers to create a cat's cradle. Bishop thought she had nice hands. Good bone structure. But then, female hands were a particular weakness of his. Always had been. Kate noticed him looking and smiled.

'You know why he left?' Bishop asked.

'Well, I found a small piece in *Variety* that said he'd gone into semi-retirement and wanted to be able to spend more time with his wife. But you know how accurate *their* stories are. Which means there could be any number of reasons why he decided to leave.'

Bishop scratched under his chin and looked out the window. There wasn't much of a view. A small car park, and beyond that a couple of empty lots overgrown with grass. 'I doubt he came out here of his own choice,' he said.

Kate pretended to look hurt. 'And what's wrong with our little town?'

'You tell me. My point is, I've never heard of a plastic surgeon going into semi-retirement. The kind of money they earn, the good ones either keep working or they stop altogether. And if this Tatem worked with a major Hollywood studio, I'm guessing he was a good one. So he either can't operate any more or he was forced out for some reason. And since he's still taking on patients, I'm going for the second option.'

'I kind of came to the same conclusion when I read it,' she said. 'He won't talk to you, you know.'

'I'm a pretty forceful personality, myself,' Bishop said. 'I think I can probably get him to open up.'

Vallejo snorted. '*I* can vouch for that.'

'What about the wife?' Bishop asked. 'You know her at all?'

Kate shook her head. 'People saw her occasionally when they first moved here. Real pretty, like you'd expect. They seemed to think late twenties, while he had to be in his late forties then. Haven't seen anything of her since, though. Could be she missed the high life and headed back to L.A.'

Bishop looked out the window again. 'That's interesting.' He turned back to Kate and said, 'Can you write down Tatem's address for me? His phone number, too.'

'Sure, on one condition.'

He looked at her. 'Let me guess. Once we get to the bottom of this, you get exclusive rights to the story.'

Kate stretched her arms wide. 'Hey, I like it here, but when I was at journalism school at Arizona State I kind of set my sights a little higher than the *Saracen Post*. And I'm not getting any younger. Look, I admit I had my doubts about Clarissa's tale when I first heard it, but now I've heard your side of the story I'm getting a feeling this could be something interesting. And I want in.'

'I could probably find that address on my own.'

'You probably could. But what makes you think you won't need my help again? In case you haven't realized, I know most of what goes on in this town. And more important, I know the people.' She slid a notepad over and picked up a pen. 'So we got a deal or what?'

Bishop paused. It didn't take him long to realize he had absolutely nothing to lose. And everything to gain. As long as there were ground rules.

'Selina's name doesn't get mentioned anywhere,' he said. 'And I mean *any*where.'

'Agreed.'

'Same goes for me. I prefer it in the shade.'

'Okay.'

'Then we got a deal,' he said. 'Give us his details.'

FORTY-SEVEN

Once they were back in the car, Vallejo said, 'I think she likes you.'

'What's not to like?' Bishop said distractedly. He was looking out the windshield and thinking of how to get rid of Vallejo for a few hours. Suspended or not, she was still a cop and there were some things she just wouldn't stand for. And he really needed to see this Tatem alone. Because one way or another, the man was going to talk.

Vallejo looked down at the paper Kate had given her and said, '28 East Parsons Avenue. I think I've driven down there before. If I remember right, Saracen High School's on the same street. So you want to go there now?'

'Not yet. I really need some wheels of my own again, and now my Chevy's history I don't think the rental companies are going to exactly welcome me with open arms.' He turned to her. 'When I was driving out to the medical centre before, I remember passing a couple of used car lots. You know the ones I mean?'

'Yeah, real classy places. I got the impression you could go there with five grand in your pocket, drive away their best vehicle and still have change left over.'

'Sounds perfect,' he said. 'Let's go take a look.'

Forty-three minutes later, Bishop left the mobile trailer that served as the main office of T.J. Singer's Autos and Trucks. In his hand were the keys and registration to a twenty-year-old, pale grey Buick LeSabre with over one hundred and fifty thousand miles on the clock. T.J. had given him a big smile when he handed over the $900 in cash. As well he should. Bishop had probably made his week.

Bishop walked back over the car lot and saw Vallejo standing next to the boxy monstrosity, shaking her head. 'I can't believe you paid money for this heap, Bishop.'

He shrugged and opened the driver's door. 'As long as it gets me from A to B, I don't care what it looks like. Besides, I only need it for a few days.'

'Uh huh. So can I assume we're about to go in different directions from here?'

'Only temporarily,' Bishop said and got in and manually wound down the front windows. The vehicle had an unpleasant, musty odour mixed in with a faint aroma of stale tobacco. 'I've been thinking it might be a good idea to make the most of Kate's knowledge now that she's offered to help.'

Vallejo leaned on the window frame. 'And that's where I come in, is it?'

'Well, the hard drive's back in your room. Tell me, how easy is it to split movie files up into sections?'

'You mean like .mpegs? Pretty easy, I think. I could download a program from the net. There's probably hundreds of them.'

'Okay, so what I need you to do is copy that final hour onto your laptop, then isolate the footage from where the SUV pulls up to the moment before they pull Hewitt's body from the rear. It's probably a couple of minutes' worth, but make sure there's nothing incriminating on there. Then show Kate the footage and see if she recognizes any of the bad guys or the vehicle. But don't let her keep a copy.'

'Okay. But you know she'll ask questions.'

'Then answer them as best you can. Maybe mix a few half-truths in there to keep her happy. I trust you to know what to say and what not to. We can meet up later and exchange information.'

'So you're going to try and see this Tatem alone, huh?'

'I think it's best.'

Vallejo let out a long breath. 'Meaning I don't need to know any more than that, right? Look, Bishop, promise you'll try and be gentle with him, okay? It's possible he's not actually involved in what's going on. We just don't know.'

Bishop's smile didn't quite reach his eyes. 'Sure, Vallejo, he could be entirely innocent.'

'Okay, okay. But have you even thought about how you'll get in to see him? Kate said the guy's surrounded by walls.'

Bishop pulled the door shut and started the engine. It caught first time, which surprised him. 'I'll think of something,' he said, before slowly pulling out of the lot.

FORTY-EIGHT

Bishop parked under one of the ash trees dotted along East Parsons Avenue and watched the entrance to No. 28 in his rear-view. The steel gate, set in a recess in the perimeter wall, was just out of sight from his current position. But he'd studied it as he passed and hadn't spotted a keypad or intercom anywhere.

Surrounding the property on all sides was an eight-foot high stucco wall, topped with elaborate wrought-iron spikes. No. 28 wasn't the only large, walled property on this street, but it was the best protected. Tatem was clearly a man who took his privacy seriously. Bishop had already checked the next street down for a rear entrance, but hadn't found one. Which meant the front gate was the only way in or out.

Directly opposite, behind a chain-link fence, was the Saracen High School athletic field with some school buildings in the distance. Nobody was playing today. The field was empty. In fact, the whole street was quiet. That was something, at least.

He picked his cell phone off the passenger seat, blocked the caller ID, then dialled the number Kate had given him.

On the ninth ring, a male voice said, 'Hello?'

Bishop spoke fast. 'That you, doc? 'Cause we need you down at Garrick hospital, ASAP.'

'Who is this? I don't recognize your voice.'

Bishop noted Tatem's own voice had a peevish, slightly nervous edge to it. Along with a submissive quality he hoped he wasn't just imagining. Sounded like whatever the good doctor was involved in, he wasn't exactly an equal partner.

'This is Tyrone,' Bishop said. 'I'm new.'

'I usually only take instructions from Abraham.'

Abraham. Now he had a name. It was a promising start.

'So is that a no, doc? Or do you want me to go interrupt Abraham so he can tell you himself? I think we both know how he'll react.'

'No, no. There's no need for that.' Tatem gave a sigh. 'So has another one arrived already?'

Every part of Bishop wanted to ask him what he meant, but as usual, good sense overrode his impulses. There'd be time later for questions and answers. 'Not my department,' he said. 'Look, I'm just telling you what Abraham told me, and that's to get your ass down to Garrick as soon as we finish talking. That okay with you, doc, or you wanna waste some more time and ask me something else?'

'No, no, I'll drive over there now,' he said, and then the line went dead.

Bishop smiled to himself. Injecting a little authority into your voice often did half the work for you. He placed the cell in the glove compartment, got out and locked the car. Then he opened the trunk and pulled out an army green ten-litre jerry can. He'd bought it from a service station on the way here. Filled it there, too. After locking the trunk, he walked over and stood under cover of the next tree down. It was about ten yards to the left of the recessed entrance. He placed the jerry can on the ground next to him and waited.

Bishop had counted off two hundred and ninety-six seconds before he heard the barely noticeable sound of the gate mechanism being activated. *A little tardy there, doc.*

He picked up the fuel container, moved over to the wall and peered round at the entranceway. The double gates were swinging slowly inwards where a silver, two-door Mercedes coupé was waiting, engine idling so quietly he could barely hear it. Through the windows, he saw the male driver was wearing a pale shirt and dark tie.

Once the gap was wide enough, the driver edged the Merc through and stopped just before the kerb. As he reached up and pressed something on the overhead control panel, Bishop ran towards the car, closing the distance in two seconds. He pulled the passenger door open and slid into the spare seat before the driver even knew what was happening. His first impression was that the interior smelled a hell of a lot nicer than his Buick.

Tatem gaped at him and said, '*Hey*, what are you doing? Who are you? I'm warning you – you'd better get out *now*.'

'Afraid I can't do that, doc,' Bishop said, placing the jerry can between his legs. 'And I'm the guy you just spoke to on the phone. Now be a good boy and take us back up to the house.'

'I'm not taking you anywhere,' Tatem shouted, gripping the wheel so hard his knuckles were turning white. 'You're in my car. Get *out*.'

Bishop almost felt sorry for the guy. It clearly took some people a little longer than others to adapt to new situations. Well, that was okay. Bishop sighed, and with his right hand reached back into his waistband. 'You gonna make me bring out my gun, is that it? 'Cause once it comes out, it stays out.'

Tatem's face went slack. 'Gun?'

'Right. A shiny .357 Colt Python. Great for close-up work. Want to see it?'

Tatem closed his eyes and shook his head. 'God, no.'

'Wise call. Let's keep things civilized.' Bishop pulled his hand back out and looked up. There was a small remote stuck to the overhead panel. On it were two buttons. He pressed the top one, turned his head and saw the gate opening behind them. 'Now reverse through the gate and drive us back to the house.'

Tatem opened his eyes and looked straight ahead, moving his lips silently as though talking to himself. He looked as though he'd expected nothing less. Like karma was finally catching up with him. Bishop didn't like that look.

'Are you going to kill me?' Tatem asked in an even tone.

'That depends on you, doc. Are you going to do what I said and reverse this thing?'

It seemed to Bishop that Tatem visibly deflated as he adjusted the gear stick, the anger from a moment ago a distant memory. Bishop watched him carefully as he slowly reversed through the gate, made a K turn and advanced down the long driveway. He looked to be in his mid-fifties, with short, steel-grey hair turning white at the temples and sideburns. The distinguished look loved by successful doctors everywhere. Bishop also noted the gold wedding band on the fourth finger of his left hand and the spare tyre round his waist.

Bishop pressed the other button to close the gates and faced forward. Up ahead, Tatem's single-storey house had a Spanish hacienda feel to it. There was a portico entranceway at the front and a sheltered patio area on the left. Lots of glass. The house was surrounded on all sides by low maintenance gravel and paving stones, with citrus trees and Mexican fan palms dotted around. The driveway ended in a double garage jutting out on the right. The door opened automatically when they were within twenty feet and Tatem took them in. Theirs was the only car parked there.

Once Tatem turned off the engine, Bishop removed the keys from the ignition. Grabbing hold of the jerry can, he got out first and saw a connecting door at the back.

'Okay, doc,' he said. 'Let's go inside now. You first.'

While Bishop waited for Tatem to join him, he studied the garage floor on the empty side and couldn't see any oil stains anywhere. It was practically spotless. Which more or less confirmed Tatem was on his own out here. Yet he was still married. *Interesting.*

Tatem led him through the door and into a laundry room. Through the open doorway, Bishop could see a large kitchen beyond.

'Where are we going?' Tatem asked, turning to him.

'Where do you keep your gun? And don't insult my intelligence by telling me you don't own one.'

Tatem sighed and said, 'I keep a revolver in my work desk in my office.'

'Then that's where we're going. Lead on.'

Bishop followed the doctor through the house, passing through a dining room and a large, stark living room, until Tatem opened a door and led them into a spacious office area. Inside, a single window looked out onto the backyard. A large oak bookcase filled with medical texts took up one side of the room. Framed photos took up the other walls. Many of them featured a striking young brunette with prominent cheekbones in a variety of poses and natural shots. Bishop had no doubt he was looking at Mrs Tatem.

Taking up a large part of the room was a mahogany work desk with the customary computer and accessories, and two chairs. Lining one of the other walls was a row of matching mahogany filing cabinets.

Lots of wood, Bishop thought. That would speed things along nicely.

Bishop pointed to the visitor's chair and said, 'Sit there. Move and I'll shoot you in the ankle. You're a doctor, so you know how much that'll hurt.'

He waited as Tatem sat. Then he walked round the desk, moved the chair out of the way and saw three drawers on each side. 'Which one?'

'The bottom drawer on the left,' Tatem said.

Bishop opened that one and saw a number of new and used note-books separated into two neat piles. There was also an ornate, nickel-plated letter opener in there, which he took out and pocketed. *Never know when something like this might come in handy.*

Further in he saw the glint of metal. He reached in and pulled out a stainless steel .38 Special with a two-inch barrel. Not a bad choice for home protection. He could tell by the weight it was empty. Reaching in again he brought out a forty-round box of Speer Gold Dot hollow-points. He opened the box and saw it was full. He loaded six rounds into the gun's chamber, clicked it shut and placed it in his waistband.

Tatem was staring at him. 'So you *weren't* armed.'

'Don't beat yourself up over it,' Bishop said as he raised the jerry can and unscrewed the top. It didn't take long for the sickly smell to permeate the room.

Then Bishop began splashing gasoline all over the desk and carpet.

FORTY-NINE

'*Wait*,' Tatem yelled, gripping the arms of the chair. His eyes were wild. 'Please. You can't do this. What have I done to you?'

Bishop didn't reply. Silence was always better in these kinds of situations. More threatening. His encounter with Addison had proved that. But at least he'd knocked the fatalism out of the guy. No good trying to get information out of a man who'd already accepted death. But possible death by fire was another matter. Nobody wanted that.

Keeping one eye on Tatem, he just kept splashing gas over the furniture. The filing cabinets. The bookcase. The drapes. The walls, too. Everywhere except the two chairs. Once he was satisfied, he shook the can. It was still about half full.

'Please stop,' Tatem said. 'Won't you just tell me why you're doing this?'

Bishop screwed the top back on and placed the can on the floor. Then he took a lighter and an opened pack of Winston cigarettes from his pocket. 'You a smoker, doc?'

'What is it you want? Money?'

'Don't blame you. Neither am I, but I don't mind making an exception now and then.' Bishop took a cigarette from the pack and inserted it between his lips. 'As for money, I already got a roof over my head, and I can afford food and clothes. What else can you offer me?'

'I can give you enough for luxuries.'

'Breathing's a luxury, doc. Don't you know that by now?' Bishop half sat on the edge of the desk and said, 'You got any idea where I was last night?'

Tatem shook his head. 'No. How could I?'

'Well, I'll tell you. I was trapped in a burning building with all the exits covered and a dead body at my feet, courtesy of some friends of yours. Now I'm returning the compliment.'

'Friends of . . . ? I don't know what you're talking about.'

Bishop took the cigarette from his mouth and began rolling it between his fingers. Looking at it, he said, 'You know, back when I was in the service, years ago this is, me and my squad were in Mogadishu, Somalia, not long after the civil war broke out. The "why" is a long story and doesn't matter now, but this one night we were in the very worst part of town when we got ambushed by a group of al-Ittihad al-Islami terrorists. You ever hear of them?'

Tatem shook his head and said nothing.

'Most of them are born sadists. At least, the ones who caught us were. They love to watch their enemies die as painfully as possible. It's like a game to them. So what they did was take us all to an empty warehouse and four of them held me down while the others tied the rest of my men up. Then I was forced to watch the youngest man on my squad being drenched in gasoline. Then they threw a lit book of matches at him and watched him burn. They were laughing all the way through it.' He paused. 'You know how long it took for him to die?'

Tatem shook his head again.

'They timed it for me. Sixty-three seconds, although it seemed a lot longer at the time. Probably felt even longer to him, don't you think?'

'I'm really sorry, but why are you telling me this?'

'Because that's what you've got to look forward to unless you answer my questions.'

'That's all you want?'

'That's all I want. And I should add that the first time you lie to me will also be the last. You understand?'

'I understand.'

'Good.' Bishop placed the cigarette and lighter on the desk next to him and said, 'These people you work for. Who are they?'

'I don't know.'

Bishop picked up the cigarette again. 'What did I just say?'

'Please, I'm telling the truth. I really *don't* know. The only person with whom I've had any contact is Abraham. That's why I questioned this Tyrone giving me instructions all of a sudden. It's never happened before.'

Bishop put down the cigarette. That made sense. The guy was a surgeon, after all. A specialist. It would be tactically unwise to tell him any more than was absolutely necessary.

'So this Abraham. What's his full name?'

Tatem shrugged. 'I only know him as Abraham. I don't even know if that's his first or last name.'

'Tell me what he looks like, then.'

Tatem closed his eyes. 'I've only met him twice, but he's about six-three and well built. Dark brown hair, but balding on top. He wears a Van Dyck beard, or he did.'

The guy in the video. The one who'd tried to kill him. And probably did the job on Hewitt and Rutherford, and God knows how many others.

'Okay. So start by explaining to me what your role is in all this.'

Tatem glanced briefly at the framed pictures on the wall. Then he turned back and said, 'Abraham calls me in to do work on female patients every now and then. They're always young. Sometimes it's just one woman a month. Sometimes two or three. Mostly facial work, but it can sometimes be more than that. And I always work from instructions handed to me by one of the two male nurses Abraham assigned to me.'

'Yeah, I met them. What are their names?'

'Robert Claiborne and Stephen Hedaya.'

'And you're only given written instructions? You never talk to the women at all?'

'Never. They're always under heavy sedation by the time I arrive. But the instructions are always very detailed and very specific.'

'Tell me about Mary Eastman in room 4–29. The woman with the bandaged face.'

'You know Mary Eastman?'

'I don't know yet.' Bishop touched his upper arms and said, 'Did she have acid burn scars here or here?'

Tatem's eyes widened a little, but he said, 'No, nothing like that. I just did some work on her cheekbones and chin, which all needed time to heal. I also removed some facial acne scars left over from her youth. I applied the bandages as a safety precaution while the skin healed. The room wasn't as sterile as I liked and I couldn't risk infection.'

So Mary Eastman can't have been Selina. But the eyes didn't lie. And Tatem's had shown recognition at the mention of the burns. Bishop thought back to his first visit to Garrick hospital. And the one name he'd seen on the database without a doctor's initials next to it. 'But you did work on the woman with the acid burns, didn't you? Angelina Eccles, right?'

Tatem was silent for a moment, his brow furrowed. 'How could you know that?'

'I know lots of things. Tell me exactly what you did to her.'

He swallowed and said, 'Well, as you can guess, I removed the welts and burn marks from her arms. The bad ones required minor skin grafts, but most of it I was able to accomplish with straightforward scar revision surgery. That's all I was instructed to do. She left the hospital after a week. I gave her a course of hyperbaric oxygen treatment so I imagine the surgery scars have entirely healed by now.'

Bishop breathed a mental sigh of relief. Up till now, he'd been working on the assumption that Selina was still alive, but he hadn't known for sure. But these people wouldn't be performing intricate scar removal surgery if they were then planning to kill her. That would make no sense at all. So she had to be still alive somewhere. But who exactly were 'these people'? And what was their purpose? These were the big questions. And ones Tatem clearly couldn't answer, that much was clear. But he had to know something more than he was telling.

'Other than the scars,' Bishop said, 'was there anything about Eccles that stood out?'

Tatem gave him a quizzical look. 'Yes. Her looks weren't too dissimilar to a patient I worked on two months before. Hardly in the monozygotic twin territory, but the similarities were there, nevertheless.'

That had to be Samantha, Bishop thought. So what had happened to her? Had she escaped her captors somehow? It was one possibility. He was about to ask Tatem her name, but didn't see much point. It would be fake, like all the others.

Instead, he said, 'What changes did you make to her?'

'Very little, I recall. I removed some moles from her chest area and buttocks and a small tattoo from the back of her neck. Also a hanging piece of skin from her left earlobe. Obviously a birthmark.'

'Uh huh. Is 4–29 the only room you use, or are there more?'

'We've got the next two along, 4–27 and 4–25. I think Claiborne and Hedaya sleep in 4–25. It's one of the bigger rooms in the hospital.'

'Which means somebody high up in the hospital administration is involved. There's no way something like that could stay under the radar for very long.'

'Oh, I agree. Somebody *has* to know. Don't ask me who, though.'

'And you've been working for them since you came out here three years ago?'

'Yes.'

'So how many patients have passed through your hands in that time? Sixty-five? Seventy?'

Tatem nodded. 'Maybe a little less. I don't know exactly. I'm not allowed to keep records of any kind.'

'Tell me, doc, doesn't it bother you, these things you do? Performing surgical procedures on patients without their knowledge? And without question?'

Tatem looked at the floor and didn't answer.

'How much do you get paid for this kind of work? A lot, I imagine.'

Tatem shrugged. 'Three hundred thousand dollars a year, deposited into an overseas account I set up years ago.'

Bishop frowned. Compared to what he must have made in Hollywood, that wasn't a whole lot. But it was still nothing to sneeze at. 'I guess a figure like that must go a long way in easing your conscience,' he said.

'No, it doesn't.' Tatem finally looked up, his eyes blazing. 'It doesn't even begin to. And if I had the guts, I'd tell them where they could stick their goddamn money.'

'Why don't you, then?'

'Because they're also holding my wife as hostage.'

FIFTY

Bishop saw fury combined with helplessness in the man's eyes. That depth of emotion couldn't be easily faked. Not in Bishop's experience. And the claim fitted in with the evidence. The missing wife. The pictures of her all over the walls. The wedding ring Tatem still wore. His self-imposed seclusion. It also explained his overriding pessimism and lack of will. This wasn't a man going through a trial separation. This was a man already very close to the edge.

'How long have they had her?' Bishop asked.

'You mean you believe me?'

'Let's say it would explain a lot of things. How long?'

Tatem sighed. 'So far, they've held Patricia for twenty-nine months and eleven days.'

'How do you know she's still alive?'

Tatem gave a sad smile. 'Because we get to spend the night with each other once a month. That much they allow us. Those two nurses I mentioned? They drive me to a different motel each time and take me to a room where Patricia's already waiting. The last time was a week ago. They've warned me that there're always four men on guard duty and that if I even think of trying to escape with her, she'll die.'

Bishop didn't doubt it. It was a brutally effective method to keep Tatem on a very tight leash. 'She must have family, though,' he said. 'Aren't they kind of curious as to why she's no longer taking their calls?'

Tatem shook his head. 'Her mother died about five years ago, after which her father moved to Vegas, married a dancer and promptly forgot about any notions of parental sentiment. Patricia's got a sister, but they fell out over something a decade ago and haven't spoken

194

since. There's an aunt in Indianapolis, but all they do is exchange cards at Thanksgiving. Fortunately, I'm able to do a pretty good imitation of Patricia's signature.'

'Maybe you should tell me how the hell you got into this mess in the first place.'

Tatem sighed. 'You recall an actor called Barrett Schaffer?'

'Sure. Big star in the seventies and eighties. Made some decent movies, I remember.'

'He did until he got old. And he was one of those that don't age well. Too much fast living and too many addictions. Well, he soon became addicted to plastic surgery and what it could do for him. After a while it only made things worse, but nobody could tell him that. Three years ago, I was called in to see if I could reverse the mistakes that had been made.'

'And something went wrong,' Bishop said.

'Badly wrong. So much had been done to his face that it practically fell apart when I went near it. Well, I got the blame, of course, even though it wasn't my fault. Everything was hushed up, as usual. Prime didn't dare fire me, but I was persona non grata around town, which means I was essentially unemployed. And then a man came into my life, offering to pay three hundred thousand a year for my services if I were to consider moving to Arizona.'

'Abraham,' Bishop said.

'Abraham. I was obviously very interested, especially as Patricia was desperate to get away from L.A. So I said yes at our first meeting. That's when he laid down the rules. I couldn't talk to the patients, although I'd be presented with signed authorization papers in every case. I'd be assigned two male nurses, and I was forbidden to discuss my work with anyone else in the hospital but them. And I'd work from written instructions, from which I wasn't allowed to deviate in any way.'

'And that didn't raise your antennae at all?'

Tatem shifted in his chair. 'It did, but the money quickly overrode any objections I might have had. I'm only human, and three hundred thousand a year's hard to ignore when you're unemployed.'

'So what changed? You see something you weren't supposed to?'

'No, I just started getting bad feelings about what I was doing. I knew there was something very wrong with the situation, but I didn't know what exactly. For a start, I couldn't escape the possibility that I wasn't the only surgeon working on these patients.'

'What do you mean?'

'I mean that I started noticing laparoscopic marks on many of the women, and they weren't my doing.'

'Laparoscopic?' Bishop asked. 'You mean the fibre-optic scope they use for keyhole surgery?'

Tatem nodded. 'It doesn't have to be for surgery, though. Sometimes it's used merely as a diagnostic aid, but it's always in the abdominal or pelvic area. You see, *lapar* is Greek for—'

'Abdomen,' Bishop said. 'Yeah, I figured that part out. And you're telling me all these women had those marks?'

'Well, I don't know for sure. Most of my work was done on the upper body so I really had no reason to look below the chest area, but once I did I started noticing these small insertion scars and after that I always made a point to check. And I'd say about eight in ten of the women had them.'

Bishop looked out the window. *Stranger and stranger.* 'And they were all in perfect health otherwise?'

'They seemed to be. I wasn't allowed to do much in the way of tests.'

'They must have had something your employers were interested in, then. Something specific to the female anatomy.' He paused, thinking. 'What about ovaries?'

'What? You mean for illegal transplants?'

Bishop nodded. 'Why not? I figure there must be plenty of rich, infertile women around who'd pay through the roof for the ability to have kids of their own.'

Tatem gave a pained smile. 'I really think you're barking up the wrong tree there.'

'Why?'

'Because the only successful ovary transplants have been between identical twins sharing the same genetic material. Anything else is doomed to failure. The host body will instantly reject the new tissue. I do remember there was a surgeon out of New York who claimed he'd come up with a theoretical model for successful transplants using non-relatives as donors, but he died a few years back and he left no papers behind to back up his claims.'

'Okay. So what's the alternative? What are they really doing over there?'

'I don't know. In all honesty, I've been afraid to think too much about it since they took Patricia. If they thought I knew anything more than I do already, there's no telling what they might do to us.'

Bishop ran a hand over his scalp and decided to let it go for now. But it was definitely something he needed to look into further. 'So did you discuss all this with your wife?'

'Yes, after about six months Patricia and I talked it over. Up until then I was able to justify what I was doing. Simple cosmetic surgery. Nothing too complex. But now I didn't know *what* I was getting into and wanted out. Patricia agreed. She said if I felt strongly about it I should walk away.'

Bishop looked at the pictures on the wall. He was beginning to understand Tatem's devotion to his wife. Regardless of whatever other qualities she possessed, if she was willing to trade a comfortable lifestyle for an uncertain future, she was clearly something special.

'And that was the second time you met Abraham?'

'Yes. It wasn't a pleasant meeting. I was told to go home and think about it, and the next morning I woke up to find Patricia missing from our bed. They must have taken her in the middle of the night and I didn't hear a damned thing.'

'Sounds like their MO,' Bishop said. 'I take it you didn't call the cops?'

Tatem shook his head. 'I got a phone call a few minutes after I woke. It was Abraham. He said Patricia would remain safe for as long as I continued to do my job and didn't talk to anybody. After he let me speak to Patricia briefly, he then laid down the new rules for me. They'd still pay me and we'd be allowed conjugal visits once a month.'

'What, till the end of time?'

'Until the four years I'd initially agreed on were up. Then they'd let her go.'

'You really believe that, doc? That once they're finished with your services they'll just let the two of you waltz off into the sunset?'

'I try not to think about that part. Besides, what else can I do?'

Bishop didn't have an easy answer to that one. He said, 'Where do they keep Patricia? You must have talked about it.'

'Over and over, but it's no good. She says they keep her locked away in some kind of secluded living quarters furnished like an apartment. Except there are no windows anywhere and the walls are made of thick hardwood. The only time she ever leaves is when they take her to the motel once a month. They drug her with a sedative first, of course. As you can imagine, her skin's bleached white by now from the lack of exposure.'

'What about sounds? Can she hear anything at all?'

'Well, she can hear people talking sometimes, but she can't tell how many. The thick walls muffle everything.'

'Does she ever see Abraham?'

Tatem paused and looked at the floor. 'She says she doesn't see anybody. Any time they deliver food, she's told to lock herself in the bathroom. It's probably for the best, anyway. Abraham's not the kind of person anybody would want to meet on their own.'

Bishop gave a thin smile as he glanced out the window again. 'Well, *I* sure would.'

'So here's your chance,' a voice said from the doorway.

FIFTY-ONE

Bishop swivelled his head to see the man from the surveillance footage standing there with a gun aimed straight at his chest. He was impressed with the man's stealth, considering his size. He hadn't heard a thing.

Bishop kept his hands in plain view on the desk either side of him. There was no way on earth to reach back for the .38 anyway. He'd be dead before he even tried.

Abraham was dressed in a dark suit over a white shirt. Bishop noticed the small eyes and the heavy creases lining his forehead. He also looked bigger than expected. Bishop could see the guy's shoulder muscles straining against his suit and the large hands looked as though they could crush a man's windpipe in a second. Or snap his neck.

'So you're the idiot who tried to kill me,' Bishop said.

Abraham smiled. 'And you're the asshole who doesn't know when to quit.'

'That's me. The second part, anyway.'

The big man kept smiling. Without taking his eyes off Bishop, he said, 'I'm disappointed in you, doctor, falling so easily for an obvious fake-out. Didn't I tell you to accept instructions from me, and only me? Lucky for you I have your phone tapped, otherwise Bishop here might have gotten Patricia killed. In fact, he still might. Where's your gun?'

Bishop saw Tatem shift in his seat. 'It . . . he's got it in the back of his waistband.'

'Fine. It can stay there for the moment. Bishop knows better than to reach for it.'

Abraham entered the room and approached Bishop's left side. The gun was a black, 9mm automatic with a stainless steel slide.

Clunky-looking. Looked like a Sig Sauer P226. When Abraham was five feet away, he reached into a jacket pocket, pulled out a pair of steel handcuffs and tossed them in Tatem's lap.

'Cuff Bishop's hands in front of him, doctor.'

Which immediately told Bishop they were going somewhere, and that he would probably be driving. Probably to his own burial site. No sense in killing him here when there were so many other locations within easy reach. They were in desert country, after all.

Bishop slowly raised both hands as Tatem got up and walked over to him. The doctor refused to make eye contact. It also took him over a minute to get the cuffs on Bishop's wrists. Bishop expected better hand control from a surgeon.

'Butterfingers,' he said.

When Tatem was done, he glanced over at Abraham like a dog to its master. Obeying Abraham had clearly become second nature to him now. Bishop had an idea his wife was the stronger half of the relationship, and that she was probably holding up a lot better.

'Good,' Abraham said. 'Now carefully remove the gun from his waistband and bring it to me.'

Tatem reached around and Bishop felt the gun disappear. Then he watched the doctor walk over and hand it to Abraham, who placed it in a pocket. 'Now search the rest of him from head to toe and show me what you find.'

Bishop remained still as Tatem clumsily patted him down. He found the wallet and keys and laid them on the desk. Then he found the letter opener. He brought it out and showed it to Abraham.

Abraham raised an eyebrow. 'Yours?'

Tatem nodded. 'I keep it in the same drawer as the gun.'

'Never miss an opportunity, do you, Bishop?' Abraham said, smiling.

Bishop shrugged. 'I just collect letter openers, that's all. It's an addiction of mine.'

'Sure it is. Okay, Tatem, hand me his wallet and keys. You can put the letter opener back in your desk.' After pocketing Bishop's meagre possessions, Abraham waved his gun in the direction of the doorway. 'Okay, Bishop, back to the garage. We'll use my car this time. And open some windows and clean this place up, will you, Tatem? It stinks in here.'

Bishop pushed off the desk and said, 'Shampoo and baking soda, doc. That ought to do the trick.' Then he began walking.

FIFTY-TWO

Abraham's car was a brand new silver Lexus LS460L with four thousand, four hundred and seventy-six miles on the clock. Bishop knew the exact mileage because it was there on the speedometer in front of him. He was the designated driver, as he'd suspected. Steering was a little problematic with his hands cuffed, but the automatic transmission balanced things out.

They were travelling south on Saracen Road, having passed the town limits about four miles back. Straight road ahead of them and desert all around. An occasional car or SUV whizzed by, heading north. Abraham was sitting in the passenger seat with his gun pointing at Bishop's side. He'd already warned that if Bishop went over 30 mph or made a wrong move, he'd shoot him in the leg. Bishop believed him.

'Fill me in,' Bishop said. 'Before you went bad, what were you? No wait, let me guess. A squid. You look the navy type: all muscle and not much upstairs.'

Abraham just smiled at him. After a few beats, he said, 'Dumb jarhead. You know what we used to sing whenever we took a dump? "Here I sit on the old latrine, giving birth to a new Marine." I always liked that song. Real catchy.' He looked out the windshield. 'Take the next left onto Terra Cotta Road. It's coming up in half a mile.'

A minute later Bishop saw the sign and slowed down. He took the turn and carried on driving.

'Where you keeping Tatem's wife holed up?' he said. 'The same place you keep Selina Clements and the other women?'

'Don't give up, do you? Forget about them. Right now, worry about yourself.'

'Sure. Is Abraham your first or last name, by the way?'

'Just drive and keep your mouth shut, asshole. You're giving me a headache.'

Bishop shut up. But he was thinking back to what Tatem had said. And what he perhaps hadn't wanted to admit to himself. For instance, that short pause after Bishop asked him if his wife had ever seen Abraham. Nothing definite, but there had been something there.

'You're screwing his wife, aren't you?' He turned to see Abraham smiling. 'And with a face like yours, I'm fairly sure it's without her consent. There's a word for that, you know.'

'Pretty quick for an ex-jarhead, aren't you? And it's not rape if she secretly enjoys it. I know what women want. Especially that one. After being married to that prick, she's bound to want someone who takes charge. And I've never gotten any complaints.'

'That's probably because she wants to keep on breathing, dickhead.' Bishop glanced at him. 'You're really the bottom of the barrel, aren't you?'

Abraham pressed the barrel of the gun hard against Bishop's temple. 'Maybe I'll just do you here. Right now.'

'And make a mess of this beautiful car?' Bishop sneered. 'Typical swab.'

Abraham took the gun away and sat back. 'I'm gonna enjoy it when your time comes, Bishop. I really am. And it'll be slow, you can believe that.'

'Just tell me we're getting close. Your body odour's getting unbearable, even with the air conditioning.'

'We're close, all right. See those old huts in the distance? That's our stop, asshole.'

Bishop had already spotted them. They were the only things on the horizon. A collection of ramshackle wood cabins about a couple of miles away to the left. He couldn't begin to guess their original purpose. Or why they'd been constructed out here in the middle of nowhere. But he had no doubt the site would make a great burial ground.

A couple of minutes later Abraham said, 'Slow down. There's a gravel road coming up on the left. There, up ahead.'

Bishop saw it. A break in the road and a dirt track leading off towards a steel gate further down and a fenced-off area. He slowed the vehicle and took the turn. Another thirty seconds and they reached the gate. Bishop stopped the car a few yards away. There was a large padlock barring entry and a *No Trespassing* sign.

'Leave the engine running and get out,' Abraham said.

Bishop got out. Abraham came round and handed him a ring with a single large key on it. 'Unlock and open the gate, then come back here.'

Abraham was waiting by the open passenger door when he was done, gun pointing nowhere in particular. 'Okay, jarhead,' he said. 'Let's go.'

Bishop opened the driver's door and got back in. Abraham was already seated and waiting. The man was quick, he had to give him that. But speed wasn't everything. Without waiting to be told, Bishop drove towards the shacks, reaching the first one a minute later.

'Well, here we are, asshole,' Abraham said. 'End of the line.'

Bishop came to a stop and Abraham pulled the handbrake and removed the keys from the ignition. He removed a small flashlight from the glove compartment, checked to make sure it was working, then motioned for Bishop to get out. Bishop opened the door and noticed Abraham locking Tatem's .38 Special in the glove compartment before he got out, too. That was good. Now he'd only have one gun to deal with. But the Sig held a fifteen or nineteen round magazine capacity. He'd have to assume nineteen. And that was bad. Very bad. But not insurmountable.

The cabins were in an even worse state than he first thought. Bishop guessed they dated back to the twenties or thirties. All one- or two-room structures. At least, they were once. There were five of them arranged in a loose semicircle, with a sixth shack on its own twenty yards further back. They all looked as though they might collapse at any second, with rusted, caved-in roofs and deteriorating window frames and doorways.

Abraham pointed to the one on its own and said, 'Over there. Get going.'

Bishop walked in front of Abraham and studied his surroundings. There wasn't much to see. Just brittlebush and overgrown weeds everywhere. There were no sounds other than the crunch of their footsteps. No cars driving by. No birds. Nothing. This was a bad place. He could feel it in his bones. People had died here recently. Probably courtesy of Abraham or one of his cohorts.

Yeah, a bad place, he thought. *And it's about to get worse.*

He slowed as he reached the remote shack. It was no different from the others. Maybe fewer windows. Beyond the doorway, he could see only darkness within. Abraham prodded the gun barrel into his back and said, 'Go inside and turn left, but move very slowly. I'm just looking for an excuse.'

Bishop walked up to the doorway, stepped inside and turned left. It was dark, but there was enough light to see. What few floorboards remained were either badly warped or broken. There were two halves of an old bicycle frame in one corner. Leaning against the south wall were a few landscaping tools. All looked rusted. A rake with only two prongs left. A hoe. A broom with no bristles. Part of an old cultivator. And a round point shovel. The type with just a staff and no handle. That stood out. It was old and rusty, but not as much as the others. And it was almost free of dust, which said it had been used recently.

'Here,' Abraham said, and threw the handcuff keys at Bishop's feet.

Bishop picked them up and unlocked the cuffs.

'Leave the cuffs and keys on the floor,' Abraham said. 'Then grab the shovel and come on outside.'

Bishop turned and saw Abraham standing just inside the doorway, gun and flashlight pointed straight at him. Realizing he couldn't do anything in here, he went over to the tools, took hold of the shovel and walked back to the doorway. Abraham kept his distance and backed out first, watching him every step of the way.

Once they were both outside, Abraham pointed east and said, 'Walk.'

Bishop began walking, watching the ground as he went. After only ten feet, he noticed some medium-sized rocks to his right, grouped together by some weeds. He memorized their position.

After another thirty feet, Abraham said, 'Okay, stop right there.'

Bishop halted. He was standing in the middle of a bare patch of land. No vegetation within a twenty foot radius. Not even weeds. Bishop looked carefully but saw no sign of recent disturbances in the earth. Not that that meant anything.

'Okay,' Abraham said from behind him, 'pick yourself a nice spot and start digging. You know what size to make it.'

Bishop looked at him. Studied the shit-eating grin of a man safe in his superiority. The illogical part of him wanted to tell Abraham to take a hike and to do the work himself, but what would that get him? A moment's satisfaction, followed by a bullet in the head and a shallow grave. Right now, he needed time. And digging would give him some. And Abraham might be more willing to talk now he believed he held the winning hand. So he took a step forward and with the shovel blade started to draw a line in the dirt.

'Uh, uh,' Abraham said. 'Not there, asshole.'

Bishop looked up. '*You* pick a spot, then.'

'I'm just saying you don't want to dig there. Trust me on that one.'

Which meant he *did* want to dig there. Just not right now. He'd find time later. Bishop marked the spot in his mind and took a few steps to the right. 'Here okay?'

'Perfect.'

Bishop studied Abraham for a moment, looking him up and down, then marked out a rectangle in the earth. Abraham was right. Bishop knew what size to make it. Two foot wide. Six foot, four inches in length. The extra inch in case his calculations were off. He didn't think they were, but you never knew.

Then he began to dig.

FIFTY-THREE

Bishop took his time. He saw no reason to make himself sweat. Besides which, it probably amused Abraham to draw this out for as long as possible.

With each excavation, Bishop put intense pressure on the shaft of the shovel while pushing his foot hard against the blade. Seeing how far it would bend. This tool was in better shape than the others, but it was still old and rusty, the wooden shaft rotten and malleable. After a few minutes testing his weight against it, he felt confident that it wouldn't take too much effort to snap it in two. But not just yet. Now wasn't the time.

'All those women you and your two pals grab in the dead of night,' Bishop said. 'Do you take a few shots at them before bringing them in to your boss?'

'Give it a rest, asshole.'

Bishop ignored him and carried on digging. 'I mean, who's gonna know? Only those two idiots, and they won't talk. Hell, maybe they even join in.'

'Maybe we're a little more professional than that, asshole.'

'You?' Bishop chuckled. 'Professional?'

'Keep going, Bishop. I've changed my mind. It's actually fun listening to a man's last words.'

'So since I'm not long for this world, there's no harm in answering my questions, is there? Like who's your boss?'

Abraham laughed at that. 'Forget it. Although I give you credit for trying. You really don't give up, do you?'

Never, Bishop thought. He said. 'So besides you three and your boss, how many more of you are there? Five? Six? More?'

'I forget. What difference does it make to you?'

'I'm the curious type. So what's the deal with you people? You dealing in black market organ transplants or something? If so, what's Tatem doing in there? Or is he just a cover for what's really going on?'

'You just got a head full of questions, don't you?' Abraham said, yawning. 'Let's just say we're a small, highly specialized organization filling a gap in the market and leave it at that.'

'Meaning what?'

'Meaning we know exactly what we're doing, and assholes like you get taken care of before you become a problem. Right now, you're just an itch that needs scratching.'

'Like Hewitt and Rutherford.'

'Right.'

'And Samantha Mathison.'

There was a pause. Then Abraham said, 'What do you know about her?'

Bishop stopped and leaned on the shovel. 'Everything.'

Abraham narrowed his eyes. Then he smiled. 'No, you don't. But it doesn't matter. She's no longer a problem. And less than thirty-six hours from now, your little bitch will be out of the equation, too.'

'You mean you're gonna kill her once she's of no further use to you?'

Abraham raised the gun. 'You're not digging.'

Bishop turned and resumed work. Today was Saturday. Which meant he now had until Sunday evening to find Selina. Added to which, he also had the little problem of escaping his current situation. But then, life was never easy.

'What's gonna happen to her?' he asked.

'Forget about the woman. She's not your problem any more. Once a couple more details are taken care of, she'll just be another footnote. Like you.'

Bishop plunged the shovel into the dirt with more force than he'd planned. Without thinking, he tried pulling it out, but the blade was stuck fast in the hard soil and began to come free of the shaft.

Shit. Too soon. It's too soon.

He'd hoped to extract more details from Abraham, but that was no longer possible. In less time than it took to blink, his instincts told him to make the best of his circumstances and go through with his performance as he'd planned. So he tried pulling the shovel out and pretended to lose his footing. He made himself fall, stepping hard on one end of the shovel with his whole body weight behind it, catching the shaft about a foot from the blade. The old wood snapped in two uneven halves, leaving a sharp, jagged edge at each end.

He landed on his ass, still holding on to the longer end. 'Shit,' he said.

Abraham let out a bark of laughter behind him. Bishop saw the blade and part of the shaft were sticking out of the ground at an angle. Still connected to each other. That was good. If the blade had come free, Abraham would have simply told him to affix it to the longer shaft piece and carry on as before.

'Get me another shovel,' Bishop said. 'This one's history.'

'You'll have to use your hands, then.'

'Uh, uh. Find me something else to use or do it yourself. You can ruin your nice suit.' He turned to look at Abraham, who was still smiling. Bishop jutted his chin at the shack twenty yards away and said, 'Get me one of those broken floorboards in there or something.'

Abraham thought for a moment, then said, 'You go and pick one out yourself. I'll be right behind you.'

Excellent. Bishop got to his feet, still holding the longer staff piece in his left hand, and walked back to the shack. He aimed for the weeds where he'd seen that group of rocks, rotating the staff between his fingers. Testing the feel of it. It was just over thirty inches long. It felt heavy enough for throwing, but wasn't nearly long enough. An effective spear needed be two or three feet longer than the height of the man throwing it. And always with a spearhead attached. Even the earliest Neanderthals knew enough to tie primitive flints to the ends.

All Bishop had was a sharp stick. Next to the rock, the most basic weapon of all. But you could only use what was at hand. And he'd been in worse positions with a lot less. It would have to do, that's all.

As they got closer to the shack, Bishop saw the rocks about three feet away. Time to exploit his newfound reputation for being accident prone.

It almost felt as though he were moving in slow motion. His right foot came into contact with the first rock and he grunted as he 'tripped'. In the half-second it took to fall, Bishop rotated his upper body clockwise so he was turned towards Abraham. At the same time, he brought the left hand back ready to throw, right arm extended for balance. He could see Abraham standing there four or five feet away. He was watching Bishop with a small smile on his lips, gun still pointing at the ground. It hadn't sunk in yet.

The moment Bishop's right knee hit the ground, it did.

Abraham's smile disappeared and he began raising the gun, while Bishop extended his left leg on the ground to keep him steady.

Then he threw the spear straight at Abraham's chest.

FIFTY-FOUR

Bishop knew his aim was off the moment it left his hand. Not much, but enough. But he didn't have time for perfection. He was up against a gun, and speed of movement counted for more than pinpoint accuracy.

Bishop immediately dived to the right. He heard a grunt and a gunshot as he rolled his body along the ground, out of the line of fire. There was another gunshot and he felt soil stinging against his cheek. He kept rolling, rolling. Once he lost momentum, he quickly got his legs under him, jumped to his feet and sprinted towards Abraham, ten feet away.

The bigger man had his free hand pressed against his upper thigh. Bishop must have scored a hit. But he was already bringing his gun round to bear on Bishop again.

Bishop darted to the left and kept running as Abraham fired off another shot. It went wide. By a couple of inches at most. But he'd halved the distance. He was almost on him.

Bishop loved soccer. A loyal New York Bulls fan, he went to see them play whenever he could. Especially as they currently had a young defender who'd barely made a bad tackle all season. He was amazing. He always got the ball, never the player. Bishop just knew his brain could process the ball's movement faster than anybody else. And with mathematical precision. He always knew where the ball was going to be. So that's where *he* would be.

Bishop's brain worked the same way. When he saw the gun moving back in his direction, he'd already narrowed the distance to three feet. He landed on his left foot, lowered his left shoulder and kicked his right foot at the place where the gun was going to be. Or more specifically, where the hand holding the gun was going to be.

The tip of Bishop's shoe struck Abraham's wrist so hard he felt sure he must have fractured something. The impact pushed the arm all the way back and the Sig flew from Abraham's grasp, landing somewhere in the brittlebush. He didn't see where.

Bishop followed through with the kick, swivelling his body round so he was facing away from Abraham. Still moving, he swung round again, this time leading with the point of his left elbow. Aiming for Abraham's left ear. It struck him on the side of the jaw instead.

Abraham fell backwards and landed on his side. Bishop stepped forward and raised his foot high before bringing it down where Abraham's head was. The big man saw it coming and got out of the way just in time. Bishop kept his balance and turned to see Abraham already rising to his feet, facing him from just a few feet away. He'd forgotten how fast the guy was. And the guy's wrist didn't seem broken like he'd hoped. Pity.

But both men were now unarmed. For Bishop, that was enough.

'It's better this way, asshole,' Abraham said. He seemed barely out of breath. 'A bullet would have been too quick, and I want you to suffer.'

Bishop glanced at the guy's left thigh and saw blood seeping through a ragged hole in his pants. 'You're leaking.'

As Abraham instinctively glanced down, Bishop turned side-on to him and delivered a sliding side-kick towards Abraham's left thigh. His heel connected with bone. Abraham grunted and jumped back a couple of feet as Bishop brought his leg back down.

'Leaking even more now.' Bishop looked around for the spear or the gun, but couldn't see them anywhere. He refocused his attention on Abraham, who was holding his wound and glaring at Bishop. If Bishop couldn't finish the bastard fast, he at least needed to wear him down. And he liked the way that thigh was looking. Bleeding nicely. Right now it was a chink in Abraham's armour. One worth exploiting to the full.

Bishop adopted a street-fighting stance. Left side facing Abraham. Feet planted shoulder width apart. Guard up. Ready. He'd already drawn first blood. And second. Time for Abraham to take the initiative. Bishop wanted to see what he had in him.

Without warning, Abraham suddenly lunged forward, swinging his right fist in a roundhouse strike. Bishop ducked his head, avoiding the punch with an inch to spare, and jabbed with his left towards the man's wounded thigh as he barrelled past. His knuckles made contact against muscle and bone again. His fist was covered in the man's blood. *Beautiful.*

Then he felt a sharp, hard blow at the base of his spine. Abraham must have got an elbow in as he passed. The pain was tremendous. Bishop went down and quickly rolled away from the danger area, then jumped to his feet and faced his opponent.

Abraham advanced again with both fists raised. Limping a little. And panting. He grinned and said, 'Got a good one in, didn't I, asshole? That's just a taster. I'm gonna break every bone in your body, then leave you breathing while the buzzards feed on your guts.'

Bishop said nothing. He was done talking. Let Abraham waste his breath if he wanted. He glanced at the man's thigh and saw blood pouring down his pants. Bishop brought his left fist back. Abraham was watching him and moved his body sideways to avoid the blow. At the last moment, Bishop swivelled on his axis, ducked inside and slammed the edge of his right elbow into the man's face instead. Just under the right eye. Abraham took a step back at the impact and Bishop followed through with a simple front kick, the heel bone of his foot striking the wounded thigh again.

The big man roared, lowered his head and simply launched himself at Bishop like a freight train. Before Bishop could get out of the way, Abraham's skull slammed into his chest. His breath left his body in a single burst and then he was falling backwards with Abraham's arms wrapped round him.

They fell to the ground and Bishop slammed his right knee twice against Abraham's wound. The man's grip loosened and Bishop rolled away, one arm around his chest. He got to his feet and saw Abraham still on the ground holding his thigh, blood seeping through his fingers. Bishop ran over and raised his foot again to stamp on his face. But with lightning speed, Abraham reached up, grabbed Bishop's foot and twisted it.

Bishop came crashing down on his stomach. He immediately hit out with his free foot and felt it connect with Abraham's face. His other foot came free of Abraham's grip, and as he raised himself up Bishop finally spotted the improvised spear. It was lying a few feet away, partially hidden by some weeds. He got up, ran over and grabbed it, and was just turning when Abraham's powerful body slammed into him again. Bishop lost his grip on the weapon and fell onto his back with Abraham on top of him. Then Abraham rammed a knee into his stomach and Bishop doubled up in pain.

He fell back, winded, then felt Abraham's hands round his neck, squeezing. With his left hand, Bishop punched upwards towards Abraham's throat. But he dodged in time and Bishop hit nothing but air. Then the pressure against his neck decreased as Abraham's fingers moved upwards, towards his face.

Bishop knew he didn't have long. Abraham was going for his eyes. He could already feel the man's thumbs on his cheeks, just inches away from his eye sockets. His left hand grabbed at Abraham's fingers to try to slow their progress. His right scrabbled around in the dirt, desperately searching for the spear he'd dropped.

It has to be close by. Has to be. If it wasn't, he was dead. Blind first, then dead.

His fingers kept groping around until, at last, they touched the jagged edge of the wooden staff. He moved his hand down its length and stopped when he reached halfway. Abraham's thumbs were at his eyes now. He clamped them shut and felt the thumbs begin to push down. He turned his head to delay the inevitable for a second and grasped the spear tight in his fist. Then he swung it upwards in an arc towards Abraham's head. He felt it make contact with something and held it there for a second before pulling it away.

The pressure against Bishop's eyeballs immediately disappeared and he felt a hot spray against his arm. He looked up, and with blurred vision saw a stream of blood pouring from Abraham's neck. Abraham had a hand pressed hard against it, trying to stem the flow.

Nice shot, Bishop thought. *Must have hit the jugular.*

He pushed Abraham off him. It didn't require much effort. Abraham simply toppled over and landed on his back, his mouth making gurgling sounds. Blood pumped out of his neck as though it was in a race to leave his body, turning the soil around his head black.

Bishop got to his feet, pressing a hand against his chest. At least his ribs didn't feel cracked. He looked down at the killer at his feet. Abraham stared back without expression, hand still clamped against the fatal wound. His eyes were already glazing over. Bishop just stood there and watched as the life slowly left his body. The image reminded him of Jean-Robert Develaux's last few seconds on this earth, half a world and a lifetime away. He and Abraham had been similar in a lot of ways. Both had enjoyed preying on women, and both had ended their odious, useless lives in pretty much the same manner. Couldn't have happened to a nicer pair. Assholes, the both of them.

A minute later, Bishop checked Abraham's body for a pulse and found nothing.

Walking back to the grave he'd started on, Bishop pulled the loosened shovel blade from the shaft and affixed it to his piece of the handle. Then he carried on digging.

FIFTY-FIVE

By the time Bishop reached the Lexus, the fading sun was turning the western horizon orange. He was hot, tired and covered in another man's blood. But at least he was breathing, unlike those two he'd just buried. Or in the case of the second body, *re*buried.

Bishop left his stuff on the passenger seat and went back and popped the trunk. As he'd hoped, Abraham kept a five-gallon plastic jug of water in there in case of breakdowns. He removed his bloodstained shirt and threw it on the ground. Maybe in future he'd be better off wearing darker colours. But at least his T-shirt was still presentable. He took that off, too, and then used some of the water to wash the blood off himself.

Once he'd done the best he could, he dried himself off, then doused the ruined shirt in gas from the tank. He used the car's cigarette lighter to set it alight and watched it burn. He didn't want his DNA anywhere around here. Then he donned his T-shirt and got in the driver's seat. He looked down at the items on the other seat. He picked up the Sig first and checked the magazine. It held sixteen rounds. He made sure one was in the chamber before placing it in the glove compartment with the .38. He'd hold on to both weapons. Neither could be traced to him, and he had a feeling they'd come in useful fairly soon.

Bishop picked up Abraham's cell phone. It was one of those fancy iPhone jobs and looked fairly new. The screen was taken up by a large chrome version of the Apple logo with a sliding lock at the bottom. Bishop used a finger to slide it to the right. A menu screen came up with row after row of application icons. He scrolled along until he found the one for 'Contacts' and opened it up.

There were no entries. None at all. Frowning, he scrolled all the way down, wondering if he was doing something wrong. He wasn't too experienced in using these touchscreen gizmos. But there was clearly nothing in the folder.

Still, there should still be some kind of call log. He tried 'Recents'. And again, all he got was another blank screen. Which indicated that whatever qualities Abraham had lacked, vigilance wasn't one of them. Probably wiped the phone's history after each and every call.

Wonderful.

He pocketed the phone. It could still come in useful. Especially since Bishop was the only person who knew Abraham was dead. Sooner or later he'd get a call from somebody wondering where he'd got to. Possibly Abraham's boss.

Finally, he picked up Abraham's leather wallet. It was slim and expensive-looking. Inside, all the credit card slots were empty, but there was a driver's licence in the ID window. The face in the photo was no prettier. And his first name had been Arjen, which at least explained why he'd preferred using his surname. The address was an apartment in Phoenix. Bishop doubted it was anything more than a billing address.

There were also eight hundred-dollar bills, three fifties, two tens and five singles in the rear pocket. Bishop pocketed the money and the licence, then wiped his prints off the empty wallet and dropped it out the window.

He sat back and tapped his head against the seat rest. He was thinking back to something Abraham had said. *Once a couple more details are taken care of, she'll just be another footnote.*

Bishop didn't like the sound of that. So far, if Samantha's situation was any kind of gauge, the way these people operated was to kidnap the victim while offing the nearest relatives. Presumably, so there'd be nobody to get suspicious and chase things up. And while there was no reason for Bishop to think they'd seen through the Selina Clements alias, something at the base of his spine told him to check anyway.

Bishop took the iPhone from his pocket and keyed in Michelle Gardiner's landline number. And waited. And waited. After fifteen rings, there was no response. It didn't have to mean anything. She could be out shopping for groceries. She could be out doing anything at all. He tried her cell phone number. This time he kept it going for twenty rings before hanging up.

She would have taken her cell with her if she'd gone out. She wasn't stupid. She'd be expecting Bishop to call her at some point with an update on her daughter. And while it was far too early to jump to conclusions, he was still getting one of his bad feelings again.

He tried Vallejo's number. She picked up and said, 'Hello?'

'It's Bishop,' he said. 'How's it going your end?'

'This isn't your number.'

'I'm borrowing someone else's phone.'

'Oh. Well, I think we might have something. What about you?'

'I've made some progress.'

'Uh huh. Positive news?'

He thought of the two bodies back there and said, 'Not really. Look, you want to meet up somewhere alone?'

'Sure. How about the park opposite the newspaper offices? I'm looking at it now and they keep it pretty well lit at night. I can wait for you at one of the picnic tables.'

'Fine. I'll see you there in half an hour. In the meantime, write these two phone numbers down, but keep them to yourself, okay?' He recited them and said, 'I'm trying to get a hold of a Michelle Gardiner, but she's not answering. Maybe you'll have better luck.'

'Okay. I'll see what I can do.'

'Thanks,' he said and hung up. Then he started the engine and began the drive back to town.

FIFTY-SIX

The drive to Olander Park took him thirty-one minutes. Along the way, he'd stopped off at East Parsons Avenue, left the Lexus and driven the rest of the way in his Buick. He parked next to a brand new BMW X5 in front of the *Post* building, crossed the street and entered the park. Vallejo was sitting at one of the concrete picnic tables about two hundred feet away. She watched him approach without expression. Which immediately put him on alert.

'What's wrong?' he asked, taking a seat opposite.

She looked down at her hands. 'How well do you know this Michelle Gardiner?'

'Just tell me, okay?'

'Okay. I called those numbers you gave me, and it took about twenty minutes of trying before somebody finally answered the cell phone.'

'But not her.'

She looked at him for a moment. 'No. It was an Officer Desmond of the New Jersey PD. After I identified myself and gave him my badge number, he told me that just over an hour ago a woman named Michelle Gardiner was the victim of a vicious hit and run about a hundred feet from her house.'

Bishop groaned. *Just a couple more details to take care of.* 'Is she dead?'

'She was still breathing when the ambulance took her off to the Somerset Hospital. But he told me there was severe internal bleeding and that it didn't look too hopeful. I'm sorry, Bishop.' She paused, then asked, 'I take it she's Selina's mother?'

He nodded and leaned forward on the table, massaging his forehead.

'Stupid, unthinking *ass*hole. As soon as you told me about how they offed Sam's family, I should have warned her to lie low. Stay at a friend's or something. But I was so sure I'd concealed every last vestige of Selina's old identity that I figured she'd be safe. But they found out somehow and decided to tie up another loose end. If she dies, it'll be my fault.'

Vallejo snorted. 'Well, that's *obvious*. I mean, how could you not anticipate the bad guy's *every* single move ahead of time and act accordingly? Jeez, what an idiot.'

'Okay, okay.' He gave a sigh and said, 'I finally met up with that man in the footage. The one with the goatee.'

'You mean Abraham?'

Bishop looked at her. 'Kate recognized him then?' When she nodded, Bishop pulled the driver's licence from his pocket and passed it over. 'This belonged to him.'

She stared at the licence for a moment, then said, '*Belonged*?'

Bishop nodded. 'Past tense. He took me out to a remote spot where events didn't quite go the way he planned. But before he died, he told me where he'd buried a previous victim of his, so I decided to check for myself.' He paused. 'I found a female body. I can't be sure, but I think it was Sam. Both upper wisdom teeth were missing. So was the lower left. I'm sorry, Vallejo.'

Vallejo stared at a spot past Bishop's shoulder and visibly slumped in the seat. She placed her elbows on the table and brought her hands to her face. She stayed like that for a while, her shoulders shaking just a little. Bishop watched her. He saw no point in mentioning that from the state of decomposition Sam had probably been there for at least a month. Or that she looked to have died from a broken neck. That kind of information could wait.

Eventually, she took her hands away and carefully wiped her eyes. 'I kind of half suspected it,' she said, 'so it shouldn't really come as a surprise. But it does. You know, Bishop, I think maybe I *did* love her.'

Bishop said nothing. There was nothing to say.

She took a long deep breath. Neither of them spoke for a minute or two. Then her eyes turned steely and she said, 'It was self-defence. Abraham's death.'

'It was, actually. Not that that would have stopped me. As far as I was concerned, that guy had already lived far too long.'

Vallejo looked at him, gave him a single nod. She was silent for a few more moments. Then she took a long breath and said, 'Okay, tell me the rest.'

Bishop quickly summarized his conversations with Tatem and Abraham. When he'd finished, Vallejo rubbed her neck and said, 'So we're still pretty much in the dark.'

'Well, we know a little more than we did. Those small insertion scars Tatem saw on the women's abdomens, for example. That's definitely something I need to check into.'

'Why, what are you thinking?'

'Tatem mentioned a doctor from New York who, before he died, said he'd possibly found a way to successfully transplant ovaries from donors who weren't related to the recipient. I'd like to know more about him. Especially the cause of death.'

'Ovaries? Is that what you think this is about? Human organ trafficking?'

Bishop paused. It was a good question. What *did* he think? His gut was telling him this was likely to be about something far older and far simpler than organ trafficking. And he'd learned to trust his instincts a long time ago. But he also couldn't afford to ignore possible leads just because they didn't fit in with his thinking. All avenues had to followed, regardless of where they might take him, if only to allow him to ultimately cross them off the list. And this idea about ovaries fit into that category. For the moment, though, he'd keep his gut feelings to himself. Too distracting otherwise. After all, you could only concentrate on one thing at any time. If the only available leads pointed to a single tree, he needed to shake that tree and see what fell out. If all he got were dead leaves, *then* he'd move on the next tree.

'I don't really know,' he said truthfully. 'It's all guesswork at this stage, but Abraham did say he was part of a small, highly specialized organization who supply a gap in the market. And there are already ways to pick up most body parts in this world if you know where to look. But from what I gather, there's no way for an infertile woman to get working ovaries unless she's got an identical twin sister. Which means if these people have somehow found a way to successfully transplant something that has been almost impossible up till now, then they can pretty much name their price. Somewhere north of the seven figure range, possibly. I mean, there must be a lot of very wealthy women around who can't have babies because of ovarian failure, and would be more than willing to pay well over the odds to change the situation.'

Vallejo shifted in her seat. 'Maybe. But it kind of means that doctor Tatem mentioned would have to still be alive, doesn't it?'

'Not necessarily. Doctors leave notes. That's why I need to find out more about the circumstances of his death.'

'Okay, so where does the plastic surgery fit in?'

Bishop shrugged. 'What if they brought Tatem in simply to provide cover while they perform tests on the women and make sure they're compatible? He did tell me none of the instructions he'd been given were particularly complex. Just some touching up here and there. But it's his name that gets logged as the consulting physician, so everything's easily explained if the law comes around and starts asking awkward questions. Whatever's going on, we're talking serious money here, so three hundred grand a year to cover their backs would be chicken feed.'

'You've really given this some thought, haven't you?'

'Not much else to do when you're digging holes.'

Vallejo ran a finger across her eyebrow. 'So what do you think is happening? Any ideas?'

'Some. How about this one? A wealthy woman with non-functioning ovaries, or maybe even the husband or boyfriend, calls these people and puts in an order for a transplant, whereupon Abraham's group set about locating a suitable donor. Somebody young and healthy with certain attributes that are required for success. They're probably able to hack into a variety of medical databases in order to narrow the search. Then, once they find the girl who fits the criteria best, they can start making plans.'

'To arrange her accidental "death", you mean? Along with the real deaths of her closest family?'

'Right. Probably by house fire like with Sam's family, since they need the bodies burnt beyond recognition. But the main thing is they don't want anybody around asking questions. My guess is they had problems in the past from close family members and figured it's more economical to snuff out potential complications right from the off. These are some bad, bad people, Vallejo. With potential millions at stake, who knows how many people they've killed already, purely as a safeguard?'

Vallejo closed her eyes. 'But wait a minute. What about the fake bodies they use as replacements for the kidnapped women? Where the hell would they get them?'

'Hospital morgues. That's where I'd go. Either on a case by case basis, or maybe they've got a stock of Jane Does stored away in a special freezer. I wouldn't put that past them.'

Vallejo nodded slowly to herself, scrunching her brows together. 'Okay. So then what? They bring the girl into hospital, right? One with all the necessary equipment for making the appropriate tests. Like the one at Garrick. Then once she's given the okay, they'd have to transport her to their main headquarters and do the real work there, wouldn't they? I mean, there's no way they could keep a major operation like that quiet for very long. Not in a working hospital.'

'That's right,' Bishop said, and motioned for Vallejo to continue. He was interested in seeing how closely her thought processes matched his. So far, she was doing fine.

Still frowning, she said, 'Which means they've built their own specialist surgery somewhere else. Maybe in a warehouse. But definitely somewhere far away from prying eyes.' She paused for a few moments, thinking it through. 'Plus there's the time element to consider. They'd want to keep the donors around for a while in case they needed them again for follow-up surgery. Like if the first ovary doesn't take and they have to extract the second one and try that.'

'They'd also need to wait around for the client to get pregnant, as well,' Bishop said. 'That would be the only surefire way to know the transplant was fully successful. After that, they could dispose of the donor.'

'You mean kill them?'

'That's what I mean. That area where they buried Sam sure looks like it could contain a lot more bodies than just hers.'

'Christ.' Vallejo puffed her cheeks and blew air out. 'But what about the physical similarities between Sam and Selina? What does that mean?'

'Well, you admitted yourself that they weren't *that* alike on second glance. But they do conform to a type. Both were pretty, healthy and young.' Bishop paused. 'There are still huge holes in the theory, though. For instance, why go all the way to Corvallis for Sam? What was so special about her? I don't know enough about organ transplant surgery, but maybe if she had an unusual blood type or something. Something that automatically put her to the top of the list . . .'

Bishop stopped when he noticed Vallejo looking at him strangely. 'What?'

'Sam was AB rhesus negative,' she said. 'I saw her blood donor card once. She said it's really rare and found in less than one per cent of the population.'

Bishop narrowed his eyes. 'That's a possibility. Maybe the buyer's part of that small percentage, too. Maybe sharing the same blood type is essential for a successful transplant. But it still doesn't explain why Selina was taken. I gave her a new identity with no medical history, so how could they know her blood type?'

'Maybe she had something else that marked her out from everybody else.'

'Yeah. That's still a lot of maybes, though. About the only thing I *do* know right now is I've got until around midnight tomorrow to find her. Abraham told me that much. That's less than thirty hours away.'

'What's supposed to happen then?'

'I don't know, but it won't be anything good. Maybe they're expecting some news that means that Selina's outlived her usefulness. But the clock's ticking and I need to start making some headway.' Bishop paused again, thinking how to phrase the next part. 'Look, Vallejo, I have to tell you that when I meet up with these people I won't be making too many citizen's arrests. You understand what I'm saying?'

Vallejo chewed on her cheek. 'Wouldn't you need a gun?'

Bishop just looked at her.

'Or don't I need to concern myself about that?'

Bishop remained silent.

'Okay,' she said, 'I get the message. So why are you telling me this?'

'To give you a choice on whether to stay with this, or go back to the life you had before you met me. I'd recommend the second one. Sam's gone, the man who killed her is dead, and you're still a cop. And even suspended cops have to abide by a set of rules.'

'And you don't?'

'I live by certain rules. Just not the same ones.' He showed his palms and said, 'You don't have to make a decision now, I'm just laying it out for you.'

She shook her head. 'If that's your subtle attempt to get rid of me, it's not working. I'm in. All the way.'

Bishop nodded. 'Fair enough. Okay, now tell me what *you* found out today.'

'I think we might have discovered who's running the show,' she said.

FIFTY-SEVEN

Vallejo said it would be better if she let Kate explain the rest, so Bishop followed her back inside to the newsroom. The place was empty now, although most of the lights were still on. Bishop noticed Kate's corner desk was also unoccupied. He looked round and saw one of the private offices on the left also had its lights on. Through the frosted glass of the door, Bishop could see the shapes of two figures within.

'What's going on?' he asked.

'The owner, Stan Neeson, arrived just as I was going out to meet you. Kate says they always meet on Saturday evening to plan for the week ahead. She said it wouldn't take long.'

'Okay.' Bishop turned and noticed a water cooler close by. He went over and poured himself a cup. Drank it and refilled it. He was pulling it out from the machine for the third time when the office door opened and Kate and her boss came out.

Neeson looked to be on either side of sixty. 'Urbane' was a good word to describe him. Grey-haired, he had a healthy, tanned complexion and wore glasses, a pastel-coloured polo shirt and pressed tan chinos. Bishop guessed he was the owner of the BMW outside.

They both saw Bishop at the same time. Kate smiled while Neeson said, 'You must be the man I've been hearing about. Bishop, yes?'

Bishop walked over and shook the hand Neeson held out. 'I'm Bishop. I don't know what you've heard, though.'

'Just what Katie's told me. As the publisher of a small local newspaper, you can probably imagine how fascinating I'm finding all this.'

Bishop looked at Kate. 'She's told you everything already? I'm not sure I like that.'

'Don't worry, Katie just asked for my learned opinion and I gave it to her. She and I have trusted each other's judgement for a long time, haven't we, Katie?'

Kate nodded. Bishop said, 'And what was your opinion on this?'

'That she continues helping you out, like she promised. And that we get to print the eventual story that comes from it, like *you* promised. I know she's been aching to move to a bigger newspaper for a while, and a big, exclusive story could be a perfect calling card for her. I'd be sorry to see her go, but I'm not about to stand in her way.'

'Thanks, Stan,' Kate said, sitting down at her desk.

Neeson smiled and found a seat nearby. 'And it would sell papers, of course. I know people around here are convinced the *Post*'s not much more than a hobby for me, but I'm actually serious about this. A rise in circulation's always welcome, even a temporary one.'

Vallejo sat, while Bishop stood next to the window. He drank half of his water and looked at Kate. He'd been very patient so far. He said, 'So I hear you got a name for me.'

'Where's the rest of the footage Clarissa showed me?' Kate asked.

'Damaged by fire. That's all we managed to save.'

Kate looked at Vallejo. 'Funny, that's what she said. I'm not sure I believe it.'

'You surprise me.'

'I'm pretty sure I recognized that street, though. I'd put money on that being Bannings' front courtyard.'

'That's wasted on me,' Bishop said. 'I don't gamble. You remember me asking about the name?'

Kate smiled. 'Okay. Did you happen to notice the name of the park across the street?'

'Sure,' Bishop said, 'Olander Park.'

'Named after our very own Grant Olander, current chairman of the Saracen Chamber of Commerce. I think it's very possible he's involved in whatever's going on.' She leaned forward, tapping her fingernails on the desk. 'Which is what, by the way? I know you like to keep things close to your chest, but at least give me something.'

Bishop looked at Vallejo. Vallejo arched her eyebrows at him.

Why not indeed? thought Bishop. *After all, it's still only a theory at this stage.*

'Okay,' he said. 'Now I'm only guessing here, but I think we could be dealing with a group that specializes in illegal organ transplants for the rich.'

Neeson and Kate looked at each other with raised eyebrows.

'Specifically, ovaries,' he continued, 'which happens to be something the medical community hasn't been able to achieve yet with any degree of success. Which means we could be talking big, big money. These are some very serious people who aren't above kidnapping and murder, but don't ask me for any more because I simply don't know enough yet. Maybe you can help me with that later, Kate. But for now, does this Olander sound like the kind of man who'd be involved in something like this? What kind of person is he?'

Neeson said, 'Shady's a good adjective to describe him. Olander's been a part of our local government for more years than I can count. He was even mayor for a long stretch a few years back. Whispers of private deals on the side and the greasing of palms have followed him wherever he goes, but he always gets voted back in somehow.'

'Right,' Kate said. 'He's also a shrewd businessman with his fingers in lots of pies, and from what I've heard, none of them are exactly above board.'

'So he's an unscrupulous politician,' Bishop said. 'I need more than that to go on.'

'I'm getting to it, Bishop. Now, about seven years ago this guy from the footage, Arjen Abraham, started working as Olander's personal assistant when he was head of the town's Economic Development Advisory Board. And any time Olander switched roles after that, he'd bring Abraham with him. Of course, everybody guessed he was the point man for Olander's private deals, but nobody ever said anything. He's a pretty scary guy.'

Not any more, Bishop thought. But he said nothing.

'He stayed in that role until about three years ago when he quit, but people have still seen him coming out of Olander's office more than once since then. Now if what you said is true, with the kind of money you're talking about it's possible Olander simply decided to assign Abraham to this new business full time.'

Bishop gulped the last of the water and threw the empty cup in Kate's wastebasket. It was certainly possible. And the time frames fitted in with what Tatem had told him. But he had a feeling there was still more. 'What else?' he asked.

'Well, about four years back,' Kate said, 'I interviewed this car dealer in Yuma. He said Olander promised him zoning permission for a dealership he wanted to set up in a sought-after section of Saracen. And all it would cost him was four brand new SUVs. Naturally, he's still waiting for the zoning permission. Poor guy can't prove anything, of course. Nobody ever can. But those SUVs he got stiffed on? They were white Mercedes Sprinter panel vans, just like the one in the footage.'

'That's a pretty common vehicle,' Bishop said.

'Maybe in the city. Not so common in these parts. And Mercs aren't cheap. You'll find just about every panel van you see out here has got a Ford logo on it.'

Bishop looked through the window at the night outside. If Olander owned the vans before, it didn't necessarily mean he still owned them. He might have simply sold them on at a profit. That was something else he'd have to look into. He turned back to Kate and said, 'Was Olander making good money from his previous schemes?'

'Oh, I think so,' she said. 'He's never exactly been on the breadline, let's put it that way.'

Neeson said, 'I believe he was a millionaire even before he entered local government. But he's one of those people who always lives beyond his means and always has an eye out for the next big chance.'

'And now? Any big changes in how he spends his money? Or any indication that he's come into a lot more of it in the last three years?'

Kate and Neeson looked at each other. 'Nothing obvious,' Kate said. 'But that doesn't necessarily mean anything.'

'That's why God invented overseas accounts,' Neeson said. 'Katie's right, though. I've had dealings with Grant many times and I can vouch that he's got very few scruples where money's involved. And if we're talking about a figure in the hundreds of millions, I'm not sure he could resist. Even if it meant being involved in something as awful as this.'

Just then a phone started ringing in one of the offices. Kate picked up hers, pressed a button on her console and said, '*Saracen Post*.' After a few seconds, she smiled at Neeson and said, 'Yeah, Ange, he is. I'll tell him,' before hanging up.

Neeson looked at her, eyebrows raised.

'Your youngest,' she said, 'reminding you the recital begins in less than half an hour, so get your ass in gear. When you gonna get yourself a cell phone, Stan?'

He stood up and kissed Kate on the cheek. 'When you get yourself a husband. Besides, I'm too old school. I better go, but you'll keep me updated on this?'

Kate looked at Bishop. 'If I can.'

'That's all I ask.' Neeson said his farewells to Bishop and Vallejo and left them.

Bishop said, 'What does this Olander look like?'

'Hold on,' Kate said and rolled her chair back to one of the filing cabinets behind her. She opened a drawer and rooted around inside. After a few seconds she came back holding a large photo. 'Here's our boy. This was taken a few years ago when he was mayor.'

Bishop took the photo from her. It was a typical publicity shot of Olander perched casually on his desk in an expensive suit, with the requisite American flag taking up most of the background. He looked to be in his early to mid sixties. Under a full head of light grey hair, he had a leathery face with small, dark brown eyes and a long, narrow nose. His teeth were white, even and plentiful. Bishop passed the photo to Vallejo and said, 'I've seen more trustworthy smiles on time-share hucksters.'

Kate grinned and said, 'The smile of the self-righteous public servant is a glorious thing to behold. Now didn't you say there was something else you wanted some help with?'

'Yeah. I spoke to Tatem and one thing he mentioned was this doctor back east who died several years ago. All I know is he claimed he'd made inroads on a method for transplanting ovaries that didn't necessitate the donors having identical genetic material. Is there any way of finding out his name?'

Kate turned to her computer and said, 'Let's see, shall we?'

FIFTY-EIGHT

It was less than three minutes later when Kate turned to Bishop and said, 'I think we got something. I found the story on the BBC site, although it's on a few others, too.'

'I'm all ears,' Bishop said.

She turned back to the screen. 'Well, assuming it's the same man, his name was Dr Kendrick Juneau and he had a tenure position at the Presbyterian in Manhattan. Specifically, the Columbia University Medical Center, where seven years ago he was granted government funding for ovarian transplant research. Then four years ago, he published a paper in the *New England Journal of Medicine* on the overuse of anaesthetics in modern medicine. In it, he also included a little footnote, hinting at how close he was to a breakthrough in organ transplant research that would aid ninety per cent of women with non-functioning ovaries. That footnote got him a fair amount of column inches for a while, but he refused to say any more. Probably didn't want his peers stealing his ideas. Then nothing more until his disappearance seven months later.'

That got Bishop's attention. 'Disappearance?'

'Right. He was on one of those solo adventure vacations in Africa. Witnesses last saw him in a canoe on the Congo River, with a guide and an unidentified dark-skinned woman. A week later, the police found the canoe's remains, but no sign of the three passengers. They put it down as possible croc attack. It happens a lot down there. Then two years ago, the day before this article was written, Juneau's wife filed a petition and had him legally declared dead by the courts.'

'What about his notes?' Vallejo asked. 'Surely somebody accessed his computer so they could continue his research?'

Kate smiled. 'Apparently he was a little paranoid when it came to computers. Only used them when it was absolutely necessary, so he wrote down all his notes in longhand and kept them hidden at home. But medical experts went though all his paperwork after he was declared dead and found next to nothing concerning his ovary research.'

Bishop sat back in the chair and looked at Vallejo. She stared back without saying anything. They were both aware of the implications.

Kate was watching Bishop with a gleam in her eyes. 'Are you thinking his death could have been faked?'

'It's one possibility,' he said. 'It's also a possibility that he was leading everybody on about his supposed breakthrough, and that he and his companions really did get attacked by crocodiles.'

'But you don't think so,' she prompted.

'I don't really know what to think yet. I generally try and stay clear of conspiracy crap, since I've found the simplest explanation's often the one to go for. But I have to admit, this does kind of fit in with what we've seen so far.' Bishop got up and walked over to the water cooler and filled another cup.

Kate said, 'Could be the people behind this read that paper four years ago and got in touch with him. Maybe they offered him a choice he couldn't resist.'

Vallejo said, 'You mean glory later, or untold riches right here and now?'

'Doctors are human like the rest of us,' Bishop said and took a sip of the water. 'With the same temptations. If nothing else, that unidentified woman in the canoe suggests he liked the ladies. Maybe he liked the thought of money, too.'

'Well, he sure wouldn't be the first.' Kate leaned back in her chair and stretched. 'Look, I haven't had anything solid pass my lips in hours. How about you guys? You want to go somewhere and grab something?'

Vallejo stood up. 'I'm not hungry, but you two go on.' She looked at Bishop and said, 'I think I want to be alone for a while, okay?'

Bishop looked at her. She'd been pretty quiet since learning about Sam. Which was only natural. He didn't think going to her room and brooding would really help her state of mind, but it was her choice. Everybody dealt with things differently. So he said, 'Okay, but do me a favour, huh? Switch to one of the other rooms, but keep your car parked outside the old one. And don't forget to take the thing with you. Maybe find it a similar home, you know, for safekeeping.'

Vallejo frowned, then smiled. 'Sure, I can do that.'

Kate looked set to ask another question, but she saw Bishop's expression and just shrugged instead. 'Looks like it's just the two of us, then. Come on, my treat.'

FIFTY-NINE

Kate took him to the Leaping Lizard, just off Saracen Road. Bishop wasn't exactly sure why. The place was clearly geared towards the younger set. And it was getting on for eight o'clock on a Saturday night, too. The place was already starting to fill up with people of Selina's age.

The Lizard was a colourfully decorated bar and diner with tables and booths for dining at one end, a central bar area, then more tables and a second bar at the other end. Widescreen TVs everywhere. All showing games or music videos. Most of them were muted at present, although that was likely to change soon enough.

They took a booth. Once the waitress finished taking their orders, Bishop said, 'You usually come here to eat?'

'Why, are you suggesting I'm not down with the kids any more?'

Bishop smiled. 'You're asking the wrong person. So, is this where you met Clarissa?'

'Yeah. I noticed she seemed quieter than usual back at the office. Something wrong?'

'A personal problem. She'll be all right in a few hours.'

'Okay, if you say so.'

The waitress came with their drinks. They each sipped their Budweisers and Kate said, 'I heard something on the police scanner this afternoon. Another Bannings employee was found dead, this time in his apartment. A Jon Rutherford. You know him?'

'No. Is there any reason why I should?'

'No reason. I just asked.'

Bishop doubted that. 'So what was the cause of death?'

'Well, he was found with his head in the oven and the gas turned on full. All the windows were shut. On the surface, it *looks* like suicide.'

Bishop took another swallow of his beer and kept his expression blank. He and Vallejo sure hadn't left Rutherford's apartment like that when they'd departed.

'But you don't believe it,' he said.

'I don't believe in the Easter Bunny, either. Come on, Bishop, I'm not stupid. That two-minute clip showed Abraham outside the Bannings place early this morning, just before the fire. Yet the police are already laying the blame at Rutherford's door. The one person who's in no position to defend himself.'

'What possible motive could he have had to kill Hewitt and burn the place up?'

'My police contact says he and Hewitt weren't on good terms, that they came to blows a couple of times. They're theorizing that maybe things went too far this time and ended with Hewitt getting his neck broken, after which Rutherford tried to cover up his crime with a fire.'

'And the next morning, he's overcome with remorse and sticks his head in an oven.'

Kate smiled. 'Doesn't sound too likely, does it?'

No, it doesn't, Bishop thought. But it was a smart play. Since Bishop had an alibi for the fire, it looked like somebody had decided Rutherford shouldn't go to waste. Somebody had to take the blame for Hewitt's murder, and who better than a suicide?

'Who called it in?' he asked.

'Why?'

'Was it a Detective Shaw?'

She frowned at him. 'Yeah, it was.'

Which pretty much confirmed what Bishop already knew. There *was* an inside man in the department. Shaw must have received orders to make sure he was first on the scene and make sure everything went as planned. But didn't cops always travel to crime scenes in pairs? What did he tell Levine to ensure he got there first?

He realized Kate was talking to him. 'What was that?' he asked.

'I said, how did you know it was Shaw?'

Bishop shrugged. 'I didn't. He was one of the cops interrogating me about the fire this morning. I just threw the name out, that's all.'

Kate snorted. 'You don't strike me as the kind of guy who just says things at random.' She watched him for a long moment as she slowly slid the side of her forefinger down the beer glass. 'You really need to give that footage to the police, you know.'

Here we go again. 'Look,' he said, 'it's a two-minute clip showing an indistinct man outside a garage that just happened to be set on fire shortly after. The very definition of circumstantial evidence. And Abraham's got no obvious motive. Any half-decent lawyer would get it thrown out in a second.'

'But it would point the police in the right direction, at least.'

He shook his head. 'If an innocent guy was facing a murder charge, I'd consider it, but Rutherford's beyond caring. And I'm not about to risk Selina's safety by alerting these people I'm on to them. Not yet.'

She seemed about to say something else, but just then the waitress came back with their meals. Cheeseburger, salad and fries for Bishop. BLT sandwich and salad for Kate. They spent a quiet minute adding various condiments. Then Kate took a bite of the sandwich and said, 'So tell me, what was it like in prison?'

That little thunderbolt threw Bishop for only a moment. He launched into his burger and said, 'You know about that?'

She nodded. 'When you first came to the office there was something about your face that struck a chord with me, so I did a little checking. You sure make interesting reading. So how was it behind bars?'

'About what you'd expect. I've been in worse places, but I've been in better. You really want to talk about that while we eat?'

'What shall we talk about, then?' she asked, taking a sip of her beer and smiling playfully at him over the glass rim.

He looked at the hands holding the glass. They were nice hands. And Kate had a nice face. Especially when she smiled. Bishop knew there were plenty of subjects they could talk about. But he also remembered why he was here and said, 'You mentioned Olander's business dealings before. Has he got his own company set-up?'

Kate sighed and put down the glass. 'Uh huh. Catalyst Incorporated, it's called.'

'And do they have offices around here?'

'Kind of. Olander's got a whole warehouse just outside of town.'

Bishop nodded. Even better. For what they were doing, they'd need someplace large. He'd already given it some serious thought, but up till now hadn't really known where to start. There were warehouses practically everywhere you looked in Arizona. But now he remembered the industrial park he'd passed on Highway 60. Just outside of town. There'd been a sign by the road with a name on it. *What was it again?* After a few seconds it came back to him. 'Gareth Rhodes Business Park? That the place you mean?'

'That's right. Olander has part ownership in the place. He's also got one of the biggest warehouses all to himself, fenced off and away from all the others. I hear he employs security guards to keep watch, day and night. People around here have always wondered what he gets up to in there.'

'That's interesting,' he said.

They both ate in silence for awhile, lost in their own thoughts. Bishop polished off the last of his burger and said, 'That car dealer in Yuma. Do you still have his number?'

Kate smiled, her salad fork halfway to her mouth. 'I've got *every*one's number, don't you know that by now? Why?'

'Can you call him and get him to give you the licence numbers for those four vans?'

Kate put down the fork and pulled out a small electronic organizer from her shoulder bag. 'I can try,' she said, and started pressing buttons with an expert's touch. 'There you are,' she said a few moments later and pulled her cell phone from her bag. Bishop watched as she keyed in a number and put the phone to her ear.

'Is that Lyle Kinney?' she said a few seconds later. 'Hi, this is Kate McGowan. Do you remember me from . . . Wow, I'm flattered. Look, I was wondering if you still had the licence numbers for those SUVs

Grant Olander conned you out of . . . Yeah, those . . . Well, I might be on to something, it's too early to tell . . . Sure, I don't mind. Take your time.'

She covered the mouthpiece. 'I caught him at his office. He's just checking for me.'

I bet he is. Bishop had no idea what the guy's marital status was, but he felt confident Kinney would make a pass before the conversation was through. Call it instinct.

'Hold on,' she said a minute later and rummaged through her bag. She pulled out a notebook and pencil and said, 'Okay, go.' She wrote down numbers for about a minute and said, 'That's great, Lyle. I really appreciate it . . .' She listened for a moment, then in a quieter voice said, 'I don't think I can, Lyle . . . No, that's okay, but I just don't think it would be a good idea . . . Exactly right. We all do . . . Okay, bye.' She ended the call and blew out a breath.

'Let him down easy, did you?'

She smiled at him. 'He really should know better. I saw the framed pictures last time I was there. Beautiful wife, nice kids. I just don't get it. Why do some guys want to risk all that for a few sweaty moments with someone they barely know?'

'Because men can be stupid. Especially when it comes to attractive women.'

She took a sip of her beer, clearly pleased with the compliment. 'And what about you, Bishop? Are you ever stupid?'

'Sometimes. None of us are perfect.'

'I meant with women.'

'I know you did.'

Kate smiled at him again. It was a great smile. One with a hint of the devil in there. She took a long slug of her beer, put the bottle down and then slowly slid her way out of her side of the booth. She came round and sat down next to him, close enough for their hips to touch. Despite the task still ahead of him, Bishop found himself enjoying the moment. He was also more than a little curious to see what she'd do next.

'Believe it or not,' she said, 'I can be stupid sometimes, too.'

'I doubt that.'

'No? Watch me.'

Then she placed a palm against his cheek and pulled his face down to hers. They kissed. Bishop didn't know for how long, but when he finally broke away he found he was short of breath. She'd tasted as nice as he'd imagined. He said, 'Pretty forward, aren't you?'

Kate shrugged. 'Grab the moment, I say. How about you?'

Bishop had never been the impulsive type, but in this particular case he was inclined to agree. Except there was still Jenna to consider. And cheating on people he cared about had never been part of his nature. But his attraction towards Kate clearly showed that long-term relationships weren't part of his nature, either. Pity. But *to thine own self be true*, as the old Shakespearean quote went. Bishop just hoped Jenna wouldn't end up resenting him for it when he told her of his decision.

And as for Kate, as much as he liked her, he couldn't afford to get sidetracked now. Not with Selina's fate in the balance. It was past nine already. He only had twenty-seven hours to play with. Maybe less. 'I say, I'll definitely give it some serious thought. But for now, do you want to show me those plate numbers?'

'Oh. Sure.' Kate reached over for her pad. She tore the page out and passed it to him.

Bishop looked at them. As he'd expected, the numbers were sequential. Straight out of the factory. Shouldn't be too hard to check who the current owners were.

'You're a journalist,' he said. 'You must know somebody at the DMV, right?'

'Wrong,' she said. 'But it just so happens I've got something even better.'

SIXTY

Kate drove them south along Saracen Road for a mile before taking a right into West Tyler Avenue. Bishop noticed a smattering of businesses and stores near the intersection on both sides, while further back it looked to be mostly private residences.

She parked her Subaru Forester outside one of the former, a small, nondescript brick building with an awning outside. Above it a sign read *Massingham Computer Sales & Repair*. It was dark inside, and the windows and door had shutters over them. Bishop had a feeling they'd entered one of the less desirable sections of town.

They both got out. Kate locked the station wagon's doors and said, 'Friendly warning. You need to be careful around Raymond, okay? I've known him a long time, but he's prickly and doesn't get on with too many people. First thing he'll do is see how far he can push your buttons. So be cool and for God's sake don't call him Raymond.'

'I'll try to remember,' Bishop said.

Kate led him down the side of the building. It was dark and went back quite a way. So far that Bishop thought maybe the place doubled as living quarters for the guy. At the rear were two small, barred windows and a steel door. There was also a spotlight near the roof that illuminated the area, and just under that Bishop noticed a very small surveillance camera behind a grille. Kate rapped her knuckles against the door and they waited.

After about thirty seconds, he heard latches being drawn, locks being turned. The door opened outwards and a medium-sized blond man stood there looking at each of them. Bishop had been picturing an older version of Milhouse off *The Simpsons*. But this Raymond was about Kate's age. His short hair was brushed forward and he had a

241

face that wasn't far off handsome. He wore glasses, though, so Bishop had got that part right.

'Hey, Lady McG,' he said, 'how y'all doin'? Who's the mouth-breather?'

'Charming,' Kate said, 'and you can drop the southern shit-kicker accent, Raymond. It doesn't suit you. This is James Bishop. Can we come in?'

'McG always be welcome here.' He opened the door further to let them through and locked it behind them. He frowned briefly at Bishop, then led them down a short hallway, past a couple of doors and into a large workroom.

There were computers, laptops, hard drives and parts everywhere. Shelves lined two of the walls, all full to the brim with items Bishop couldn't even begin to identify. Framed pictures and posters covered most of the other two walls. Books and magazines all over the floor. Raymond cleared one chair of stuff so Kate could sit. Then he took the only other one and rested an elbow on the only clear spot on his desk. 'Bishop, huh?'

'That's right,' Bishop said.

'So you known McG here long?'

'Not long. Just a few hours.'

'Uh huh. So what's the deal with you, Bishop? You law or something?'

Bishop smiled. 'Something.'

Raymond gave him a malicious grin back. 'Something. You a tough guy, Bishop?'

'Not particularly.'

'So if I were to tell you that I don't like your face, or your attitude, and to get the hell out off my property, what would you do?'

'Leave, I guess. Why, is that something you're likely to say?'

'Raymond . . .' Kate said in a low tone.

'Hey, I'm just having a conversation with the man, McG. Don't sweat it. Besides, you barely know him. He could be anyone. Maybe he's a closet pantie sniffer. He looks the type. How about it, Jimbo? That the kind of thing that gets you hot?'

Bishop shrugged. 'Sure, Ray. Whatever you say.'

Raymond's face immediately went stony. Bishop kept his a blank mask. Nobody spoke for a few moments. Then Raymond adjusted his glasses and smiled slightly with one side of his mouth. 'Yeah, thought so,' he said.

'If I can cut in on your king-of-the-castle act for just a second, Raymond,' Kate said, 'we came here hoping you could help us out with something.'

He turned to her and his smile got wider. 'Hit me, McG.'

'If only it were that easy.' She passed over the page from her note-book. 'We want to know who these vehicles are registered to. Pretty simple stuff, but I told Bishop you were better than the DMV at this kind of thing.'

He turned to his desk. 'Not better, exactly,' he said and started typing on the laptop as he spoke. 'See, it's all about who you know in this world, McG. And I happen to know one of the guys who helped design the firewalls for their servers. Met him back when I was still working for the phone company and we stayed in touch ever since. We still do each other favours, swap passwords and back doors, that kind of thing.'

Raymond went quiet and continued typing, occasionally using the touchpad. Oblivious of everything else. Jenna was the same. Bishop had seen her get wired in to the point where he could set off a fire-cracker next to her ear and she wouldn't notice.

After a while, Raymond turned to Kate and said, 'What are you expecting to find, McG?'

'That they're all registered to a company called Catalyst Incorporated.'

He turned back to the screen. 'Well, they used to be. Catalyst sold them all on three years ago. Two went to private buyers, an A. Mendoza in Glendale, and an R. Trevane in Gila Bend. The other two were bought by a company called Distar Associates.'

Kate sighed. 'There goes *that* theory, then.'

'Not necessarily,' Bishop said. 'Where's this Distar company based?'

Raymond leaned in closer. 'They got an office over in Flagstaff.'

'Any way of finding out who the owners are?'

'Sure, you just do a search on the Arizona Secretary of State website.' Raymond turned to the second laptop and went back to work. After a while he said, 'Looks like I spoke too soon. I'm getting a big fat nothing.'

Kate turned to Bishop. 'They didn't register the business in this state then.'

'Try a search on the Nevada website,' Bishop said.

Raymond said, 'O-o-kay,' and went to work.

'Why there?' Kate asked.

'Nevada's a major corporate haven,' Bishop said. 'You can get incorporated there even if your company headquarters are in another state, but you're still protected by their strict disclosure laws. Plus you don't pay corporate income tax.'

'I guess you read the right magazines, huh?'

Bishop smiled. 'I do, but that's not it. In my old life, I provided personal protection for a lot of rich businessmen, and if there was a legal way to save a buck they'd find it. This was one of the ways.'

'I knew it. Under the skin of every millionaire beats the heart of a piker.'

'That's probably why they stay millionaires.'

'Bingo,' Raymond said. 'We got us a hit.'

'We're listening,' said Kate.

'Well, the company was registered in Nevada on March 11, three years ago. That's four months before they bought the vans.' He made a face. 'And can you believe this? It's owned by a John Smith.'

Kate chuckled. 'You know, that *could* be his real name. They do exist.'

'Sure they do,' Bishop said. But he didn't think so in this case. He strolled over to a bare patch of wall and leaned his back against it. He was thinking about human nature, and how often even the smartest people often resorted to sentimentality. Even when it was against their best interests. And you didn't get any more sentimental than family.

He turned to Kate and said, 'Is Olander married? Does he have kids?'

'Yeah. He's still married to his high school sweetheart. She's not the nicest person you could ever meet, believe me. Got two kids, I think. Both boys and both grown, of course. One's a corporate lawyer in Phoenix. I don't know about the other one.'

'You know their names?'

'Um. The lawyer's Peter. The other one's Patrick. I think.'

Not what he was after. 'What about the wife?'

'What about her?'

'Would her name be Diana, or Diane? Something like that?'

Kate brought her eyebrows together. 'No, but you're close. It's Dionne.'

'And her middle name. Is it Stephanie? Or maybe Stella?'

Then Kate's frown turned to a smile as she got it. 'Hold on a second. Let me check.'

'Her maiden name, too, while you're at it.'

She nodded as she pulled her cell from her bag and pressed a number. Waited. Then she said, 'Hey, Arnie. Yeah, it's me. Look, you researched that Olander puff piece we did a few years back, right? You wouldn't happen to remember the wife's middle name, would you?' She looked at Bishop, smiled and said, 'Okay, and what about her maiden name?' A moment later, she said, 'Great. I owe you a beer, Arnie. Thanks.'

Bishop said, 'Stella.'

'Stephanie,' she said. 'Dionne Stephanie. And her maiden name was Arbor. *Distar*. Pretty cool, Bishop. So Olander sets up another company out of state to remove any annoying trails that might lead back to him. Like the change in ownership of two of Catalyst's vans. You think he uses these vehicles for his felonious activities?'

Bishop frowned. 'Possibly. Could be any number of reasons for wanting to hide the ownership.'

Raymond was watching each of them in turn. 'Okay, which one of you is gonna tell me what the hell's going on? What felonious activities?'

Kate turned to Bishop with raised eyebrows.

Bishop tapped his head lightly against the wall and tried to think why Kate shouldn't fill Raymond in. If Neeson knew, why not

Raymond? He could be a useful asset in the hours to come if he was kept in the loop.

'Okay,' Bishop said, pushing off from the wall. He looked at his watch. 21.34. Getting late. 'But, Raymond, keep what you hear to yourself, okay? It's important. Kate will explain why.'

Kate looked at him. 'You're going? I thought . . .' She paused.

'Sorry, Kate. I have to. I'm up against the clock here.'

'Well, where are you headed? I can give you a left.'

He walked over to the hallway and shook his head. 'You stay here and fill Raymond in. It's only a ten-minute walk back to my car and I need some time to think. I'll be in touch, though. With both of you.'

Raymond grinned and said, 'Can't wait.'

SIXTY-ONE

Bishop got back to his Buick and drove out to the Heritage Apartments. He parked in the same lot as before and stayed in his seat, slowly scanning the area, alert to any kind of movement. The occasional vehicle passed by behind him. Each time he noted its progress in the rear-view until it was out of sight. But other than a pedestrian here and there, he saw nothing that gave him pause. Through the rear gates he could make out that old couple again, still sitting outside their ground floor apartment. Still in the same positions. Maybe they slept there. The old guy certainly looked as though he was out for the count.

He stuck the Sig in his waistband under his T-shirt and got out the car. He walked towards the stairs and the woman looked up from her book and smiled.

'Hello again,' she said. 'Nice night.'

'Sure is,' he said and stopped. The husband remained asleep in his chair, snoring slightly. 'You must see most people coming in or out, right?'

'Oh, yes.'

'Anyone come around here today who didn't belong?'

She pursed her lips. 'Well, there was Mr Baynard at No. 12, but I'm not sure he belongs on this *planet*. Or did you mean somebody new?'

'That's what I meant.'

'In that case, no. Just the same old faces. Why, are you expecting someone?'

Bishop smiled. 'No, just checking. Thanks.' He kept walking, took the stairs, and when he reached No. 40 paused outside the door and listened. He heard nothing. Taking the Sig from his waistband, he quickly unlocked the door and pushed it open.

He could immediately sense he was alone in the apartment, but he checked the rooms anyway. Once he was satisfied, he took a quick shower and put on some clean clothes. Black shirt, black pants, black windbreaker. He also took a Brunton pocket scope from his bag and put it in his pocket. He checked the inner pockets of the bag and smiled when his fingers found the black cotton ski mask and the roll of duct tape. They might come in handy again. Then he picked up his cell and called Vallejo.

She picked up on the fifth ring and said, 'Hey.'

'Hey yourself. How you doing?'

'Not so great. I'm thinking I probably would have been better off staying with you guys and grabbing something to eat. I'm in room No. 17 now, but I'm still looking at the same four walls and thinking of Sam.'

'In that case,' Bishop said, 'I've got something that'll take your mind off her.'

SIXTY-TWO

Vallejo let Bishop drive. If something happened, the Buick was definitely the more expendable vehicle. Bishop was tired of it already. However long he kept the windows open, he could never quite get rid of the musty smell. The manual stick shift kept sticking, too.

After stopping off at a fast-food place so Vallejo could get a takeout, he took them out of town and east onto Highway 60 again. Vallejo had finished her food by the time he came to the sign for Gareth Rhodes Business Park. The clock on the dash said it was 22.19. He pulled in, turned off the headlights and cruised slowly along the paved access road, navigating by moonlight.

The main road went on for about five hundred feet before veering off to the right. Then it straightened out again. To their right was just desert. On the left were various large single-storey warehouses, broken up by smaller roads branching off from this one. By the time he'd reached the end of the main road, he'd counted three in all. And none of the warehouses he'd passed looked like the one Kate had described. There was also nobody else around that Bishop could see.

'It probably wouldn't be along this main section, anyway,' Vallejo said, sipping from a large cup of coffee. 'Too wide open.'

'I had to check,' Bishop said and made a U-turn. 'Let me have some of that.'

She passed him the cup. He took a few swallows, made a face and handed it back. Vallejo's sweet tooth was too much for him. He then took a right into the first offshoot road. It descended on a slight gradient and Bishop counted four more warehouses. Two on each side. All protected by perfunctory chain-link fencing and steel gates.

249

Again, nobody in sight. At the end of the road, he made another U-turn and came back.

'These warehouses all look fairly big to me,' Vallejo said.

'Too close to each other. Kate said Olander's got himself a little more privacy.'

They tried the next road, which also sloped down at a slightly deeper gradient. Bishop saw three warehouses on the left, all broken up into smaller units, each with its own shuttered entrance. The first warehouse on the right was a sheet metal manufacturing business. Next to that was another one with a large *For Lease* sign affixed to the side. After that was a large lot, empty except for several parked cars, two abandoned truck trailers and three large dumpsters.

But at the end of the road, at the bottom of the gradient, Bishop also saw another warehouse with no immediate neighbours surrounding it.

'That looks promising,' Vallejo said.

'Just what I was thinking.'

Bishop turned into the vacant lot and saw the parked cars weren't parked, they were abandoned. There were four of them, all rusted by the looks of it. They either had flat tyres or no tyres at all. Further along, the trailers looked to be in a bad way, too. Clearly, this lot was a designated dumping ground. Which made it a perfect vantage point for Bishop. He parked next to one of the cars facing the end warehouse and turned off the engine.

The moon was approaching its last quarter, so visibility was reasonable. He took the scope from his pocket and pointed it down the hill. The warehouse was at least two storeys and took up a much larger area than the others. A large section of the south wall facing them was made up of a huge door that would have looked more at home on an aircraft hangar. There were also two smaller, windowless buildings to the left and right of the warehouse, with shutters instead of doors. The entire plot took up four or five acres, maybe. There was six-foot high cyclone fencing all round, with razor wire on top. There were no lights anywhere on the premises, not even spotlights. There were about fifteen vehicles parked in an area out front, close to the left-hand building. Bishop didn't see any guards on patrol.

He took out his cell, called Kate and put it on speakerphone. When she picked up, he said, 'It's Bishop. I forgot to ask you what kind of car Olander drives.'

'Well, he owns two that I know of,' she said. 'A BMW and one of those big Jaguars. Olander's a bit of an Anglophile so he usually prefers the Jag. It goes hand in hand with his fake mid-Atlantic accent.'

Bishop thanked her and ended the call. He adjusted the scope's magnification to get a better look. One of the vehicles down there definitely looked like a Jag. One of the big XJ models. Probably the only one for hundreds of miles. They weren't exactly common.

He passed Vallejo the scope and she took a look. 'Hmm, looks like Olander's taking care of business personally tonight,' she said. 'I don't see any of those vans, though.'

'Maybe they keep them inside.' Just then, he saw a gleam of light in the rear-view and said, 'Somebody's coming.'

They both lowered themselves and waited as a car passed by. Bishop then got up and looked through the scope. He watched the car follow the road until it stopped at the fence. A man in a suit got out and walked up to the front gate. Bishop now noticed a small keypad on a pole. The man stood in front of it, blocking Bishop's vision, and a few seconds later the gate slowly opened. Very slowly. The man impatiently kicked at it, then got back in his car.

So the fence wasn't electrified. That was puzzling. Bishop had expected more security. Or maybe they thought the razor wire was enough. Surveillance cameras were a possibility, but he couldn't see how that would work without some kind of exterior lighting. Unless they were using thermal imaging cameras. But it seemed unlikely. Decent T.I. cameras were beyond most people's budgets and they'd need a lot of them to cover such a large area. And what would be the point? It would be easier and more economical to install some muted lighting and use normal night-time cameras.

Bishop didn't really know what to think just yet. Not without more information.

Once there was enough space, the driver drove through the gap in the direction of the other parked cars. Bishop kept the scope on the gate and saw it close as slowly as it had opened. He tracked the car again and saw it come to a stop in the parking area. The driver got out. Another man got out the passenger side. Bishop noticed movement to the left of the main warehouse and then another man emerged from the shadows. He was wearing a guard's uniform and a side holster. He approached the two men and they had a brief conversation. Then they all walked into the shadows of the main warehouse and disappeared from sight.

Bishop lowered the scope. 'Looks like Saturday night's a work night,' he said.

'No rest for the wicked,' Vallejo said and glanced in the side mirror. 'Shit, here comes another one.'

They both ducked down briefly as the vehicle passed. Bishop saw it was a van this time. No way to tell the make from the back, but it looked similar to the one in the footage. The driver, another man, performed the same routine on the gate and drove on through. He parked next to the previous car, and the security guard emerged from the deep shadows again. The driver got out to talk to him, while another man exited the van's rear door. Bishop saw him motion to somebody inside and then a woman stepped out onto the tarmac. Then another woman, with her arms wrapped tight around her chest, followed by a third man who shut the door. They were too far away for Bishop to make out any features other than gender. Then they all walked towards the main warehouse, the third man closely behind the two women.

Bishop passed the scope to Vallejo, who looked for a few seconds and said, 'If body language means anything, I'd say those women would very much like to be anywhere but here. What do you think they've been doing?'

'Who knows?' he said.

Vallejo nodded. 'Maybe it's . . .' she began, and stopped at the muffled, tinny sound of Vivaldi's *Four Seasons* coming from the glove compartment. 'That's not me,' she said.

'Me neither.' Bishop reached over to open the glove compartment and the music filled the car interior. Inside was a hands-free unit for his cell, a new toothbrush he'd bought earlier and Abraham's iPhone, pulsing with light. He pulled out the phone. There was no number displayed on the screen. Obviously withheld.

He looked at Vallejo, then took the call.

SIXTY-THREE

'Abraham?' the male voice said. 'Where are you? You're late.'

Bishop gave a noncommittal grunt to give himself more breathing space. He was thinking back to Abraham's voice pattern, wondering if there had been a hint of Kansas or Missouri in there, when the caller said, 'Who is this?'

'Abraham,' Bishop said in what he hoped was the right pitch.

'I don't think so. He's never been the grunting type. Where is he?'

'Disneyland,' Bishop said in his own voice. 'Poor guy needed a break.'

There was a second's pause. Then, 'You're Bishop.'

'If you say so.'

'I do.'

'So what shall I call you?'

'My name's not important,' the man said. The clipped voice came with a slight echo behind it. He sounded amused. In control. Which he clearly was at present. Bishop hated him already.

'In that case, why don't I just call you Merv? There was a kid in high school by that name who got caught flashing in the girls' toilets one time. Your voice reminds me of him.'

The man sighed. 'Sticks and stones, Bishop. You'll have to do better than that.'

'Sticks and stones were all I needed to deal with Abraham. Might make more of an effort when you and I meet up, though.'

The man snorted. 'Do you want some friendly advice?'

'Love some.'

'Disappear,' he said. 'You may think you're a threat to me, but you're not. Not even close. Believe me, you're totally out of

254

your league on this, so your best bet is to go home and forget all
about it.'

'Sounds like great advice. Oh, just one thing, though. Selina has
to come with me.'

'Selina? Oh, you mean Sonja Addison.' He chuckled. 'Yeah, I know
all about her real history. You'd be surprised at how successful we are
at getting people to pour out their secrets. As for letting her go, well,
that's not really possible at this late stage. Not now that everything's
been squared away. You understand.'

'Sure,' Bishop said. 'I can't really walk away, either. I've just realized
I can't have you breathing the same air as me. Especially not after
what you did to her mother.'

The man chuckled again. 'You heard about that, did you? Well,
that's life for you. Just goes to show you can get killed cross—'

Bishop pressed the red button and dropped the phone back in the
glove compartment. He wouldn't get anything else from the bastard
except more empty threats and smug retorts, so why prolong things?

Vallejo said, 'Who was that? Olander?'

'Not unless he's lost his mid-Atlantic accent. But he sounded like
a man clearly used to giving orders and having those orders obeyed.
Maybe a partner of some kind. Olander might have provided the seed
money and the clout, but the guy on the phone is running things.
I'm sure of it.'

'So you get anything useful from the conversation?'

Bishop shrugged. 'Not much. There was a slight echo when he
spoke, so I got the impression he was in a room with a high ceiling.'

'Like a warehouse?'

'Could be. Also, he used the term *everything's been squared away.*'

'So?'

'So that's not normal-speak. Your average person might say
"arranged" or "taken care of". But not "squared away". I've never
heard that one used outside the Marine Corps.'

'You're right. I've heard my dad use the phrase sometimes, but that's
about it.' Vallejo frowned. 'Does that make a difference?'

'Not sure. I know Abraham was ex-navy.' He tapped his fingers against the steering wheel. 'I guess it just means that I'm likely to be up against some well-trained men.'

Vallejo turned to him. 'You mean *we'll* be up against them.'

'That's what I said. We.'

SIXTY-FOUR

At 23.27, Bishop saw two men emerge from the shadows of the warehouse and walk towards the parked cars. He grabbed the scope from the dash and said, 'Wake up, Vallejo. We got something.'

'I am awake,' she said. 'Just resting my eyes, that's all.'

'Sure.' He looked through the eyepiece and saw both men were making plenty of arm movements. Looked like they were arguing about something. One of them had very light hair. Possibly white or light grey. The other looked nondescript from this range. He handed the scope to Vallejo. 'One of them could be Olander.'

She looked in silence for a few moments, fought a yawn, then handed it back to Bishop. 'Looks like it. We'll know for sure in a second.'

Bishop put the scope to his eye again. The two men were just standing there, about twenty feet from the cars. Still arguing. Then the light-haired man shook his head and walked over to his car, while the other man watched.

The light-haired man got into the Jag and pulled away as the other man walked back to the warehouse. The front gate opened automatically when the Jag was within a few feet of it, and as soon as there was enough space he drove through. Bishop kept the scope on the front windshield all the way. When he was about to pass by, Bishop could see from the Jag's dashboard illumination that it was the same man as in the photo.

'Now there's a man clinging to the past,' Vallejo said. 'Check out the vanity plate.'

Bishop lowered the scope and got a flash of the licence plate. *AZMAYOR.*

'Real subtle,' Bishop said. 'I guess it must make him feel important.'

He aimed the scope down the hill again. The gate was closed. The man had retreated back into the building. Everything was still.

Vallejo turned to him. 'Frightened women arriving with escorts. Armed guards. Security fencing all around. Grant Olander on site. I don't know about you, Bishop, but this is looking more and more like the place.'

But was Selina in there? That was the question foremost in Bishop's mind. He leaned his elbow on the armrest and rubbed a palm over his buzz cut. 'Hmm,' he said.

'And what does "hmm" mean?'

'It means I need more intel. I don't like the thought of going in blind and there's only one way to solve that.'

Vallejo gave a single bark of laughter. 'There it is. I *knew* you brought me out here for a reason. Don't tell me. I'm picked for lookout duty. And here I was, actually believing we were gonna go in together.'

Bishop sighed. 'And we will, Vallejo. This is just a recon. I'm not prepared for anything more than that right now.'

'Sure. And what if you happen to see Selina in there? You telling me you'll just leave her where she is and come back out again?'

'That's something I can't answer until I get an idea of the layout. If she's in there and she's under the watch of a single guard and I think I've got a chance, then yeah, I might try and bring her out. But only if I think I can do it without getting us both killed in the process. I've come too far to risk her life unnecessarily with a half-assed rescue attempt.'

Vallejo watched him for a moment, then nodded. 'Okay, but what if there are surveillance cameras? They'll make you the moment you get over the fence.'

He shook his head. 'Night-time cameras need ambient light to work with, and I don't see any lights out there.'

'But you don't *know*.'

'No, I don't. But that's why I've got you here.'

Vallejo gave a deep sigh. 'Why do I get the feeling you had this planned from the start, Bishop? And why am *I* the lookout?'

Bishop reached over, opened the glove compartment again and pulled out the hands-free cable with microphone and earpiece. 'Because you got better night vision than me,' he said.

'Oh, yeah? How do you figure that?'

'I saw you driving last night, remember? With no lights. In the dark. Like it was day. Or am I wrong?'

She shrugged. 'You're not wrong. My dad always said I was born with the eyes of a cat. So we going to keep in contact by cell phone? That's pretty low-tech, isn't it?'

'You can only work with what you've got.'

'And what about the armed guards? You given them any thought?'

'Sure,' he said and pulled the Sig out from under the seat. He checked the magazine again. It still held fifteen rounds, with one in the pipe. Same as the last time he'd checked.

'Don't suppose you got a licence for that thing.'

He blinked at her. 'Would it make any difference?'

She smiled. 'I guess not. You know as soon as you use it, the whole world'll come crashing down on you.'

'If I have to use it, everything's already gone to hell. This is strictly for insurance. But I learned long ago it's better to have a gun and not need it than the other way round.'

'Right out of the police manual,' she said. 'So when you going in?'

'The moment somebody else opens that gate.'

SIXTY-FIVE

It was 02.07 when Bishop heard Vallejo whisper in his ear, 'Heads up, we've got company.' He looked to his left and two seconds later spotted the faint hint of headlights coming his way.

'I see it,' he whispered into the microphone, and turned his face away in order to retain his night vision. He just concentrated on the sound of the tyres crunching along the road as the vehicle got closer.

Bishop was lying flat, next to the fence, about twenty-five feet to the right of the front gate. Far enough away for an approaching car's headlights not to reach him. He had the ski mask on, so all anyone looking would see was a black mass on the ground. He hoped.

'He's about thirty feet from the gate,' Vallejo whispered. 'Two-door sedan of some kind. I can only see the driver in there. Twenty feet.'

'Copy that.' Bishop just lay there. Waiting. Listening. The sound of the engine became steadily louder until the vehicle came to a halt. A door opened. No other sounds. Guy was probably wearing sneakers. Or shoes with rubber soles. Like Bishop.

'He's putting in the code now. And no, I can't make it out.'

Bishop smiled under the mask. After a few moments he heard the sound of a lock being disengaged, accompanied by an electronic whine. Then Bishop heard the car door slam shut. The engine idled for eleven more seconds before the driver began moving the car forward. The electronic humming continued. The sound of the engine grew fainter.

'He's heading left, towards the other parked cars.'

Bishop moved his head and saw the vehicle's rear lights getting smaller. The gate stopped moving.

'No sign of the guard yet,' Vallejo said.

The electronic hum started up again and the gate began to close.

'I still don't see him,' she said. 'Come on, you . . . Okay, there he is. Approaching from the left side of the warehouse. You should be able to see him any second now. He's about two hundred yards from you. Gate's half closed already. You've got a clear run. If you're gonna move, better do it now.'

He saw the guard in the distance with his back to Bishop. Just as Vallejo described. Bishop jumped to his feet and sprinted for the gate, covering the twenty-five feet in three seconds. He dived through the gap and kept rolling. He heard the gate click shut behind him, got up and kept running towards the right-hand building a hundred yards away. The length of a football field. Easy. He focused on the building and nothing else. Just went full out. He reached it fifteen seconds later, slightly out of breath, but still alert. Still ready for anything.

'Nice going, marathon man,' Vallejo said in his ear. 'Guard's talking to the new arrival. Another guy in casual clothes.'

'Uh huh.' Bishop checked his immediate surroundings. Vallejo wouldn't be much help to him now. Too many blind spots from her position in the car. If there was another guard working the perimeter, he'd know about it before she did.

He was in front of a concrete building with two steel roll-up doors, one on either side of him. No light coming through the cracks. The eastern wall of the main warehouse was about forty or fifty yards away, shrouded in deep shadow. He stayed where he was for a few moments. Just waiting. Ready to act if he saw movement. His theory regarding surveillance cameras had sounded good, but if he was wrong he'd find out soon enough.

Seconds passed and nothing happened. Vallejo was quiet. The guard must still be acting as normal. Which meant there was no alert out, and no cameras.

He ran over to the warehouse. Once he reached it, he stayed close to the steel wall and moved towards the northern side. He didn't pass any doors or entrances along the way. When he reached the end, he peered round the corner and saw movement. A human-shaped silhouette about fifty feet away.

Bishop quickly pulled his head back and said, 'Is the guard still talking to the guy?'

'Yeah, they're walking back now. Where are you?'

'Main warehouse. North-east corner. We got a second guard back here.'

'Copy that.'

Bishop crouched down and poked part of his head round again. The shape was bigger. The man was about twenty feet away now and getting closer. Ambling along. Bored, probably. Looked about five-ten. Thick build. Bishop ducked back again and stood up, back against the wall. So either two guards were patrolling the same part of the warehouse, which made no sense, or one guy stayed inside and only came out to check when a new arrival came in. Probably from an electronic signal whenever the gate was activated.

Bishop stayed totally still, breathing through his mouth, listening to the faint sounds of feet on gravel.

He waited.

When the guard came round the corner five seconds later, Bishop made a fist of his left hand and jabbed upwards, the middle knuckles of his fingers striking the guard just under his right ear. Where the nerves were. The guard made a soft grunt and began to crumple. Bishop grabbed the unconscious man round the waist and slowly lowered him to the ground.

He got up and peered round the corner again. Just in time to see two more distant silhouettes disappear into an opening in the warehouse.

Bishop took off his ski mask and looked down at the guard. Last time he'd tried that move, the victim had stayed unconscious for over half an hour. And he'd been a lot bigger than this guy. Should give him enough time. Still, he couldn't leave him out here in the open.

The guard was wearing a dark nylon windbreaker over a pale shirt and dark pants. Bishop removed the jacket and placed it on the ground next to him. He also removed the man's duty belt and holster. The gun was a new-looking Taurus 909 9mm. Bishop checked the contents of the belt pouches. They contained a pair of handcuffs, a Maglite, a Cobra walkie-talkie, a set of keys, and a thin vial of pepper spray.

Everything a growing boy needs.

Bishop fastened the belt round his own waist, but turned off the walkie-talkie. He didn't need it going off at the wrong moment. Then, after making sure he held the only keys, he turned the guard onto his stomach and cuffed the man's hands behind him.

Hefting the man over his shoulder, Bishop carried him fifty yards to the concrete building and set him down against the rear wall. He took a few moments to get his breath back. The guy was heavier than he looked. Then he took the small roll of duct tape from his jacket pocket and spent a minute binding the man's feet and gagging him.

He was painfully aware that knocking out a guard was the best way of alerting the enemy of his presence here, which would inevitably mean an increase in security. But if the guard couldn't be found anywhere on the premises, and if nobody actually saw Bishop, they wouldn't know what to think. They might presume the guard just upped and left for whatever reason. Possibly. But it meant that once Bishop had seen what he needed, he'd have to take this guy back with him and keep him on ice. It wouldn't be easy, but he couldn't see a way round it.

Bishop jogged back to his previous spot and peered round the north-east corner. Nobody in sight. He picked up the guard's jacket and put it on over his own. The sleeves were a little short, but it would do. Then he turned the corner and began walking along the north side of the warehouse, towards the entrance the other guard had used.

He passed a featureless steel door he figured had to be the fire exit and kept going. He found what he wanted at the far end. At first glance, it looked like another fire door, except this one also had a small window at about head height. There was a suggestion of light coming from within. There was also a keypad affixed to the wall to the left of the door. Bishop sidled up to the window and glanced inside. All he saw was a narrow hallway that ended in a windowless door about thirty feet away. The dim light came from a single ceiling light at that end. Either a low-wattage bulb or one near the end of its life.

And beyond that door was what? Part of him expected to find Selina in there somewhere, but the lack of security concerned him.

Correction: lack of *visible* security. He could have already tripped a dozen alarms on the way here. The enemy might already be aware of his presence, calmly waiting for him to enter the trap. Like a spider welcoming the fly. No way of telling. Well, he'd just have to risk it. There were no other options.

Bishop studied the keypad. It was the standard configuration. Twelve buttons. One to ten, plus a star and a hash. If he had the time and an unlimited number of attempts, he could probably get in. But he didn't have time, and he probably only had three tries. That was usually how it worked. Pursing his lips, he thought of the guard back there and wondered if he was the type of person who trusted his own memory. Lots of people didn't.

Bishop felt the man's inner jacket pockets, pulled out a wallet and opened it. There was a driver's licence for a George Ross, a couple of credit cards, some cash. But in one of the pockets there were some business cards. Bishop slid them out and slowly flipped through them. Nothing caught his eye. He turned the cards over and flipped through again. Halfway through, he stopped. Went back one. There. Some numbers written on the back.

'What's going on?' Vallejo said, interrupting his thoughts.

'I'm at the rear entrance,' he said. 'About to go inside. Probably best if we maintain radio silence from now on. I'm gonna hang up now, so only call if there's an emergency, okay? Anything else, you can text.'

'Got it. Out.'

Bishop closed the connection and put the earpiece in his pocket. Then he looked at the numbers. There were three sets of figures, jotted down at various angles. 037889, 7249 and 11072. The middle one looked like a PIN number, so he tried the first one. Nothing happened. Maybe it was the combination to the exterior gate. He tried 11072 next. A second later, he heard a metallic click in the door and smiled.

He checked his watch. It was 02.11. With one hand resting on the holstered gun, Bishop pulled the door open and entered the warehouse.

SIXTY-SIX

Vallejo checked the time again. It was 02.24. Almost fifteen minutes since she'd last spoken to Bishop. And no other vehicles had arrived. It was just her out here.

She was getting antsy now and hated herself for it. It wasn't like her. She'd been on countless stakeouts before and had always been the cool and collected one. Always. She never got nervous. Her male colleagues had even awarded her the nickname *Icegirl*, after one of the characters in that superhero team movie from a while back. She had a feeling it wasn't meant to be entirely complimentary, but she actually considered it a huge honour. Not that she'd ever admit it to anyone, of course. *So what makes this situation any different?*

Maybe it was because she was the sole back-up. Bishop had said to give him half an hour. After that, if she still hadn't heard from him, the ball was in her court. Call in the police or do whatever she thought best. Sure. Like she had a wealth of other options from which to choose. Part of her wanted to call him for a status update, but she wasn't about to do something that dumb, either. She was only to contact him in an emergency, and feeling anxious didn't really qualify.

So just be cool, Icegirl, she told herself. *You've still got another fifteen minutes before you have to make a decision.*

Leaning her head back against the seat rest, Vallejo stared out the windshield as she thought about Bishop. They'd only known each other for just over twenty-four hours – *Jesus, was that all?* – but she felt she'd gotten to know him as well as anybody in that time. And she still couldn't figure him out. Not entirely. All she really knew for sure was that he was pretty much capable of anything. Which was both good and bad, depending on the circumstances. He didn't give too much thought to going outside the law, either, and that still made her a little uncomfortable. Like last night, when he'd talked about questioning Selina's husband and that drug dealer back east, he'd kept it all pretty vague. Vallejo got the feeling the methods he'd used to get them to talk had probably been fairly extreme. Had he resorted to torture to get the information he wanted? And if so, did she really want to know?

And present company excepted, his deep-seated antipathy towards the police was a big puzzle, too. The wrongful arrest four years ago and subsequent imprisonment only partly explained it. After all, the police weren't the ones who'd set him up. She had an idea there was something else in his past that had turned him against them, but she didn't feel too comfortable probing him about it. And it was really none of her business anyway.

She checked the time again. 02.27. *What is he doing in there?*

Vallejo closed her eyes and forced herself to relax. He was doing what he set out to do. Getting a layout of the place before both of them went in for real. Despite what he'd said earlier, she didn't think he'd try to bring out Selina yet, even if he felt it was possible. Not when there were still other women in there in the same situation. *That* much she knew about Bishop. It would be all or nothing.

Inevitably, her thoughts turned to Samantha again. And the empty hole that had opened up in her psyche since learning of her murder. She'd told Bishop she'd more or less been prepared for the worst, but that was a lie. She hadn't at all. Up till now, she'd been surviving on bravado and false hope. It was what had kept her going all this time. And now, to be faced with the fact that Sam was gone forever was almost unbearable.

But she wouldn't cry. Not any more. That part was over with. Bishop had disposed of her murderer, but there was still the man who'd given the order. The one on the phone. One way or another, he'd pay. That was all she cared about now. That, and the other women still in there.

Vallejo snapped her eyes open at the sound of feet on gravel. Running feet.

Straight ahead, she saw a dark figure jogging up the shallow hill towards the car. It was Bishop. Had to be. The perimeter gate was closing behind him. He had his gun in his left hand. She couldn't see his pursuers.

Without thought, she started the engine and immediately put it in reverse. The rear wheels fought against the earth as she backed up, then she spun the wheel left and accelerated towards the road. Just as she reached it, Bishop came level and yanked the passenger door open and jumped in.

'Let's go,' he said. 'Now.'

SIXTY-SEVEN

Once they were on Highway 60, Bishop said, 'Ease down, nobody's following us.'

Vallejo checked the rear-view, but gradually slowed a little. 'You sure about that?'

'Pretty sure.' He rubbed a hand over his face and looked out at the darkness ahead. 'Make that *definitely* sure.'

'So you're saying nobody saw you?'

Bishop made a harsh sound through his nose. 'Not exactly.'

'I don't get you.'

He took a deep breath and slowly blew it out. 'It's not Olander.'

'It's not?'

'Uh, uh. The guy's no saint, but he's not responsible for the missing women, and he sure hasn't killed anybody. That much I'm certain of. To be honest, I had my doubts from the first, but I needed to know for sure.'

'But those girls in the van . . .'

'. . . are paid employees, same as everybody else in that place.' He turned to her. 'You want to know why they've got security guards outside? Why they work mostly at night and try and keep a low profile? They're shooting porn movies in there. There's probably other shady stuff going on, but mostly it's just simple voyeurism for the masses.'

'*Porn* movies?'

'Porn movies. And pretty extreme ones, from what I saw. Maybe that's why those women we saw arriving didn't look too enthusiastic about the night ahead.'

'Okay. Tell me what happened.'

268

Bishop told her about getting into the warehouse, and went on, 'I passed through some empty offices and ended up in a stockroom containing dozens of wooden crates. Then I heard this girl screaming and crying in the next room and pushed the door open. It was decked out like a schoolroom. Cameras and lights everywhere. About five or six people all focused on the action at the head of the class, where this really young-looking girl was lying spread-eagled on the teacher's desk, getting "gang-raped" by three naked old dudes.'

Vallejo winced. 'Please tell me she wasn't underage.'

'Uh, uh. She was just one of those undeveloped girls who look a lot younger than their years. She showed me her driver's licence later and she'd celebrated her eighteenth birthday ten months before. Even so, it was pretty sick stuff. I can only assume there's a big market out there for schoolgirl rape fantasies.'

'Yeah, there is. Makes me despair of the human race sometimes. Where am I going, by the way? Back to the motel?'

'Might as well. All your stuff's there.'

'So what happened next?'

'One of the camera operators noticed me standing there with a gun in my hand and cried out. Everyone froze in their tracks. Even the actors. It was almost funny, the positions they were in. The girl was looking at me like I'd just landed from another planet. Things got kind of weird after that. Or should I say weird*er*.'

'What do you mean?'

'I mean one of the camera operators just looked at me and said, "*So Ramirez finally found us then.*" I didn't know what the hell he was talking about, so I just said nothing. I think they all assumed I was from some rival outfit, or maybe a cop on the take, come to close them down or something. They were all scared shitless. Which was fine by me. Made them easier to control. Then I noticed one of them whispering into a walkie-talkie so I took it from him and waited by the door. When the guard came through I knocked him out, then accused the others of filming kiddie porn. That's when the girl ran over to her clothes and showed me her licence. Then I noticed a couple of other doors on the other side of the room. I ordered everyone to walk in front of me and for the girl to open the doors and show me what was behind them.'

'Which was what?'

'More "locations". One room was laid out like a Turkish bath. The other one was a fake gym. People were actually filming some kind of orgy in that one, so we closed the door without alerting them. I already had enough on my hands. The girl told me there were about fifteen more film sets spread around the warehouse and I believed her. By that point, I already knew I was wasting my time.'

Bishop rubbed his palm through his hair and said, 'Then I was about to make my exit when one of the men came over and placed a fat envelope in my hands. Said he hoped five grand would be enough to convince me not to tell my boss that I'd found them.'

Vallejo took her eyes from the road and looked at him. 'Bishop, you didn't.'

He reached into his jacket pocket, brought out the envelope and placed it on the dashboard. 'Seemed rude not to. Besides, it should cover my expenses.'

Vallejo shook her head and said, 'But why were you running back there? I thought you were being chased.'

'No, I wasn't being chased. But I was fairly sure an alert had been sent out and I wanted to get us away from there ASAP. I don't need more complications right now.'

After a few moments Vallejo said, 'We got problems, don't we?'

'We sure do. Less than twenty-four hours to find Selina and I'm right back where I started.'

They drove in silence for a while. They passed the turnoff for Saracen and kept on going. Another few minutes and Bishop noticed the familiar motel sign, all lit up like a beacon for the marooned. That's how he felt at the moment. Stranded. Treading water. And what about Selina? What had been done to her? And what was supposed to happen to her tomorrow? What he needed to do more than anything was make new plans to locate her, but he was exhausted and his mind felt sluggish. He had to get some rest. Just three or four hours would be enough. And then he could start again. From scratch, if need be. Giving up simply wasn't an option.

Vallejo said, 'We've made *some* progress, Bishop. I think you had the right idea, just the wrong location. We're still looking for somewhere that's big enough to hold a lot of women for long periods, and a warehouse is still our best bet.'

'Lot of warehouses in this part of the country. You want to check every one?'

Vallejo slowed as they got closer to the motel entrance. 'Well, there must be some way we can narrow down the possibilities. There has to be.'

'Yeah, you're right,' he said as she pulled into the court and steered them towards her Fusion, still parked outside her old room. 'Maybe we'll think of something in the morning, when we're fresher.'

Vallejo stopped the car, but left the engine running. 'It's already morning.'

'Later *this* morning, then.' Bishop tapped a finger against his lower lip as he looked around the empty forecourt. He'd already planned on finding alternative lodgings for himself. In a situation like this, it was a good idea not to stay in one place too long. For the same reason, he didn't feel too comfortable about leaving Vallejo here on her own. That felt like just asking for trouble. 'Look,' he said, 'I was going to find another motel for myself. I know you're tired, but I'd feel a whole lot better if you came with me. Better safe than sorry.'

She frowned at him for few moments, then said, 'We-e-ell, there's a town called Salome about ten miles west of here. I only passed through the once, but I'm pretty sure I saw a motel sign along the main drag. I think I could probably stay awake until we got there.'

'Fine,' Bishop said. 'Grab your gear and I'll follow you.'

SIXTY-EIGHT

The owner of the motel in Salome clearly wasn't too happy about having his beauty sleep interrupted. But in the current economic climate, he wasn't about to turn down an easy eighty bucks, either. They got two rooms right next to each other and parked their vehicles directly outside. Bishop grabbed his toothbrush from the glove compartment, locked the Buick and walked over to his room. Vallejo already had her own door half open when she turned to him and said, 'Shit. The hard drive. I hid it in the new room's air-conditioning vent like you suggested, and then promptly forgot all about it. It's still there.'

'And it'll still be there tomorrow,' Bishop said. 'Get some sleep first.'

Vallejo gave him a weary smile. 'Yeah, you're right. I'll go get it in the morning.'

Without another word, Bishop entered his room, undressed and fell into bed. Next thing he knew, it was five hours later and he felt a little more like his old self. After a quick shower, he dressed and left the room. He was about to knock on Vallejo's door when he noticed her Fusion was gone from the bay. She'd obviously gone to get the hard drive from the other motel. So the question was, wait here or follow?

Bishop didn't think about it for long. Given the choice, he usually opted for movement over inertia. He got into the Buick, pulled out onto the highway and headed east. It was a typical Sunday morning, which meant he practically had the road to himself. When he finally pulled into the Amber Motel forecourt a short while later, it was 08.55.

And her Fusion wasn't there. And it hadn't passed him on the way in, either.

It didn't have to mean anything. Vallejo could have simply decided to get some coffee or an early breakfast in town. But even as he thought it, it didn't ring true. Today was the last chance they had of finding Selina, and she would have waited for him so they could discuss their next move. As sure as taxes.

He scanned the courtyard and the only other vehicle was the Lincoln he'd seen twice before, parked next to the front office. He glanced in there as he passed, but couldn't see the manager. Probably still asleep in the back.

Bishop slowly circled around the pool and parked in front of No. 17. He took the .38 Special from under the seat and checked the chamber. Then he got out and approached the room. He tried the handle. It was unlocked. Left hand gripping the gun, he pushed the door open until it banged lightly against the wall.

The room was empty. The bed was still made. Bishop stepped inside and listened. No sounds other than the occasional vehicle passing by outside. He quickly checked the bathroom. Empty. But he detected a familiar medicinal odour in the air. Barely noticeable, but there. He didn't like that smell at all.

He came out and stepped over to the desk and saw the chair underneath was at angle. He pulled it out and saw Vallejo's shoeprints on the cushion. He picked it up and set it down under the air conditioning grille in the wall. Bishop stood on the chair and saw the four corner screws were still jutting out slightly. He reached up and used just his thumb and index finger to unscrew them. When the third one was out he let the aluminium grille swing free, then reached in and moved his hand around the vent. As he'd suspected, the hard drive was no longer there.

He replaced the grille and stepped off the chair, frowning as he wiped the dust from his hands. Again, no real evidence of anything untoward. Vallejo had come here for the drive, after all. So why was his gut telling him this was all wrong? That she'd been interrupted in her efforts by the people they were after? Well, there was that smell.

He knew from personal experience that chloroform gave off that kind of odour. It was pretty dirty inside the vent, too. So it was a good bet that after extracting the hard drive she'd gone into the bathroom to wash her hands. With the tap running, they could have taken her by surprise. Simply come up from behind, chloroformed her and then taken her to wherever.

He began to search the room, looking for a sign. Looking for something. *Any*thing. If she'd been snatched, then the enemy would have guessed Bishop might come back here to check on her. Which meant they would have left a message of some kind. He tried the side drawers. They held nothing but a bible and a free magazine advertising local attractions. In the refrigerator he saw two cans of coke and an unopened bottle of wine. He took a good look under the bed. Checked under the pillows and mattress. Went over the bathroom again, inch by inch.

Nothing.

He cast his eyes around the main room once more, stopping when they landed on the front door. It was still wide open. He went over and gently closed it. And there, taped to the back, was a small sheet of notepaper, folded in half. Bishop took it off and unfolded it.

There was a single word on it. Written in large capitals.

WAIT.

SIXTY-NINE

When Bishop pulled up outside Raymond Massingham's place twenty minutes later, he saw Kate's Subaru was already there. He'd kept it short over the phone, just asked her to meet him at Raymond's and not to tell anybody else.

He took a moment to rein in his anger. It wasn't easy. Not now the enemy had two people he cared about in their grasp. But above all, he needed a clear head if he was going to get them back. Giving in to his emotions would just slow him down. And he had just over half a day left on the clock. Willing himself to remain calm and objective, he got out and walked back to the rear entrance where he pounded twice on the door. Kate opened it, looking good in a generic long-sleeved shirt and combat pants. He barely noticed.

'What's wrong?' she asked.

'Everything,' Bishop said, and slipped past her and on into Raymond's workroom.

Raymond looked up and waved a hand at Bishop as he entered. He was wearing Bermuda shorts and a T-shirt and sitting in the same seat as last night, sipping from a cup. Bishop smelled coffee. Kate went over and perched against Raymond's desk, watching Bishop.

'So what's this all about?' she asked. 'And how come Clarissa's not with you?'

Bishop took the only other seat and said, 'We had a busy time of it last night and finally crashed about six hours ago. In a different motel from where we'd been staying. But Vallejo said she'd left something in her old room and went back for it this morning, before I got up.' He took the note from his pocket and handed it over. 'I've just come back from there, and found her car gone and

275

this left for me. I also noticed a faint chloroform odour in the bathroom.'

Kate looked at the piece of paper, then showed it to Raymond. 'You mean these people just kidnapped her? How can they do that?'

'Easily. It's what they do. Believe me, they're specialists at this kind of thing.'

Raymond started at the note and said, 'Wait for what, exactly?'

Bishop sighed. 'Wait at the motel. Wait for a phone call. Wait for further instructions. It could mean anything. Or nothing.'

'What are you going to do?' Kate asked.

'Well, I don't plan on answering my phone for a while. If they can't get hold of me, they can't give me instructions. I've got a feeling whatever they want me to do, I won't like.'

'But you won't be able to hold them off forever. There's no telling what they might do to Clarissa if they can't get reach you.'

'Yeah, I'm walking a tightrope, but I need some time to think and plan. The most important thing is to figure out where their headquarters are. Unfortunately, I'm still no closer to that than when I arrived two days ago.'

Kate bit her bottom lip. 'Well, I could drive you over to Olander's house. Maybe if we confront him direct . . .'

'It's not Olander,' he said.

'What are you talking about?'

'We were at his warehouse last night. I managed to find a way in and look around. I know exactly what he's doing in there and it isn't holding women against their will.'

Raymond leaned forward in his seat. 'So what *is* going on in there?'

Bishop quickly described everything he'd seen last night. When he'd finished, Kate looked as though she'd just stepped in something.

'So Olander's nothing but a *porn* merchant?' she said. 'I expected something more . . . more . . . Actually, I don't know *what* I expected. Just not *that.*'

'Well, I saw some large crates in one of the rooms. No idea what was inside, but it could be he's got all kinds of stuff going on on the sidelines. Counterfeit goods, maybe. Whatever it is, I don't care.' He leaned back in the chair and sighed as he stared at the ceiling. 'All the signs were telling me I was on the wrong track, but I had to check and make sure. And now I've got to start all over again.'

'You lost me,' Kate said. 'What signs?'

He turned to her. 'Yesterday, you and Neeson told us Olander hasn't really acted any differently in the last few years. Yet he drives around in an imported Jaguar, probably the only one in the whole state. And he's got a vanity licence plate to remind everyone what an important figure he used to be. This is clearly a guy with an ego.'

Raymond looked at Kate and said, 'That sounds like Olander, all right.'

'Okay,' Bishop said, 'so if he's at the head of a racket that's bringing in untold millions every year, why isn't he flashing his money around more? Like buying a bigger house, for instance? He doesn't strike me as the kind of guy who quietly spirits his money away in an offshore account; he needs people to see what a big man he is. Also, there wasn't nearly enough security at the warehouse. Just a couple of guards. That's enough to deter casual trespassers, but not much more than that.'

Kate stared at one of the pictures on the wall and tapped her fingernails on the desk. 'But what about his clandestine meetings with Abraham? And Distar? That can't just be coincidence.'

'Yeah, well, I've been thinking about that.' Bishop told them about his brief phone conversation last night with Abraham's boss and said, 'The main impression I got from this guy was that he's somebody who doesn't leave much to chance. It could be he set up Distar purely as a decoy to wrong-foot anybody who follows the paper trail route, like we did. Kind of like a tripwire to give him advance warning that somebody's looking in places they shouldn't. Then he can act accordingly. I mean, he's known about me practically since I arrived in town, but so far he's felt secure enough to label me a minor nuisance. But he must have got word somehow that I broke into Olander's warehouse last night, and that tells him I've made the Distar connection. I'm getting close to him and he doesn't like that. So since he couldn't find me, he took Vallejo as extra insurance.'

Kate was shaking her head. 'But we only made the Distar connection because I knew about those vans he screwed out of Kinney.'

'We got lucky and just fast-tracked it, that's all. But it's dollars to doughnuts that if you were to dig into Distar further, you'd find plenty of signs pointing to Olander.'

'Okay, so how do you explain the relationship with Abraham?'

Bishop shrugged. 'I think, there, we just added two and two together and came up with five. They worked together a long time, don't forget. They could simply have remained in friendly contact ever since. Nothing more.'

Kate was silent for a few moments, looking at the floor with a single line visible across her brow. Bishop could almost see the wheels turning. Then she said, 'Look, Bishop, the more I'm hearing, the more I'm convinced we should bring the police in on this. If they've kidnapped Clarissa, who's *also* a cop I might add, then this is a damn sight more serious than I imagined.'

'You don't know the half of it,' he said. 'But no police. I don't exactly trust them right now.'

Kate and Raymond exchanged a look, then she said, 'You're right, we *don't* know the half of it. So why don't you fill us in on what's really going on here? You never know, we might be able to help.'

Bishop looked at her. Journalist or not, it wasn't an unreasonable request. Truth was, he needed all the help he could get right now. But he couldn't expect them to give it without knowing the facts.

So he told them what he knew. Or most of it. About what Hewitt had seen at Selina's place a month before, and the connection with the hospital in Garrick. He mentioned the similarities between Selina and Sam, then described the murders of Hewitt and Rutherford, and how he'd almost joined them thanks to that fire. He also gave them Tatem's version of events, and told how his employees kept him in line by imprisoning his wife. He spoke about their MO of 'accidental' house fires to cover their tracks. He told them what little he'd learned from Abraham and the unnamed man on the other end of Abraham's phone. He also told them of his own suspicions that somebody on the Saracen PD was somehow involved.

When he was finally done, Kate said, 'Wow. But look, why do you assume . . . ?'

'Hey, time out,' Bishop said and held up a hand. He turned to Raymond. 'Before we go any further, how about making us some more of that fine-smelling coffee?'

'Don't see why not,' Raymond said and got to his feet.

SEVENTY

Vallejo awoke to the muted sounds of running water coming from a nearby room. She had a headache and her mouth felt dry. She slowly opened her eyes and stared at the ceiling. She was lying on a bed, but clearly not in her motel room. Then she remembered. She'd been leaning over the bathroom sink of No.17, soaping her hands, when it happened. She hadn't even heard them enter the room. All she knew was when a thick arm grabbed her round the neck and pulled her up. Then somebody smothered her face with a damp cloth and pressed a hand against it. The medicinal smell was overpowering. She had time enough to think *chloroform*, and then there was only oblivion.

And now she was here. Wherever *here* was.

She slowly turned her head and saw she was in a sparsely furnished bedroom. The first thing she noticed was the lack of windows. Just blank walls all around, except for two doors on opposite sides of the bed. She raised herself to a sitting position, the pounding in her head increasing with the movement.

The sound of water stopped and the door to her left opened. A woman in a long-sleeved sweater and black jeans came out and said, 'Oh, you're awake.'

I guess I am, Vallejo thought, but said nothing. The woman was about Vallejo's age and very pretty, with the high cheekbones of a model, and large, sad eyes. Her skin was as white as alabaster and she wore her shoulder-length brown hair in a ponytail. From the decor and from what Bishop had told her, Vallejo figured this must be the surgeon's wife. Which meant Vallejo was in a whole heap of trouble. She wondered if Bishop was even aware she was missing yet.

'Are you okay?' the woman asked. 'Do you want anything? Some water?'

'Water sounds good,' Vallejo said.

The woman smiled and said, 'Wait here.' Then she disappeared through the other doorway, returning a few seconds later with a large tumbler of water.

Vallejo took it and drank it in one go. Plain water had never tasted so good. Even the headache didn't seem so bad any more.

She handed the glass back and said, 'Thanks. Is your name Patricia Tatem?'

The woman frowned. 'That's right. How do you know me? Who are you?'

'I'm Clarissa Vallejo.' She swung her legs off the bed. 'And your husband mentioned you to a man I know. I don't suppose you've got the time?'

Patricia showed her bare wrists. 'No watch. And no clocks. Besides, what difference would it make in here?'

'You've got a point.' Vallejo looked around the room and sighed. 'It looks like we might be roommates for a while, so how about giving me the five-cent tour?'

'Okay, but there's not much to see.'

Vallejo got up off the bed and let Patricia lead the way. She opened the door through which she'd gone to fetch the water, and Vallejo stepped through and found herself in the main living area. It was about twice the size of the bedroom. There was a kitchenette off to one side and a steel door in the far wall. To her left was a large TV with piles of DVDs stacked against the wall. Another wall was taken up by two large bookcases filled with paperbacks and magazines. Everything looked neat and tidy. Orderly. In the centre of the room was a large couch, an easy chair, and a coffee table with a single, open paperback on the surface.

Vallejo turned to Patricia. 'Guess you don't get too many visitors, huh?'

Patricia wrapped her arms across her chest. 'None that I want to talk about.'

'You been here a long time?'

Patricia made a harsh sound through her nostrils. 'You can't imagine.'

She was right. Vallejo couldn't. At least in prison you were allowed out for exercise. But to be stuck within these walls for what might be forever? *Jesus. The poor woman.*

'So my husband, Adrian. Is he all right?'

'Far as I know,' Vallejo said. 'He was . . .'

She stopped at the sound of a heavy bolt being drawn. Both women turned their heads towards the steel door. It swung open and a blank-faced man stepped into the room. He was holding an automatic pistol and took his position by the side of the doorway. All Vallejo could see through the opening was a grey wall. Then another man came in, carrying a large cardboard box, which he took over to the kitchenette and placed on a counter.

He left and a third man entered. Vallejo knew instantly that this was the man in charge. Possibly the same guy Bishop spoke to on the cell last night. He was about six feet tall and wore a dark grey shirt and black pants that fit his powerful physique perfectly. His dark hair was cut short and his features were regular, except for a drooping right eyelid which only made him seem more threatening. But both eyes were the kind that looked right through you.

He nodded his head towards the kitchenette and said, 'Your latest food supplies, Patricia. Why don't you go and unpack?'

Vallejo watched as Patricia shuffled towards the kitchenette and said, 'So what do I call you?'

'You don't,' the man said. 'Where's Bishop?'

'How the hell do I know? Some other motel, I expect. He didn't see fit to tell me which one. He did tell me he doesn't like staying in one place too long, though.'

Those merciless eyes of his just bored right into her for a few moments. Then he smiled and said, 'Sit down, Clarissa.'

She took a look at the impassive guard, then sat on the couch. 'You know me?'

'Naturally.' He took the easy chair, pulled a slim cell phone from his pocket and placed it on the armrest. 'For a cop, you're a long way from home, aren't you?'

'And it's all thanks to you and your dead friend Abraham.'

Vallejo heard a noise and turned to see Patricia watching them both, open-mouthed.

The man chuckled and said, 'I was hoping to keep that little fact a secret for a while longer. Never mind.' He turned back to Vallejo. 'I think it's about time we contacted Bishop, don't you?'

He picked up the cell phone, pressed a button and put it to his ear. His eyes watched her as he waited. His face gave nothing away. Clearly, nobody was answering. He waited a full minute before ending the call. Then he pulled a piece of paper from his pocket, referring to it as he keyed in a new number.

He waited longer this time, but still there was no response. He hung up and said, 'He's not answering. Why is that, Clarissa?'

'Well, if one of those numbers was for Abraham's phone,' she said, thinking fast, 'you're wasting your time. Bishop threw it in the desert after his chat with you last night. And the only other one he's got he keeps in the glove compartment most of the time. He doesn't like cell phones much.'

The man just looked at her without expression. No doubt calculating whether she was lying or not.

'Don't worry,' she said. 'He'll check it for messages. Once he sees the missed call, he'll keep it close to him. Try again later.'

The man just watched her. After a while he pocketed the phone and stood up. 'That's exactly what I plan to do,' he said. 'And if he doesn't answer next time, you lose a limb.'

SEVENTY-ONE

When it became obvious the caller had hung up, Kate said, 'I hope to God you know what you're doing, Bishop.'

'You and me both,' he said, pocketing the phone. He took another sip of the warm coffee. 'No point in worrying about it now.'

'I guess not.' She stood up and rolled her shoulders. 'But if what you say is right, one thing I still don't get is why it's taken over three years for somebody to figure out something screwy's going on. Surely one of the fire investigators would have noticed something somewhere along the line. These guys are trained to spot the smallest irregularity.'

'People generally see what they expect to see, Kate,' Bishop said. He was recalling the car 'accident' he arranged for Selina back in Louisford. And how he'd contrived the evidence to look exactly how he wanted it. It already seemed an age ago.

'But still—'

'Look,' he interrupted, 'if there's no motive for arson and no evidence of foul play, they're unlikely to put too much effort into the possibility of murder, aren't they? And one thing I can pretty much guarantee is the man running the show has got the whole process down, with every little detail covered. If he wants the fires to look like accidents, they'll look like accidents. Believe me, I recognize the mindset.'

Raymond smirked. 'Kinda like looking in the mirror, huh?'

Bishop didn't answer, but the same thought had occurred to him. Thorough planning and an attention to detail were clearly characteristics they both shared. Except the man he was after had taken a wrong turn somewhere. At some point he'd decided his fellow humans were nothing more than pieces of meat to be used and disposed of as he saw fit. Bishop wasn't sure if that was why he hated him, or because of their similarities. Probably a combination of both. But it didn't matter. Bishop knew he wouldn't be able to rest until one of them was dead. Maybe both of them. Just so long as Selina and Vallejo were safe. That was all that concerned him now.

'And you really think the police are involved too?' Kate asked.

'Possibly only one.' Bishop pictured Shaw's face again. And then there was that odd encounter with Chief Emery at the station. It could conceivably be either of them. Or even both. 'But I'd say somebody over there's definitely got his feet in both camps. And for a number of reasons. For instance, how did they know Vallejo would be at the Amber Motel, unless they got a peek at the sworn statement she gave to the police to spring me? That's the only place I can think of where she referenced it.'

He reached for his cup and finished the last of the coffee before it got cold. 'Anyway,' he said, 'let's get back to the problem of finding out where their base is. Time's running short.'

Raymond leaned forward in his chair, elbows on his knees. 'Well, let's see now. It has to be some place big, right? If they're holding all these women in reserve for possible follow-up surgery? Like a converted warehouse or something.'

'Right,' Bishop said. 'If they can afford to keep Tatem's wife locked away in comfortably sized living quarters, it's a safe bet the other women have got similar accommodations.'

'And it has to be somewhere remote,' Kate said.

Bishop nodded. 'That's another reason I wasn't convinced about Olander's place. Too many neighbours. So forget industrial parks. It'll be on its own.'

'It still doesn't help much,' Kate said. 'The further out you go, the more solitary warehouses you see. And that's just those within the town borders.'

Bishop stood up and leaned against the wall. 'Good point. So far, everything's been kind of centred around Saracen, but there's no reason they couldn't be located over in Garrick. Some place not too far from the hospital, maybe.' He fell silent for a few moments, taking in this new possibility. It wasn't a comforting thought.

'Who are their customers exactly?' Raymond asked, picking up a pen from his desk and tapping it against his palm. 'And how do they get here? Maybe if we can figure that part out, it'll help us narrow the search.'

'Well, they'll be wealthy,' Bishop said. 'And they'll come from all corners of the globe. And one thing I know is that rich people prefer to fly whenever possible, even for domestic travel. So probably by corporate jet or private plane. Status is everything, after all.'

Kate said, 'So they land at one of the smaller airports and drive the rest of the way?'

'Or they get chauffeured in. Maybe our boy . . .' Bishop stopped. He was thinking back to his days as a close protection officer. Specifically, the times when he'd have to accompany clients in their private jets as they exited and re-entered the country.

After a while, Kate said, 'What?'

Bishop turned to her. 'Who says it has to be an airport?'

'Uh, let's see, now,' Raymond said. 'U.S. Customs? Homeland Security? You heard of them?'

'That's not what I mean. Look, all private aircraft coming to the States have to land at a specified airport of entry for Customs inspections, right?'

'Right,' Kate said. 'There are about ten here in Arizona, I think. Most of them along the Mexican border.'

Bishop nodded. 'And once they go through all the formalities and get the green light, where do they go next?'

'Anywhere they want, I guess.'

'Exactly. They can land the aircraft on an old airfield if they want. Or even just a flat stretch of land if it's a small enough plane.'

Raymond smiled and began nodding his head. 'So if our boy found himself a warehouse right next to a clear, flat stretch of land, he'd pretty much have *all* his bases covered.'

'Pretty much,' Bishop said. 'Minimal exposure for himself and his customers, and nobody around to ask awkward questions, especially if he arranges it so the clients land in the dead of night.'

Kate said, 'But they'd need landing lights for that. Somebody would have spotted them by now.'

'Not if it's remote enough,' Bishop said. 'And they wouldn't be turned on for very long. Once or twice a week at most. Each time no longer than half an hour, tops. Rest of the time, they could cover them up.'

'Okay,' Kate said, 'you've convinced me. So what now? Do we each drive around town and check out the likeliest suspects?'

'No need for that, McG,' Raymond said, turning to his monitors. 'Can you say *Google Earth*?'

'So three possibles,' Raymond said, finally turning from his monitor. 'That ain't so bad, is it?'

'I don't know,' Bishop said. 'We'll see.'

But he had to admit this Google Earth application was one hell of a useful tool. After Bishop instructed them to look for large structures with no nearby neighbours, and with adjoining land at least two thousand feet in length and two hundred feet wide, they'd each taken a section of town. It took the three of them less than half an hour to explore Saracen in full.

Raymond had found two possibilities: a cardboard box manufacturer and a wholesale supplier of building and construction materials, both on the outskirts of town. Bishop had also found a seemingly vacant building south of them, about a mile away from the Bannings place. And all were surrounded by flat land large enough to serve as a make-do landing field.

It was a start. But Bishop still needed to narrow it down further.

He turned to Raymond and said, 'When you gather information for Kate, is it always through legitimate sources?'

Raymond smiled and shared a look with Kate. 'Not always.'

'So you're a hacker.'

Raymond looked uncomfortable. 'Hey, I know my way around a mainframe, but I wouldn't go that far. I just got plenty of friends who know stuff and don't mind sharing information.'

'Okay, so say I wanted to see the monthly electric bills for these three warehouses, how hard would that be?'

'Well, it's no walk in the park. You'd need to get into the Arizona

Public Service main server and access customers' private accounts. That's serious security right there. It can be done remotely, but we're still talking some major firewalls.'

'What about through one of those back doors you mentioned?'

Raymond frowned, clicking his teeth together. Looked at Kate. 'I'd have to call a certain pal of mine, but, yeah, I could probably do it. But I wouldn't want to be in there for long.'

'What are you thinking, Bishop?' Kate asked.

'We're searching for a round-the-clock operation, aren't we? And supplying lighting, heating and electrics to a structure that large on a permanent basis adds up.'

Raymond was nodding. 'So if one of these places has a monthly utility bill that can feed a small country, we've found our scumbags.'

'Well, it would put them top of the list. How about it, Raymond? Are we go?'

Raymond looked at a point above Bishop's head as he tapped the pen against his palm. The tapping got faster and faster until he threw the pen on the desk and reached for his cell phone. 'Let me make a couple of calls,' he said.

SEVENTY-TWO

'Okay,' Raymond said, tapping keys as computer code filled the screen, 'I'm in the accounts directory, but let's keep it short. No telling when the automated sentry starts making its next sweep. Right, hit me with the first address.'

'114 Radcliffe Avenue,' Bishop said. He watched Raymond key in the box manufacturer's address and hit 'Return'. There was a short wait, and then lines of text filled the screen.

'Great,' Raymond said. 'You have to scroll though the whole goddamn street. Here we go. I might have known, 114's right at the end. Okay. There. That look normal to you, Bishop?'

Bishop leaned in and looked at the new page onscreen. He saw a month-by-month costing for gas and electric at that address. The highest bill was for January, generally Arizona's coldest month. $847. February was significantly less, and the rest of the year they were able to keep it under $500.

'That looks about average,' Bishop said. 'Try 93 East Roderick Street next.'

Raymond tapped his fingers against the keyboard and used the trackpad. Finally a new page opened up and Bishop scanned the entries. The building supplies wholesaler forked out over a grand in January and February, but the bills shrank in the following months, closely matching that of the previous business. Not nearly enough to keep a large concern lit and heated around the clock.

'Try 232 Valencia Avenue,' Bishop said. That was the one Bishop had found. It had looked vacant from above, but maybe it was supposed to look that way.

Raymond keyed it in. Got the whole street again and scrolled down to 232. Clicked on it. The page opened up.

Damn, Bishop thought. The building was listed, but there were no bills for this year. Which meant the place really *was* vacant.

'That's it,' Raymond said, 'I'm outta there.' He quit out of the system, then disabled and unplugged his router. He sighed and sat back in his seat. 'Three strikes. But it *had* to be one of them, didn't it?'

'Not necessarily,' Bishop said, staring at the wall. 'We just played a hunch, that's all. One that didn't come off.'

Silence filled the room. Kate looked at the floor as she combed a hand through her hair. Raymond gazed at the ceiling, shaking his head. But Bishop couldn't afford to feel discouraged. Now now. Besides, something was currently scratching away at the base of his spine. He wasn't sure what, exactly. Something about the pictures on the wall.

It seemed Raymond was a fan of Raquel Welch back in her prime. The man had good taste. There were four posters of the actress running across the wall, including that one of her in a fur bikini. But in between these were framed photos of friends and family. Bishop focused on two in particular. They were both black and white. One was a studio headshot of a handsome, blond man wearing an air force uniform. He looked confident and ready to take on the world. Bishop glanced at Raymond and noticed a definite family resemblance around the eyes and mouth. The other photo showed the same man standing next to a P-51 Mustang, with a hangar taking up much of the background.

'Who's the pilot?' Bishop asked. 'Your grandfather?'

Raymond sat up and looked where he was pointing. 'Great-grandfather. Jack Massingham. My grandpa says he notched up a shitload of Nazis during the war.'

'And the shot of him next to the Mustang. Where was that taken?'

'Uh, Luke Field at Luke Airfield Base. Why?'

'I'm a history buff.' Which was true. It had always been his favourite subject in school. Military history, especially. Bishop stood up and moved closer to the photo. Part of him was thinking of that old scar on his shoulder and how long it took him to notice its hidden shape.

How sometimes the answer's right there in front of you, but you're too close to see it. He saw it now. And the itching at the base of his spine had stopped.

Bishop said, 'I remember reading how the government spent months on feasibility studies before finally choosing Luke Field as a major training base. They'd find a likely spot, build a temporary hangar and fly in all kinds of specialists to check the area thoroughly before making a decision.'

Kate was frowning. 'So?'

'So this area could have been one of those locations they studied. Evening before last, when I was driving east along the highway I noticed an ancient-looking aircraft hangar in the distance. About five miles out of Saracen.'

'That's a new one on me,' Raymond said, turning to his monitor, 'and I've lived here most of my life.'

'I know which one you mean,' Kate said. 'It's on your right. Not all that obvious unless you're looking for it.'

'That's it.' He turned and said to Raymond, 'You on Google Earth again?'

'Yeah. You say it's located about five miles outside of town?'

'Give or take a mile.' Bishop went over and stood behind him. Kate joined them.

Raymond had zoomed out and was slowly scrolling east on Highway 60. When the scale at the bottom of the screen told him he'd progressed five miles, he started to zoom in again.

Bishop noticed a speck that could have been a building and pointed. 'There.'

'I see it,' Raymond said and increased the magnification further.

It was still blurred, but Bishop could make out a few more details. The hangar was set back about a mile from the highway. Situated close to the southern side of the building was a much smaller annex. Other than that it was on its own. No other structures for at least a mile in each direction. And there was a long, barely defined area alongside going from east to west that must have served as a landing strip. And maybe still did.

Raymond zoomed to the maximum setting so the roof took up half the screen. It was in the standard curved shape of the era. Most of the tiling had fallen away over the years, leaving much of the wooden sheathing underneath exposed. From the scale, Bishop quickly calculated the building covered about thirty thousand square feet.

'That's one big mother,' Raymond said.

Bishop nodded. 'About half the size of a football field. Too big for a temporary hangar. So maybe this once served as a reserve training base instead.'

Raymond started scrolling to the left and then down and to the right. Bishop could now see what had to be fencing going all round the property. And there was also a small structure close to the north fence, possibly a guard hut of some kind, and the faint markings of a dirt track leading from there to the highway.

Bishop pursed his lips. 'I'd sure love to get a look at that place from the ground.'

'Maybe we can,' Kate said. 'Our photographer, Richard, was planning a book on Saracen's history three or four years back and he took a whole bunch of shots of the surrounding area.' She sat at one of the other laptops, opened a browser and typed in an address. 'I'm sure I saw something on his website that looked like an old hangar.'

Once the site loaded, Kate clicked on the 'Gallery' link on the side and was taken to a page of photo thumbnails. She moved in closer and a few seconds later said, 'Here we go. I was right. Richard's got two shots of the place.'

She clicked on one of the thumbnails and a photo immediately filled the screen. Bishop could see it had been taken at dusk. It showed a tattered and weather-worn sign affixed to a barbed wire fence. The faded lettering on the sign read *NO ENTRANCE* and underneath, *Government Property*. The hangar in the background was out of focus.

'Very artsy,' Raymond said, while Kate clicked on an arrow to the right of the screen.

The next photo was a front shot of the hangar itself, again taken at dusk. It showed a low, wooden building in desperate need of a paint job, with overgrown sagebrush all round. The large hangar doors were closed. Bishop saw smaller doorways and gaps for windows along one side of the building. All were boarded up. Bishop smiled. Assuming the place still looked the same from the outside, he liked what he was seeing.

'*Government property,*' he said quietly. 'I wonder if it still is.'

'Easy enough to find out,' Raymond said and went straight to the official website for the County Assessor. He clicked on a link for 'Real Property'. The resulting page gave them a variety of search options in order to access specific property data: by address, by owner name, by parcel number, by agent name, or by subdivision name.

'McG,' he said, 'see if you can find out an address for the place. It's gotta have one.'

Kate went to one of the map sites on her computer and quickly navigated her way down Highway 60. A minute later, she said, 'It's listed as 67206A, East Highway 60.'

'Right.' Raymond typed the address into the appropriate box and pressed 'Return'.

Immediately a page came up showing the basic property data for No. 67206A. Parcel number, property class, and so on. Next to the owner's name, it said *Outrun Corporation*.

'Looks like it *is* privately owned,' Raymond said.

'The government must have auctioned off the land at some point,' Bishop said. 'This is looking better and better.'

Kate leaned in closer. 'Click on the name, Raymond.' Her voice sounded tense.

Raymond did as he was asked and they were taken to another page. It gave Outrun's address as a box number in Phoenix.

'Son of a bitch,' Kate whispered.

Bishop turned to her. 'You recognize the name?'

'And the box number. That's one of Stan Neeson's companies.'

SEVENTY-THREE

Bishop watched from the back seat as Kate steered the Subaru into Carter Drive. It was a long cul-de-sac with high concrete walls enclosing the vast, expensive properties lining each side. Kate pulled into the third recessed entrance on the right. There was a keypad and an intercom on the left-hand wall. Bishop looked through the windshield and couldn't spot any cameras. But that didn't mean there weren't any.

Kate had told him Neeson lived alone since his divorce, except for a long-term housekeeper who never worked weekends, while his two grown-up daughters had moved out long ago and now lived locally with their own families. She'd also mentioned that Neeson had held a prominent position on Garrick hospital's board of directors for a number of years, which explained the ease with which those three hospital rooms were set aside for private use. Finally, all the pieces were coming together.

Kate rolled her window down, reached out and pressed the buzzer. Twenty seconds later, a thin voice came from the speaker: 'Is that you, Katie?'

Which immediately told Bishop they were being watched right now.

'Hey, Stan,' she said in a light voice, 'got something I want to run by you. It's about Olander and how to prime the readers for when the story breaks. But I need your okay first.'

'Not that I don't enjoy seeing you, Kate, but couldn't you have just phoned?'

'It's kind of sensitive. Best we discuss it in person.'

'I see. Just you out there, is it?'

'Just me.'

'Then come on up.'

Bishop heard a brief hum, then the gates began to open and Kate drove slowly through. He saw perfect lawns on either side, with palm trees all around providing plenty of shade. Up ahead, the gravel drive ended in a circle in front of a single-storey, white stucco house. It was in a similar Spanish style to Tatem's place, but covered a much larger area, with a lot more wings protruding out from the main body. To Bishop it looked more like a modern scientific research centre than a home.

Through the car's tinted windows, he spotted Neeson standing outside his front door with a faint smile on his face. Kate circled round and stopped the vehicle a few feet away. She got out and Neeson looked behind her and his eyes grew large.

Knowing he'd been spotted, Bishop reached for the .38 Special under his shirt as he shoved the car door open. But Neeson moved faster than his years. Before Bishop was all the way out, the older man had ducked back through the front door and slammed it shut behind him.

'Shit,' Bishop said and turned to Kate. 'He'll want to get to a phone and call his people. Where will he go?'

Kate looked at him, open-mouthed.

He grabbed one of her wrists. 'Where are the phones, Kate? I need to know. *Now*.'

'Uh, there's one in the hallway just behind that door. There's another one in his study.' She pointed and said, 'That room over there on the far right, just past that big palm. That's all, I think.'

Bishop thought fast. Neeson wouldn't use the hallway phone. He'd expect Bishop to shoot out the front door lock and enter that way. No, he'd make for the study. Bishop turned right and ran along the front of the house, hoping there wasn't a third phone Kate didn't know about. Bishop reached the large palm and stopped just short of the room at the end. He peered through one of the windows and saw Neeson already in there, locking the door. Then he came round to the desk with his back to Bishop. He grabbed a cordless from a base unit with one hand while reaching down for one of the drawers with the other.

There was a sliding glass door a few feet to Bishop's right. He stepped over and tried the handle. It was unlocked. He slid it all the way open and pointed the .38 at the man's head.

'Freeze,' he said.

Neeson froze, his hand halfway in the desk drawer.

Bishop stepped into the room. 'Now bring your hand out of there. Slowly.'

Neeson did as he was told, his right hand coming out empty. Bishop stepped round to his side and saw he was still holding the cordless. 'Now put the phone down.'

Neeson stared at Bishop's gun and carefully placed the cordless back in the base unit. Then he slowly raised both hands in the air. Bishop saw a movement in his peripheral vision and then heard Kate come through the doorway.

'Oh, Stan,' she said. 'No. It *can't* be you.'

'It's him, all right,' Bishop said, and pointed to a leather couch positioned against one of the walls. 'Plant your ass over there, Neeson. And keep it there.'

Neeson looked at Kate with an unreadable expression and then walked over to the couch. When he sat, Bishop checked the drawer he'd been reaching for and pulled out another .38. With a four-inch barrel, this time. He was getting quite a collection. He tucked it in his waistband and saw Kate walking towards Neeson.

'That's as far as you go, Kate,' Bishop said.

She stopped, and Neeson said, 'Look, if you're thinking of exchanging me for—'

'Exchange? I can't see your partner caring too much what happens to you, can you? After all, he's the one running things these days, am I right?'

Neeson closed his mouth and glared at Bishop. Which proved he'd hit the mark.

'Now. Why don't we start things off with his name?'

'What good will—?' Neeson was beginning, when the phone started ringing.

SEVENTY-FOUR

Kate and Neeson stared at the handset as though it might jump off the desk. Bishop motioned with the gun and said, 'Get over here, Neeson.'

The older man got up and walked over, keeping his distance from Kate. Bishop plucked the handset from the base unit and said, 'When you answer, put it on speaker. I'm not in the best of moods right now, so I hear one wrong word out of you and I'll snap your neck like a chicken's. Understand?'

Neeson took a deep breath and nodded.

'Answer it, then.'

Neeson took the phone and pressed a single button on the base unit. He said, 'Yes?'

An amplified voice said, 'Neeson?' Bishop immediately recognized it as the man from last night.

'It's me, Alex.'

'So have you gotten off your ass and spoken with that McGowan woman yet? Has Bishop been in contact with her?'

Neeson looked over at Kate as she sat down on the couch. 'I've just gotten off the line with her and she hasn't heard from him. She said she tried calling a couple of times, but got no answer.'

The caller sighed. 'That matches with what the dyke said. Okay, check back with her again soon, but keep me updated. I'm rapidly running out of patience with this bullshit.' The man called Alex clicked off and Bishop took the phone from Neeson's hand.

'Good,' he said. 'So what's Alex's surname?'

'Hallaran.'

'Alex Hallaran,' Bishop said, nodding. 'He sounds like a man with a short fuse.'

'Yes, he gets aggravated easily, like most control freaks. He could take the pressure off by delegating some of the workload, but it's just not in his nature. And you're the one testing his patience right now. He needs you out of the way before the client arrives tonight. That's why he took the Vallejo woman. For leverage.'

'Yeah, I figured that much out myself. And how does he plan to neutralize me? He can't possibly believe I'd be dumb enough to turn myself over to him.'

'How should I know? He doesn't tell me his plans. But he'll try and contact you again and I'd advise you to answer next time. Hallaran's got a hair-trigger temper and if he can't get hold of you, he'll take it out on your friend. That much I know for sure.'

Bishop thought about that as he watched Neeson, who didn't look quite as urbane as before. In fact, he looked as though he'd aged ten years in the last ten minutes.

Neeson swallowed and said, 'So what are you going to do with me?'

Kate came over, her eyes reduced to slits. 'I want to throw you down a deep well, you bastard. All these years I trusted you and never even suspected what you're really capable of. How could you do it? All those deaths. All those innocent people and children wiped off the face of the earth, just so some rich women can get transplants and have kids of their own. Jesus, what kind of monster are you?'

Neeson just stood there with his mouth open, staring at Kate. '*Transplants? Kids?* What on earth are you talking about?'

SEVENTY-FIVE

Bishop studied the genuine look of shock on Neeson's face and immediately knew his initial instincts had been correct. That the missing women were in fact serving a far simpler need. A far more ancient need. From the start, he hadn't been entirely convinced about the ovary transplant angle, especially after Tatem nixed the idea as unworkable. Nevertheless, when the few facts available to them had started to go in that direction, he'd preferred to stay open-minded about the whole thing and see where it led. But Neeson's reaction confirmed Bishop's belief that the simplest explanation was usually the correct one.

'Stop there, Kate,' Bishop said. 'He really doesn't know what you're talking about.'

Kate turned to him, disbelief in her eyes. 'What? You're saying he's *innocent*?'

'Not hardly. I'm just saying this was never about organ transplants. They're not dealing in body parts, they're dealing in *bodies*. That's right, isn't it, Neeson?'

The older man looked at him and said nothing. Which was all the answer he needed.

'You mean human trafficking?' Kate said. 'But what about Kendrick Juneau's suspicious disappearance? And those scars on the women patients?'

Bishop shrugged. 'Juneau and his companions probably *did* die on the Congo River, which means his research died along with him. End of story. It was an odd death, but not necessarily suspicious. And the scars were probably routine internal tests to make sure the women were in perfect health. Tatem's merely there to wipe away all the so-called imperfections whenever necessary, like the acid burns on Selina's arms and the tattoo on Samantha Mathison's back. Making sure the buyer doesn't get damaged goods.'

Kate was still glaring at Neeson. 'But in that case, why kill Samantha? In fact, why not grab women with no physical imperfections at all? They must exist.'

'Yeah, but Abraham told me they're a highly specialized service, so maybe it's not so simple as that.' Bishop thought for a moment, watching Neeson. 'What if it's a case of providing women to order? Then grooming them for the customer, both physically and mentally? You can't get more specialized than that. In which case, they could have found out about Samantha's sexual orientation too late, then decided to get rid of her and start looking around for a suitable replacement while they still could. That would fit.'

Kate was nodding slowly. 'Then somebody spots Selina at the diner and decides her resemblance to Samantha is good enough for their purposes.'

'Possibly. But we don't need to guess any more, do we? Not when we can get it from the horse's mouth. How about it, Neeson? Are we getting warm?'

Neeson just stood there without answering.

'Take a seat,' Bishop said, pointing his gun at the chair behind the desk. He waited as Neeson sat down, then said, 'Okay, Kate, go and see if you can find me a kitchen knife, will you? And make sure it's a sharp one.'

Kate looked at him for a few moments, then began walking for the door.

'Wait,' Neeson said. 'What do you need a knife for?'

'For every time you don't answer a question. You already owe me a finger.'

Neeson's face immediately lost what little colour was left. 'No, please. There's no need for that. I'll tell you what you want to know.'

'Hold it, Kate,' Bishop said, and she stopped and came back. 'Okay, Neeson, but I hear one false note and Kate goes back for the knife. I don't have time for any more screwing around.'

Neeson took a breath. 'I won't lie to you, Bishop. I'm no hero. And you're actually fairly close to the truth already. But it's not really human trafficking, as such. Hallaran once called it an exclusive match-making service for the discrim—'

'*Matchmaking* service?' Kate blurted out. 'Are you in*sane?*'

Bishop held up a hand. 'Just let him talk, Kate. Go on, Neeson.'

'Look, I know how it sounds, but Alex Hallaran's the real brains behind it all, not me. I came up with the seed of an idea and provided the initial start-up money, sure, but it's Hallaran who handles the day-to-day running of the operation. It's not like Eastern Europe where they grab girls off the street and sell them on to the highest bidder. Hallaran's refined things to a much more concentrated level, targeted to a specific client's wishes. Usually from rich businessmen looking for their perfect partners.'

'I bet the girls appreciate that distinction,' Bishop said, leaning against the sliding door. 'So take me through the process from start to finish.'

Neeson glanced briefly at Kate, swallowed and said, 'Well, as you can imagine, a business like this relies heavily on word of mouth. A client might hear about us from a friend who's used us and he'll contact Hallaran and put in a very specific request for a certain type of women. And not just the physical aspects. The woman's personality is just as important. Our clients are looking for lifelong partners, not sex slaves. Then, once he's wired over a deposit, Hallaran can start . . .'

'How much?'

'One million dollars, with the second million to be paid on delivery.'

Bishop whistled. 'And how many women, on average?'

'Hallaran limits it to one new client a fortnight, maximum. He says this enables him to stagger the extractions to a manageable level and keep the rolling stock to no more than eight women at any one time. There are seven onsite now. Not including your friend and the surgeon's wife.'

Kate shook her head and turned to Bishop. 'Lifelong *partners*? *Extractions*? *Rolling* stock? Can you believe the shit that's coming out of this man's mouth?'

'It's pretty amazing, I have to admit.'

But it also confirmed Bishop's impression of this Hallaran character. He was a details man. And he wasn't overly greedy. He knew his limitations and stayed within them, regardless of the temptations. Which meant he was smart. Besides, a yearly turnover of fifty million wasn't exactly chicken feed.

Bishop said, 'And these customers of yours. Where do they come from?'

'Anywhere but here. Right from the start, Hallaran was very specific about servicing overseas clients only.'

'Figures,' Bishop said. 'Otherwise, too much chance of somebody from the victim's past running into her and recognizing her. Or of the woman running to the Feds. So how does he go about finding a particular woman for a particular customer?'

'Well, the client receives a special graphics program to design his perfect mate. Then once he gets that back, Hallaran's able to hack into the State Department and the DMV, who between them hold photos of most of the adults in this country. He also uses some of the big social network servers, too, like Facebook, Twitter and MySpace, to cover all those who don't hold driver's licences or passports. I don't know all the details, but he eventually narrows the final candidates down to just one.'

'Unbelievable,' Kate said. She was looking at Neeson as though he were a lower life form. Something reptilian, maybe. 'Like it's a game show or something.'

Bishop ignored her. 'At which point Hallaran plans her fake death and the real deaths of her immediate family, so nobody will be around to raise awkward questions. Right?'

Neeson lowered his eyes. 'You have to believe I had nothing to do with those deaths. Nothing at all. That was all Hallaran's idea. At first we kept it simple. Abraham would wait for the perfect moment, then simply grab the designated woman and bring her here and that would be that. Women go missing all the time in this country, and we figured what's one more? But the husband of one of them actually tracked Hallaran down somehow and came very close to killing him. After that Hallaran became very paranoid. He came up with the idea of arranging house fires so it couldn't ever happen again. That way, he could erase the woman's old identity and any interested parties in one fell swoop. I thought it was far too risky and unnecessary, but what could I say? He doesn't listen to me.'

'Sure, I understand. So once you people have wiped out everyone and everything the victim's held dear up till that point, that's when you *really* go to work on her, right? What do you use? Drugs? Brainwashing?'

'Just a very intense hypnotherapy programme,' Neeson said, 'combined with various drugs and mood enhancers to help break down the person's psychological barriers. I don't know the names of the drugs. But Hallaran has two hypnotherapists he uses. By the time they're done, the women are almost looking forward to their new lives. He's never had any complaints from any previous clients, I know that.'

'I bet he hasn't,' Bishop said. 'Over how long a period is this programme?'

'Between three to four months for each woman.'

Which meant Hallaran had to be housing at least half a dozen victims at any one time. His 'rolling stock', as Neeson had put it. 'I was right about Samantha Mathison, wasn't I? You people killed her when you found out she was gay, and grabbed Selina to take her place.'

'*Hallaran* had her killed,' Neeson said. 'I didn't even learn about it until a week later.'

'Sure. And tonight, her buyer's coming to the hangar to collect his prize and take her away, right?'

Neeson nodded.

'What time? And how will he arrive?'

'He's due at one a.m. and he'll be arriving by private plane. They usually do.'

'Who is he?' Kate asked.

'A Portuguese businessman called Poleina. I hear he's big in steel manufacturing.'

'So he'll fly in with his pilot and bodyguards, pick up his prize and leave?'

'Not straight away,' Neeson said. 'He'll check over his girl and make sure he's satisfied with everything while the plane's being refuelled. It usually takes about half an hour.'

And it was noon now. Which meant Bishop had between thirteen and fourteen hours before Selina was out of his reach for good. Not to mention Vallejo. And all the other women. Added to which, he'd have to be prepared for whatever handicap Hallaran threw his way, too. Neeson was right about that: he couldn't avoid him for much longer.

'And what about you, Neeson? Are you usually there for the handover?'

Bishop waited for the lie, but Neeson just sighed and said, 'Sometimes. Not always. Hallaran leaves it up to me.'

'Okay. How many men has Hallaran got over there? Be exact.'

Neeson closed his eyes and said, 'There are two guards outside. Inside there's Hallaran, of course. Then Abraham, his second-in-command and about the only one he really trusts, and four more armed men. Plus Ryan, the programmer. That makes nine. And the two hypnotherapists. So eleven in all.'

Ten, Bishop thought. Neeson obviously hadn't gotten the news about Abraham yet. And Bishop wasn't about to update him. 'And they all live out at the hangar?'

Neeson nodded. 'The only exceptions are myself and the two orderlies who stay at the hospital. Hallaran believes it's more secure that way.'

'All part of his four-year plan, huh?'

Neeson shrugged his shoulders. 'Hallaran says the longer you keep something like this going, the bigger the risk of getting caught. Besides, everyone's prepared to tolerate the accommodations in return for the big pay day at the end.'

Bishop was about to burst his bubble on that little point when he felt a vibration in his pocket. He pulled out his cell phone. The caller was unidentified. But he already had a pretty good idea who it was.

This time, he took the call.

SEVENTY-SIX

'So *there* you are,' Hallaran said. He sounded his old, smug self again. 'You're a hard man to get hold of, Bishop.'

'I could say the same about you.'

Hallaran chuckled. 'Listen, I've got someone here who's *real* glad you answered your phone. Things were about to get nasty. Hold on.'

Bishop kept his eyes on Neeson as he listened to silence on the line. Five seconds later, a familiar voice said, 'Sorry, Bishop, I should have waited for you.'

'It doesn't matter now. You okay, Vallejo?'

'Yeah, but for how long, I don't know. Like you said, these are some serious people.'

'That's enough,' Hallaran broke in. 'Now she's confirmed what you already knew, we can get down to it. You got a pen on you?'

Bishop didn't need one, but he said, 'Go on.'

'You know a place called Queen Creek?'

He did. 'Small town, south-east of Phoenix.'

'That's the one. Now there's a street in that town called South Greencrest Road, and halfway down you'll find a place called McWilliams Diner. Next to that's a general store. Outside that store, there are three payphones in a row. You'll want the middle one.'

'Will I?'

'At three o'clock this afternoon, you will. I'll be calling that number and if you haven't answered before the tenth ring, your friend here will be taking a long trip to see her old girlfriend. A *very* long trip.'

Bishop checked his watch and saw it was now 12.09. 'I only met

Vallejo less than forty-eight hours ago. What makes you think we're friends?'

Hallaran gave a deep sigh. 'Is that really how you want this conversation to go, Bishop? Because we can end it right now. Right this second. That what you want?'

'No.'

'Wise man. Don't ever test me, Bishop. You'll come off worst, I guarantee it.'

'So what happens after I pick up the phone? I get one in the back of the head from a long-distance rifle?'

'Now there's a thought,' Hallaran said and chuckled again. 'I only wish I could spare the manpower. No, we'll just talk for a while, is all. I'll let you swap a few words with Vallejo and then you put the phone down again. But stick around, because I *will* be calling again.'

'When?'

'Whenever I feel like hearing your voice. Could be any time. Tonight's a busy night and I can't have you running loose. Come morning, we'll arrange something more concrete.'

'You'll kill her anyway,' Bishop said. 'You can't afford to let her go now.'

'I haven't decided one way or the other yet. And besides, it's not the going, but how you go. You were in the Corps, so you know what I'm talking about. And one thing I can promise is if you don't answer when I call, Vallejo here will die a long and painful death. I've got a fellow here whose record so far is a week, and I know he'd love to beat it if he could. Do you believe me, Bishop?'

'Yes.'

'Good. You better get moving, you got a long drive ahead of you.'

The connection went dead.

Bishop looked at a point a few inches above Neeson's head as he carefully placed the cell phone back in his pocket. With his other hand, he slowly pulled the hammer back on the .38 Special, then just as slowly returned it to its original position. Then he did it again. And again. He was thinking about Hallaran, who was right about one thing. That it wasn't the going that counted, but how you went. Bishop wondered how long he could make it last once he got his hands on this Hallaran.

'So are you going to tell me what he said?' Kate asked.

Bishop turned to her and came back to the present. Then he quickly recounted the conversation, minus the street and place names.

'What are you going to do?' she asked.

'Take the call. What other choice is there? I can't get into that hangar during daylight hours, anyway.'

Kate looked out a window. 'Won't he try to kill you now he knows where you'll be?'

'If Abraham was still around, I'd say it was a certainty. Now I'm not so sure. He's already a man down and he can't afford to take either of the outside guards away from their posts, which just leaves four other men. And Hallaran will need them all tonight. No, he can afford to wait and take me out at his leisure. He holds all the cards right now.'

But as Bishop spoke the words, he was thinking of a way he might have his cake and eat it, too. Although he wasn't sure it was even possible. But right now he had to move fast if he was going to make that phone before three. He just hoped the Sunday traffic would be on his side. But first, he had a small detour to make.

He turned to see Kate watching Neeson with unconcealed disgust. 'What do we do with him?' she asked. 'We can't let him go.'

'No, we can't. Has he got a cellar in this place?'

'Yeah. I think there's an entrance to it from the kitchen.'

Bishop motioned with the gun for Neeson to stand. 'Let's go take a look.'

SEVENTY-SEVEN

At 14.59, Bishop downshifted into third and swung the Buick hard into South Greencrest Road. The back end fishtailed and the rear tyres skidded on the asphalt as Bishop jerked the wheel left, then right. The moment the car straightened out, he slammed his foot down again, quickly taking it back up to fifty, sixty.

It had been an intense ride all the way, with Sunday drivers doing their damnedest to bring his blood pressure up to critical levels. The only positive was he hadn't been pulled over for speeding yet. But he was late all the same. Less than a minute before Hallaran would call and he still hadn't reached the convenience store. He swerved round an old pick-up doing thirty, looking in both directions for what he wanted.

The dashboard clock changed to 15.00.

Shit. Bishop knew the clock was accurate to the second. He'd made sure of that before he left. But he had to keep going. There was still a chance. *Where's that goddamn store?*

There. Coming up about five hundred feet ahead on the left. And before it, another building with *McWilliams Diner* in big red letters outside. Bishop kept the speed up and watched the sparse oncoming traffic, picking his spot. He sped by the diner and when he was almost at right angles to the store entrance yanked the wheel hard left, narrowly avoiding a Volkswagen as he cut diagonally across the street like a scythe, over the sidewalk and straight into the forecourt. He heard angry car horns behind him as he skidded to a stop at an angle. Leaving the engine running, he jumped out and sprinted towards the three red public phones on poles outside the store.

A middle-aged Latino guy was using the middle phone, watching the action with wide eyes. He saw Bishop running at him and held the phone away from his ear, looking increasingly panicked.

Bishop halted a few feet from him, looked around wildly with his eyes bugging out and shouted, '*Put the phone back. Put it back. No calls, no calls. Not safe.*'

'Sure, man, sure,' the man said. He left the phone dangling as he backed away, patting the air in front of him. 'Whatever you say. It's all yours, okay?'

Bishop kept staring at him as he placed the phone back on the hook, hoping the crazy act would be enough to keep the guy from calling the cops. He watched the man get into his work van and pull out onto the road. When he was gone, Bishop looked down at his watch. It was already 15.01. It changed to 15.02 as he watched.

He was too late.

Bishop slumped against the phone box and looked up at the clear blue sky. When Hallaran had got a busy signal, he would have hung up and assumed Bishop wasn't playing. Which meant he'd blown it. And Vallejo would be the one who paid. He shook his head in mute anger, wondering what to do next. All he could do was wait on the off chance that Hallaran would try again and hope for the best.

The phone started ringing.

Bishop turned and just looked at it. Not quite believing it. He let it ring once more and then picked up the receiver. 'I'm here,' he said.

'So you are,' Hallaran said, chuckling. 'Had my doubts for a moment there. Who was that on the line before?'

'Some guy. I chased him off.'

'Ha. You sure like living close to the edge, don't you? Okay, that was me giving you a break, but don't get used to it because it won't happen again. Here's your dyke friend. Keep it short.'

There was a couple of seconds' silence, then Vallejo said, 'Hey, stranger.'

'How you doing, Clarissa?'

'*Clarissa?* You're not going soft on me, are you, Bishop?'

'Never.'

'You'd better not. Things are pretty much the same here. Shame you can't come visit.'

Before Bishop could answer, Hallaran came on and said, 'Yeah, well, that's life. Now you be sure to stick around and make sure nobody else uses that phone. No second chances in this game, you got that, Bishop?'

Yeah, I got that, he thought as the line went dead. *No second chances.*

He carefully replaced the phone and looked back at the car. And the passenger he'd brought along with him.

SEVENTY-EIGHT

Bishop sat on the Buick's hood and checked his watch again for the thousandth time. 18.34. Almost three and a half hours since the last call. But he had a strong feeling Hallaran would try again pretty soon. He'd want to know Bishop was still where he was supposed to be. Which he was, for the moment.

Whether that continued to be the case depended on Raymond.

After locking Neeson up in his own cellar and assigning Kate as temporary watchdog, he'd sped over to Raymond's place, outlined the situation and asked for his help. Raymond was currently kneeling before the middle pay phone a few feet away, wearing his old work overalls with the phone company logo on the back.

He also had an open laptop on the ground in front of him and a tool bag by his side. Earlier, he'd removed a steel panel from the front of the post, exposing five cables. A single USB line ran from his laptop to a port within. Two more wires connected two of the cables to a handheld, digital multimeter. Raymond held an orange phone to his ear. One of those giants with the keypad on the back. He was still trying to gain access to the main server of TransSouthcom's nearest switching station. The method he was using was something Jenna had mentioned trying more than once, back in her bad girl days.

Raymond hung up. Without turning, he said, 'I'm gonna run out of employees at this rate. *And* it's a Sunday.'

'We have to keep trying,' Bishop said.

'I know.' Raymond sighed as he looked at the laptop screen. Then he keyed in another number on the phone and put it to his ear. A few seconds later, he said, 'Yeah, who am I talking to? . . . Oh, Leonard, I finally got hold of you . . . Yeah, this is Al from tech support. Heard you got a problem with your access . . . You *do*? Well, that's what I'm here for . . . Yeah, I know, but it's worth it for the double time. What's the problem, buddy? . . . Right . . . Right . . . well, that don't sound too bad. Let's see now, if you wanna give me your user name and password, I'll dive right in and see what I can do.'

Bishop came over and watched Raymond key in some letters and numbers on the laptop. Then the welcome screen disappeared as Raymond scrolled through some code. After a few moments, he said, 'Well, Lenny, I can tell you right now this ain't the same operating system I been trained on. I think I'm gonna have to hand it over to another technician when he gets in tomorrow . . . Yeah, real sorry to get your hopes up like that . . . Sure, I'll tell him. So long.' He put down the phone and continued keying.

'So you're in?' Bishop asked.

'I'm in. Let's see now, I need to find . . . ah, *there* it is. Okay, baby, talk to me.'

Bishop stood up and let him work. *Quid pro quo*, Jenna had called it. A simple social engineering technique. You phone random numbers at a company and claim to be somebody from technical support. Eventually, you're going to hit a grateful somebody with a computer problem that needs solving. And as soon as they've given you their network user name and password, you can pretty much go where you want.

The payphone started ringing.

Bishop turned to Raymond. 'Is that you?'

'Uh, uh. Not me.' Raymond was frantically navigating his way through the company's system using just the touchpad. 'Just let it ring, okay? I think I'm almost there.'

Bishop stepped forward and grabbed the receiver, ready to take it off the hook. It rang a third time. He pulled the cell from his pocket with his other hand. Four rings. Raymond pressed the touchpad and then keyed in some text. Five rings. A pause. Six rings.

It rang again. 'That's seven,' Bishop said.

'I know, I know,' Raymond said, still typing rapidly. Then he took his fingers away from the keyboard and sat back. 'All done.'

The pay phone rang an eighth time. Bishop and Raymond looked at each other.

Then Bishop's cell phone started ringing, while the pay phone remained silent.

'See?' Raymond said, smiling.

Bishop smiled back and took the call on his cell. 'It's me.'

'Catch you mid-flow, did I?' Hallaran said.

'Something like that. You gonna gloat or are you gonna put her on?'

'Patience, Bishop. Here she is.'

'Hey, partner,' the familiar voice said, 'wish you were here.'

'Me too, Vallejo. How you holding up?'

'Well, I'm still breathing. They haven't laid a hand on me yet, but that's just . . .'

'And she'll stay that way as long as you do as you're told,' Hallaran interrupted. 'But for now, go grab a bite at the diner next door. I promise not to call back for at least an hour.'

'You're all heart. You know, I'm really looking forward to meeting you.'

'Don't look forward to it too much. You might not like how it comes out.' Then the line went dead.

I could give you the same advice, he thought, pocketing the cell. He turned to Raymond, who was screwing the front panel back on the post. 'Real good work, Raymond. I'm impressed.'

'Hey, I wasn't sure I could do it for a moment there. Things have changed a lot since I left, but rerouting a line's the same once you're in the system. Now any incoming calls on this phone will get transferred to your cell, but it'll still be logged as coming to this site.'

'What about outgoing?'

Raymond got up and rubbed his forehead. 'Well, we might have a problem if somebody comes along and makes a collect call. The operator won't be able to make the connection and will disconnect it, then report a fault in the line. A way round it is to put an *Out of Order* sticker over this box, but then the store owner here might get curious and check back with the central office. Either way's risky. It's up to you.'

Bishop thought for a moment and shrugged. 'Keep it as it is, then. Okay, let's wrap it up. We got some driving to do.'

SEVENTY-NINE

It was 23.43 when the next call came. Bishop answered the cell and Hallaran's voice said, 'Answered on the third ring, this time. You're improving. So you been keeping busy over there?'

'Sure,' Bishop said. He was currently standing by the empty fireplace in Neeson's large, spacious living room. Kate was perched on the coffee table, watching him. Raymond was sitting on the couch, still in his overalls, sipping a coke. 'Mostly thinking of what I'm gonna do to you once we meet.'

'Very productive. But then, it's always good to have goals, even if they *are* unrealistic.'

'Uh huh. You want to let me talk to her now?'

'Why not? Just keep it short, like before.'

Vallejo came on. 'Hey, again. So how's things on the outside?'

'Same as always. How about you? Still keeping bad company?'

'The worst. But at least I got Patricia with me. We're having a slumber party. You're invited, but only if you bring some booze.'

There were some muffled sounds and then Hallaran cut in. 'Cute. As you can hear, we're all having a wild time here. Gotta hang up now, but let's talk again soon, huh?'

The line went dead and Bishop pocketed the phone. This was the second call since they'd left Queen Creek. Both times he'd been listening carefully for any sign that Hallaran might suspect something was amiss. But he still sounded the same. Like he was untouchable. So it looked like Bishop might be in the clear. At least, for the time being.

He checked the wall clock above the fireplace. 23.45. Getting close to game time. He also reflected on how well Vallejo was holding up. She had to know how close she was to the abyss, but she was playing it as cool as ever. As though she trusted Bishop to have a plan to get her out of this mess. That kind of faith left a deep impression on him. Not that he needed any more motivation. He'd originally come into this with the express purpose of finding Selina and bringing her back. But it was bigger than that now. Much bigger. He couldn't afford to let Vallejo down. He couldn't afford to let any of them down.

He sat in one of the easy chairs and took Abraham's Sig from his shoulder holster. He was wearing the same clothes as last night. Black combats, black shirt, black windbreaker. The holster was new, though. He'd picked it up at a gun store just outside Phoenix on the way back. Along with a few other items. Like the Ka-Bar knife and ankle holster.

As he checked the magazine again, Kate asked, 'So Clarissa's still okay?'

Bishop nodded. 'For now.'

'I still can't believe you're going in there alone, Bishop.'

'Who else is gonna help? And don't bring up the cops again, because we've been through all that. There are too many lives at stake. You'll call them, just not yet.'

He'd already gone over it with her in as much detail as he could. About when to call in the alarm. And to make sure to stay well clear of the hangar until they arrived. Then she could go in with her photographer and do all the filming and reporting she wanted. Assuming things went to plan. Which they probably wouldn't.

Plans were all well and good, but there were too many unknowns in this instance. Like the placement of the guards. He knew a lot of it would come down to improvisation in the end, but he couldn't tell Kate that. She had to believe he knew what he was doing all along or she'd go straight to the cops right now.

'When you aiming to go in?' Raymond asked.

'Neeson says this Poleina is arriving at 0100 hours, so the closer I can time it to that, the better. When everybody's attention will be focused on the plane's arrival.'

Reholstering the gun, he took from his pocket the rough plan Neeson had drawn for him and looked it over again, making sure he had it all down. The interior's six-by-six grid format looked deceptively simple at first glance, but Bishop knew Hallaran must have put a lot of thought into the layout and location of each room.

The hangar was a square split up into four quadrants by two central corridors, running from north to south and east to west. The south-east quadrant contained nine equal-sized rooms in rows of three, with each block separated by a smaller corridor running the length of the building. The bottom six were numbered and reserved for the captured women, then three apartments for Hallaran's people. The main east-west corridor then acted as a partition for the north-east quadrant, which featured three more staff apartments, followed by rooms 7 to 9. And then something called a 'games' room, a storage room, and a utility area. Making eighteen rooms altogether.

The other half of the hangar kept to the same grid layout, but with several differences. The south-west quadrant contained just three long areas running across: an open space Neeson called the reception area, then a gym area, then Hallaran's large apartment. Naturally, it was three times the size of the others. Finally, in the north-west quadrant, a long garage area took up the west side, followed by six more rooms in three rows of two. Two of these were apartments, plus the medical room, the kitchen, Hallaran's office, and the comms room.

All those corridors, and any one of them could contain a guard on his rounds. The place was wide open in there, with few hiding places. Not exactly ideal conditions, but then they never were. Bishop would just have to live with it.

Or not, as the case may be.

Sticking the paper back in his pocket, he stood up and took another look at the clock. 23.56. 'Okay,' he said, 'I think it's time we brought Neeson out.'

EIGHTY

Neeson drove the BMW X5 slowly down the dirt track with his headlights off. More of Hallaran's rules. Bishop was crouched in the back of the SUV, watching Neeson via the side mirror. He'd already made it clear that if he spotted any sign that his captive was trying to alert the guard, or leave his seat, he'd get two in the back.

Ahead, Bishop saw the dark shape of the hangar looming larger. Before that was razor-wire-topped barbed wire fencing – also electrified, according to Neeson – stretching off to the left and right. And the guard shack by the entrance gate. Fifty feet away now. No lights anywhere. Just the kind of set-up he'd expected to see at Olander's place.

'Remember what we talked about,' Bishop said. 'Just act normal and say the lines and you got nothing to worry about.'

'I understand,' Neeson said, drawing in a deep breath.

'Good.' Bishop got down on the floor, between the front and rear seats. He grabbed the section of black carpeting he'd cut from the rear of the vehicle and pulled it over himself. He also had the fibre-optic scope he'd used at Gaspard's embedded inside the driver's seat. The insertion tube peeking out from behind Neeson's left shoulder was aimed towards the side mirror. Bishop picked the eyepiece off the floor and brought it to his left eye.

The image was clear enough, and the lens gave him a wide angle view of the side mirror and part of the hangar up ahead. Bishop saw the fence getting closer, and ten seconds later they came to a stop. The guard hut was left of shot, about ten feet further in. Suddenly, light played over the vehicle from that direction and fixed itself on Neeson. Then it went away and Bishop saw the gates open inwards.

Neeson drove through and stopped by the shack.

Bishop watched his face in the side mirror. The smile didn't look too convincing, but Bishop figured his nervousness would work in their favour.

'Hey, Mr Neeson,' a deep male voice said. 'Wasn't expecting you tonight.'

'Couldn't sleep,' Neeson said. 'So I figured I'd come out and meet out latest client. Make sure everything goes smoothly.'

Bishop couldn't see the guard, but he saw a light playing over the vehicle again. Had to be a flashlight. He watched Neeson's face. Anything more than a cursory inspection and it would be obvious there was something in the back of the vehicle. He'd have to move fast and cut them both down. Bishop got ready.

Then, just as suddenly, the light disappeared and the guard said, 'Well, you cut it close, Mr N. Plane's due pretty soon.'

'I know. Look, Lane, do me a favour, will you? Don't report to Hallaran that I've arrived yet. Truth is, I'm really here because I want to spend some time with that little brunette in No.7 and I don't need Hallaran giving me hell. You know how he gets. Right now, he'll be occupied with No. 3 and he won't care where I am.'

'Hey, I don't know, Mr N. I've got orders to call in any time I open that gate. It's my ass if I don't.'

'Come on, Lane. Help me out here. Just let me have fifteen minutes with her, then you can report I've just arrived and I'll go and wait with the others for the plane to land. Besides, I've heard you and Baldwin like checking in with certain girls occasionally, so I know you understand.'

There was a pause of a few seconds. Then the guard said, 'I don't know what you're talking about, Mr Neeson. But I'll give you the fifteen minutes. Starting now.'

Bishop saw Neeson breathe a sigh of relief. 'I owe you one, Lane. Thanks a lot.'

'Sure, Mr N,' the guard said. 'Have fun.'

Neeson put the car into gear and moved off slowly. Bishop checked his watch. 00.41. So if the guard kept his promise, Bishop had until

00.56 before Hallaran got the word. He raised himself up and peered through the rear windshield. The guard was watching the departing vehicle as he walked back to the hut. But he wasn't talking to anyone. Maybe this would work. 'That was real good, Neeson. You might make it through this yet.'

'I plan to. I'm not about to do anything stupid.'

'Glad to hear it,' Bishop said, facing front.

Neeson was steering them to the right of the building, past the main hangar doors. They had to be there just for show now. Probably boarded up from the inside as soon as they moved in. Neeson took them round to the west side of the hangar and stopped. Bishop saw three wide wooden doors alongside each other, near the north-west corner. These had to be the garage entrances. He looked around and couldn't see the other perimeter guard, but then it was a big area to cover.

Neeson took a remote from the passenger seat and pressed a button. All three doors began to roll back automatically and Bishop saw a number of vehicles parked inside. Too dark to see what they were, though. Neeson started forward again and aimed for the third door. It looked fairly empty on that side.

Once they were in, Bishop said, 'Lower the doors.'

Neeson obeyed and a faint electronic hum accompanied the doors back to their original positions.

'Switch on the sidelights and get out,' Bishop said.

Neeson did as he was told and he and Bishop exited the vehicle at the same time. In the dim light, Bishop saw they were in a long area with vinyl flooring and wood-panelled walls all around. There was enough space for about fifteen vehicles. Maybe more. He counted twelve, including theirs. Five had protective coverings over them. The six that didn't consisted of an SUV, a sedan, a pair of very familiar ambulances and a Mercedes Sprinter van. Plus a gleaming black stretch limo with heavily tinted windows at the end. No fuel tankers, of course. Neeson had told him they were both housed in the small building on the south side, separate from the main building.

There were also two doors. The one on the right would lead directly into the reception area, smack dab in the heart of the enemy. Too soon for that. The door straight ahead was the one he wanted.

Bishop raised the covering on the nearest vehicle and glanced at the interior. 'I don't see any keys,' he said.

'Hallaran keeps them all locked in his desk in his office.'

'Not too big on trust, huh?' Bishop lowered the canvas and said, 'So this Ryan, the computer specialist. He doesn't go out and meet the customers with Hallaran?'

Neeson shook his head. 'There's no need. He mostly stays in his room, either working or sleeping.'

'Good. Take me there.'

'Take . . . ? But I already gave you his location on that map.'

Bishop pointed his gun. 'So is that a no?'

Neeson's eyes grew wide. '*No, don't.* I'll take you.'

But as soon as he turned in the direction of the door, Bishop raised the Sig and brought it straight down, the grip striking Neeson just behind his right ear. The older man collapsed silently to the floor, his head coming to a rest against Bishop's feet.

'On second thoughts,' Bishop said, pulling a roll of duct tape from a pocket, 'I'll find him myself.'

EIGHTY-ONE

Bishop worked fast. Using his Maglite for illumination, he turned off the sidelights and secured the bound Neeson in the BMW's rear cargo area. Two cars down, he found a similar-sized vehicle and removed the protective canvas tarpaulin, which he used to cover the BMW. With any luck, nobody would notice there was an extra SUV in here until it was too late.

Gripping the Sig, Bishop jogged over to the door straight ahead and opened it a crack. He saw a well-lit, narrow corridor receding into the distance with doors on either side. The nearest one on the right was open. He spotted the main corridor intersection about four hundred feet ahead. Nobody was in sight. He pulled the door open and stepped through.

Now he heard the faint sounds of human voices from the open doorway ahead. To his left he saw, affixed to the wall, a red fire-pull station under a clear tamper cover. He went over and tapped a knuckle lightly against the wall. White plywood. Probably wood panelling underneath. Sounded like it was at least a couple of inches thick. Looking up, he studied the ceiling fifteen feet above, and saw sprinklers placed at hundred foot intervals.

Bishop frowned at that. Sprinklers were all well and good, but Hallaran would know better than most how quickly fires could get out of hand. What if the sprinklers malfunctioned? Where were the back-up extinguishers? There should have been some around here. A meticulous type like Hallaran would insist on it. That was definitely something worth thinking about. But it was already 00.44. Twelve minutes before the guard called in. Maybe less. He needed to move. Four rooms between him and the intersection ahead. Two on either side. According to the plan, the medical room and Hallaran's office were on the left, communal kitchen and communications room on the right. The voices were coming from the kitchen.

Bishop crept along the right wall until he was able to peer in. He saw a large, cavernous dining area with the usual furnishings and plenty of tables and chairs. Further in, he could just make out the back of one guy as he sipped from a cup of something. He was standing up, and wore a light blue shirt, jeans and a shoulder holster. Bishop couldn't see the other guy. Then the man who was drinking laughed at something and Bishop darted past the opening. The impulsive part of his brain was urging him to bring down the odds now, while he had the chance. But he wouldn't be able to do it quietly, and anything less would raise the alarm too soon.

Just stick to the plan, Bishop. Change it only when there's no other choice.

He kept moving. Up ahead, he noticed a small window next to the comms room door. That was a detail Neeson had neglected to mention. Bishop edged along the wall until he reached the window. Crouching down underneath, he raised part of his head for a look inside. He saw maps pasted on the walls, with communications equipment and monitors on a long table against the far wall. A man in a baseball cap sat at the table with his head down, his attention on the newspaper before him.

That's it, brother. You just keep on reading.

Still crouching, Bishop moved past the door and along the wall to the junction. The north–south corridor was much wider than the one he was in. He looked to the left and saw one more intersection down there. He turned the other way and saw another three corridors on the left and one near the end on the right. But just past the comms room was a large open space, which had to be the reception area. He heard more voices and various sounds coming from that direction.

Bishop suddenly saw part of a foot materialize from the last corridor and quickly pulled his head back. He stood up with his back against the wall and looked left. He was acutely aware that the two in the kitchen could discover him at any moment. But he couldn't move now.

He focused on the footsteps coming down the corridor towards him. Just one man, it sounded like. Then they stopped.

Bishop waited. And listened. He couldn't hear anything except muffled conversation.

He was about to poke part of his head round when the footsteps started up again. Two sets this time. And they were moving away from him. Bishop chanced a look and saw an overweight man in deep conversation with the man beside him as they walked back down the hallway. This one was wearing a dark shirt and pants and looked in much better shape. He wasn't wearing a sidearm, either. Bishop thought this could well be Hallaran. He had an air of authority about him that was hard to fake.

Bishop watched for a couple more seconds, absently fingering the trigger of the Sig as he weighed the pros and cons of direct action. But he quickly discounted it and ran across the passageway and entered the opposite corridor. There were six doors along here. Three on each side, and no windows. Another fire pull station at the end. One for every corridor, he guessed. But still no extinguishers in sight.

The first door on the left had the number 9 stamped on it and two heavy duty, steel fence latches at the top and bottom. No locks. So everybody had easy access to the victims whenever they felt like it. With beautiful women behind every door, that kind of arrangement was open to abuse. And from what the sentry had said, some of the men in here were happy to make the most of the situation. Maybe all of them. Bishop stored that thought away.

The door opposite was Abraham's old room. It had no markings and a deadbolt lock in addition to the steel latches. These were probably added once Patricia Tatem took residency. She and Vallejo were possibly in there right now. Maybe just a few feet away from him. He fought the urge to unlock the door and kept walking down the passageway. He passed rooms 8 and 7 and two unmarked doors. At the end, he saw what looked like another corridor running along the hangar's east wall. Neeson hadn't mentioned that, either. He peered round the corner and saw it travelled the entire length of the building.

So all the rooms on this side of the building could be accessed from this corridor. That was useful to know.

Bishop walked back to the last unmarked door and took a look at the lock. Another deadbolt. Well, there were ways around that.

From one of the pockets of his combats, he pulled out the manual lock pick gun and double-ended tension wrench he'd also picked up in Phoenix. The gun worked on the same principle as the bump keys, but could access a much wider variety of locks. Like deadbolts. With one eye on the kitchen doorway at the other end of the passage, Bishop carefully inserted the tension wrench into the keyhole. Then he inserted the needle of the gun just above and kept pressing the trigger, applying rotating pressure to the tension wrench with his thumb. On the fourth attempt, he felt the pins jump into the hole casing.

Pocketing his tools, Bishop carefully turned the handle and opened the door.

EIGHTY-TWO

Inside, the lights were on. Sweeping the room with his gun, Bishop quietly shut and locked the door behind him. He was in a large living area with some futuristic-looking leather furniture in the centre, a home theatre system at one end and a pool table in the corner. It was a mess. The whole place stank of stale food. Books, magazines and dirty clothes everywhere. But no Ryan. And no sounds other than his own breathing.

There was an entranceway to his immediate left. Bishop stepped through into another similar sized area. And just as messy. There were unwashed clothes on the king-sized bed and more all over the floor. Against the wall was another widescreen TV and there was an en-suite bathroom to the right. But straight ahead was a set of heavily tinted glass sliding doors running from one side of the room to the other. Behind these was another large room, the centrepiece of which was a large conference table filled with hardware of some kind. Bishop could see somebody sitting at the table with his back to him, working on a computer. That had to be Ryan.

Keeping his gun aimed at the man's back, Bishop edged over to the bathroom and glanced inside. It was empty. Then he crossed the bedroom, grasped the handle of the central glass door and slowly slid it to the left. He heard the air conditioner blasting away inside first, followed by the sound of fingers tapping rapidly on a keyboard. Ryan, a long-haired, skinny guy in T-shirt and shorts, sounded as though he was going for a speed record. Computers of all sizes, monitors, scanners, hard drives, cables, and various other accessories covered every inch of the table, with even more stuff stacked underneath. There were box shelves against one wall, containing a mass of manuals and yet more paraphernalia.

Bishop stepped inside and walked towards the programmer, not caring if he was heard or not.

When he came abreast of Ryan, the younger man looked up from his screen and shrieked. He jumped off the seat and hit the floor just as the seat toppled over and landed next to him. Staring at the gun aimed at his head he raised a hand and shouted, '*Don't shoot*. Please. Who *are* you? What do you want?'

'My name doesn't matter,' Bishop said. 'And what I want is for you call up the files of every woman you people have snatched since you started. I want current locations, names of family members you had killed, everything. And if I hear the words "I don't know what you're talking about", I'll shoot you right now.'

Ryan blinked at him. His mouth moved but no words came out. Finally, he said, 'Look, whoever you are, I don't know what you been told, but we don't hold on to that kind of information. It's too risky. Each time we finish a deal I wipe everything. That's the truth.'

Bishop smiled for the first time. It wasn't a friendly smile. 'A smart guy. I knew it as soon as I saw you. I really like smart guys. Their instinct for self-preservation is second to none. And I figure a smart guy would keep a copy of everything tucked away on one of these hard drives, or email it to himself, just in case he ever felt vulnerable. Am I right?'

'You got it all wrong, man. Hallaran watches over my shoulder when I delete the stuff and always makes sure there's no trace left on my server. I'm not lying to you.'

Bishop nodded and set the chair back on its wheels. 'Okay, sit down with your back perfectly straight, facing the computer.'

'Huh?'

Bishop pulled back the hammer and said, 'Want me to repeat myself?'

Ryan swallowed and stood up. He sat on the chair and straightened his back until it was at a ninety degree angle to the floor. Bishop then gripped the man's right shoulder tightly with one hand, keeping him in place. With the other, he pressed the barrel of the gun against the top of Ryan's spine, between the first and second cervical vertebrae. Pointing straight down.

'What are you doing?' Ryan asked. He was shivering now, and Bishop didn't think it was because of the air conditioning.

'Making sure I've got the angle right. I've done this before, and if you twitch at the wrong moment it could pierce your heart. I only want to sever your spinal column so I need you to take a deep breath and keep your body completely still. Ready?'

Ryan swivelled his head round and stared wildly up at Bishop. '*Jesus, no.* I've got it all hidden away, like you said. I sent them to different accounts in pieces. I'll show you. Just take the gun away. Please. I'll do it now.'

Bishop narrowed his eyes and looked at his watch. 00.49. Then he reached into a pocket, brought out two flash drives and dropped them on the desk. 'Okay, copy the information onto both of these. You got three minutes.'

Ryan nodded eagerly and rolled the chair over to the largest monitor and switched it on. Then he unrolled a silicone rubber keyboard and got to work. Once Bishop saw the home page for an email service, he turned away and studied the other items on the desk. Most of it was beyond him, of course. But then, he'd never exactly been computer literate. Sometimes he thought he'd been born in the wrong century. Most of the time, in fact.

He looked up. Sprinklers in here, too. And the bedroom. Everywhere, it seemed. Hallaran really was the obsessive type.

But there was something else bugging him. Anomalies always did that. 'Hallaran has an office a few doors down, right?' he said. 'Next to the medical room?'

'That's right.' Ryan was scrolling through a list of emails.

'Why? He could convert a room in his living quarters like you. And it's three times the size of this place.'

Ryan shook his head. 'How should I know? Maybe that's what he did. I know he doesn't use that office much these days.'

'He doesn't, huh?' That was interesting. Bishop rubbed a palm over his head as he considered Hallaran's working methods. So far, he'd proved he was all about preparation. So why would a person like that build an office he knew he'd rarely use? There had to be a good reason.

After Bishop was done here, it might be worth checking that room out. He had a hunch it might hold some answers.

When he checked his watch again, it was 00.51. 'Time's almost up.'

'I'm nearly done. Just this last folder to detach and then I'll drag them onto the flash drives.'

'I want to look one over before you do it.'

Ryan nodded. Bishop waited as he finished up, then quit out of the internet browser. Bishop saw the desktop contained seven untitled folders that hadn't been there before. Ryan turned to him and said, 'Ready.'

'Move aside,' Bishop said.

Ryan rolled his chair to the right. Bishop came over and clicked on the third folder down. Inside were about thirty files categorized by date. Each one had a woman's name as its title. Bishop clicked on one of two named *Victoria*. A page opened up in the format of a purchase order, giving the amount paid, the woman's full name of Victoria Elizabeth Connor, and the name of the new owner. As if she was a piece of meat. The sheer arrogance of the thing made him sick. And angry. He scrolled to the next page and saw a list itemizing the surgical procedures undertaken by Tatem. The third page gave names and addresses of family. The fourth showed before and after photos. There was more, but Bishop had seen enough.

He closed it off and went through each of the other folders until he found Selina's file in the very last one. He dragged that file to the trash and was about to close the folder when he noticed the very last file: *Expenses*. Bishop clicked on it and a spreadsheet opened up. It listed outgoings on a month-by-month basis. Fuel. Food. Electrics. The usual. Except there was also a listing for *Police*.

And underneath that was a name. But not the one he'd expected to see.

Levine.

So he'd been right about the inside man, but wrong about Shaw. It was his senior partner with the heavy-lidded eyes and the relaxed manner. And with the money he was being paid on the side, why shouldn't he be relaxed? Levine must have entered Rutherford's place first and closed the windows again to make it look like suicide while Shaw called it in. Another riddle solved. No doubt Kate would find this all very interesting. He'd give her one of these flash drives later for her story. Assuming he got out of this alive. But then you had to stay positive, or what was the point of anything?

'Okay,' Bishop said and moved out of the way. 'Finish up.'

Ryan rolled the chair back and Bishop waited as he transferred everything over to the first flash drive. He repeated the process with the second, then handed both sticks to Bishop.

'Whatever you're here to do,' he pleaded, 'maybe I can help.'

'I don't think so,' Bishop said, and struck Ryan on the base of the neck with his gun. The man fell forward in the chair, unconscious. 'But thanks, anyway.'

EIGHTY-THREE

Bishop entered the 'office' and carefully locked the door again behind him. The deadbolt had given him about as much trouble as the last one. He found the light switch and saw he was in a big, cavernous room, about fifty feet by fifty. There was a massive oak desk against one wall, with a computer, monitor and telephone on the surface. Three director's chairs surrounded it. Another one behind it. That was all. The rest of the room was empty. Every movement of Bishop's caused a minor echo. He looked up and saw eight circular lights. And no sprinkler. *How about that?*

He checked the time. 00.53. Three minutes left before the guard, Lane, reported in. If he hadn't already.

Bishop walked behind the desk and moved the chair out of the way. This would be the best place to put it. Where nobody was likely to discover it by mistake. He knelt down and studied the carpet tiles. They were about twenty-four inches by twenty-four. He took the Ka-Bar knife from his ankle holster and inserted it in the one of the cracks and lifted a little. He levered the rest of the tile up with his fingers and put it to one side. Underneath was standard concrete flooring.

It took five more tiles until he found the trapdoor. Bishop smiled. The steel panel was exactly the same size as the tile above and perfectly flush with the floor. The surface was featureless except for two recessed hinges on the left and a quarter-inch hole on the right of centre, about a half-inch deep. He got up and stepped over to the desk. There were two large drawers at each end. The first one he tried was unlocked. It was also empty. He tried the second drawer, but this one was locked. He had it open in less than five seconds.

It was full of keys, like Neeson said. Mostly car keys from the looks of it. There was a strip of white plastic attached to each key ring with a vehicle make and licence number written in marker. Only the keys for the limo were missing. But he kept sifting through until he found what he was looking for. A five-inch long iron key with a triangular handle and a rectangular-shaped end. The kind of tool used to prise open light-duty manhole covers. Or trapdoors set in the floor. He'd expected Hallaran would keep a spare. The man was nothing if not thorough.

Bishop went back, inserted it into the hole and turned it clockwise until it clicked into place. He then pulled the trapdoor all the way open until it rested against the floor. He also saw a large locking bar connected to the inner part of the door, allowing it to be opened and locked from the inside.

Inside, there was a steel stepladder leading down to a narrow, makeshift clearing seven or eight feet below. Bishop took out his Maglite, descended a few steps and shone it around the interior. It was a tunnel. Or the starting point for one.

Hallaran's personal escape route.

Like he'd suspected. A thorough man would always have a Plan B in case everything went down the crapper. One only he knew about. And this was Hallaran's.

The tunnel was about five feet wide and pointing north, with concrete foundation pillars every few feet. The Maglite only let him see so much before darkness took over. But it probably led to a grille somewhere beyond the perimeter fencing. No doubt safely camouflaged from accidental discovery. Bishop also saw three heavy-duty flashlights and a large plastic water jug on the ground. And one other item: a bright orange, twelve-gauge flare gun with a spare cartridge affixed to the side.

Bishop took the flare gun and came back up. It all made sense now. Everything. Including this. He was just confirming it was loaded when he caught sight of his watch. It was 00.56 already.

Shit. He was out of time. He had to get to Vallejo, fast.

Then he heard the sound of a key in the door.

EIGHTY-FOUR

Bishop moved quickly, edging along the wall until he was halfway along. He was side on to the door, which meant they'd have to enter the room before they saw him. Bishop heard the key turn in the lock and cocked the flare gun's firing pin. Aimed the flare gun at the door.

The door opened part of the way and a man wearing a light blue shirt and jeans stepped into the room. The same man Bishop had seen in the kitchen. His eyes landed on Bishop and he immediately reached for his shoulder holster.

Bishop pulled the trigger. There was a brief flash, accompanied by a sharp *pft* sound, and then the flare was embedded in the man's chest. He fell back against the wall making 'uh, uh' sounds, while his hands scrabbled for purchase on the incandescent, 1100-degree candle burning though his shirt. Dropping the gun, Bishop sprinted forward, closing the distance in less than a second. He gripped the sides of the guard's skull in both hands and violently twisted it clockwise until he heard the snap.

The man immediately went limp. Bishop checked his pulse and felt nothing. After a few more seconds the flare went out, too.

Bishop breathed out. *So much for making plans*, he thought. Still, they were a man down now. Two, if you counted Abraham. Three, if you counted Ryan, currently bound and gagged in his bathroom.

Bishop got up and shut the door. Then he came back and searched the man's pockets. The billfold contained a driver's licence for Patrick Baldwin, one of the rapists Neeson had name-checked at the gate. He put it back and pulled the gun from the holster. It was a black Walther PPS. Looked fairly new. He ejected the magazine and counted fifteen rounds. The holster also held a spare magazine, so he took that, too.

And the Midland two-way radio attached to his belt. Then Bishop got up and dragged Baldwin along the floor and dropped the body through the trapdoor. He closed it up and slipped the key into his pocket, reloaded and pocketed the flare gun, then ran to the door.

He opened it a crack, heard nothing, and slipped out. Crouching as he passed the comms room window, he heard the guard in there speaking to somebody on the radio. The plane had to be close to landing now. He checked his watch again. 00.59. He didn't have much time. He checked the main corridor was clear and dashed across.

Standing in front of the door to Abraham's apartment, he carefully slid the latches across. After using the pick gun on the lock, Bishop opened the door and quickly entered the room.

The lights were on in here, too. He saw Vallejo sitting on the couch. A woman with the same face as the one in Tatem's photos sat in an adjoining chair. Both were looking at him. Bishop raised a single finger to his lips as he shut the door, then Vallejo was up off the couch and jogging over to him, a grin plastered over her face.

'Unbelievable,' she said, slowly shaking her head. 'I could actually kiss you right now, Bishop. On the lips.'

'Better not,' he said, 'you'd only regret it later.' He turned to the other woman, who was coming over to join them. 'You're Patricia Tatem?'

'Yes,' she said. 'How did you get in here? What—?'

'No time for explanations,' he interrupted. 'We're up against it. You both ready to move?'

'You bet your ass we are,' Vallejo said.

Bishop nodded and handed her Baldwin's Walther and the spare magazine. 'That makes thirty rounds, including one in the chamber.' Vallejo pocketed the spare, still grinning, while Bishop took the fully loaded .38 Special from a jacket pocket and showed it to Patricia. 'This is your husband's. He ever teach you how to use it?'

She gave a tight smile. 'More like *I* taught *him*.'

'Excellent,' Bishop said. He'd been right about her. Tough as nails. He handed her the gun. 'Just don't get trigger happy. Use as a last resort only.'

'I understand. So are we leaving now?'

He shook his head. 'Not without the other women. Apparently, there are seven more locked in their rooms, including Selina. Vallejo, I assume you know what this is about now.'

'Yeah, Patricia filled me in on what this place is. So what's the plan?'

Bishop passed her the sketch Neeson had made and pointed to their current location. 'This is us. The numbered rooms are where the women are held, except for 8 and 9, which are both vacant. So to start with, you'll need to wake them up and drag them back here in batches. There's no telling how they'll react after being doped up for so long, so Patricia, you'll need to stay with them so they don't freak out.'

'Okay,' she said.

Vallejo frowned at the map. 'No. 7's easy, but what about these ones at the other end?'

'Well, Selina's in No. 3, so you won't be able to do anything until they've taken her out to meet the buyer. His plane's coming in now. Then you'll just have to gather the rest, somehow, and bring them back to join the others.'

'While avoiding the armed goons,' Vallejo said.

'It might not be too bad. The head man, Hallaran, is short-staffed now, so they'll all be busy preparing for the plane's arrival. That's the theory, anyway.' On the map, he pointed at the hangar's east wall and said, 'The good news is there's a passageway along here that runs the length of the hangar, so you can access those rooms without going down the main central corridor.'

Bishop turned to Patricia. Pointing at the office diagonally opposite the room they were in, he said, 'This is where you want to take the first group of women. There's a steel trapdoor by the desk that leads down to Hallaran's personal escape tunnel.' He gave her the key. 'This opens it, and there's a locking bar on the other side. You'll also find the body of one of the guards down there, so you better take a bed sheet to cover it with.'

Vallejo looked at him. 'You've been busy.'

'Idle hands,' he said with a shrug. 'Patricia, once you get yourself and those women down in that tunnel, you wait for Vallejo and the rest. Arrange a code so that you'll recognize her when she knocks. Otherwise, keep it locked. Once you're all together, follow it to the end and out. I don't know where it leads, but it'll be better than here.'

'*If* everything goes as planned,' Vallejo said. 'So where will you be during all this?'

'Going after Selina. She's the main reason I'm here, remember?'

Vallejo snorted. 'What? All on your own?'

'Don't worry about me.' From his windbreaker pocket, Bishop pulled out one of the flash drives and a spare cell phone he'd brought along. 'Keep these safe. If you get into trouble and need to contact me, just speed dial one. I'll try to—'

Just then, the two-way radio in Bishop's pocket crackled to life. He brought it out as a voice said, '*Grieco, status report.*' Bishop recognized it immediately. Hallaran.

A deep, baritone voice came back: '*Just got off the radio with the pilot, sir. He said he sees the lights and estimated they'll be on the ground in three minutes or less.*'

'*Good. You'd better go now if you're going to meet them.*'

'*Yes, sir. Out.*'

Perfect. Bishop turned the volume down and said, 'That's my cue. Remember, if it comes down to the wire, shoot to kill. 'Cause they'll do the same to you.'

'I won't forget,' Vallejo said and touched his arm. 'You be careful, huh?'

'You too,' he said and jogged over to the door. He opened it and peered left. Six seconds later, he heard the sound of another door opening and pulled his head back. When he heard footsteps getting fainter, he peered round again. He saw a stocky, well-muscled man in a baseball cap marching down the corridor towards the garage door. He wore one of those nylon hip holsters on his right side and was twirling a key ring around his finger.

Grieco. The man from the comms room.

The moment he stepped through the doorway and into the garage, Bishop followed.

EIGHTY-FIVE

Bishop glanced both ways at the junction, saw it was clear and then sprinted all out for the door straight ahead, reaching it four seconds later.

He turned the handle and opened the door a crack. The lights were on inside: six industrial-sized fluorescent tubes running along the length of the garage. To his left, about fifty feet away, Grieco was walking towards the limo at the end, still playing with the key ring.

Bishop silently pulled the door shut behind him and ducked between the two vehicles directly ahead. When he reached the trunks, he raised his head and saw Grieco turn near the end and approach the driver's side of the limo.

As soon as he opened the door, Bishop began moving at a half-crouch from car to car in that direction. He was four vehicles from the end when he heard the limo's engine start up. He moved to the next vehicle. Then he heard the car door open again, accompanied by the *bing, bing, bing* of an electronic warning chime and the sound of footsteps. Bishop figured Grieco was under orders to turn off the interior lights before opening the garage doors.

He moved to the next car's rear bumper. Stopped. Then on to the next. He was halfway along the second-from-last vehicle's bumper when the lights went out. Good. Bishop liked the dark. Peering over the trunk, he saw the only illumination was coming from the limo's interior. He kept his eye on the open door, listening to the man's footsteps as he came back. Then he watched as Grieco got in the driver's seat and reached for his seat belt.

As soon as he shut the door, Bishop turned into the space between the cars and crept up to the driver's side. Behind him, he heard the sound of the garage doors opening and he placed the Sig back in his shoulder holster. Better to keep things quiet if he could.

He watched as the garage shutters arced up, placing his hand on the door latch. Before they reached the top, he stood up and yanked the door open.

The car's interior light came on. Grieco looked up and gaped at Bishop at though he'd just seen the Rapture. Bishop pulled his right arm back and chopped at the man's larynx with the hard edge of his palm. Grieco made a gagging noise and lurched forward as blood erupted from his mouth and onto his pants. Bishop reached in with both hands and finished him, using the same move he'd used on Baldwin.

Bringing down the odds, one at time. That's the way to beat them.

Bishop pulled the lever to pop the trunk, placed Grieco's baseball cap on his own head and clipped the man's holster to his belt. This one held a Glock 23 with a full magazine of seventeen .40 S&W rounds. And another spare mag in the side pocket. In situations like this, you couldn't have too many guns, or too much ammo.

Bishop dragged the body back and stuffed it in the trunk. Then he got behind the wheel and backed the limo out. There was a remote on the passenger seat and Bishop pressed the button that closed the shutters. He aimed the limo in the direction of the front gate and checked himself in the mirror as he drove. The cap and the tinted glass should help at the entrance. If not, he'd simply have to reduce the enemy's ranks by one more. But he hoped it wouldn't come to that just yet. Nice and quiet was how he wanted it. For now.

As he got closer to the gatehouse Bishop tried to make out Lane, the guard, but saw no sign of him. When he was within a hundred feet of the fence, the gates began to automatically open inwards. He looked to his right and saw Lane lean out of a window and wave him through. Bishop lowered the visor on his cap and waved back as he drove by.

Just business as usual.

Bishop hung a left as soon as he was through, refusing to dwell on how easy that had been. It wouldn't last. He just kept the limo at a steady twenty, and when the perimeter fence turned left again, so did he. He pressed the button to lower the window and tried to discern the sound of a plane, but couldn't hear anything yet.

Another thirty seconds and he was past the hangar. Movement over there caused Bishop to turn his head. But it was just the fuel tanker coming out of the annex at the rear. A six-wheeler with maybe a three or four thousand gallon load capacity. He'd almost forgotten about the refuelling. Now he was glad he hadn't had to kill Lane.

Fifteen seconds more and he was past the perimeter fence. Ahead was just darkness and desert. Except he could now make out faint landing lights in the ground a half mile away, arranged in an east–west direction. Faint from his position, but probably as clear as day when seen from above. And he could also hear the distant sound of a prop plane coming from the east. Sounded like a single-engine, but he couldn't be sure.

Bishop aimed for the most westerly part of the strip and spotted lights in the sky about half a mile away. When he was about a hundred feet from the landing strip Bishop stopped the limo, but kept the engine running.

1.06 a.m., according to the dashboard clock. Looked like they were right on time.

Less than a minute later, Bishop watched as the plane came in at a perfect angle. It touched down, decreased its speed and finally came to a stop with fifty feet to spare, perfectly placed in the centre of the airstrip. Bishop put the limo in gear and drove over to meet it.

The corporate jet was a single-engine turboprop, as he'd guessed. Most had twin propellers, one on each wing, but this only had the one. Possibly a Pilatus. Bishop remembered one of his old clients having owned something similar. He pulled up outside the passenger door on the port side. There were four small windows along the body and a cargo door at the rear. He didn't have to wait long before somebody inside opened the passenger door and lowered it to the ground.

A large, shaven-headed, dark-skinned man in a sports jacket and slacks appeared in the entranceway and glared at the limo. Bishop leaned out and touched a finger against his cap visor. 'How you doin'?' he said.

The bodyguard disappeared for a moment and then came back out, taking the steps two at a time. He came up to Bishop and said, 'Name.'

'Mine or yours?' Bishop said.

The bodyguard's expression didn't change.

'Hey, I'm just screwing with you. I'm Grieco, your limo driver. Call Mr Hallaran if you don't believe me.' Bishop pulled the two-way from his belt and offered it to the man.

The bodyguard ignored it, turned to the plane and nodded to another steroid abuser waiting at the top of the steps. He had the exact same build and dress sense, but he had long hair tied back in a ponytail. Even in the darkness, Bishop saw facial similarities. Maybe they were brothers or something. Ponytail said something in Portuguese, then moved aside as a third man came down the steps. He wore an expensive-looking suit and looked to be in his mid-fifties. He had grey, receding hair. His face was heavily lined and his expression sombre. He looked like a man used to getting what he wanted. This had to be Poleina.

Shaved-head went back and opened the limo's rear door. Poleina quickly ducked inside and sprawled out on the back seat like he owned it. Shaved-head followed him in, closed the door and took the jump seat opposite. Ponytail came round the front of the vehicle, opened the passenger door and sat next to Bishop. 'Drive,' he said.

'Way ahead of you,' Bishop said and started back the way he'd come. He looked in the rear-view. Poleina was looking out the right-hand window at the hangar in the distance.

'Nice landing,' Bishop said.

'Thank you,' said Poleina without turning from the window. 'Gerardo?'

Ponytail turned to Bishop and said, 'No more talk. Drive.'

Bishop shrugged and drove. Halfway back, they passed the fuel tanker coming the other way, also with its headlights off. Less than ninety seconds later, he reached the entrance gates and Lane opened them and waved the car through like before. Bishop didn't wave back this time. He just kept going towards the hangar, passing the garage shutters and stopping outside a nondescript door a couple of hundred feet further along. Bishop was only guessing, but this had to be the entrance to the reception room.

'Here we are,' Bishop said. 'Door to door service, as advertised.'

Without another word, all three men exited the car and approached the hangar door. He watched Gerardo open the door and go in first, followed by Poleina, then Shaved-head.

Bishop rolled his window back up and turned off the engine, hoping Vallejo and Patricia were making progress. He looked at his watch. 01.13. This was the worst part. Waiting for Poleina to deliver Selina to him. Neeson said it usually took half an hour to finalize everything. Once they were all inside the car, he could take care of Poleina and his men. Then it was a simple matter of taking out Lane at the gate and driving on through. Hallaran was a luxury he'd have to save for later.

Sure. Nothing easier.

Except Bishop had been on countless missions during his eight years in uniform, and something invariably went wrong somewhere along the line. It was inevitable. Life wasn't like the movies, and human error was just something you had to factor in right from the start. And right now, there was too much happening over which he had no control. Too many people. And the fact that it had been plain sailing thus far only added to his uneasiness.

Experience told him they were due for a slip-up. So Bishop sat back and tried to anticipate all the ways that could happen. The possibilities were almost limitless, but that didn't stop him. He had nothing else to occupy his time.

He was still thinking on it at 01.26, when he heard gunfire coming from inside.

EIGHTY-SIX

Bishop pulled the keys from the ignition and jumped out of the car. As he was locking it, the radio on his belt burst into life again.

'*Grieco, Baldwin, Kiervan,*' Hallaran yelled, '*get your asses to the south side of the hangar right now. We got a shooter in room 2. The dyke cop.*' More gunshots. '*She's got some of the women with her. Sullivan, cover the main entrance. Lane, you stay in position at the gate and make sure Poleina gets out okay. And keep your eyes peeled for a male intruder. He'll be around here somewhere. Everybody report your positions now.*'

'*This is Kiervan,*' another voice said, sounding out of breath. '*Pilot's still in the middle of refuelling. I'm running back now. Be there in four minutes or less. Lane, get ready to open that gate for me.*'

'*Lane here. Copy that. Am waiting at the gate.*'

'*Sullivan here. Making for the main entrance now.*'

Bishop pressed 'Transmit', rubbed the speaker back and forth over his cheek stubble to mask his voice and said in a baritone, '*Grieco here. Coming in now.*' Then he clicked off.

He turned the volume down, ran over to the hangar and pressed himself against the wall a few feet from the door. He held the Sig Sauer to his chest and just stood there, waiting. With Grieco and Baldwin down, that left Hallaran and one more goon inside. Plus two more, Kiervan and Sullivan, on their way. As for the civilians, Ryan was out for the count and if the two hypnotherapists had any sense they'd have locked themselves in their rooms at the first sound of gunfire. One of them had probably been the fat man he'd spotted earlier.

Bishop saw movement at his left. A tiny human silhouette about two or three hundred yards away, running towards the hangar door.

Bishop heard more gunshots coming from inside. He'd given Vallejo thirty rounds. How much did she have left? He needed to get to her fast. But first, he had to wait for this Sullivan to close the distance. *Come on, boy. Your boss is calling.*

The shape had halved the distance already. He was moving at a good clip. Bishop watched him get bigger and bigger. When he judged Sullivan was about twenty feet away, Bishop pushed away from the wall, raised the Sig and aimed it dead centre at the man's chest area. He fired three times in quick succession and Sullivan went down soundlessly in heap, like the strings had been cut. Bishop ran over, gun aimed at the spot where he'd fallen. When he saw the body, he pointed the gun at the man's head and fired again. The man's left leg jerked once and then was still.

It was always best to be thorough. Bishop had learned that lesson the hard way a long time ago. He didn't need any nasty surprises creeping up behind him.

Bishop knelt down and checked for the man's gun, but the holster and both his hands were empty. He found his Maglite, played the beam around the body and still couldn't see it. He knew it had to be here somewhere, but he didn't have time. He ran back to the door and heard shouting from within. And it didn't sound like English.

As he pulled the door open he also grabbed Grieco's Glock from his hip holster. He re-entered the hangar with a gun in each hand, covering everything in front of him.

The 'reception room' was a vast open space resembling a modern loft conversion, with oak flooring, and white walls and ceiling. There were carefully designed nooks here and there, stocked with modern seating and tables. Fifty feet away, Poleina stood in one of these recesses, gripping the shoulder of a blonde woman in a white, spaghetti-strap dress.

It was Selina. Even from a distance Bishop could tell.

Finally, he was able to confirm she was alive with his own eyes. The sense of relief he felt was almost palpable. Because he knew that whatever happened next, history wouldn't be repeating itself. He wouldn't be finding Selina in the same state as he'd found Laurette

Chounan all those years ago. That was what he'd been dreading the most. But he didn't waste time with further reflection. That was all in the past. There was still too much to do in the here and now.

Poleina was shouting at Gerardo, who was busy tying a piece of bloody material around his associate's wounded shoulder. In the light, they really looked like brothers. Which meant they probably were.

Then Poleina noticed Bishop and turned with the girl. Both bodyguards instantly raised their weapons in his direction. Bishop kept his guns pointed at the ground and jogged over. He was still one of Hallaran's men as far as they were concerned. Not a threat. As long as Selina didn't blow his cover.

As he got closer, he watched her face. She looked confused and scared. Still as pretty as ever, but the eyes looking back at him were different. Not just drugged, but older. The spark he'd seen before was missing. Maybe forever. Then Bishop saw a glint of recognition enter them. Slowing, he stared hard at her and gave a minuscule shake of his head. *Say nothing.* He had no idea if she understood.

'Stop there,' Poleina said. 'Hallaran said we leave now. He wants you inside. Where are the keys for the car?'

Bishop came to a halt ten feet away. Help Selina or Vallejo? Or more to the point, help who first? But he already knew the answer. They had two guns trained on him. One of them looked like a micro Uzi machine pistol, but smaller. The moment he brought his arms around, they'd cut him to pieces. He was no good to Selina dead. And Vallejo would be out of ammo soon.

'They're still in the ignition,' he lied, edging to the left. Keeping his eyes on Selina, he said, 'I'll come back for you.'

Poleina frowned and said, 'Thank you, but we will be fine on our own.' Bishop hoped Selina had understood what he was saying, but she made no response.

Bishop left them and ran towards the sounds of gunfire. She'd been inches away from him. Almost close enough to touch. He told himself he had no choice. That with the car keys in his pocket, they'd have to make for the plane by foot. With a wounded man and a girl in heels. That would take at least five minutes. And the pilot would have to finish refuelling, too. Then prepare for take-off. It would all take time. He checked his watch as he ran. 01.28. From now on, every second counted.

At the back of the room were two wide entranceways leading to the main north–south corridor. By the time he reached the right-hand opening, the gunfire had stopped. Temporarily, at least. He poked part of his head round and looked to his right, towards the south side of the hangar. He saw nobody. He heard faraway voices, but they were indistinct.

Holstering the Glock, he pulled his cell from a pocket, pressed the 2 button and held it to his ear. After what seemed like minutes, the ringing tone was replaced by Vallejo's breathless voice. 'I was just about to call. We're in bad shape here, Bishop.'

'I figured,' he said. 'What's your situation, how many of you are there, and how much ammo have you got left?'

'We're in room 2. I had the last four women with me, but two of them panicked and ran out of here screaming when the gunfire started. They're both dead, about ten feet away from me. I'm down to my last six rounds. I think two bad guys. One each end of this passageway. We're blocked in with no way out. Wait one.' Bishop heard two loud shots, followed by a burst of return fire. Then Vallejo said, 'Down to four rounds now, but I think I might have hit one of them. I live in hope.'

'What about Patricia?'

'Far as I know, she's at the tunnel with the other two, waiting for me.'

'Okay, maybe I can help get you there. I'll call you back.'

He hung up and peered round again. Still nobody in sight. There were two intersections to his right. The first allowed access to rooms 4 to 6. The last led to rooms 1, 2 and 3. To his left was the main east–west corridor. He ran for that one.

EIGHTY-SEVEN

When Bishop reached the end of the corridor he checked both ways. The left was clear. But so was the right. Yet if Vallejo had been right about being flanked at both ends, Bishop should have been able to see one of them, even from this distance.

Then he looked more carefully. There *was* somebody down there, but he was lying on the floor. Easy to miss at this distance. Maybe Vallejo was a better shot than she gave herself credit for. Still holding the Sig, Bishop ran to the other end of the corridor, finally reaching the figure almost thirty seconds later.

The man was lying on his back, a Glock forgotten in his right hand. He was staring calmly at the ceiling. Blood was pumping steadily out of the gunshot wound in his neck and pooling around his head. It wasn't the same guy he'd seen talking with the fat man earlier. Different clothes. Which meant this probably wasn't Hallaran. Pity.

Bishop reached down and plucked the gun from his hand. The man was too far gone to notice. Bishop checked the magazine. Almost empty. There was a spare magazine in his pocket, though, so Bishop took that and tossed the gun. He then stepped over the dying man and peered round the next corner, scanning the length of the corridor. He saw two female bodies in nightwear lying on the floor, halfway down. Blood everywhere. There was no sign of Hallaran. The door to the second room on the left was wide open. From this position the angle was too acute to see inside.

He brought out his cell and said, 'Vallejo, you there? Vallejo?'

'I'm here,' she said. 'Where are you?'

'On your right, at the end of the corridor.' He looked back at the gunman. The flow of blood had already stopped. 'The man you shot is history. I need you to count to five and then run towards me, okay? I'll cover you.'

'Got it.'

Bishop pocketed the phone and stepped into the corridor, aiming the Sig towards the spot where the other gunman was supposed to be. Bishop had a strong feeling it was Hallaran. It was also possible he'd doubled back to come up behind him. Bishop took a few steps back to the corner so he could see in both directions. There was nothing behind him.

Then a pair of barefoot women in light nightgowns burst out of the room with Vallejo at the rear, shouting, 'Go, go, go.' As they ran towards him, Bishop kept his gun trained on Hallaran's position, expecting gunfire, but there was nothing.

When they reached him, Vallejo saw the body on the floor and said, 'Where's the other one?'

'He'll be around,' Bishop said. He unclipped the belt holster with the Glock and the two spare magazines and passed it to her. 'This is everybody?'

'All except Selina,' Vallejo said, clipping the holster to her own belt.

'Yeah, I saw her when—' Bishop stopped at the faint sounds of gunfire coming from somewhere behind them. Two shots. Then a pause. Followed by three more shots. What did they signify? It couldn't be Patricia. She wouldn't be dumb enough to leave the safety of the tunnel.

Then Bishop looked up as the closest sprinkler twenty feet away suddenly erupted and began spraying the floors and walls. Simultaneously accompanied by the other sprinklers. All of them. In every corridor.

Except he knew it wasn't water pouring out of the sprinkler heads. It was gasoline.

EIGHTY-EIGHT

'Are you kidding me?' Vallejo said, turning in a circle as she held a hand over her nose. The stench of gas was already overpowering, the air already thick with fumes.

'Hallaran's Plan B,' Bishop said. 'He's decided it's time to cut his losses.'

Bishop had already assumed the place was booby-trapped. It had to be. It was the smart move. So, remembering Hallaran's MO up till now, Bishop had simply put two and two together and come up with the only possible answer. This one. It explained the lack of fire extinguishers, as well as the absent sprinkler in the office. And then there was the flare gun he'd picked up earlier in the tunnel. In an emergency, Hallaran could have retreated to that room, fired a flare towards the other side of the hangar and immediately set the place alight. Meanwhile he'd casually make his getaway, confident that all the evidence and any potential witnesses would be destroyed in one go. Especially his own personnel.

Except he couldn't access his tunnel now. Bishop had removed that option. But Hallaran would still be here, somewhere. He wouldn't leave until he was sure Bishop was dead. Until they were *all* dead.

Bishop turned to see Vallejo looking at him, still shaking her head. The two young girls, one a redhead, the other a brunette, were also staring at him as though he had all the answers. *If only*, he thought.

'What are your names?' he asked.

'Emma,' the redhead said.

'I'm Melissa,' said the other one. Her pupils looked like black pearls.

'Okay, Melissa and Emma, we're gonna have to run past these sprinklers. Try and get as little on you as possible. Melissa, take my hand.

348

Emma, take Vallejo's there. I don't want anyone getting left behind. Vallejo, cover our backs as we go, okay?'

'Right,' she said.

Emma said, 'Are we going to die?'

'Eventually,' he said, 'just not today. We ready?'

Emma nodded. Melissa didn't respond. Vallejo said, 'Let's do it.'

Without another word, Bishop set off and they all followed. They progressed down the passageway at a decent speed, splashing through the steadily growing pools of gasoline every few seconds. They kept to the right so the falling rain only came into contact with their feet and lower legs. But even that was too much.

Bishop checked his watch as he ran. It was already 01.32. Selina would be at the plane within a couple of minutes. And not long after that, they'd finish refuelling and take off. He forced himself not to think about it. There was nothing he could do right now. Instead, he focused on Hallaran, who'd be waiting for them. Bishop would have to be ready.

When Bishop reached the corridor that led to the garage, he stopped before it and peered round the corner. He saw a man lying next to an open doorway about fifty yards down, with blood all over his face. One of the hypnotherapists, possibly. Which explained the gunshots he'd heard. Hallaran was just being his usual thorough self. No loose ends allowed.

He turned back to Vallejo. 'Keep an eye out. Hallaran's around here somewhere.'

'I kind of figured that,' she said.

Bishop clutched Melissa's hand again and took off down the corridor at a fast jog, all his senses alert. He slowed at the open doorway, gun aimed at the darkness within, then speeded up again knowing Vallejo was covering their backs. But there were no more shots.

He passed Abraham's room and slowed his pace, stopping just before the end. Above the four-way intersection ahead was another working sprinkler. The floor underneath was drenched in gas. Letting go of Melissa's hand, Bishop took a few paces forward and glanced round the corner. Then immediately dropped to the floor as an automatic weapon sprayed the wall beside him, the bullets barely missing his head as small chunks of plywood rained over his body. It was coming from the reception room to his left. Bishop aimed the Sig in that direction and returned fire. As he crawled back to the safety of the corridor, he got a glimpse of the same man he'd seen earlier. Hallaran.

Then more shots, but from a semi-auto this time. The two girls screamed behind him. Vallejo shouted, '*Get down*,' and then started firing at the hallway directly opposite. Bishop looked up and saw a man shooting back before ducking into the comms room doorway. That had to be Kiervan. There was nobody else left.

The moment Vallejo stopped shooting, Kiervan reappeared and fired back. Bishop raised himself up and let off another volley. Vallejo joined in. Bishop kept shooting, hitting nothing, until the trigger clicked on empty. He ejected the magazine, pulled the last spare from his pocket and rammed it home. Then he saw Kiervan fall back against the wall with a red bloom on his chest. He got off two more shots before Bishop aimed carefully at his head and fired once. Kiervan's head snapped back and he fell to the floor, unmoving.

Behind Bishop, the screaming had turned to crying. He turned and saw Vallejo leaning against the wall with a hand against her side, the blood already staining her shirt.

'Bastard gave me a little something to remember him by,' she said, wincing. 'I'll be okay.'

Bishop saw Melissa had been hit, too. She was crying as she held a bloody hand against her upper right arm. Emma looked dazed, but unharmed.

They were so close. Just a few more yards to the office. And only Hallaran left now. Except he had a sub-machine gun, which trumped two semi-automatic pistols every time.

'You're too late, Bishop,' Hallaran called out from round the corner. 'Your little woman's gone, but at least she'll be alive. Can't say the same for you, though.'

Bishop heard something heavy hit the wall and then a *whumpf* sound. Probably a flare. Bishop could already smell burning. The fire would spread quickly. The intersection would be impassable in a matter of seconds. They needed to move. Right now. He turned back to Vallejo and said, 'This whole place is about to go up. The office is just there on the other side. You can make it.'

She took her hand away from her side and stared at the blood. 'Can't argue with a confident man,' she said.

'Come on, let's go,' he said, helping her up. 'I'll give you cover.'

He also pulled Emma and Melissa to their feet and got all three to hold hands. Then he took a quick look round the corner. The flames were rising up the walls and steadily advancing along the floor like flowing lava. Less than ten feet away and gaining fast.

'Run,' he said. '*Now.*'

He emerged from the corridor and started firing at the spot where he'd last seen Hallaran. Everything was now obscured by flames and smoke. From the corner of his eye, he saw Vallejo dragging the two girls across the main passageway. There was another burst from the machine gun and Bishop ducked and fired off a continuous volley of shots. He risked a glance and saw the girls had reached the safety of the next corridor. Still shooting, Bishop ran across the intersection, through the pool of gas, and reached the other side just as the Sig clicked empty. The fire was still advancing towards him. He dropped the gun and ran over to the office door and saw Vallejo already pushing the girls inside.

'Shut this door and get them out of here, Vallejo,' he yelled over the noise of the flames. 'I have to go.' He didn't wait for a reply, just kept on running. When he reached the door at the end, he yanked it open and re-entered the garage.

The place was still in total darkness. Bishop felt around the wall until he found the switch he knew was there. The lights came on and he ran over to Neeson's BMW and removed the canvas. He retrieved the keys from his pocket, unlocked it and got in. After pressing the button to open the shutters, he pulled his seat belt across and pulled Neeson's .38 from his waistband. Just six rounds, but they'd have to do. He placed the gun on the seat next to him. As he started the engine, he remembered Neeson was still unconscious in the trunk. Then put him out of his mind. At least this way the guy wouldn't burn to death.

Once the garage shutters were halfway open, Bishop switched on the headlights and backed out. He swung the wheel hard to the left until he was pointing towards the airstrip. In the distance, he saw the plane was still on the ground. The tanker was still out there, too. There was still time. But not much. A plane that size would only have about a five hundred gallon fuel capacity, so they'd be finished refuelling the thing any second now.

He put the stick into Drive and stepped hard on the gas. The BMW took off over the bumpy ground, the hangar soon whizzing by as he increased the speed. No time for subtlety any more. It was the direct route or nothing. That's why he'd chosen the SUV over the limo. A four-wheel drive had a much better chance of smashing through that fence. Then it was just a few hundred yards further to the plane. He'd make it. He *had* to.

Bishop had got the thing up to seventy and was just reaching the end of the hangar when he saw a large, dark shape suddenly come out of nowhere from the left. Less than five yards away and on a collision course. The second fuel tanker.

Bishop swore and stamped hard on the brakes with both feet, at the same time yanking the wheel all the way to the left. But he was going way too fast. And the tanker was too close. And no room to manoeuvre. The SUV went into a four-wheel drift, still heading for the tanker at speed. They were going to collide. Bishop had just enough time to relax his body in readiness for the pain to come, then the BMW smashed broadside into the side of the tanker at fifty miles an hour.

EIGHTY-NINE

It was like hitting a brick wall. Or any other immovable object. The noise from the collision sounded like the end of the world. Bishop's body jerked so hard against the safety belt he felt a rib crack. At the same time, the front airbag exploded from the steering wheel like a shotgun going off, slamming him back in his seat and smothering him in less than a second. Bishop had time to see the right-hand side of the SUV instantly flatten against the tanker like paper, then everything turned white.

Silence.

Bishop breathed out and opened his eyes. He was still in one piece. Just. The airbag immediately began to deflate and he turned to his right. That whole side of the vehicle looked as though it had just been inserted partway into an industrial crusher. The .38 was gone, sucked into the mess and probably half its original size now. And Neeson in the back. He must have died immediately on impact.

The only noises were the sound of the truck's idling engine and a heavy drumming on the SUV roof. And he smelled gasoline again. Not kerosene. Probably Avgas, the highly flammable aviation fuel used to power piston-engined aircraft like Poleina's. The force of the crash probably ruptured the tank. Bishop figured it had to have been Hallaran driving. Bastard must be serious about making sure Bishop was dead.

Bishop unlatched his seat belt and shouldered open the door, the move instantly inflaming the pain in his rib. Then he fell out the car onto the gas-soaked ground. More splashed onto his clothes in a steady spray from above.

Have to get up. Have to finish Hallaran and get moving. The plane won't be there much longer.

Bishop heard a crunching sound nearby. Then a boot suddenly smacked into his right side, forcing the air from his body and knocking him onto his back. Bishop wrapped an arm around his cracked rib and looked up. The figure he'd seen before was standing over him. Hallaran. He was unarmed. Behind him, Bishop could see the damage the crash had caused. There was an uneven fissure running down the centre of the tank and the contents were spraying out in a wide are, drenching everything within range. Including both men.

'I told you you're too late, Bishop,' he said. 'She'll be airborne in a minute, by which time you'll be beyond caring anyway. Tell me, how does it feel to have gone through all this effort for nothing?'

'It's over, Hallaran,' Bishop said. 'You're done.'

'You think?' Hallaran smiled. 'All you did was speed things along, that's all. Another year like I planned would have been perfect, but I'm already richer than God, and thanks to you I don't even have to share any of the profits. But you still stuck your nose into my business, and that's something I can't let you get away with.' He gave another hard kick to Bishop's stomach. 'Come on, get up. It's no fun if you don't try, and I want this to last. I want you to see that plane take off and know how close you came before I finish you.'

Bishop winced and slowly raised himself to a sitting position. Making as though he was still sluggish from the crash. Then his left hand darted down towards his ankle holster and pulled his knife free. He lunged forward and stabbed at the man's legs. But Hallaran had anticipated the move and was already stepping back out of the way. He kicked out and his foot struck Bishop's inner wrist. The knife flew from Bishop's hand and he saw it skitter along the wet soil and finish up under the wreckage of the car.

Bishop kept moving. With one hand on the ground for support, he delivered a side kick aimed at Hallaran's right knee. Hallaran turned to avoid it and Bishop's boot glanced off the inside of the leg instead. But Hallaran lost his balance and fell, landing in one of the puddles of fuel. Bishop clambered over and dived on top of him, pressing his elbow against the man's Adam's apple, pushing down with every inch of strength while his other hand tried to grab hold of Hallaran's left arm. But Hallaran used his other fist to deliver a rocket to Bishop's ribcage.

The pain was unbelievable. Bishop released Hallaran and rolled off, his left arm holding his chest. This was like Abraham all over again. Except now he was on the receiving end. He forced himself to his feet and saw Hallaran already moving in. Bishop had no time to get out of the way as Hallaran delivered a roundhouse kick to his ribs again.

But Bishop managed to clutch the leg just as it made contact and hold on to it, swivelling his body to the left and downwards. Bringing Hallaran down with him. As soon as he hit the ground, Hallaran quickly kicked out with his other foot, catching Bishop perfectly on the chin. A follow-up kick caught him in the stomach and Bishop fell back, winded. Then Hallaran got up and stamped his right foot into Bishop's groin, causing him to double up in agony.

Hallaran knelt down and rammed a knee into Bishop's abdomen, and all the air left his lungs in a nanosecond. He only managed to take in a couple more quick gulps of oxygen before Hallaran clutched his throat in both hands and began squeezing. Bishop grabbed at Hallaran's arms and tried to prise the hands away, but they didn't budge an inch. He reached for the man's eyes, but Hallaran simply moved his face out of reach. He punched at Hallaran's midsection, but it was like hitting bone. He opened his mouth to try to take in more much-needed air, but only ended up swallowing more of the jet fuel raining down on them. He began coughing, gagging, losing what little oxygen he still had left.

Hallaran just kept squeezing, grinning like an idiot as he steadily choked the life from Bishop. 'Don't think I can wait for Poleina's plane to take off, after all,' he said, panting. 'I'm enjoying this too much. Been a while since I used my bare hands on a man the way I was trained. Forgot how good it feels. How natural.' He laughed. 'Didn't I say you'd come off worst if you tested me?'

Bishop was barely listening. What strength he still possessed was fast draining away with his air. He was nearly finished. Hallaran was clearly the better fighter. Or at least the fitter of the two. Whichever way you looked at it, he was winning. But Bishop couldn't give up yet. Not with Selina still out there.

If only I had a gun, he thought. *Or a weapon of some kind. Something to equalize the odds. Anything.*

And then Bishop remembered he *did* have something. It was still down there in his jacket pocket. And that single spark of hope gave him a sudden surge of renewed strength. He let his whole body go completely limp for a second, long enough for Hallaran's grip on him to relax a little. Then he grabbed hold of Hallaran's shirt with both hands, planted his right foot on Hallaran's waist and used all his strength to roll his body backward, pulling Hallaran up and over in the classic circular judo throw.

He turned and saw Hallaran land on his back and roll forward, about to get to his feet again. Bishop took a deep breath and sat up, both hands feeling around his windbreaker. *There* it was. Left pocket. His clothes were wet and slippery, and he managed to get his hand inside just as Hallaran rose to his feet and turned to him.

Bishop pulled out the stubby orange flare gun he'd used on Baldwin. He aimed the gun at Hallaran's midsection and pulled back the hammer.

Hallaran's eyes grew wide. He knew what was coming. He took two short steps back, raised a hand and shouted, '*No. Wait.*'

'No time,' Bishop said, and pulled the trigger.

The flare hit Hallaran right in the chest. He fell to his knees, hands scrabbling around frantically as he tried to get the white-hot candle off of him. But it was too late. He screamed as his shirt immediately caught fire. It spread quickly to his pants. Then the top layer of skin underneath. Hallaran fell to the ground, his screams rising in pitch as the flames spread rapidly up and down his body. He was still screaming when they engulfed his head.

Bishop thought of all those families of his victims who'd suffered death by fire on his orders. Men. Women. Kids. Now Hallaran knew. He was finally seeing the light.

Bishop got to his feet and moved back out of the danger area, where the ground wasn't damp. Watching Hallaran's movements become weaker and weaker as he rolled his body around the ground, shrieking like a banshee, unaware he was feeding the flames further and making his own funeral pyre. The sickening stench of burning flesh filled the air and it wasn't long before the screams died off. Bishop took his eyes away, then ran round the tanker and jumped up into the cab before it caught fire, too.

The plane was still on the ground. He could see it out there, still pointing west. But for how much longer, he didn't know. He jammed the tanker's gear stick into first and pressed down on the accelerator. The truck moved off slowly and gradually picked up speed as Bishop turned the wheel and steered it towards the airstrip.

By the time he neared the fence, he'd got the vehicle up to a decent speed. He kept the pedal pressed to the floor and aimed the truck dead centre between two of the concrete posts. The vehicle struck the fence at fifty miles an hour. There was a brief electrical discharge as the tough fencing tore away from the insulators on each side, followed by an angry sound of stretching and grinding metal that vibrated all the way through his legs. Bishop didn't slow, just ploughed through the gap, urging the thing to go faster. The truck was his only weapon now. He'd use it to ram the plane and disable it. As long as Selina stayed on American soil, that's all that mattered. After that, he'd have to improvise.

Through the windshield, he saw the plane at least two hundred yards distant. Still pointing east. Then the wing lights came on. They were preparing to go.

Then he noticed the truck was rapidly losing speed. He pressed down on the pedal and nothing happened. And the metallic grinding sound was back, and getting louder. It hadn't been the sound of the fence breaking. Something in the engine must have been damaged from the crash. Then Bishop heard a loud crack out front and the engine died completely, leaving the truck to silently rattle along under its own power, slowing with every foot.

In the distance he could hear the sound of the plane's starter motor as it caught. And the sound of the turboprop engine began rising in pitch. The pilot was preparing to take off.

And Bishop was still a hundred and fifty yards away. With no possible way of reaching it before it did.

NINETY

Bishop jumped out the moving cab and started running for the airstrip. He tuned out the stabbing pain in his ribcage. It didn't matter. He had to keep going, that's all. He'd never given up before and he wasn't about to start now.

There's still a chance, he thought. *As long as you keep your eye on the ball and stay focused, there's always a chance.*

Almost immediately, Bishop heard the throaty sound of another engine behind him. He turned and saw a dark sedan speeding through the gap in the fence, heading his way. But there was nobody left in the hangar, and it was too soon for the cops. So who was this?

As the vehicle got closer, Bishop was getting ready to jump out of its path when the driver suddenly veered left and the car skidded to a complete stop just a few feet away.

Bishop ran forward, yanked open the passenger door and saw Vallejo looking back at him from the driver's seat. Her face was haggard, but she was smiling.

'Come on,' she said. 'I don't have all night.'

Bishop shook his head and jumped in. 'You're really something, Vallejo,' he said. 'Back up to the truck first. Let's take this door off at the hinges.'

'Right.' Vallejo didn't ask why, just put the car into reverse, turned her head round and pressed down on the accelerator. Bishop kept the door open with his hand and watched the tanker getting closer and closer. He pulled his hand back as the car scraped against the side of the cabin at thirty miles per hour. A loud, metallic, screeching sound assaulted his ears as the open door immediately reversed back in on itself and smacked against the front fender. The inner springs and hinges pinged free of the chassis and the door fell away and into the narrow gap between both vehicles.

'Okay,' Bishop said, 'punch it.'

Vallejo braked, slammed the gearshift into Drive and stamped her foot down. They quickly picked up speed as she pushed the engine to its limit. Through the windshield, Bishop saw the plane in the distance turning in a semicircle until it was pointing west. They were still more than a hundred yards away, but closing fast.

'Tell me you brought your gun with you,' he said.

'I borrowed Patricia's. Mine was empty. It's somewhere down by your feet.'

Bishop leaned forward and felt around on the floor until he found the .38 Special. He sat back and flipped open the chamber. Five rounds. But five was better than nothing.

'Not that I'm complaining,' he said, 'but shouldn't you be in the tunnel with the others?'

'And miss all this excitement?' She gave him a quick glance before facing front again. 'I've come too far to quit now and besides, I thought you still might have use of my driving skills. Looks like I was right. Patricia can handle the women fine by herself.'

'Did you at least call 911?'

'Yeah. The dispatcher told me it had already been logged and that emergency vehicles were already on their way. Including the police.'

'Kate,' he said. 'She must have called it in as soon as she heard shooting.'

'Good of her. So what's the plan?'

'For now, just keep pushing this thing. We can't let that aircraft get off the ground.'

Vallejo shut up and concentrated on her driving. They were already at fifty, the harsh terrain rocking them back and forth in their seats. Giving the car's suspension a real workover. Bishop prayed they didn't blow a tyre. Or even worse, an axle. Just thirty yards from the first fuel tanker now. Twenty. And just past that was the plane. It had already begun taxiing, getting ready for take-off.

Bishop gripped the dash with his free hand. 'They're moving.'

'I know.'

'Faster.'

'I *know*.'

Then they were whizzing by the fuel tanker and crossing over the first row of ground lights. As soon as they hit the airstrip the terrain wasn't so rough, but it was still a bumpy ride. Vallejo straightened the car out and increased their speed. The prop plane had to be going at forty miles per hour already, but they were gaining on it. Bishop braced a foot against the door frame and leaned part of the way out. The cold desert air blasted against his face and the noise of the jet engine filled his ears.

They were ten yards behind and closing. Five yards now. Four. Vallejo turned the wheel slightly and they began to approach from the port side. A few seconds more and the car was level with the rear cargo door, just behind the left wing. The engine was at half throttle now and rising in pitch as the plane increased its speed. Vallejo kept pace with it.

'What now?' she yelled over the noise

'Just keep up,' he shouted back.

But it was a good question. Bishop thought furiously, going through the few options available to him. The plane was going too fast for Vallejo to get in front and force it off course. And there wasn't time enough to get onto the wing and screw with the port-side flap. And the flaps were already lowered, which meant he wouldn't be able to stop it from taking off anyway. All that was left was to fire on the cockpit and try to hit the pilot. Not much of a plan, but it was all he had.

Bishop was about to order Vallejo to increase their speed when the cargo door started to slowly open outwards. And then upwards. The ponytailed bodyguard, Gerardo, was on one knee, holding it open with one hand. The other hand held the Micro Uzi Bishop had seen earlier. It was pointing right at them.

'Pull back,' Bishop shouted. 'Now.'

Vallejo swerved and momentarily took her foot off the accelerator. They dropped back a few yards and both ducked down as a stream of bullets riddled the hood of the car. Then the bottom of the windshield developed a neat row of cracks from right to left. More rounds smacked against the door behind Bishop and he heard the rear window smash. Then nothing. He glanced to his right and saw Gerardo take his free hand from the door and pull the now empty magazine from the gun's housing. Bishop sat up and saw an unharmed Vallejo staring back at him.

'Bring us level again,' he yelled. 'Get close enough that I can jump across.'

'Christ,' Vallejo said. But she immediately speeded up until they were once again parallel with the cargo door. Both machines were travelling at about eighty now. She edged the car closer until they were only ten feet away.

Gerardo was already pulling a new clip from his rear pocket and bringing it round. Bishop aimed the .38 at the man's chest and fired. The bodyguard jerked back and fell on his ass, one hand against his right hip, where there was already a dark stain forming. Bishop counted himself fortunate he'd hit anything. At the speed they were going, and on this terrain, pinpoint accuracy was impossible.

'Get closer,' Bishop shouted.

Only six feet separating them now. Five. Four. *Come on, baby, come on.*

Bishop aimed the gun at the man's midriff and fired again. This time, he was too close to miss. Gerardo fell onto his back with an ugly hole in his chest. The Uzi fell onto the floor and bounced twice before it disappeared out the doorway and was gone. That was one less problem to worry about, at least. Bishop holstered his gun and raised himself to a crouch, facing the plane. Both hands gripping the door frame. Glancing to his left, he saw they were running out of airstrip. And the throttles were at full thrust. They must be doing close to ninety. Vallejo edged the car closer still. Only three feet away from the opening. It was now or never.

Bishop took a deep breath and held it. Then he leapt across.

He landed hard on the floor of the cargo area and kept rolling until Gerardo's body stopped him. Ignoring the pain in his chest,

Bishop raised his head and saw he was in a space about eight feet long and six feet wide, sectioned off from the rest of the cabin by a thick, black net running from floor to roof. Across the way, Vallejo was still keeping pace and darting looks his way.

Bishop clambered over Gerardo and used his feet to push the body out through the opening. He stood up and began waving at Vallejo to drop back entirely when he heard an inhuman roar at his right. Then a sledgehammer smashed into his side, just below his ribs. He fell to the floor in agony and when he looked up, saw the other bodyguard standing over him. His expression was a mixture of torment and pure, naked fury. He must have seen Bishop throw his brother's body out the plane.

Shaved-head shouted something in Spanish, then pulled his right foot back for another kick. Bishop quickly rolled his body towards the rear of the cargo area, but it was too late. The man's foot connected with the base of Bishop's skull and his head bounced off the floor. Fighting the dizziness threatening to overtake him, Bishop kicked out with both feet and felt them connect with something solid. Bishop took a deep breath and shook his head. A mistake, as he almost lost consciousness right there. He turned to see Shaved-head a few feet away. He had a bloody mouth and was already halfway to his feet.

Time to end this, Bishop thought, reaching for his shoulder holster. *Right now.*

Then the plane lifted into the air and the world shifted on its axis by twenty degrees.

Shaved-head lost his balance and fell back against the starboard side while Bishop slid back until he hit the rear wall. Bishop sat up and reached for his gun again, but before he could get anywhere near, Shaved-head was on him like a dervish. A roundhouse punch to the skull was followed by another kick to his stomach, followed by intense pain. Bishop fell onto his back and then Shaved-head was on top of him, shouting obscenities in Portuguese and pummelling his face with both fists. Left. Then right. Then left. Then right. Each punch like a freight train. Bishop tasted blood in his mouth and felt something snap in his right cheekbone. He knew he couldn't take too much more of this.

But the cargo door was still open above his head, the noise of the engine still drowning out all other sounds. Remembering how he'd dealt with Hallaran, Bishop decided to try the same move again. But he had to do it now, while he still had some strength left.

Just before the next punch made contact, Bishop moved his head two inches to the right. Shaved-head's fist glanced off his temple and hit the floor instead. Bishop immediately made a claw of his left hand and thrust it upwards with the palm exposed, the heel bone striking Ponytail right under his chin. He felt the man's teeth click together and used the momentary respite to grab Shaved-head by his shirt lapels. He pulled him forward and at the same time kicked his legs up, using all his weight and strength to launch Shaved-head's body up and over his head.

And out through the opening.

The scream lasted for a fraction of a second and then it was just the sound of the jet engine again. Bishop looked out into the darkness and figured they were about a hundred feet from the ground and rising. No way he could have survived that fall.

Bishop slowly got to his feet and touched his right cheekbone. His fingers came away bloody. Something was definitely broken in there. And a couple of his back teeth felt loose. Most of his face felt numb, though, which was probably a good thing. He reached up, grabbed hold of the door's inner handle and pulled it down, fighting the heavy turbulence outside. It took a few seconds, but he finally got it closed and turned the handle clockwise until it clicked into the *safe* position.

The sudden silence was almost deafening as he pulled the .38 from his holster.

Two down. Just one to go.

NINETY-ONE

Bishop parted the net partition, creating a gap large enough to step through. Beyond, the main cabin was about as plush as you'd expect. Everything in light tan. Four leather upholstered seats, each with its own glass table. A large LCD screen affixed to the wall ahead, with a small bar and a fridge in the corner. And plenty of space in which to move around.

Selina was standing in the aisle a dozen feet away, watching Bishop with round eyes. Poleina was behind her, gripping her shoulder while the other hand held a Beretta to her ear. He was half crouching so only part of his head and right shoulder was visible.

Bishop stepped into the cabin, keeping his own gun trained on Poleina's right eye.

'Drop your gun,' Poleina said in a shaky voice. The hand holding the Beretta didn't look at all steady, either. With his bodyguards gone, the man was clearly well out of his comfort zone. Which made him all the more dangerous.

'Sure,' Bishop said. 'Right after you drop yours.'

'I . . . I will kill her.'

'I don't think so. Not after you've just laid out two million bucks.'

'I *will*. I know you came for this girl. Hallaran told me. You will not let her die, and you cannot shoot me without hitting her.'

Bishop said nothing, but Poleina was right. Bishop had always been highly proficient with light arms, but right now they were in a jet that was still climbing, with constant turbulence hitting the hull every few seconds. If he shot at Poleina and the plane hit an air pocket at the wrong moment, he'd take Selina's ear off. Or worse. He couldn't risk that.

Bishop needed to get closer. He took a tentative step forward. Then another.

'*Stop*,' Poleina shouted, jamming the barrel into Selina's neck. '*Stop there*. I will shoot her if you keep walking.'

Bishop halted and said, 'We really don't need to do this, Poleina. I don't care about you. So why not set this thing down somewhere and let us both off? Then you go your way and we'll go ours.'

'No. You drop your gun and I let you live. Or I shoot you, using her as a shield. I am the one in control here. Not you.'

Bishop hadn't really thought he'd go for it, but he had to try. He shifted his glance to Selina. It was up to her now. Except her eyes were glassy, as though she was having trouble focusing on him. God knows what Hallaran had given her to keep her placid. Bishop could only hope she still possessed enough of her wits to do what was needed.

He stared at her, and without moving his head made a show of lowering his eyes to his right hand. It was next to his leg, just out of Poleina's line of sight. But Selina would be able to see it if she tilted her head a little to the left. Keeping the thumb and pinkie hidden he started tapping the middle three fingers against his leg. Selina frowned, clearly not understanding. He stared hard at her and then slowly lowered his eyes again.

Follow my eyes down, he willed, *and look at my hand.*

Poleina was watching him too, not taking his eyes off Bishop's face. Which was all to the good. He pulled back the hammer of the Beretta and said, 'You will drop your gun.'

Bishop ignored him and kept his attention on Selina. He figured he still had a few seconds left, so he continued tapping his fingers against his leg. Still frowning, she finally tilted her head a little to the left and moved her eyes slowly downwards. They stopped at his hand. Once Bishop knew he had her attention, he stopped tapping and tucked his ring finger into his palm. Followed by the middle finger. Then the index finger.

She raised her eyes to his, her brows still together. Bishop moved his eyes towards the .38 Special in his other hand, then down to his leg again. Went through it all again quickly. Ring finger. Middle finger.

Index finger. Gun. Then he looked at her, willing her to fight through the fog and understand. He did it a third time and locked eyes with her. Ten seconds had passed already. Poleina wouldn't wait much longer.

Selina lost the frown. Instead, she started moving her lips with exaggerated mouth movements. Bishop didn't need to be a lip-reader to understand the words.

Three. Two. One. Bang.

Good girl. She'd got it. He gave an almost imperceptible nod and she gave a thin smile back. Then she lowered her eyes to the three fingers of his hand. Waiting for the signal.

'Enough thinking,' Poleina said. 'Drop the gun or I shoot.'

Bishop looked at Poleina. Picked his target and held the gun steady. Took a deep breath. Held it.

Three. He tucked the ring finger away.

Two. The middle finger followed it.

One. The index finger disappeared.

Then everything happened at once. Selina suddenly screamed at the top of her lungs and lurched her body forward as though about to vomit, instantly freeing her shoulder from Poleina's grip. Poleina clutched at the space where her neck once was. The other hand was already lowering the gun in her direction when Bishop fired his. The .38 hit Poleina in the shoulder and he yelled and fell back against one of the glass tables, gun still in hand, then rolled off and hit the carpeted floor.

Bishop was already moving. He sprinted past Selina's prone body and reached Poleina before he even knew what was happening. Stepping on the man's right wrist, he pulled the Beretta from his grip and tucked it in his waistband.

Poleina clutched his wounded shoulder, moaning softly. A small amount of blood leaked onto the light-coloured carpet underneath. He'd live.

'Don't move,' Bishop said and turned to Selina. She was still lying on the floor a few feet away and looking up at him. Her eyes looked a lot clearer. The short burst of adrenalin must have temporarily counteracted whatever was in her system.

'Bishop,' she whispered.

'It's me,' he said, helping her to her feet. 'Are you okay?'

Instead of answering, Selina suddenly wrapped both arms around him tight and pressed her face against his chest. Bishop could hear muffled sobs and smoothed her hair as she let it all out. She deserved this moment of relief. And if he was honest, so did he. He was dog tired. But holding her in his arms like this, knowing she was physically safe, made everything he'd gone through worth it. And he knew he'd do it all again if he had to.

Bishop let a few moments pass, then said, 'You want to ease off a little, Selina? I think you just cost me another rib.'

'Sorry,' she said and loosened her grip. She used a hand to wipe her eyes and said, 'I thought I'd never see a friendly face again.'

'Yeah, well, blame me for not checking in with you regularly. That's a mistake I won't make again.' He pulled away and took the small roll of duct tape from his jacket pocket. 'But right now, you can do me a big favour and bind this guy's wrists and feet for me.'

She nodded and went to work while Bishop covered him with the Walther.

Once she was done, Bishop said, 'Okay, Selina, grab yourself a seat and yell if he moves.'

'Where are you going?'

'To persuade our friend in the cockpit to take us back to earth.'

NINETY-TWO

As it turned out, the young pilot didn't need much persuading and they were on the ground five minutes later. As they were taxiing back, Bishop yawned and looked out the window. He saw two vehicles with flashing red and white lights approaching the airstrip. In the distance, the hangar was totally ablaze, with flames reaching high into the night sky. He spotted at least two fire engines and plenty of other vehicles moving about. No doubt Kate and her photographer were over there, too, getting valuable footage to sell on to the networks.

Bishop glanced at the unconscious Poleina in the seat across the aisle, then at Selina in the seat behind. She was staring out the window without expression, having barely spoken since they'd turned back. Bishop guessed it might be some time before she was back to her old self. She'd probably need some professional help to get rid of the shit Hallaran had put into her head, too. And, of course, he still faced the unenviable task of telling her about her mother's possible murder. That was something he *really* wasn't looking forward to.

When the jet finally came to a complete stop, Bishop sighed, got up and went over to the cabin door. He turned the locking bar, lowered it to the ground and saw four uniformed cops in a line. Two were pointing handguns at him. The third held a shotgun. The fourth was the man he'd seen briefly at the station after being arrested. Captain Emery. He was watching Bishop with one hand resting on the gun in his belt holster.

Bishop put his hands up and turned to see Selina watching him. 'Time to go,' he said. She silently unbuckled her seat belt, then came over and followed him down the steps.

At the bottom, Emery approached, shaking his head. 'I should have known *you'd* be at the centre of this,' he said. 'Who else is inside?'

Bishop said, 'Just the pilot and his boss, a Portuguese businessman named Poleina. He's also got a bullet in his shoulder. This is the woman he was kidnapping. There should also be five more women around here somewhere.'

Emery looked at Selina, then turned back to Bishop. 'Yeah, we found them climbing out of a hole in the ground, four of them doped up on Christ knows what. Paramedics are looking them over right now. We're finding a lot of dead bodies, too. You have anything to do with that?'

'Depends. Am I under arrest again?'

Emery gave him a look, then turned to the uniforms and said, 'Sienkewicz, Boyd, you two search the plane and bring out whoever you find. Thorson, get on the horn and get another couple of ambulances down here, pronto.' All three uniforms lowered their guns and went into action. Emery turned back to Bishop and said, 'So who lit the match?'

Bishop lowered his hands. 'A man named Alex Hallaran. He had the whole place booby-trapped. That was his body next to the smashed SUV you passed. Or what's left of it after he caught fire. I assume Kate McGowan's clued you in on what's been going on here.'

'Just the basics. Hard to believe something like . . .'

Both men turned at the sound of another approaching car, coming from the same direction as Bishop had come.

Bishop had to smile when he spotted the missing front door panel. The vehicle pulled up behind one of the black and whites and Vallejo got out and began walking towards them, holding a cell phone to her ear. Bishop noticed the large bloodstain on her shirt hadn't gotten any bigger and figured she must have applied a makeshift bandage at some point. But seeing her still upright suddenly put Bishop's own aches and pains into perspective.

Once she'd closed the distance, she turned to Selina and held out the phone. 'Got somebody here wants to talk to you.'

Selina glanced at Bishop, then took the phone. 'Hello? . . . Hello? . . . *Mom*? Is that really *you*? . . . Oh, Mom, you can't believe how *good* it is to hear your voice . . .'

She turned away from them, still talking, and Bishop said, 'You're kidding.'

Vallejo shrugged. 'Thought I'd check with the hospital again before you said something you might regret. Turns out the paramedics got to her mother just in time. She's got a lot of broken bones, but she's conscious and off the critical list. Doctor said she could be right as rain in a few months.'

Bishop smiled. 'That's good news, Vallejo. Real good news.'

Emery said, 'And just who the hell are *you?*'

Bishop saw Vallejo's face change and broke in before she said something *she'd* regret. 'She's your white knight, Captain,' he said. 'Meet Clarissa Vallejo, currently on suspension from the Corvallis Police Department. She's been after these people for months, on her own time, and long before I came into the picture.'

'Is that so?' Emery said, looking thoughtful.

'And since this is going to be a pretty big deal once the news gets out, I'm thinking the two of you could put your heads together so you both come out of it smelling of roses. That way you can keep me out of it entirely, and everybody gets what they want.'

'I must be delirious from the pain,' Vallejo said. 'What are you talking about?'

Bishop looked at Emery. It was obvious from his expression he was already on the same page. And that he hadn't reached the rank of captain by missing golden opportunities when they were presented to him.

Emery turned to Vallejo. 'Why were you suspended?'

'For slugging my superior officer.'

He gave a slow smile. 'That's not too good, but maybe we could work around it.'

'What do you mean?'

Bishop said, 'He means you were working off the books for the Saracen PD all along. He'd suspected something like this was going on under his jurisdiction for a while now and decided to enlist an out of town cop to investigate further, incognito so as not to alert the bad guys.' He turned to Emery. 'Something like that?'

'Close enough. We can go over it in detail later if Vallejo here's agreeable. I could also be persuaded to submit a glowing, personal recommendation to her own captain if she thought it would help her case.'

Vallejo looked at each of them in turn. Then she smiled and said, 'You won't find anybody more agreeable than me. Maybe we could come to an arrangement at that.'

'Good,' Bishop said and turned to Emery. 'Now you can do me a favour.'

Emery looked as though he'd just swallowed a spider. 'Do *you* a favour.'

'Don't worry, you'll get something of equal value in return.' Bishop pointed to Selina's back and said, 'That woman over there's been through enough hell already. Even before all this. Now I spent a lot of time and effort to give her a new chance at a life without violence, and the only way that'll ever happen is if she doesn't get mentioned in your report. So what I need is for you to forget you ever saw her.'

Emery snorted. 'That's all? Just falsify a police report? In a major murder investigation? You don't ask much, do you?'

'You're already bending the truth regarding Vallejo here. All I'm asking for is one small omission. Besides, you got four other female victims to work with. What's one less?'

Seconds passed as Emery frowned at Selina, who still had her back to them. Then he turned to Bishop again. 'And what do I get out of it?'

'The jackpot. Names. Dates. Financial details of everybody involved. Details and locations of scores of women who've gone missing over the past few years. In addition to details of hundreds of murders that were listed as accidental deaths.'

The cop raised an eyebrow. 'Are you serious?'

'Very,' Bishop said. 'Do we have a deal?'

'If you can give me that, then we *defi*nitely have a deal.'

Bishop turned to Vallejo and said, 'Better hand him that flash drive I gave you.'

She reached into a pocket and passed the stick to Emery.

'And if I were you,' Bishop said, 'I'd send some men over to the Garrick Hospital before word of this gets out. Room 4–25. There are two men in there, Claiborne and Hedaya, who you really want under lock and key, ASAP. Trust me on that.' Bishop saw no advantage in ruining Emery's present good mood, so he didn't bother mentioning Levine's involvement. Emery would find out himself soon enough. And so would Kate, once he gave her the other flash stick. Or an amended version, at least. After all, he didn't want her stealing all of Emery's glory. Or Vallejo's. There was enough for everyone.

Emery paused, nodded once at Bishop, then went over and started giving Thorson new orders. Bishop turned and saw an ambulance shape silhouetted against the fire in the background. It drove through the gap in the fence and made its way towards them.

'You two better take that one,' Emery called out. 'I'll speak to you both later at the hospital. We got plenty to talk about.'

Bishop gave a mock salute in response. Selina came over and handed the phone back to Vallejo. Bishop noticed she looked more upbeat. Good news generally had that effect.

'Your mom okay?' he asked.

'She says she will be,' Selina said, 'but I've got to go back to New Jersey. I know the rules, Bishop, but I just *have* to see her.'

'I think we can probably arrange something,' he said, quickly thinking it through. With her new identity still safe, he couldn't foresee a problem if she wanted to stay near her mother for a short while. Once Michelle was well enough, Selina could then use Addison's stash to settle wherever she wanted. Maybe even back here in Arizona. It was as good a place as any, despite recent events. He'd even give her the Buick for the cross-country trip.

As for Carl Addison, Bishop felt certain his days were numbered now that Gaspard knew he'd spilled his guts to Bishop. That's if he wasn't dead already. He'd have to check once he got back. After which, an anonymous call to the cops advising them to look into Joshua Gaspard for the murder might be a good idea. At the very least, it would place him under the spotlight he'd been avoiding up till now. And if that didn't work, Bishop would simply try something else. There were always options.

He smiled at Selina and said, 'In fact, I'm *sure* we can arrange something. I'd drive you myself, but I'll probably be here for another day, at least. We're off to check the damage now.'

The ambulance came to a stop behind the police vehicles. A paramedic got out and stood next to the driver's door, waiting for them.

'Do you mind if I come with you, then?' Selina asked. 'I can wait an extra day or two. I just don't want to be alone just now.'

'Hey, the more the merrier,' Vallejo said.

'Let's go, then,' Bishop said. The three of them began walking back to the ambulance. Another young paramedic already had the rear doors open. He came over and gently helped Vallejo aboard and onto a stretcher. Bishop and Selina followed and sat on a small bench along the other side. Vallejo laid her head back on the pillow and shut her eyes.

Bishop knew how she felt. He yawned as the paramedic went over and shut the rear doors. Once the ambulance finally began to move off, Bishop leaned back and thought he might pay his sister a visit once he got back to the city. Selina's talk with her mother had reminded him he hadn't touched base with Amy or the kids for a while. After all, family was important. And while he was at it, he might actually give Equal Aid a call, too. He still had that open offer, along with a contact number for a guy named Giordano. Maybe he'd see what was what. Couldn't hurt to at least listen.

The ambulance suddenly hit a bump and Bishop felt something sharp dig into his butt. 'Almost forgot,' he said and reached into his back pocket. He brought out the pentagram necklace he'd been carrying around all this time and dropped it into Selina's hand. 'I figured you might want this back.'

She looked down at it and smiled. 'I think you might have been right the first time. It's not really doing its job, is it?' After a short pause, she leaned forward and affixed the chain around her neck. 'But maybe I'll just hang on to it, just in case. Thank you.'

'Least I could do,' Bishop said, and closed his eyes, his head swaying gently with the motion of the vehicle.

And within seconds, he was asleep.